# FALLING FOR MEADOW

IMPACTFUL LOVE STORIES

@authorkelsdenisestone     kelsdenisestone.com

# FALLING FOR MEADOW

*a novel*

KELS & DENISE STONE

BETWEEN THE SHEETS
PUBLISHING

Published by Between the Sheets Publishing

kelsdenisestone.com

Copyright © 2024 Between the Sheets Publishing LLC

All rights reserved.

Paperback ISBN: 978-1-964675-03-9

eBook ISBN: 979-8-9864169-1-5

No part of this book may be reproduced, distributed, or transmitted in any form or by any means, including photocopying, recording, or other electronic or mechanical methods, without the prior written permission of the author, except in the case of brief quotations in book reviews.

This is a work of fiction. Names, characters, places, and incidents are the product of the authors' imagination or are used fictitiously. Any resemblance to actual events, organizations, locales, or persons, living or dead, is coincidental and is not intended by the authors.

Falling for Meadow

Editing & Proofreading:

Caroline Acebo at Brass House LLC

Caroline Knecht

Isabella Bauer

Cover Design: Chloe Friedlein

*Cherish your friends—the ones who see all the ugly, scary, shameful parts and love you endlessly. The ones you grow with. The ones who pluck through all your weeds and collect the dandelions.*

*Love you, bestie.*

# Authors' Note

This book deals with mature themes such as grief, guardianship, and anxiety. We hope that we've taken great care in addressing these topics.

# Prologue
## Ollie

**seventeen years ago**

"Last call for Heathrow routing to Logan!" The airline employee's shout echoes in the deserted departures terminal.

My eyes ransack the place for a flash of chestnut brown hair or pearly skin.

*Where the fuck is Meadow?*

"Another minute," I plead, shooting him a tight-lipped smile. "Please."

The employee's face softens with pity. "One more minute and you're either boarding the plane or staying in Inverness."

Today marks the beginning of the life Meadow and I spent the past year dreaming about. Sure, the next few months won't look exactly like we'd planned, but it's temporary.

We'll still be together. Finally sharing a bed in the tiny flat we're leasing near MIT. The one with extra cabinets for her pans. The waitressing job she got at a nearby restaurant to pass the time and save up money until she can reapply for culinary school. Lobster rolls, late nights, watching baseball at Fenway

Park. The reruns of *Beck*, her favorite crime series, on our TV. Ticking off our long list of cool foodie spots.

I can't go to the States without her. Especially to live in the city where she was born and raised.

The collar of my wool jumper strangles me no matter how hard I yank at it. Worry corrodes my chest.

For fuck's sake. Maybe she got stuck behind a herd of sheep? Or perhaps the car broke down?

Ha! The excuses sound ridiculous.

Meadow's word: that's something I never had to doubt before.

The ground beneath me billows. I stare down at my feet. The same old hiking boots I've had since I was seventeen barely fit.

At a freshly turned nineteen, my limbs are wild weeds, stretching and growing in every direction. As if warning me that I'd outgrow Thistlehill if I didn't leave as soon as possible.

My hometown is a microscopic enclave nestled deep in the Scottish Highlands, about an hour from Inverness. Tall mountains with peaks, rolling hills stretching as far as the eye can see, and the tranquil Loch Flora, which reflects the ever-changing sky. The most exciting thing that happened here in the past decade was that the Macraes, a family from America, moved in right next door to me.

I scrutinize the leather that is caked in the mud that was outside her house when I kissed her goodbye yesterday.

*This may be our last kiss in Scotland, Ollie.*

*We better make it special.*

Meadow promised we'd leave this town *together*.

What happened in between last night and right now?

She would've tried to reach out. *That's it*—she must have already. I yank open the zipper of my duffel and spot the box with the blue sapphire ring I saved up for all year.

The one I plan on giving her as soon as we get the keys to

our flat. Time slips around me. The employee's impatience hammers into the back of my head.

I move the box aside and grab the cell phone my parents gifted me as a going-away present.

I flip open the damn device, barely managing to steady the tiny metal thing in my damp palms, and turn it on.

Nothing.

No calls. No messages.

I hit her contact in my recent calls, but the line is dead.

A tap slaps my shoulder. *Meadow.*

I spin on my heels. Instead of her deep blue eyes, I see the same perturbed airline employee.

"Mate, the plane's leaving."

My brain rattles for an excuse that'll extend this purgatory for a moment longer. Nothing comes. There had to be an unforeseen delay. Perhaps she'll catch a later flight.

"Alright, sorry, I'm coming." I grab my duffle bag and sling it over my shoulder.

At the first step, my heart doesn't follow. It's as if I'm trudging through wet cement. On the second step, the hollowness in my chest turns numb. When I reach the air bridge, I force a large gulp of air into my lungs.

A ping comes from the phone.

> DOE
> I'm sorry Ollie, but I'm not coming.

I slam the call button, but it goes straight to voicemail. Her singsong voice plays through the receiver.

*This is Meadow's phone. Guess you couldn't catch me. Leave a message...if you dare.*

My girl. My everything.

My muscles ache, coaxing me to run out of this airport and all the way to her house, where I'll beg her to change her mind. Then a deep anger rises from me; an ache plunges into my gut.

Meadow doesn't care—she's a coward. I'm humiliated. A fool to believe that dating my best friend's little sister was going to end with me and her flying off into the sunset together. It's like I'm one of her cooking experiments, meticulously crafted only to be disapproved of and tossed aside like unwanted leftovers.

My ridiculous plans. The ring.

*Fuck.*

Four years I've known this girl. Loved her in secret until her brother went off to university and I stayed back because I was deferred from my dream school. It was going to be the worst year of my life, but it ended up being the best because, finally, I could be with her. Fall in love.

All so she could ditch me.

I swallow around a dry throat and step onto the plane.

Over time and with distance—almost five thousand kilometers' worth—I'll forget about her. I have to. By this time tomorrow, I'll begin the life I've been dreaming about since Fox and Meadow Macrae moved in next door.

A life of money, success, and prestige.

And I'll be damn sure that one day, when she passes some newsstand wherever she ends up, she'll see a picture of me with an innovation that has changed the world and she'll regret abandoning me.

No more small towns; no more same old.

And now, I guess there won't be any more Meadow.

# Chapter 1
# Ollie

"It's been nearly seventeen years, I doubt she even remembers me." The lie sounds convincing enough.

Outside the kitchen window, the Macraes' porch light flickers in the blackness, as if luring me next door. Unease buoys in my chest. I place the dirty dessert plates in the sink and spin around to face my parents at the table.

Da hums and cocks his eyebrow.

"Sure." Ma raises the left side of her mouth in a smirk that's far too presumptuous for the occasion.

No chance the girl I fell in love with as a naive teenager has thought about me once over the years. Especially after everything that unfurled between us. Surely the best I can hope for tonight is a friendly hello. A chance to suss out how things will be during my very temporary return to Thistlehill.

"Right, well..." I drum my hand on the counter, trying to work out my nerves. No point in wasting any more time.

"Ye'll be fine. Ye're doin' the right thing by going o'er there and breaking bread with the Macraes." Da lumbers over to me. His hand lands heavily on my shoulder. "Nane can refuse yer ma's whisky cake. Not even Meadow."

I force a smile, and he does the same—crooked and uneven. A replica of mine. The decades have grayed my da's hair and dented creases into his cheeks. He still has my vibrant brown eyes, the sulfur and wood on his skin. A scar above his brow I don't remember.

"Better to get the reunion o'er with, Ollie. She's already not expecting you, and it's gettin' late. Rare to catch her home most weeknights," Ma chimes in.

"Should I wait until tomorrow?" I ask nervously. How is Meadow going to react when I show up at her door? "Did you even tell her I was coming?"

"'Course we did. But we weren't going to be arranging a playdate for ye two. It's better tae go o'er there now than wait around for her to come tae ye; she's very busy." There's a sharpness to Ma's words as she crosses her arms over her chest. Her white plaited hair drapes across her right shoulder.

"Aye." I wave off my parents, grab the glass container filled with Ma's famous whisky cake, and head to the front door.

"I thought he'd get here and change his mind." Ma's hushed whisper comes from the kitchen. "I near want to cancel our trip so we can get more time with him."

"No, *mo ghràdh*; I'm not givin' up the trip ye've wanted a second time. I will not. You've been waiting for a chance at a real honeymoon for seventeen years."

"Oh, Seamus." My mother's voice trembles.

"Our boy ne'er bothers coming home, and we've made our peace with our life here not being good enough for him. He's a man now; he can make his own decisions."

"Then we'll have to make the most of the week we have with him," Ma resolves.

I'm not a good son. It was easier to hide from that truth across an entire ocean.

I pull on my new, freshly waxed Barbour jacket before slipping on the matching hiking boots. When I step onto the porch, a cold gust of wind worms its way into my jacket. I yank the fabric closed with my free hand, keeping the whisky cake tucked under my right arm, before starting the forty-seven steps to the Macrae house.

Forty-seven steps.

That's exactly how long it took each morning before I'd pick up Fox and Meadow and we'd walk to Grace Academy. Exactly the number of clumsy steps I'd take to sneak into Meadow's bedroom when Fox left for university.

I wince. Memories are fickle and useless. I'm not the boy I once was, and I won't be him again.

The thick moss between our houses is covered in a thin layer of old snow, not marked by three pairs of boots as it once had been. The ground is soft, and mud clings to my rubber soles as muscle memory carries me to a place I never thought I'd go again but has never left my mind.

Neighbors again.

Thirty-nine steps.

Neighbors with my ex-girlfriend. The woman I wanted to marry, more accurately.

Ridiculous. I doubt either of us would give a lot of weight to the true eighteen months we spent in a relationship. So what if we'd been head over heels for each other since we met? We were kids. We had barely developed our prefrontal cortexes.

Thirty-one steps.

It's been years. Seventeen of them. I drill the reality into my mind.

This is simply a neighborly hello.

I avert my gaze from the path that snakes down to what was once our place on Loch Flora.

Our place.

*No.*

*Stop.*

I shake my head. Where's my mind run off to? The fucking

yellow brick road of memories I doubt she even remembers. The sooner I get this over with, the better. One single peek at the girl I used to love will quash my curiosity, bury the hatchet, keep me from any awkward encounters in town.

Meadow and I could only ever be cordial anyway.

On step twenty-four, my left boot drowns in thick mud, and I misstep.

"Fucking hell," I growl into the hazy gray sky. Small towns are the bane of my existence. "That better be mud and not cow shit."

Clutching the container close, I yank my foot out of the brown muck. A hefty rain droplet lands on my face. Then another comes down. In a blink, the swollen sky bursts open, turning the snowflakes into heavy rain.

I cinch my hood. A huge gust of wind whips at me, taking Ma's hand-embroidered towel that I'd been using as a lid.

I belt out a loud groan. The elements are punishing me for having been away from home for so long. Thanks, Mother Earth; it's not like I've never advocated for your protection.

What was the point of cleaning up oceans for the past decade if the planet is going to take out its bad mood on me?

I push forward.

Thirteen steps.

Twelve.

Eleven.

The Macrae house is exactly how I remember it when the family moved from America. Two stories, an angled brown roof, and bright white trim that shines even in the pitch darkness. The porch has a new swing, slathered in fresh red paint. Everything else is trapped in the past I left it in. Windows with white grilles. A big wooden door and a brass handle.

I hesitate at the threshold. My eyes land on Fox's old window on the second floor. Regret taps on my shoulder like a forgotten ghost.

It was a different time.
Now, she's alone in there.
Meadow Macrae.
I swallow the nervous fisherman's bait speared through my throat. As I finally will myself to knock, a loud, shrill sound comes from inside.
*Was that a scream?*
My heartbeat matches the pace of the drumming rainfall. I lean in, pressing my ear against the front door, hoping to make sense of the sounds coming from behind it. The wood creaks beneath my soft touch and swings open to reveal a nearly dark house.
The fluorescent light of the television flickers in the background. An image of—I rub my free palm into my eyes. Is that Tormund from *Game of Thrones* standing next to Peter Haber frozen on the screen?
The strained noises return, deepening with each passing second, as if begging for freedom from suffocation.
"Hello?" I call out, keeping half of my body out on the porch.
Someone leaps from the couch like a frightened cat. "AHHH!"
"AHHH!" I yell in return, shuddering under the force of their wails.
Our screams boom around the house, growing wilder with each passing second.
"Who are you?" the voice yells.
From the glow of the screen, I barely make out an arm swinging something overhead. I don't have time to find out what it is before it thuds against my chest.
"What the fuck was that?" I recoil, dropping the cake, which clatters to the floor. I take a step inside the house, running my hand along the wall.
Where's the light switch? It used to be here.

"I know how to use a knife. Very fucking well, mind you. I'm a goddamn knife-wielding professional." The voice turns familiar—an American accent I'd recognize anywhere. "And I've been waiting for the perfect opportunity to test my skills on some unlucky bastard."

Buzzing echoes in the room. I can't tell where it's coming from.

My eyes narrow, struggling to adjust to the dark. The blur of a tall body in the middle of the living room begins to take shape.

Meadow.

Chestnut brown hair sits atop her head, pieces hanging loosely around her face. A jumper drapes over her shoulders. A halo of television light glows around her ample legs and the voluptuous curves of her hips—those are new.

"You threw something at me," I chuckle, but the sound is cut short. "Guess you always had your brother's rugby arm."

"What?"

Fuck. Mentioning Fox was not on the itinerary of this brief hello.

"It's me, Meadow," I explain.

"There's a whole lot of me's around this town, plenty of them waiting to get right in front of my knife collection." She darts like a lion around the couch and toward a side table.

"Ol," I clarify, clearing my throat.

"Ol who?"

Her words slash through me—I didn't matter to her.

"Ollie Anderson, uh, from next door?"

A light flicks on. Recognition crosses her face as she stares at me. Beside my boot, there's a bright blue vibrator flinging around whisky cake.

A laugh traps itself in my throat.

I just walked in on Meadow Macrae touching herself to—to *Beck*? She was obsessed with this show when we were younger.

"They're still making episodes of *Beck*?" I ask.

"Huh?" There are markings of age on her skin that match my own, but the confused eyes peering at me belong to the same girl I fell in love with.

"Never mind." I clear my throat, avoiding her stare. "Your door was open; I didn't mean to barge in here and frighten you."

"I don't lock it."

Right, nobody in Thistlehill locks their door.

"No, I guess why would you when you're waiting to unleash those knife skills on someone?" I joke. If we can get our old banter back, perhaps we'll be fine. "Is the Japanese blade I bought you all those years ago too dull and rusty, or would you at least whip it out for me?"

Most of the women I've dated over the years wanted flowers, lush perfume, or weekend getaways—Meadow wanted a Japanese chef's knife. It was my first real gift to her.

She sneers at me.

"Every single knife I've ever owned is in immaculate condition." Her voice carries a tone like I've further offended her. I try to not let my pulse respond to the fact that she may still have the chef's knife I gifted her. After all these years? No way. "Which is too bad, since you barging in here would've made a little rust on my blades useful." Her voice is filled with a humorous exaggeration.

"Wouldn't matter anyways; I got my tetanus booster last month."

She yanks down her jumper, covering her thighs. She sure as fuck looks pissed off. "Are you seriously talking about vaccines right now? Why are you in my house?"

Yeah, I definitely should've waited until morning to speak with her. Coming here tonight was a big mistake.

"Look, I thought I could swing by and say hello. I see that you're buzzy—I mean, busy." *Ol, you're making things so much worse.*

"I—" Her voice catches in her throat. The Meadow I knew

never ran out of quips to throw at me. "Yes. I was extremely busy. My TV got stuck while I was watching *Beck*, and I was trying to fix it."

"Didn't know screwdrivers come shaped like this nowadays." I nod to the vibrator, which is still flinging cake all over her hardwood floors.

Meadow's nostrils flare, and she crosses her arms over her chest. The movement bungee jumps the jumper up to the tops of her thighs. My gaze lands on her bare legs. A rush of blood surges beneath my belt, and my throat dries.

Fuck.

Her pale skin looks smooth to the touch. It was once.

"There's a lot you don't know about how things are nowadays," she bites out. Her comment strikes a nerve. Sure, I've barged in on her private time, but I didn't expect her to have her fangs out. We both made mistakes. I sure as hell am ashamed of mine, but I thought we'd be able to put that behind us. "What are you doing here?"

"I'm runnin' the distillery for the next three months." A useless explanation. Surely our parents already told her I was coming back.

Anderson Distillery has been in our family for four generations. Da took it over from his father, who took it over from his own. It's always been expected I'd be next in line, but I never wanted that. That's why this visit is temporary.

The distillery ends with my da, but I can at least make it very successful while he's still alive. A stabbing pain shocks through me at the thought.

"I already knew that. Doesn't explain why you're breaking into my house at eight o'clock in the evening. Have you ever heard of knocking? Or texting, or calling?"

I suppress the bubble of anger bursting in my throat. She's one to talk about texting or calling. Never mind. That's the past. *Focus on fixing this horrid interaction and get out of here.*

"You're right. I thought I'd bring over some of Ma's cake." I gesture to the mess—my peace offering—on the floor. "It was obviously a mistake to interrupt your night without prior warning."

Her hands shoot up to her head, and her fingers rake through her hair. The jumper lifts again, revealing a pair of cotton boxer shorts hanging off her waist. Fuck, that annoyed look on her face used to be my kryptonite.

"Mom?" A small voice interrupts the interrogation. Looking over my shoulder, I find a child standing on the porch, glaring up at me with suspicion. Her long brown hair is soaked from the rain outside. Her eyes are a carbon copy of Meadow's. "Are you one of Mommy's friends?" She directs the question right at me, throwing her hands on her hips.

She's my first love's duplicate. *A daughter.*

It can't be.

I take a step back in disbelief. My spine collides with the edge of the doorframe.

Meadow rushes over to us, kicking the vibrator beneath a set of drawers in the entryway.

"He's just a friend of the Andersons. What are you doing home, plum?"

A friend of my family's. Ouch. This brief hello has turned into a full-blown disaster.

"Tap got done early, so Gram dropped me off." The girl makes her way around my frozen stance and enters the house. Her accent is a mix between Scottish and American. The flat, nasal, and staccato pronunciation of her words sounds exactly like Meadow's American cadence. It's fucking adorable, that's what it is, but none of it is making any sense. Why didn't my parents say anything about Meadow being a mother? "I'm Maisie." She flashes me a toothy grin.

*Maisie.*

My jaw refuses to hinge closed.

"Is she mine?" I whisper because I genuinely have no other words to say.

The look on Meadow's face is back to daggers. "You must be joking."

"Uh—"

"She's seven years old," Meadow says frankly.

"Almost eight." Maisie beams, and her eyes skip to the floor. "Is that Nan's cake?"

*Nan?*

"It was." Meadow sighs and tips her head back up to look at me. "Thought that MIT degree was meant to teach you some basic math." That's a low blow coming from her.

My cheeks flame. Shock spins my mind out of this world. "It did. I—"

A car horn pulls my attention to the driveaway. A white Ateca is facing off with the rain. From the driver's seat, Ivy Macrae waves at me. I force my hand into action, mimicking the gesture, but nausea churns in my stomach.

If Meadow is this hostile with me, then the thing I was most afraid of must be true. The entire Macrae family hates me for what I did. Or, more accurately, what I didn't do. But Fox told me to stay away.

Shame weighs heavily on my chest.

Coming to this house was a mistake.

Returning to Scotland was a mistake.

Ivy speeds off, and when I glance inside the house again, Maisie holds a curious gaze on me, while Meadow is visually uncomfortable. I need to get out of here.

She has a child. Probably happily married too. How did my parents manage to keep this from me for all these years?

"Maisie," Meadow says, breaking the silence, "go throw on your jammies, and I'll make you a hot cocoa before bed."

"Mmm, I like that a-choco-lot." The girl twirls around where she stands and giggles. "Nice to meet you, friend of the

Andersons. Maybe you can come over for cocoa another time."

I nod, not knowing what else to do.

Maisie skips down the hall to Meadow's old room.

Meadow plants one hand on her hip, copying her daughter's earlier posture. Marks cover her fingers, some a deep red, some faded. Proof of a life lived—without each other.

Last time I held that hand, the only scar she had was on the underside of her left thumb. A burn mark from when she attempted to make us porchetta after school.

I have an overwhelming desire to ask her how she got the rest, but I doubt she'd tell me anything. I doubt I want to know. What good will it do me? I've already pried my way into the fabric of her life with one small misstep.

"What do you want, Oliver?"

No one ever uses my full name anymore. I'm always Ollie, just Ollie. Except as a kid, when Meadow was mad at me. Or when the partners from my first finance job would scold me.

Another blast from the past I don't want to remember.

"Look, let me at least help you clean this up." I bend down. The hardwood floor is plastered with thick globs of Ma's whisky cake, with shards of glass sticking out of some. The low hum of Meadow's vibrator continues beneath the chest of drawers.

She frowns. "No. Go. Please."

I fucked this whole thing up. So bad.

"Sorry." I bullet out the door, rushing through all forty-seven steps. When I reach my front door, I storm into the house and kick off my boots.

"How'd it go?" Ma calls out.

I burst into the kitchen. "How could you not warn me that Meadow has a seven-year old?!"

"Maisie was home?" Ma's eyes shoot open as she glances at Da. "She wasn't supposed to be back from her wee tap dance class until much later."

*Were they hoping this happened?*

Da looks at me over *The Thistlehill Daily* in his hands. "Ye told us not tae share any news about her."

"I meant things like…I don't know. How she takes her coffee." It used to be pitch black. "Or whether or not she put up a Christmas tree this year." She used to love to do that with Fox. "Small, meaningless details I wouldn't want to be kept apprised of. But a daughter was definitely worth mentioning. Who's the father?"

"Ollie, sit down." Ma pulls out the chair beside her and invites me in.

A tic pricks my jaw. I don't have time for lengthy explanations.

"Can you please tell me? I'm exhausted, and I just found out my parents withheld serious information from me for years." I haven't slept in almost twenty-four hours, and who knows how much sleep I'll get tonight after that horrific encounter.

"Maisie is Fox and Penelope's daughter," Da says.

"Meadow is her guardian," Ma adds, wringing her fingers. "She's been raising that wee girl after…well, after their car accident. Maisie was only six months old when her parents were taken from her."

Fuck. That little girl looked exactly like Fox and Meadow. Those Macrae genes run deep.

Uneasiness ripples through me in a suffocating cloud. I palm the back of my neck, thinking about the last time I saw my childhood best friend. As a boy I knew everything about Fox, but as a man I didn't even know he had a daughter with his girlfriend from university.

*Your own fault*, I remind myself. I stayed away. I kept this old life, this history of mine, at a distance. Because I wanted to and Fox wanted me to.

Why is that not enough to stop the ache in my chest?

"Just simmer down, Ol," Da sighs, giving me a look I can't decipher. When I was a boy, with no siblings to keep me occupied, I became fluent in my parents' glances. Their secret world of forehead creases and narrowed eyes. That's the gift with any family —a language only the natives can speak.

I sigh. "A heads-up would've been nice."

"You're the one who's stayed away for so long," Da barks.

After I began my new, shiny life across the ocean, those whispered looks of my parents got lost in translation. Each time they visited me in Manhattan, a little more distance percolated between us.

"We're not tryin' to snap. We missed our only son being back home, back where ye belong, and—" Ma's expression thaws slightly as she continues the same conversation we had the entire dinner. "When ye told us that ye're coming back to run the distillery while we're away on our trip, I hoped that meant ye'd be moving back permanently."

No clue where they got that impression. For months, I made sure to stress over our calls that this is temporary—a break while I'm in between jobs. I have no intention to move back to Thistlehill and give up my high-rise apartment in New York. This town and I don't belong together. We're like oil and water—no possibility of fusing.

But after I helped my friends, Matthew Hudson and Molly Greene, with a whisky connection for the On Cloud Nine conglomerate's annual party, the hoteliers wanted to make the Anderson product a signature at all of their resorts. A partnership that could make my parents wealthy and secure their retirement. *Finally.*

"I know, Ma," I say gently because there's no use arguing about this anymore. "I missed you too, but I have a job lined up in the city in June. I can't give it up. It's the one."

She rolls her eyes. I ignore the disappointment growing in

my gut. It's not the response she was hoping for, but it's all I've got.

"That's what ye said about yer previous job too, Ollie. They're all yer dream jobs." Ma frowns. Their scrutiny has me feeling less like a thirty-five-year-old man and more like a lanky kid again—anxiously anticipating how a conversation will turn sour and how I'd be responsible for it.

"Maybe none of them are quite right because you belong here," Da grumbles. The room fills with a terse uneasiness.

*Nonsense.* I won't have this argument again.

"I'm keeping my promise." I ignore his sly dig. "When you get back from your trip, the distillery will be self-sufficient, and you'll have lots more time and money. Like you've always wanted."

My heart stops. The topic of finances and our access to them has never been an easy one in this house.

"I told ye we are fine—we didn't need that new business," Da bites.

"The partnership with On Cloud Nine could set you up for life. It's the largest hotel chain in the world," I explain for what feels like the hundredth time.

Da's complained about the new business ever since the first order came in three months ago. He told me that the current state of the distillery couldn't handle a large influx of orders because of dated machinery. He stubbornly insisted that he doesn't need the money or the contract. The only way I could convince him not to turn down the business, which my parents so desperately need, was to come back to Scotland and deal with it myself.

"We like our life," Da grumbles, and I sigh. "Money isn't everything."

That's the biggest lie I've ever heard.

When I was seventeen, my parents used their travel fund to pay me to work at the distillery. I spent most summers as a boy helping out at the family business for free, but Da and I fought all the time—I had ideas for the distillery that he didn't care for. All too modern and innovative for his tradition. However, I couldn't turn down the opportunity to save some money before going to university.

I've always felt guilty that Ma insisted we use their sparse travel fund to pay me for work I used to have do for free. But it's time for me to pay them back for their sacrifice.

"If we cannae change yer mind, maybe Meadow will." Ma's gaze shifts to the window behind me, to the Macrae house. "She could be good company for you, since you were on your own in the States."

It's only been two hours, and I'm already aching to be back in New York.

In the city, most of my nights are spent alone, hunched over my computer as I try to distract myself with a show I can barely remember while eating the same meal from the Mediterranean place down the street. *Lamb leg and tabbouleh salad*, the waiter's unchanging voice echoes in my head.

My life in the city, although a little lonely, is too nice to be away from for long. I wouldn't trade it for Thistlehill.

After my team dissolved at the Oceanic Research Organization, friends started their own lives and ventures. I was getting left behind, and I was not going to be abandoned again.

Something I never managed to figure out for myself. My life is my work.

So, when I got invited to interview for the Director of Sustainable Innovation position at Viggle, I jumped at the chance. A dream career move. One I've counted on since I was a kid with a plan to leave this town. One I've worked tirelessly toward for the past two decades.

It's the ticket to ultimate success. The job to make me forget the hollowness in my chest. Half-a-million-dollar salary, two hundred thousand as a signing bonus, Viggle shares, an office overlooking Central Park, and my own assistant. Sure, I'll be behind a desk most of the time, but I'll have what I always wanted—my name smeared all over successful projects.

I signed the job offer and quit ORO after a couple weeks of negotiations. My start date is the first week of June. That gives me three months to fix things here and start a legacy of my own.

"I doubt it, but I still wish you'd told me about the kid," I say.

"It didnae feel right tae tell ye, son," Ma explains. "That's Meadow's business to share."

There's nothing for me to say. I want to get out of this house and away from the guilt I spent so many years outrunning.

Only ninety-one days until I can leave again. I'll be counting down each one.

"I'm gonna call it a night." I turn on my heels.

"Remember, braw and early the morn," Da shouts from the kitchen.

"Aye."

The familiar stairs creak beneath my weight as I make my way up to my old bedroom. My shoulders barely fit, and I knock into the picture frames on the wall. I push open the door at the end of the hall.

The room seems smaller than it was when I dropped off my bags a couple hours ago. In one corner, there's a measly twin bed with my three suitcases next to it, a desk, a bookcase, and a chair.

On the dusty shelves, my old film camera stares at me. The nicest possession I had as a boy. Beside it, my ancient woodworking figurines that I'd spend hours fiddling with—small animals carved out of oak that I'd find in the shed behind the house. Framed photographs crowd the shelf. Most are of me, Ma, and Da, but Fox is in a few. Meadow too.

A photo of all three of us at Loch Flora…we must only be fifteen then. Fox is holding a trophy, and I have my arms looped over Meadow and him. We'd won a rugby championship that day.

How times have changed.

The reminder of our happy faces makes me dig my wallet out of my back pocket. The tattered picture of her is hidden behind cafe reward cards and business cards I never filed. I pull it out and trace the rips and bends in the small Polaroid of her at the loch. The one I took of her before our first kiss.

What was I thinking?

Why did I even keep this thing in here?

This place—hell, just Meadow—used to be my home, but it's apparent that our wounds are etched into us. Naivety has always been my pitfall with her. That's what I was tonight—naive and foolish to pretend that I'd have a handle on this. That almost two decades away from my hometown weren't going to make me feel alien.

I tuck the picture of her deep into the shelf and flip each of the frames face down.

Fox was right. The cry of his voice is a faded memory in the back of my mind, but I still feel its hurt.

*Don't ever fucking talk to me or my sister again.*

I shudder. No. There will be no more memories haunting me tonight.

## Chapter 2
# Ollie

> **AVE**
> Hey, sent over the design layouts for the distillery's ordering system.
>
> **OLLIE**
> Great, just in time
>
> **AVE**
> Good luck! :)

THE DISTILLERY IS A FIVE-MINUTE DRIVE DOWN AN UNFINISHED road. My head bobs against the roof of Da's old Rover, the same truck he used to let me borrow as a teenager. It took ten minutes to warm up and a lot of angry blabbering about the lazy engine.

He should've let me buy him that new Munro MK1 pickup truck for his birthday, but Da's always been a *why mend it if it's not awry* kind of man. Whereas I'm more of an *improved safety features and self-driving mechanisms* kind of guy.

Something that's kept us from seeing eye to eye all these years.

My parents were always far too proud to accept my financial help, even as my life across the pond was budding with wealth. I could easily pay for their retirement ten times over. But my da refuses. *Honest work or nothing* is his motto. Even if that honest work almost ended their marriage and bankrupted our family. The memories of their late-night fighting and talk of sacrifice cause acid to trickle up my throat.

The forest hiding the distillery is thicker than I remember, burdened with heavy, giant elm trees laden in snow. In the distance, the cerulean Loch Flora sits half frozen in the center of rugged mountains. The sky is brushed gray, moody and miserable.

"Aye, Kleptocow." Da tsks, pulling my attention from the landscape and onto a pale brown cow. A bushy fringe covers its face. The furry animal, the color of oolong doused in far too much milk, stands in the middle of the road, chewing her cud.

"What did you say?"

"That's Madame Belle, but everyone in town calls her Kleptocow. Got a tendency to steal, that beast. She's always waltzing around town, taking things off people's porches," Da says with a straight face, like a thieving cow is as normal as a subway pickpocket.

"The cow *steals* things?"

"The other day Ma caught her walking away with our *Thistlehill Daily.*"

*Only in small towns.* "That makes perfect sense." I sigh in exasperation. "Drive around her." I'm antsy to get into the warm office. My fingers are about to fall off from the cold. "Or use the horn at least." Part of me wants to slam down on the steering wheel myself. It may feel like I'm back in the city again. It's eerily quiet here.

"Yer ma would hear the horn and get worried. Plus, road's too narrow." Da puts the car in park and unbuckles his seatbelt. "She belongs to the Cameron twins. They'll deny their beast has the personality of a greedy crow if you ask 'em. You remember Kenna and Lorna, don't ye, son?"

"Mhm," I grunt, attempting to stretch my legs in the tight space of the passenger seat. My knees press against the dashboard.

"Oh, stop fussing, Ol." Da shakes his head disapprovingly. "Why are ye in such a hurry?"

"I didn't sleep well last night." My mind kept dredging up old memories of Meadow and Fox. Ones that used to only resurface after one drink too many, or whenever that chestnut brown hair looked all too familiar in the sea of people in New York.

Memories that I would've preferred to keep as ghosts.

"Is that the jet lag we have to look forward to on our trip?" Da asks, pulling my foggy mind back to the present. "Hope it won't upset your ma."

"I'm sure she'll be too happy to be traveling somewhere warm to care," I say lightheartedly, but the words clearly upset him. This isn't a conversation for right now, or ever. I deflect, asking, "Are we gonna sit here all day and wait for this master cow burglar to plot world domination or what?"

The cow turns its head toward me, blinking its beady, greedy eyes at me. No way it heard me.

"This cow has a mind of her own. No need tae taunt the ol' lass." Da opens the door, grabs something from the trunk, and approaches the cow. He slaps her haunch, but no dice. In his free hand, he shows her a bright red apple, shiny even in the dim light of morning, which finally catches her attention.

Belle moves with the speed of fresh molasses, but she follows Da's apple off the road. He's seriously bribing a thieving cow on the way to work. How often does this even happen?

Two minutes later, the monumental white-brick building comes into view. My great-great-grandfather bought this place after he started selling homemade whisky at an outdoor market in town. Now, the labels are stocked at a few special restaurants and stores all over Scotland.

I spent my entire childhood running through these halls,

learning about the distillery. Broke my arm climbing up the copper stills, learned how to drive in the parking lot, tasted my first drink, and snuck kisses to Meadow in the barrel room.

The memories pour back all too fast. The summer days we'd spend at the loch, Meadow scribbling in her notebook, me sneaking glances at her while doing some rugby training with Fox. Or that one time, after we began dating, when we snuck out with a bottle of whisky and went running through the hills howling at the moon. She ripped my shirt off my shoulders. I lost her leather belt in the grass.

I swallow, resist the images flashing in my mind, and focus on the black letters painted on the side of the building:

**Anderson Distillery**
*est. 1895*

My legacy. At least according to my parents.

Da parks, and we hustle through the battering wind to the entrance.

The crisp, dewy air mixes with the peat smoke escaping the building. Birds screech in the distance, and the loud turbines that process water from Loch Flora vibrate the ground beneath my feet.

When I step through the entryway, the rank fermentation blasts my senses. Sweet and musky. Heat begins to defrost my icy nose.

"Ain't it just how you left it?" Da beams, walking me through the distillation room. The copper stills with big swanlike necks overtake the room.

"It is." Everything in Thistlehill is exactly how I remember it.

"The stills will need replacing in a couple years. At least the bottling is still doing its best to hold fast. We can squeeze a few more years out of those machines." Da looks away, probably calculating the costs in his head. This particular expression of his has never left my mind. Growing up, our family was always in between wanting and needing. Frequently, because of how costly running the distillery was, only the needs got met.

I'm here to fix that.

"Replacing the bottling facility is one of the things I plan on doing so we can keep the On Cloud Nine contract and get this place into consistent profitability for you and Ma. I was doing some research, and there are modern bottling and capping machines that are energy efficient and emit less $CO_2$—"

"What was good enough for Gran Craig is good enough for me," he snaps.

I wince. "But if you're going to keep the business of the largest resort conglomerate, then I'll have to make changes. Trust me, Da. I know how to handle people like that."

The discomfort in his posture multiplies. Tense shoulders and solemn expression. "Aye. This business was meant to be yours one day, so you can do what you think is best. But don't go changing things so much that I won't be able to manage them when I'm back and ye're gone again."

"I won't. I'm only trying to help."

We pass Callum Paterson, the head distiller, already at work near the spirit safe. The brass box with sight-glass panes hides the whisky's distillation flow. A couple years ago, Callum started overseeing most of the distillation process with Da. Since the recipes have been in our families for years, he mostly ensures quality control.

Despite the pillars of time, he hasn't aged a day. A brick for a forehead, and a thick mustache sitting on the sill of his lips. The man's known for having few words and a dry tongue.

He grunts as we pass.

"Long time no see, Cal."

"I thought that was you," a cheery voice calls from around the corner. Elspeth, Callum's daughter, walks over to us from down the hall. She's her father's opposite. A straw-haired ray of sun in the grim distillery.

Da and I probably have the same contrast.

"Elspeth, last I saw you, you must've been what? Eleven?" I smile at her.

"Now I'm working here like you were! Pa couldn't get enough of us hangin' out together," she jokes and nudges Callum. A flicker of a smile graces his face. "Tours in the summer and taking orders the rest of the year. I'm even helping out as mash-woman while we're in the off season. Anything to earn some extra cash to help my band tour." Turning the barley and making sure the peat is burning properly is quite the hands-on job. Most of the work here is that way—manual. I was in the best shape of my life growing up and learning the ropes of this place.

"Sounds like you've got a lot on your plate," I chuckle. "But don't worry, I'll be making some changes that should lighten up your workload."

"Does that mean pay cuts?" She tilts her head, and her eyes open wide.

"No, not at all," I clarify.

"Seamus, thought you turned down that fancy contract," Callum says, looking confused. "Those people were demanding some kind of online thing and turnarounds that don't work for us. Our way of doing things isn't good enough for them. Figures. No other client of ours has ever asked for us to change."

It's an ordering system, not an infringement on their values.

"My son insisted that he'd make sure the distillery can supply those hotels with our whisky."

Get in. Update the distillery so my parents can maintain a sizable amount of business for the first time in their lives. Get out.

"He hasn't been here in almost two decades; what's he going to know about managing the distillery?" Callum says.

I knew I'd be met with pushback, but I didn't think they'd be so blunt about it.

"I assure you, Callum, the years I spent here as a boy will pay off. And, thankfully, you and Elspeth will be here."

The response doesn't seem to satisfy him at all.

"I guess it would be nice to have some more time to practice the bass. Right, Pa?" Elspeth slices at the tension and shoots me a hopeful look. Maybe I will have an ally after all. "Change isn't so bad."

"The Greenes could help transform Anderson into a household name, like Johnnie Walker or even Macallan," I add.

"Nae harm in being a small shop," Da grumbles. Callum nods in agreement. "Makes our whisky more exclusive, artisanal, homemade."

I want to explain that his *exclusive* whisky barely made a profit *ever*, but I know all too well that'll start an argument.

What he won't say is thanks for making the On Cloud Nine contract happen and letting him take his wife on the honeymoon they never got. He won't even acknowledge that this is a way for me to pay them back for the sacrifice they made when I went to university.

*Stay focused, Ol. Fix what you can. There's no point in trying to change his mind. You know better than that.*

"On Cloud Nine will put our contract on hold for a month. That'll give me enough time to meet their demands," I assure them.

Luckily, Matthew's new wife, Molly, was able to convince her dad to give us an advance for the large order we have to deliver at the end of the month. That should cover the cost of the updates and get their whisky to them as soon as possible.

"Not everythin' is better with *new* machines and online systems. Especially if we cannot understand them. Our clients like chattin' to Elspeth. A personalized touch," Callum says.

Elspeth gives me an uncomfortable smile.

"Sure, I get that. But how do you make sure something hasn't fallen through the cracks?"

Da taps his finger against his temple. "It's all up here."

I refrain from rolling my eyes. Stubborn ol' fools.

"I already coded the bones for the ordering system. My friend sent over the layouts. Elspeth can still talk to the clients, manage those relationships. She simply won't have to write down every order and track them in a notebook." I sigh. "It'll bring Anderson Distillery into the future."

"Ye're not gonna put us out of a job, are ye?" Callum's eyes pierce me with disdain, and even though I probably have a full twelve inches on him, his stare sends a shot of terror into my chest.

"Never," I promise. "We can learn how to operate the new machines in the bottling facility together, and I'll teach you the systems. Elspeth's always been the brightest in her class, if I remember right."

"Ye don't think we're good enough to do things our own way?" Callum bites.

"Of course not, I meant, I—" I did not expect such hostility. I'm helping them, not replacing them. Why wouldn't he want his job to be easier? "Trust me, it'll be beneficial for everyone."

"Trust is built over time." He leans forward.

He's right, but I'm here for the right reasons. I'll have to make him see that.

"Anyway, won't keep ye two. Gotta get my city-slicker son and his cannoli jeans up to speed on some things," Da amends.

"They're Canali," I clarify, but it's no use. He caught me cutting off the tags on them this morning, and the judgment was stark. I figured my parents would be happy to see how I've done for myself, but so far it seems like I was wrong.

"Cheerie, Ollie. Glad to have you back. If you're ever in the mood for a rock show, I play at Tavern some weekends." Elspeth forces a wave and jolts off.

I grit my teeth and follow Da to his office.

Inside, my father's desk is a slab of wood set atop two oak barrels. In a frame on the wall is a newspaper article: "Plastech and Oceanic Research Organization Partner up to Eliminate the Great Pacific Garbage Patch." In the picture, my arm is slung over my friends' shoulders. Matthew, Avery, Robert. I miss them.

At my MIT graduation, Da told me he was proud of me. That was one of three times in my entire life I've ever heard him say those words. The first time was when I performed my first high kick in rugby practice. The second time was when I participated in the Thistlehill caber toss competition.

I guess this little clipping means he is still proud of me, in his own way. Feelings go unspoken more often than not in the Anderson family.

He sits back in his chair, assessing me. "Look, ye ken how I feel about machines and this business, son. I'm happy ye're back, and I can concede that this On Cloud Nine account would be good for the distillery, but we already have a way of daein' things."

"Aye, but these new updates will be better for you. We've already signed the contract."

"We are daein' just fine." He swats at the air.

"Yeah, but you're letting *me* run things. Not Elspeth or Callum."

"Because the girl loves her music more than whisky, and Callum's not great at managing clients. But he's worked here for longer than you've been alive. Remember that."

I tap my boot against the hardwood floor. I need to make him see reason.

"I'm only looking out for you, the way you looked out for me the year I was deferred. You made sacrifices for me, and I'm trying to pay that back. Let me handle this, Da. I've helped run a start-up and worked at one of the most prestigious financial firms on Wall Street. I know what I'm talking about."

"Aye, ye and yer Ivy." Da shakes his head.

My chest expands on my next breath, and I straighten my spine.

"MIT isn't an Ivy," I remind him and pick up a folder from his pile.

He waves me off, and I square my shoulders. My ego is dented by his dismissal. It was much easier to deal with his brushing off over the phone.

Ninety days until I'm in my lie-flat seat back to New York.

A name on the contract in my hand catches my attention. *Fox Den.*

"What's this?" I flash him the paper.

He takes it from me and pulls it close to his eyes. "Meadow's new place. Didn't you say you talked to her?"

"Her place?" The lack of clarity roils my stomach.

"Meadow's new restaurant. Anderson is set to be her exclusive supplier, giving Fox Den a signature malt. Need to go through the stock in the barrel room to figure out something special." Meadow always dreamed of having her own place. Even with all of her big dreams, she found her way back to Thistlehill. I refuse to let that happen to me. "It'll be open two Saturdays from now. Ma's torn up 'bout missing it."

"She named it after him?" I swallow.

"Keeping that boy's memory alive. When she announced it at Town Hall a few months ago, the entire town was sniffling." He trails his gaze over my face.

How could she stand to be reminded of her brother every day? When Fox's death swept through my life, his memory kept me lucid through sleep. It was torture being that close to the reminder of him. "Speakin' of the Macraes, ye ought to say hello tae Ivy and Harris. They practically raised youse. Don't offend them by not stoppin' in."

"Probably better I steer clear of that whole family." I'm not ready to address that shame yet. I'll get around to it...eventually or never.

He plants his hands on the desk. "Ye can dae what ye like for the business, son. But be nice to Meadow and the Macraes. Life's been tough for her, losin' her brother and takin' care of that sweet lass."

*Why didn't her parents take Maisie when Fox passed? Why did Meadow choose to come back to Thistlehill? Is she truly happy here?*

Questions I've been ruminating on since last night. All pointless. Getting close to her or her family again won't be good for anyone.

"Meadow's got no interest in me."

"Believe whatever, but we all help each other here. Ma and I watch Maisie from time tae time when Meadow's busy; ye'll no doubt offer tae dae the same."

"Okay," I say dismissively.

"Good." His serious posture melts.

I wish Fox and I hadn't had that fight after Meadow and I broke up. Being around his family—especially his sister—is daunting. If I could turn back time, truthfully, I don't know what I would do.

Anything to lift this chain of guilt from around my neck.

## Chapter 3
# Ollie
### twenty-one years ago

I PULL MY CAMERA'S VIEWFINDER TO MY EYE AND ZOOM IN ON the ground below, inspecting the new neighbors.

Among the beehive of men in overalls carrying large brown boxes is a girl. She has to be about my age. Short brown hair. A huge gray sweatshirt hangs off her shoulders, covering her jeans, with the letters "MIT" printed onto it.

Her face is scrunched together like she's bit into the sourest lemon as she drags a suitcase nearly half her size up the stone pathway. A wheel gets stuck. She grunts and tugs until a burst of pots and pans erupts from inside.

"No, no, no!" she groans, scrambling to her knees.

There's no way I'll miss out on making new friends. I bolt downstairs and out of the door.

"Let me help!" I shout. The girl's eyes peel open so wide it looks like she put toothpicks in her lids.

They're blue. So, so blue. I glance up at the sky for a second to make sure it hasn't fallen into her eyes, then look back down at her.

"I got it," she says, standing up. The way the sun hits her hair makes her look like she's glowing.

My body feels warm. Very warm.

"You're tall," I gulp.

"So are you." She bends, waddling around like a duck, hauling the pans into her arms.

"I'm Ollie."

*You're tall. I'm Ollie?!* I sound as empty-headed as a log. I grab the biggest pan and pass it to her.

"Thanks. My name's Meadow."

Her accent is unfamiliar, and she says the ending of her name as though she's mouthing the word "doe." I want to hear her say it again. Better yet, I want to spend the whole afternoon staring at her. She's so pretty. Like maybe the prettiest girl I've ever seen.

Ever.

"Where are you from?"

"Uh, Cambridge." She fists her sweatshirt out for me to see. I read the word "MIT" again.

"Isn't that near London?"

"Um, no. America. Maybe you heard of Boston?"

"Cool. I mean, yeah." I cough. "I've heard of Boston, for sure." I'll have to look it up on a map when I get home. I don't want her to think I don't know my geography.

"My parents decided to move here since my grandparents used to live in this house."

"That's cool." I eye the pans. "Um, what's all of this for?"

"They're my special pans. All-Clads. Bought them for my thirteenth birthday last December," she says with excitement. "I cook with them."

"Look pretty normal to me." I inspect the bottom of a small one; my reflection stares back at me.

"Sure, they're not the copper version but they're still extraordinary." Her eyebrows scrunch up as if I've offended her.

"Um..." I'm blowing this. "Is it because they're *pantastic*?"

She stares at me with the straightest face. The world stills. Of course a girl like this wouldn't like my silly jokes. But then a bubbly giggle pours out of her as she keels over with laughter. A boom of accomplishment fills my chest.

A friend.

"Thanks for helping. I have something for you," she says, standing up. Out of her pocket, she retrieves a plastic bag filled with golden, scone-looking pastries. "Want a biscuit?"

"Those aren't biscuits."

"Right. My dad said you guys have different names for stuff here." She hands me one. "Try it. Promise it's not poisoned." There's a flicker of playfulness in her eye.

"That's something someone who's tryin' to poison someone would say."

Her brow lifts. "Are you brave enough to risk it?" I fist the buttons of my flannel, trying to rub away the warmth that's spreading across my chest, but it's like a sunburn—persistent and hard to ignore. "Oh, go on, take it, I'm only messing with you."

I take a bite. My tastebuds erupt. Flaky, buttery, sweet, and definitely no poison.

"Woah." I already want another one.

"I made them at the little hotel we were staying at. The oven wasn't great, and I didn't add enough salt to this batch, but maybe the next." She sounds like my da sipping whisky and assessing how many more years the liquid has left to age. "I'll promise to leave out the poison too." She snorts.

"I think it's perfect," I blurt.

"Thanks." She hoists the zipper of her luggage shut. "I better get going."

"Here, let me help you with this. Hard to roll wheels over the stones. Trust me, you don't want any more *panxplosions* happening."

"It's heavy," she contemplates.

"I'm sure I can handle it."

"Then follow me, Ollie." My name from her mouth sounds as good as her biscuit tasted.

I hoist the suitcase off the ground and follow her. "If you want more salt for your scones—or *biscuits*, as you say—you can get some at Honeydew Market. It's the only store in town."

She stops at the threshold of the front door, and I set her bag down. "Only one? In Boston we had stores on every block. My mom and I would go shopping every Saturday morning, and I'd get to pick all the groceries for a new recipe each week."

"I've never been to a city before," I admit.

"Oh, don't worry, I'll tell you all about it."

"I'd like that." Anything to keep her talking to me.

She surveys the mossy grass, the forest at the far end of my house, Loch Flora in the distance. I watch her. I can't stop watching her. "Can I ask you a question?"

"Aye."

"Do you enjoy living here? Moving to a new country is a big change for me."

"I've never known anything else."

Possibly that will change with her living next door. I'll learn about places where they have stores on every corner, and what other words we use differently than she does.

"Meadow?" Another kid's voice echoes off the walls inside the house.

"That's going to be my brother," she says.

I still. More than one kid. "Brother?"

"Fox. He's fourteen."

"So am I, at least for the next two months. My birthday is on July twenty-third."

"Cool, I'm still thirteen. My birthday is on December thirteenth." She turns. The smell of rain hits my nose. I glance up at the sky, but it's clear. "Fox, I'm out here," Meadow calls.

A tall, lanky boy appears in the hall. His eyes are the same color as hers. The chestnut strands of his hair drape his eyes, and he pushes the locks out of his vision. He's wearing jeans, a sports jersey, and sneakers that look like they've never seen Highland mud. The boy's almost golden.

"Who's this?" He inspects me, leaning against the doorframe.

"I'm Ollie," I say. "I live right over there. We're neighbors."

He looks over my shoulder at my house and then back at me. "Not many people here, are there?"

"Not down our hill."

"Huh, I guess you're our first friend," Fox says. "Do you know how to play Scrabble? We got a new box of it."

"Yeah, I love Scrabble."

"Cool, come in." I go to follow Fox, but Meadow hesitates at the doorway.

"You want to come too?" I ask.

"Meadow isn't very good at spelling or adding up numbers," her brother answers.

She looks away. "Yeah, I'm not good at that game."

"I can help you keep score. I'm pretty good at maths." I don't want to leave her here alone.

She eyes her brother, who shrugs. "Okay. Thanks."

"No need to thank me. You can pay me back with whatever you're going to be making in those pans." I wink and run after Fox.

Best new neighbors ever.

## Chapter 4
# Meadow

"Earth to Mommy!" Maisie claps her hands together from her booster seat in the back of the car.

"Sorry, Mais." I give her a small smile in the rearview mirror and sip my pitch-black coffee. I'll need seven more cups to get me through today. The sky is drained of light as we ascend the windy road up the hill to Grace Academy. "I didn't sleep well last night."

Or at all.

On my one day off in weeks, my worst fucking nightmare came to life before my head even hit my pillow. Since January, all the town could talk about is Ollie Anderson—the prodigal son, Fox's best friend, the ocean-cleaning, big-city rich boy returning home. A man my parents would be proud of because he clearly followed in my father's footsteps. Unlike me.

Even from our brief interaction, it was obvious he's successful.

I'd painstakingly planned the welcome-back recital: Stop by the Andersons'. Bring over an ale brisket, the most neutral cut of meat I could think of, and simply say hello. Be civil. Don't get into the past.

Instead, my bright blue dong did a happy jig in his mother's cake. *Just perfect.*

"Take a nap today," Maisie says frankly.

"Maybe I will," I chuckle. Even if I found an hour in my day, there's no way I could lie still for more than thirty seconds.

"What were you saying before I zoned out there, plum?"

"I can't miss my first rugby practice tonight." She kicks her booties around, flashing me her blue doe eyes. For a seven-year-old, Maisie's plate is as full as mine with school, tap dancing lessons, friend dates, and now rugby.

"Of course. I'll be there to drive you."

"You're the best, Mom."

"Love you."

We pull up to the white brick school. Students pile into the arched entrance as parents chatter. A few of the moms outside of pickup wave, and I return the gesture.

Maisie unbuckles her belt, the one we double-check is strapped in every single time she gets in the car, and places a warm kiss on my cheek. A seatbelt saved her life once. "Do not forget my practice. Please, please, please. Coach Neil says this is going to be my most important season yet."

"I won't. Have a good day, okay?"

She shakes her head vigorously, her ponytail whacking around the car. "Run the pass, Ma."

"Heard." I wink, indulging in my favorite part of the morning.

Those nights she spent doing homework at Ramona's restaurant while I prepped for the dinner shift paid off in her learning all the kitchen lingo. The phrases are so much sweeter coming from her mouth than the rage-filled head chefs who screamed at me for most of my twenties.

She bounces down the pavement, and the sparkly pink faux fox tail attached to her book bag swings with each step. Before going inside, she gives me another small wave.

Making this little girl happy is my favorite thing to do—next to cooking.

I circle back down the gravelly road. In the silence, my mind returns to him again.

America was good to Ollie—which is exactly why I need to avoid him at all costs.

What happened with us was foolish young love, if I could even call it that. We were kids, barely on the brink of adulthood. We both made mistakes.

I turn onto the town center's roundabout. In the middle, the famous statues—two fifteen-foot metal thistles intertwined together—are covered in ice. In July, the national flower blooms in thick purples and greens all over the mountainsides.

I continue down the left side of the road, passing Tavern and Betty's Bed & Breakfast. A handwritten chalkboard scribbled with today's pastries sits under the green awning. I circle past Honeydew Market, an ivory-faced structure that takes up half a street.

Finally, smack dab in the center of downtown, between Paul's flower shop and the secondhand bookstore, Fox Den—my dream—comes into view, with bare vines crawling over the deep redbrick exterior.

When Lenny and Iris Georgette put their old sweater shop on the market five months ago, I couldn't resist putting in an offer. I quit my head chef position at Ramona's the second my signature went on the deed.

It was terrifying quitting a steady-paying job that gave Maisie and me a comfortable life, but I deserved to take a chance on myself after all these years of putting someone else first. I've poured all of my blood, tears, savings, and my parents' loan into making my own restaurant a reality. I cringe, hating that I had to borrow money from them. But they offered, probably trying to make up for the fact that they refused to pay for culinary school. It was college or nothing in the Macrae house. I swore I'd never take a dime from them, but things changed after Fox's death, our relationship caught somewhere between the old and new.

Owning my own restaurant is my dream, and I couldn't sacrifice not going after it any longer. Which is why Fox Den needs to be a flaming success.

It will be. It has to be.

Everything is riding on this.

I park the car in my spot behind the restaurant, loop around to the front, and make my way inside. A soft light emanates from the bay windows. Brooke and Fi must've arrived early. A nag settles into my gut. I should've been here sooner.

Tomorrow, I'll get Maisie and myself out the door faster.

The front room is spacious, with a fireplace and a newly installed bar. Sheets of plastic cover the beautiful oak floors, which will be filled with furniture this week. An artisan woodworker in Glasgow has been building our tables. The dining chairs are in transit from a used online marketplace, a fusion restaurant going out of business. Hopefully that's not a bad omen.

One man's trash is another woman's treasure.

"Good morning. Sorry I'm late." My voice echoes in the empty space.

"What do you mean? You're right on time." Brooke, my sous chef, flashes me a cheeky smile. Her curly blonde hair is combed back into a high ponytail. "Besides, you can't be late for painting day. We'll be high on fumes in about an hour; then the concept of time won't exist," she sings into a clean paintbrush as she wiggles her shoulders at me. "Energizer Bunny" was the nickname she got when we were at Le Cordon Bleu together. She was the only other American student in my program, making the trek to France all the way from Florida.

"She's been this cheery since we walked in a half hour ago," Fi, my pastry chef, groans. Her Scottish accent rises and falls with a songlike quality. She comes out from the back room with two steaming mugs. She hands me one, and I gulp down the pitch-black brew.

"I can't get over the notes of cherry in this espresso," I moan into the cup.

*Perfection.*

"With the dark chocolate mousse, it'll be fantastic." Fi's black pixie haircut is pushed out of her face with a purple bandana, making her green eyes pop.

"Agreed."

"Unlike you two addicts, I don't need coffee this morning. I'm over the moon because I saw some hunky man meat leaving the bus station last night," Brooke says, emptying her paint canister into a plastic pail. "So, perhaps I won't need to drive to Inverness this week for a date."

My pulse fizzles out. She can't possibly mean Ollie.

"Really? Man meat?" Fi narrows her eyes on Brooke, looking positively repulsed. "You're so crude."

Brooke shoots me a playful eye roll, her round brown eyes scrunching up playfully.

I wasn't sure how they were going to get on when we all agreed to take the plunge a few months ago and become business partners, but despite their light banter, I think they've taken a liking to each other.

That's what a kitchen needs—harmony.

I clear my throat. "What are you talking about?"

"When I was walking home last night, this guy, Meadow," she gasps with amusement. "He must've been seven feet tall—a mountain come to life, basically. Anyway, he was lugging three suitcases into the back of a truck parked outside the bus station like they were bags of hen feathers."

That confirms it. She saw him.

"Probably didn't get the memo that tourist season doesn't start for two more months." Fi shrugs, slipping plastic covers over her boots.

I shuck off my jacket, plop down on the ground, and pull the protectors over my soles. My friends will find out about my run-in last night anyway, so I may as well be the one to tell them.

"That was Oliver Anderson." I avoid their stares, fidgeting with the plastic for far longer than necessary.

Brooke drops her rolling pail and sprints over to me. "No. Fucking. Way." She squats down to my eye level and grabs me by the shoulders. "The Ollie? *Your* Ollie?"

The mere mass of him occupying my doorway returns to my mind. His shoulders are considerably larger than I remember, his jaw sharper, covered with a full beard of auburn peppered with gray. A shiver runs through my body at the memory of how his coarse hair used to feel across my cheek, chest, and inner thighs.

He looked grown. Obviously he would be; I'm grown up too. But something about him was different, and it wasn't only the fancy clothes and glistening smile—it was his attitude. Sassy and sharp. Even still, underneath that new exterior, I caught a small glimpse of the boy who'd try anything to make me smile. The moment he spoke, a dam broke, and memories poured out, threatening to drown me.

*You always had your brother's arm.*

Why'd he decide to bring up Fox? He hasn't cared about him all these years. After our plans to move to America collapsed, my brother told me that he and Ollie never spoke. He didn't even bother coming to his funeral.

My mind is positively sabotaging me.

"He's not mine," I snap, swatting Brooke's hands.

Panic floods her brown eyes. "By the way, I didn't mean anything by that hunky man meat comment."

"It's fine," I assure her.

"You've gotta admit, the sight of him was something else. Looked like a tight end on a football team. My hometown Florida Gators always had big boys like that."

Fi looks confused by Brooke's American football reference. "A flanker in rugby," I explain.

"Doubt he has any trouble flanking anything," Brooke snickers.

Her eyes draw down, as if she's remembering those first few months in Paris. Brooke helped me heal when I was still raw with heartache. While I taught her to perfect her brunoise, she taught me how to flirt with men who weren't my first love—a skill that served as a lazy distraction for when my mind was stuck on Ollie.

We spent the next eight years blistering our fingers and yapping about our back pain like two old ladies while we gave our twenties to Michelin-starred restaurants all over France.

She was my first call when I signed the deed to Fox Den. She was exhausted from the fast-paced chef life and agreed to pool her savings and move here immediately.

"My pa mentioned he was coming back." Fi looks at me with concern. "Didn't realize it was so soon."

"Yep."

We marinate in the awkward silence.

Fi was born and raised in Thistlehill. She's a few years older than me, so we never connected in school, but she hung out with Fox and Ollie.

It was her sticky toffee pudding that kept me going when Maisie's infant wails could be heard all through town. She connected me with Ramona, who needed a new head chef, and we've worked together for the last six years. But, like me, she always felt she wasn't utilizing all of her exemplary baking skills at one of the only restaurants in Thistlehill.

Ramona's is the closest thing to a decent dinner service in town. The restaurant has served the same six menu items since my family moved here. It's reliable. A town favorite for locals. However, I could go my entire life without smelling the stench of her secret-ingredient stew.

"Can we get started with the painting? We have a long day ahead of us," I remind them, deflecting the conversation from Ollie as best I can. "Fi, why don't you get on the kitchen pathway, and Brooke, that wall is going to need a lot of work." I nod to the freshly dried concrete farthest away from me.

"Yes, chef." Brooke bounces up and gets to work. After a breath of silence, she says, "I can still ask you questions from all the way over here."

Great. "Must you?"

She ignores me. "Did you talk to him?"

I pick up a roller and dip it into the milky sage color in the tray. "Not exactly. More like we had a few awkward jokes, and then I yelled at him."

"Is he staying with Seamus and Riley?" Fi turns up her speaker, and music fills the dining room. I've never met anyone who can't stand the silence as much as Fi. It's as if without a soundtrack, her life is empty.

I guess if I didn't have cooking, my life would feel the same way.

"Yes." I smash the roller against my wall and begin painting.

"The Andersons are in the house next to Meadow." Fi paddles the information to Brooke given the confused expression on her face. She's only lived in Thistlehill full-time for two months, and learning all the ins and outs of the town is a lifelong process.

"You're neighbors. Brilliant. Is that why you yelled at him? He show up with an outstretched tree trunk arm and beg you for a cup of sugar you didn't feel like sharing?"

"No. He—" I inhale a long breath. No point in putting off the inevitable horror story. "Walked in on me while I was, uh, watching *Beck...*"

"You mean hanging out with your blue rabbit on the couch and catching glimpses of Kristofer Hivju?" Brooke teases, and Fi laughs under her breath.

"I threatened to use my knife skills on him."

They gasp. "*No.*"

I roll my lips together and nod. "He didn't even knock, just barged into my house as if he's been back home for ages."

"Then what happened?" Brooke's excitement is far too perky for the shitshow that unfolded last night.

"I threw the rabbit at him."

A carnival of laughter erupts out of the both of them. Instead of being mortified, I join in. It is ridiculous.

"Oh, man, did he volunteer to use it on you?" Brooke wipes the tears in her eyes and returns to her wall.

"No. Maisie came home early."

The hollering dies.

"It'll be a hello he'll never forget," she jokes.

The comment pours salt on a wound that's never healed. Ollie hasn't returned to our small town in decades. Not for my brother's funeral, and not even to visit his parents.

"Watch out for the bricks." My breath halts as Brooke's paintbrush gets too close to the beautiful fireplace at her side. "We want to keep those exposed."

"I remember the plans." She shrinks and glides her roller neatly against the wall. The same way she got small when she brought up adding more unique flavors to our appetizers and I lost my cool at her. Thistlehill can't handle the things we did when we were in France. Doubt circumvents my chest. No. An execution-strong menu with classic flavors is the way to succeed.

Not being experimental.

"I know you do, I'm sorry," I say. Brooke has the hands of a surgeon, but I have the nerves of a starved polar bear. One wrong move, and we're back into damage control. "I only want to get this wrapped up and tackle everything else we have going on today. We open in two weeks, and we still have so much to do."

"We're going to get it done, chef. We're capable," Brooke reminds me. "Try to take it easy, okay?"

The reminder of my fried nerves and razor-thin patience sends a tic into my jaw.

"I think Colette coming to the opening has me on edge. I want her to be proud of us." I credit my entire culinary career to Colette Dubois hiring me and Brooke. She encouraged me that this was the best time to take the plunge. If she believes I have what it takes to run my own place, then I believe it.

"Meadow, you were always her favorite," Brooke says.

"How are you feeling about the fact that you'll be seeing Ollie around now?" Fi watches me. The green of her eyes is laced with concern.

"I have no time to think about him or the past. What happened between us happened. And it's not my job to make it right. We've got a restaurant to run."

"But how are you feeling?" Brooke asks.

"Busy. Very fucking busy."

Fi flashes Brooke a look before saying, "You know what happens when you work too hard. What if your panic—"

"No. It won't. I know how to handle myself," I promise.

When I get stressed, my nerves rev up their engines. When I was a teenager, the panic attacks would happen in the midst of nasty fights with my parents—a tsunami waiting to envelop me. The episodes continued after I ended things with Ollie, through the exhaustion from culinary school and my work-for-tuition program. After Fox passed, panic would corrode every fiber of my being for days, and I'd just push through.

Anxiety is a part of me, and that's okay. It has been a constant in my life, like a dull, aching bruise that never heals. But I learned to manage my mind when it spins off its hinges.

Deep breaths. Staying present.

Sure, sometimes I feel the crest of panic itch up my throat when I work too hard or my lack of sleep catches up to me, but I can always maintain it. I always have it under control. I need to. For myself, for Maisie, for the people counting on me.

Besides, there hasn't been a bad episode for a few years.

"Remember that busy is a verb. Not a feeling." Brooke gives me a concerned glance.

"Most businesses turn over in a year, so it's a feeling for me. After we open, we have about twelve months to make a name for ourselves. If we don't, our miniscule funds are going to send us into bankruptcy." I remind them what's at stake. A year to make Fox Den a permanent stop on the famous North Coast 500 route, a 516-mile scenic route around the north coast of Scotland, starting and ending at Inverness Castle.

Between October and April, it's quiet. But once the annual Thistlehill Festival commences, the town swarms with tourists. My favorite time of year, and the best way to get our name out there.

"There are three of us, and the new staff. We can rely on each other to succeed," Brooke promises.

"I won't believe you until I see it with my own eyes."

Everything is riding on this going perfectly, and it's up to me to make sure that happens.

## Chapter 5
# Meadow

"Argh," I groan and wince as pain stabs through my lower stomach.

"Another shooter?" Maisie asks.

I nod, breathing through the aching cramp. This period is a nightmare.

"It's fine." A sweat bead drips along my neck.

My premenstrual dysphoric disorder and fibroids consume my life. A sick punishment for a chef who stands all day and works late nights. But my uterus decided to be a cunt one day and left me with *fun* symptoms—debilitating cramps, severe mood swings, a surge in my anxiety, sciatica that makes me want to rip my leg off, crippling nausea, and tender breasts that can't even handle being in a bra—that last weeks at a time. Sadly, nothing helps. Not even the birth control pills my doctor insists are meant to manage the unsettled hormones.

*C'mon, painkillers. Kick in already. There's no time to waste.*

"My boots are outside."

"Go get 'em and come back here; we have to pack up your school bag. What would you like for lunch today?" I rise slowly, waiting for my menstrual cup to flip a coin on staying in place or dislodging and soaking me in blood. Wouldn't be the first time that's happened. Yes, it's horrific and graphic. Worst of all, it's my life every single month until these wretched periods go away all together. Or, better yet, someone decides to invest a ton of money into women's health instead of dismissing the issues as a typical woman's problem.

"Grilled cheese," she sings as she opens the front door, letting in the cool air.

"How about we do that for dinner so the cheese is all nice and pull-y?"

"Okay, a tomato roll-up then. With extra cheese puffs."

"Yes, chef," I laugh.

Maisie hesitates, tiptoeing and stretching out her neck. "Mommy, look, it's the friend of the Andersons again."

I prance to the living room window like a starved cheetah and hide behind a curtain, looking over to the Andersons' front porch. Ollie is wrapped in a thick wool blanket, sipping out of a mug. I guess our three-day streak of avoiding each other had to end sometime. Why on earth is he sitting outside at dawn in this weather? Doesn't matter. He can catch a cold for all I care.

"Yep."

"Let's say hello."

"We have to finish getting ready for school, plum."

"But it would be rude not to." Maisie skips out onto the porch, her oversized book bag bouncing on her shoulders. Before I have a chance to stop her, she bellows at Ollie's porch, "What's your name?"

*Dammit.*

"Ollie." His voice drifts over to me through the open front door. Thank god we don't have any other neighbors with how loud these two are shouting.

"I've never met you before," Maisie yells back. I hesitate. Should I pull her back into the house? No. This is fine. We have to be neighbors while he's here. This was bound to happen eventually."

"Except on Monday, but you didn't introduce yourself."

"Sorry about that. I was a little tired from my flight. It's good to be meeting now."

She giggles. "You have a cool beard, but it's a little too bushy," Maisie remarks.

I snort at her frankness and continue watching from behind the living room curtain. Ollie stands, drapes the red blanket around his broad shoulders, and meanders to the banister with a smile plastered on his face. I'm definitely giving creeper vibes, but what am I to do? Go out onto the porch and give him a warm hello?

Him showing up here after all this time, looking like a lumberjack mountain man, is unfair. This whole ignoring him thing would be easier if he'd grown a second head, or maybe a tail. Yes, a tail would help distract me from his messy auburn waves, strong nose, stout forehead, and deep throaty laugh.

"That so?"

"Definitely," Maisie says.

"I'll have to fix that as soon as possible." He nods to her backpack. "You have a neat keychain right there."

Not this.

Not now.

My daughter yanks her backpack off her shoulder and holds up the pink faux fur accessory. "Grandpa gave this to me. He said my dad used to have one on his backpack too."

"He sure did."

"You knew my dad?" Her voice escalates. Hopeful but small. Now he's done it. Opened a door even I won't be able to keep locked. *How dare he bring up Fox again.*

"I—"

"Maisie," I call out. "Come inside, we have to leave soon."

"But, *Moooom*," she pleads. I don't respond. "Fine. Bye, Ollie."

"Bye, Maisie."

These interactions cannot happen. I won't allow it. Maisie's past has never been a secret. Anything she wants to know about Fox and Penelope, I tell her. But the way things were left between me, Ollie, and Fox are too complicated to explain.

Once Maisie is back in the house, I give her my phone. "Why don't you put some music on? I need to go have a word with Mr. Anderson."

"Can I play any song?" There's a positively mischievous glint in her eyes. I've made my bed, and I'm going to lie in it. I swore if I had to listen to *The cold never bothered me anyway* in the middle of winter one more time I'd scream, but I need a second.

"Any song."

When she plops down on the couch to scroll my phone, I hurry out the door to his side of the lawn, ready to strike.

Ollie readjusts the blanket. One frayed edge collapses, revealing a sliver of his bare chest and thick neck. I blink, stunned. That blanket is the same one we snuggled under after losing our virginity together in the back of his dad's pickup truck right after our first official date. His warm skin pressed against me. He was so sweet, and tender and—No, that was the old Ollie.

The man in front of me, however frustratingly handsome, is not someone I know.

*Eyes up, Meadow. Stick to the plan. Tell him to stay out of our way. Do not stare at his unruly chest hair.*

I'm mad. Furious. Embarrassed. Heartbroken.

"You hiding a knife in your pocket?"

"Maybe I should be," I bite. The porch is high off the ground, but with him standing at the edge of it, I'm microscopic. I'm five eleven, and he's the only man who's ever made me feel small. It used to be one of the things I loved about him. Now, I fucking hate it.

"Look, I was only being polite. Can't exactly ignore a child." He pauses, tipping his head to one side awkwardly. "That keychain was something."

"How dare you," I whisper, not wanting Maisie or his parents to be privy to this conversation. My mom immediately phoned Riley after I gave her an abridged version of our reunion. There won't be any more gossip about Ollie and me.

"Meadow, I didn't mean anything by it."

"Listen, Oliver, you can show up here and act like Prince Charming on his high horse, coming to do a good deed for your parents, but you will not—"

"Prince Charming?" he laughs, though there's a hard glint in his eyes I've never seen before.

I ignore him. "Do not talk to Maisie about her father. I know you didn't care about him." The words are harsh, but he needs to hear them. Hear the words I've kept inside all this time.

Ollie straightens, his face flushing. "Must be hard for you to talk the big talk, considering you're a coward."

"Coward? You gotta be kidding me." His words sear me, charring any fiber of rational thought. My palms slam onto the curves of my hips. The torrent of old and new anger rips through me, and there's no way to hold it back. "*You're* the coward who spent two decades hiding across an ocean—"

"You left me at the airport, alone, with nothing but a heartless text."

"I was seventeen. A child. I did my best to make things right between us." My pulse batters my chest. Another cramp shoots into my abdomen, weakening my legs. "I had reasons, and you didn't want to listen to them. You ignored me, over and over again. What did you want me to do when you refused to hear me out?"

"Not abandon me in the first place, especially a couple weeks after my birthday," he says coldly.

That's such a petty response. "You don't think I felt guilty?"

"Not guilty enough to do the right thing and end it with me in person. I was a fool standing in the terminal, begging them to keep the plane on the ground a moment longer."

Melancholy washes over me, but I can't let him see it. He's not allowed that part of me. As kids, we only knew each other for four years. Eighteen months of that time was spent in a real relationship. Did that small past affect us both so much that we can't handle things like two grown adults in the present?

"And you never returned my phone calls. Not even on the night I found out Fox had died. You—" My pesky emotions catch in my throat. Dammit. "You were the first person I called, the only one who would understand, and you didn't pick up. For someone who's acting all scorned, you sure as hell didn't seem to care about me back then. So don't act like you want to try and be my friend now. Don't talk to my daughter, don't strut around here and expect things to be normal."

The words seem to break his ironclad exterior. "What?"

"Honestly, Oliver, who cares about what happened with us? This was *Fox*. Not a single phone call from you, no text, not even one of those fucking generic baskets you can buy online that say something like *Sorry for your loss*. Don't you dare call *me* a coward."

I need to get out of here. This is all too much.

"I—" He exhales, rubbing his forehead with his palm. "I changed my number when I got to the States."

"It doesn't matter." I'm not prepared for his excuses. "That girl is my entire world. If you want to take a trip down memory lane with Maisie, you need to run it by me. You don't have the right to share whatever personal tidbits you still remember about my brother with her."

"You're right." The calm tone in his voice is surprising. "Look, I shouldn't have stormed your house on Monday, and I shouldn't have called you a coward. Being back here is a lot. I haven't been sleeping, my folks aren't pleased with me, and all

I'm trying to say is that I didn't mean to escalate the situation."

I take a step back, narrowing my eyes on him. An apology was the last thing I expected. As a teenager, he always tried to defuse situations. Maybe a part of the boy I used to know is still in there somewhere. "Okay," I concede.

"We don't need to speak about the past. We were way over our heads at that age; it was nothing. We meant nothing." His words slow time around me. He was my first everything, and that meant *nothing*? "How's that sound? No need to ever recall your date with the vibrator either."

Is he trying to piss me off? "You're the worst."

"Aye, maybe I am, but I'll be out of your hair in three months."

"Not soon enough."

Our gazes blaze with the same fire.

How is it after all these years I want to scream and yell and bash a pan over his head, but, in the same breath, I sort of want him to hold me? To tell me everything is fine, we'll figure it out, to make me laugh?

He always seemed to know how to do that so much better than anyone else.

A faint whisper of longing ebbs through my body. Alight, raw, and consuming.

A need.

I slam the door on that feeling, locking it away.

"Let's be cordial until I leave," Ollie says.

"Fine by me."

"Fine."

"Great." I leave him, his auburn waves, and his unruly chest hair on the porch.

His stare scrapes against my back the entire walk to my house. My hand finds the necklace my brother gave me when he dropped me off at Le Cordon Bleu. He told me that Ollie would come around as he clasped the chain around my neck. Guess he was wrong.

Once I'm inside, I grab Maisie's lunch in the kitchen, throwing in extra snacks. My kiddo eyes me across the living room.

"What was that about, Mommy?"

"I have no idea what you're talking about."

"How does Ollie know Dad?" Maisie strolls over to the kitchen, climbing up onto a wooden counter stool beneath the island.

I can tell her the facts and leave the heartbreak in the margins.

The past, that far back, rarely felt relevant enough to bring up. Ollie simply stopped being a part of our stories when he left. Even if the three of us were inseparable for years. We could hang out for hours with no real responsibilities. A part of me yearns for that freedom sometimes.

"When your gran and grandpa moved us to Scotland, we lived in this house," I remind her. She hangs off of every word, the same way my brother did when you told him a story. It was as if it was the most interesting thing in the world to him. "Ollie lived next door."

"Why would Pops and Nan have a friend living with them for that long?"

"He's actually their son."

"Oh." She thinks. "Was Ollie really friends with Dad?"

My hands work on autopilot as I slice an apple, the same way I'd mindlessly cook at Ramona's. I hope cooking at Fox Den doesn't become this monotonous. Maisie's cerulean eyes are intent on me. She's a spitting image of my brother. Her smile is the same one Ollie used to keep permanently glued onto Fox's face.

A wave of sadness washes over me. I miss my brother so much.

Grief is a fickle thing. Weeks can pass without remembering the deep emptiness inside of me, and in the next moment, it's as if I'm that twenty-seven-year-old girl, inconsolably crying on a plane back to Scotland to attend her brother's funeral and become a guardian to his baby. I left a job I loved and an apartment right on the Rhône, one I shared with Brooke.

And I'd do it all over again for Maisie and for my brother, even if a small part of me never actually mourned the life and the future I gave up.

That's what Fox Den is. A piece of my old dreams that I can try to make work in this reality.

"They used to be inseparable." I steady my voice, tossing the apples into a container with a spritz of lemon juice to keep them fresh.

"You said Dad was your best friend when you were a little girl. That means Ollie must've been your best friend too." She comes to the conclusion any other seven-year-old would, easily seeing past the fragments of why it's not quite that simple. My throat seizes up, and I swallow. "Do you not like him?"

"Ollie?" My brows sew together.

"Duh, Ollie, who else? The not-friend of the Andersons who's actually their kid who also happens to be Dad's best friend."

Far too smart to let me get away with anything. "Why would you think that?"

"You seemed pretty mad when you talked to him. You had your hands on your hips and everything." So much for tempting her with the playlist. I should've known she was going to keep watch through the window.

"I—he—we had to talk about the missing flowerpot. The one we bought in Inverness, remember? It had a beautiful, shimmering red glaze," I lie, etching another carving into my bad mom trophy.

Although I *have* been missing a flowerpot since Ollie

arrived. At first I thought it may have been the Camerons' Kleptocow, but she couldn't possibly move an entire pot. Unless her jaw was made of steel. Ollie must've kicked it over as he rushed out of my house on Monday and was too much of a coward to tell me.

*Coward.*

How dare he call me that.

"Hmm." She crosses her small arms over her chest, probably not believing a single word I'm saying. "You also haven't dropped off a welcome gift for him."

"I don't give everyone a welcome gift."

"Not true. You gave Brooke a huge welcome dinner when she moved here."

She has me there.

"Fine. Ollie and I had a small fight many, many years ago. Way before you were born."

"And did you apologize?"

"What?" I say hastily.

"Did you say sorry? You always tell me to say sorry, Mommy. *Share your feelings and move forward together.*" She does her best to imitate me.

Curse those damn gentle parenting books!

A simple apology won't be enough to dig through the decades of scorned resentment both of us are so clearly clinging to. There's also no time.

He's going to leave again, and I don't have time for friends who aren't going to stick around.

"You're right, plum. That is what I say."

"So, I think—"

"Get over here." I put the lunch and extra snack in her backpack. "I need to use the restroom, and then we'll go."

Maisie's gone into full interrogator mode. I knew I shouldn't have let her sneak in a few episodes of *Beck* before bed. That settles it. I'll definitely keep my mystery shows and novels far away from her.

I rush upstairs, empty my already full menstrual cup, and take my birth control because I can't remember if I have already taken one this morning or if this is my second one, before going through my to-do list.

After I train the staff, I need to deep clean the new fridge that was installed yesterday. That'll be at least two hours of work, but I do have a new audiobook in the Highland and Hearth mystery series.

*Why did Ollie come back?*

No. Focus. We want to run through the menu one more time. Something isn't quite right, but it may only be nerves. It's a step up from Ramona's, that's for sure, but I don't want to scare the townsfolk with cuisine that's too inventive. Classics with perfect execution.

*Can we even keep our distance when we live right next door?*

Stop. Stop it, right now! I need to finalize the deal with Seamus before he leaves next week. Otherwise, I won't have my own whisky for Fox Den. Seamus wouldn't put Ollie in charge of that. *Right?*

I stifle a yawn. Nausea burns my throat. Coffee and a ginger honey tea are all I need.

It'll be alright. I'll get it done, and it'll be perfect. I always manage.

## Chapter 6
# Ollie

RAMONA'S RUSTIC RESTAURANT IS FOSSILIZED. SEPIA-TINTED photographs line the walls, capturing the town's uneventful history. The floorboards creak with memories I'm not upset about missing over the years. Timeworn tables and chairs are filled with familiar faces. It seems barely anyone's left Thistlehill.

After evading a few curious stares, my parents and I reach an empty table farthest from the entrance. Instead of three place settings, we're seated for seven.

"I thought it was going to be just us," I ask as Da pulls out a chair and gestures for Ma to take a seat.

"Change of plans." She shrugs, fumbling with the cloth napkin beside her plate. Her usual blue jeans and thick braid have been replaced by her special dress and curls. "I suppose I forgot tae mention that the Macraes are seeing us off."

They've got to be joking. "Right, of course."

I should've expected this; they've been best friends for years. Shame coats my face. What am I going to say to them? *Sorry I missed your son's funeral and never called to wish you my condolences or even catch up—even though you were like second parents to me, sometimes better parents than my own—all because your daughter broke my heart and I never moved past it?*

I need to make peace with this and put it to rest once and for all. I'll simply say I'm sorry. There's nothing else to do.

A cactus of nerves prickles my chest. Maybe this dinner is exactly what I needed. A way to iron out some of this shame that's been haunting me. I had no room to process Fox's death. Not a second to spare on grieving the man who—apart from my parents, Harris, and Meadow—had the biggest impact on my life.

I'd worked too hard to get to where I was—

*No, where you still are, Ollie.*

I roll out the tension in my neck.

Meadow's words echo in my mind. *You were the first person I called, the only one who would understand, and you didn't pick up.* I wasn't there for her. I wasn't there for Harris and Ivy Macrae. I haven't even been there for my own parents.

I stumble into the chair opposite Ma.

A high-pitched voice screams through the restaurant, "Ollie!" Maisie's little face weaves through the tables, Ivy and Harris right on her heels. *Where's Meadow?* Unease mixes with something else. Hopefully she's cooled off since our run-in on Friday. Avoiding each other was never going to work. This town has always been too small for the both of us.

"Hi, Maisie." I smile and remember Meadow's firm instructions. Don't overstep. Don't bring up her dad.

"Hi, Nan! Hi, Pops!" Maisie bounces on her toes, flashing her barely toothy smile at them. "Can I sit with you guys? Coach Neil announced my rugby position today. Guess what it is! Guess. They made me the fullback! Can you believe that?"

Fox's old position.

"Come and tell us about it here." Da pulls out a chair for her and pats the seat.

She called them *Nan* and *Pops*. They're obviously close. I guess my parents really have been watching Maisie. Perhaps that's why they've never bugged me about grandchildren; they have one living right next door.

An entire life happened without me. Of course time went on after I left. My neck strains. I chose this. Never mind. My parents leave tomorrow. When they come back from their cruise, I'll have two days with them before I fly home to New York City. We'll return to a superficial family in no time.

"Ollie, look at you, all grown up." Ivy's familiar American accent is a warm surprise. "A whole man you've got here, Ri."

"It's good to see you," I say. She ignores my awkward pause and bends down, wrapping me in a hug. Harris slings over her shoulder and lands a heavy pat on me.

"Ollie, my boy, I've missed you. We have, we've missed you so much." The man who was like a second father to me beams. His grin is the same, but his once raven-black hair is lush with gray. When we were kids, he was monumental, able to hold his own on the rugby field with us, but he's half the size of the man I knew so long ago.

Words latch together like a bin of paperclips in my throat.

"What? Did you already dig into Ramona's stew? Trust me, son, it's darn good, but it rushes through you with the speed of lightning. Always has my face seizing up like yours is right now."

He laughs, and the colorful image cracks me. "I'll keep that in mind."

Surely Ivy and Harris are only being cordial for my parents' sake. They bid hello to my parents, stripping off their scarves, beanies, and gloves before finding their place around the table.

The weathered entrance swings open, and Meadow walks in. My breathing slows. Her ivory skin glows beneath the warm yellow hue of the pendant lamps above. Her chestnut hair is curled at the ends, picking up streams of light as if they were fire.

"Ah, there she is," Ivy sighs. "Kleptocow fell asleep in the parking lot again. Meadow had to drive down the street and use her own spot at Fox Den."

"That darn cow," Da laughs.

She's a vision striding toward our table, which has suddenly become the best seat in the house. Her full hips swing around chairs, hypnotizing me. She never used to wear makeup, but on her cheeks and lips there's a tinge of pink.

I grip the edge of the table. *Where is the waiter with some bloody water?*

When I finally tear my eyes away from her, I catch Ma and Ivy conspiratorially whispering to each other.

Not this again.

Those same hushed exchanges happened after we announced we were dating. They heard wedding bells bellowing loudly through the cobblestone streets of Thistlehill.

Meadow and I were barely on the brink of adulthood, and our folks were already mapping out an entire life for us. Especially since her parents didn't exactly agree with her culinary pursuits. A part of me thinks they hoped that when we moved abroad, I'd make Meadow change her mind about university.

I never planned on doing that.

Maybe that's why she left me. The expectations of our parents were always overwhelming. It's the reason we kept our relationship a secret for as long as possible.

"Hey, everyone." Meadow kisses Da and Ma's cheeks, eyeing the only empty seat, which is next to me. She glares at Ivy, probably jumping to the same conclusion I have. This is looking less like a goodbye dinner and more like a setup.

"Hi, Mommy," Maisie sings.

"Hey," I say with a forced grin.

"Hi." Meadow avoids my gaze and reaches for the chair next to me. I clamber for it and pull it out for her. "Thanks."

Out of the corner of my eye, Ma hides her smile.

Meadow shrugs off her jacket. Underneath is a dark purple dress wrapped around her lush curves. A small thistle charm dangles from her neck. She reluctantly slides into her seat.

We used to love sitting together. We'd play footsie, hold hands under the table, whisper inside jokes and hushed *I love yous* to each other.

*Focus on anything but her.*

Her arm grazes mine.

My body heats. A shock zips through my chest, and my hand smacks into the glass in front of me.

S*mooth. Real smooth.*

"I had no idea about any of this," I whisper, leaning toward her.

*Big fucking mistake.*

Damp earth. Fresh rain. My mind reignites like a city regaining power. Meadow.

*You're home*, my thoughts scream. Her scent. Petrichor. *My home.*

The most peculiar thing about her. It's as if the earth from when she foraged for mushrooms or the dirt she cleaned off vegetables while cooking implanted itself into her skin. It hasn't changed at all.

"It's fine." She shakes her head dismissively. "It's only dinner."

A waiter cuts the small distance between us, dropping off the menus. The table laughs as they boast up Ma about her knitting, and Da orders a bottle of champagne. I order whatever he's having and fall back into my daze until the waiter leaves.

"Ollie, tell us what you've been up to." Ivy props her palms beneath her chin and rests her elbows on the table. "We already know you graduated from MIT in only three years, then went into finance, and of course you sold that cool ocean-cleaning technology. Busy, busy man! We need more details. There's a lot of lost time to make up for."

Meadow's hands, marked up and scarred, fumble with her cloth napkin. I attempt to rile my sluggish heartbeat.

"That's the gist of it. I wasn't going to make a big thing about it, but after I help Da with the distillery, I've got my dream job lined up in New York City. I start in June," I recite with the formality of a job interview. I want to impress them so badly. More than my own parents.

*Relax, Ol. These people know you. They're not strangers.*

"Dream job?" Harris asks.

"Director of Sustainable Innovation at Viggle. Won't be anything like Silverman Sachs, that's for sure." Though I will be taking on the same kind of workload as I did in the dog days of my finance years. But it'll be worth it. The success of making a big name for myself at the most important company in the world will be worth it.

"Ah, I remember those old stomping grounds," Harris chuckles, nudging Ivy. "Was the New York office as soul-sucking as I said the Boston one was?"

"Even more than you described." I stretch out my legs under the table, uneasiness coating my muscles.

Meadow's father was the inspiration for my need for success. The Macraes always had it so much better than us. All the smartest, wealthiest men worked at Silverman, he used to tell me. I wanted to be one of them. I wanted to be just like Harris Macrae. That's who I had to be if Meadow and I were going to make a life together. I wanted to provide her with the things she was accustomed to. For both of us.

"You lasted almost as long as I did. Once you pass nine years, making it to ten is hell." He cringes, pushing his aging hands through his hair.

I definitely agree. A decade at the place, for all the wealth it brought me, was wearing on me.

"I wasn't going to let you spend another second in that dungeon." Ivy snorts. Beside me, Meadow's napkin fumbling has turned into a full-blown fabric strangulation. I suppose after all these years, the memories of her life back in Boston haven't shaken loose. "I still remember those nights when you'd stumble in, exhausted, at two in the morning and try to get that one"—she nods at Meadow—"to bed before leaving at seven to do the day all over again."

"One of the best decisions of my life was quitting and moving here. And marrying my Ivy." Harris places a kiss on his wife's cheek.

I heard this story a couple times over as a kid. I was never dissuaded from thinking I could tough it out myself. I had what it took. Harris said he saw himself in me back then. I wanted to make him and myself proud.

"It helped get me to where I am now," I laugh.

"Good on ya, son. Everyone's gotta push through the corporate pipeline and pay their dues."

Ivy senses her daughter's discomfort from across the table. "Well, Meadow knows all about paying her dues." She smiles, interrupting the moment of reminiscing. "Don't you, dear? All those hours in the kitchen have finally paid off, and you can have your own place." There's something in her voice that feels awkward. As if she's overcompensating.

Meadow's been a chef for the better part of two decades; there's no way her parents still disapprove of her culinary career.

"Yeah," Meadow says dismissively and forces a smile. "Seamus, did you have a chance to peek through that contract I sent over last week?"

Ivy and Harris share a brief glance. Clearly there's still some tension between them and her career.

I figured if they're this involved in her life, the rift between them had healed. Meadow and her parents didn't get along much when we were teenagers. Much like my da didn't understand my desire for more than we had, her parents didn't approve of her choosing cooking over university.

But maybe she's still in the same position with her parents as I am with mine. Still misunderstood, after all this time.

I can't help but look at her. The tension in her jaw. The fumbling with her napkin. I itch for the small telepathic phone line we used to have. When we'd be able to speak in just looks. But there's no point in digging that up.

I doubt she wants to answer questions that personal.

Da drums his hands on the table. "Oh, dear, we've been busy. Ye ken, I was thinkin' that since Ol will be here for the next few months, and he's got a technical eye, that he can take over yer contract for Fox Den."

Ding! Ding! Ding! The award for the most obvious parents goes to these noodles. Da hasn't been anywhere near busy this week. We've been leaving the distillery early every night to spend time with Ma. Hell, I saw the contract on his desk the second day I was here.

Meadow will surely be clawing my throat out in no time. Nothing cordial and distant about a business partnership. The bright side is, that's the first time Da's mentioned my technical eye as good for something.

Meadow sips water, her shoulders deflating. "We can talk about something special for my restaurant when you're back."

Da frowns.

"No, if the distillery is in negotiations with your restaurant, then it's only right that I take over," I say, glancing up at her.

Meadow's full lips roll together into a straight line. "My menu goes to the printer on Thursday. I'll need something before then."

"I have plenty of time," I assure her. There's no denying her restaurant will be a success if she's at the helm. No point in having the distillery lose out on meaningful local business.

"You sure?" The annoyance-laced glare she's currently directing at me is heating up the room one degree at a time.

"Shouldn't be a problem," I lie. "I'll guarantee that Fox Den gets some of Anderson's best for its opening."

Meadow scans my face. Her gaze drops from mine to my lips. It rolls over my neck, shoulders, and hands before she shakes her head quickly and looks back up into my eyes. Straightening, she flattens her palms over the wrinkled napkin in her lap and throws on a curt smile.

"Great. Meet at the Den tomorrow...let's say two o'clock?"

"Aye."

Perhaps we can quash the past. Spending time around Meadow doesn't seem all that bad, as long as I stay on her good side and don't bring up our history.

"Mommy has a date," Maisie laughs, watching our tennis match of glances.

"Work, plum. Mommy has work," Meadow corrects her.

"Excellent." Ma nods. "A match made in heaven."

"Thank you, Seamus." Meadow nods uncomfortably.

"Don't worry, dear. Ol here will make sure tae take good care of ye."

Ivy and Ma snicker together. Meadow ignores them.

"Are you getting nervous for the big opening night next Saturday?" Ma asks, rubbing the back of her neck.

The hardness in Meadow's face melts away, and she gets that twinkle in her eye that's impossible to miss. She was always wistful and ablaze whenever she had a chance to talk about food. "Hard not to be. There's so much to do, but Fi and Brooke have been amazing." Must be her staff? "The menu will be elevated classics. I hope it's not too much for Thistlehill," she says with a smile that doesn't feel genuine. "I used to trial all sorts of recipes in the past, but we're not exactly a foodie destination that can handle too much creativity." She looks back down at her plate.

The Meadow I knew never let her confidence in her recipes falter. She was inventive. An actual artist with a knife and a pan.

Involuntarily, a grating scoff bolts out of my chest. "Too much?"

"You think they're going to hate it?"

"No, the opposite. It would be preposterous if everyone didn't love whatever you put on your menu."

Her cheeks flush. It's barely noticeable. "What's that supposed to mean?"

I fumble with the fork in front of me until it clatters against the plate. "Only that I'm sure your restaurant will be much better than…d'Or."

The neatly sculpted points of her brows clap together in confusion. "How do you know that I worked at d'Or?"

Another big fucking mistake. Why don't I have a single filter for my thoughts tonight? "Uh." I pause. "I'm sure Ma told me about it in passing." I shoot her a pleading look.

"Never heard of it." Ma sips her wine.

"Me either," Maisie chimes in, looking as devious as the rest of the table. Though far too adorable for the devilish plotting our parents are in on.

Caught red-handed. Now my ex-girlfriend knows I kept tabs on her over the years. That's normal, right? Everyone has one of those nights when their restless fingers lead them down a rabbit hole of internet searches until they're suddenly on StreetEasy checking how much their ex is paying for rent.

According to a deep dive I did over a decade ago, Meadow had an eight-hundred-euro-a month two-bedroom in Lyon. That particular tidbit I plan to keep buried as deep as I fucking can.

Meadow's brows are still raised in a question mark curve.

"There's no chance your menu won't be great. So you have nothing to worry about." I nod. *Yeah. That's good.* "Sometimes, I can still taste the lamb you made me for my eighteenth birthday."

So much for not bringing up the past.

Our parents' burning stares sear my cheek. Meadow's own expression looks positively flabbergasted.

"Uh." She swallows and bats her lashes away from me.

I remember it like it was yesterday. We spent the afternoon playing house for the first time while our parents were away.

"I agree with Ollie." Harris comes to my rescue, nodding with a pride I haven't seen directed at Meadow before. "Every single person in town is going to love it. You've been busting your butt making sure that this opening goes perfectly. No way it won't be exactly as you've planned."

Maisie leans her head against Harris's arm and smiles. "Yeah, Mommy."

The unease returns to her posture. Something about her restaurant and her parents is making her uncomfortable. Sure, it's been almost twenty years, but I can tell. I see it on her. I know her.

"It's going to be the best restaurant in all of Scotland," I say.

"Eventually. There's an actual consortium of judges; they work to publish the Best of Scotland guides. No restaurant ever gets picked within their first year of business." Her voice is almost dismissive.

Does she think Fox Den wouldn't be a match against some of the best? Impossible.

"Regardless of the prizes, we're so proud of her." Ivy nods feverishly and theatrically throws on the widest smile for Meadow. "We are, sweetheart. So proud."

Meadow's leg jolts nervously beneath the table. "Thanks, Mom."

The waiter returns, setting plates down in front of us. I glance down at the plate in front of me. Ramona's infamous stew.

*Ah, for fuck's sake.*

"If ye'll let me say a few words." Da raises his glass of champagne. "This is a bittersweet occasion." He begins his speech, recalling Ma and his wedding, the decades at the distillery, and how they had to postpone their honeymoon.

Meadow's leg hasn't stopped bouncing. She's not alright. My visceral reaction to her feelings, the one in which every protective fiber of my being would light up around her, returns.

I hate seeing her worked up like this. I itch to be able to help calm her like I used to. My chair vibrates like one of those foot massage machines at the airport from her excessive foot tapping.

Enough. I have to say something. Let me brighten the mood; I'm good at that. I can make her laugh. Besides, if we're going to be working together, then we can't exactly have bad blood.

This is good for the partnership.

One joke. A smile. It'll be alright.

"I'm going to regret eating this, aren't I?" I whisper and tip my head toward the stew.

"I worked in Ramona's kitchen for a long time," she says in a hushed voice. "The one thing I was never allowed to prepare was that stew." *Oh jeez.* I squirm and catch the faintest, nearly invisible lift of her lips at my reaction. "She has her own very special blend of spices."

"To mask the arsenic?" I suggest, pulling on a terrible memory from long ago. One that Meadow shared with me after reading one of her mystery books. They always had funny titles like *A Cookery Conundrum* or *The Scone Scheme*.

She doesn't react to the very distant callback. I've obviously overplayed my hand here. Of course she doesn't remember an inside joke from who knows how many years ago.

Just as I scramble for another quip to remedy the awkward silence, Meadow leans an inch closer, her expression turning devious. "Are you brave enough to risk it?" I snort loud enough to catch the attention of the people at the table beside us. "So why'd you look me up?" Meadow murmurs as Da continues his speech.

"I didn't look you up."

She fiddles with her fork. "Kinda sounds like you did."

No avoiding that observation. "Maybe I came across something online—"

"Didn't realize food blogs were of interest to you."

*You. You were of interest to me.* "What reason would I have to go scouring the internet for something like that?"

She regards Maisie, who's munching through her bowl of pasta. "How would I know? You're the one who seemed to know a lot about my career at d'Or even though you hate me."

*Hate her?* No. "I don't—"

Da's voice cuts through our conversation. "If awbody could raise their glasses." We do as he says.

"You two are celebrating so much, I'll need to drive home," I say, feeling frustrated by the interruption.

"They have the Tipsy Taxi now," Harris says, red in the face. "Those schoolkids could always use a couple of extra bucks driving the drinking crowd around."

"Tipsy Taxi?" I ask.

"Kids in golf carts. Town Hall voted on them being designated drivers, to avoid any driving under the influence. After what happened with—" Ma stops, and her gaze darts to Ivy. *After a drunk driver took Fox and Penelope's lives?* Meadow flinches, confirming my suspicion.

"Oh," I say.

Da continues, "To our pals who've been with us through the good and the bad, we'll miss ye. To ma lad, I'm glad tae have ye back, even if it's only for a wee while. To Meadow, we'll miss yer cooking and yer wit. And this little lass"—he smiles at Maisie—"farewell temporarily. We promise no tae think of ye too much as we're cruisin' through the Mediterranean. *Slàinte mhath*!"

"*Slàinte mhath,*" we cheer in unison, clinking our glasses.

Harris sets down his flute. "Feels good to have our kids here together again."

The table falls quiet. It's as though Fox's ghost has pulled up a chair and joined us.

"Fox would've loved this." Ma gives Ivy a soft squeeze of the hand.

Ivy's eyes brim red, but she puts on a bright smile. "Wouldn't he?"

Can they stomach talking about Fox as if he's still here? The reality of him being gone never provides me comfort. Instead, it's as if an anvil has been thrust into my chest.

"Let's dig in, shall we?" Da nudges his nose at the food, and we all follow suit.

The rest of the meal rushes by in a blur, with the majority of the conversation revolving around my parents' travel itinerary. Whenever I catch a glimpse of Meadow's eyes, she spins her gaze away from me, pretending to be interested in all the hiking trails my parents have planned.

I have an unquenchable curiosity for what I've missed about Meadow's life. All the things I couldn't quite capture from drunken internet searches.

Is she truly happy? What was it like moving back here after losing her brother and becoming a guardian to his child? It could not have been easy at all. Sure, she's tough, but that's the kind of sacrifice only a few people can stomach. Does she wish things were different? Are any of the dishes on her menu from the days when she'd use Fox and me as guinea pigs? Her imagination had no limits back then. Is it the same now? Is she still the same at all?

Did she miss me?

The last one doesn't matter. I'll be gone soon. Eighty-five days, to be exact.

## Chapter 7
# Meadow
#### nineteen years ago

HE LEAPS INTO THE AIR, PALMS OUTSTRETCHED TO THE SKY. Sweat glistens off his muscular back as he lands in a steady plank on the pebbled loch shore. His calves—which over the summer turned into the size of logs—flex as he starts doing push-ups.

Longing sits in my chest as I watch him. It's impossible not to. He's gorgeous. Even drenched in sweat, curls toppling all over his head. I'd like to be the ground he's sweating on.

Ollie Anderson is *perfect*.

Ugh, this crush of mine is getting out of hand. Sickeningly out of hand. Why can't I like any other boy? One who's not Fox's best friend?

For two whole platonic years, Ollie hasn't thought about me like that.

I guess, sometimes, those brown eyes linger on me in a way that seems more like *I want to kiss you, Meadow* and less like *Hey lass, you're my best friend's little sister.* He remembers when I have a test at school and what cuisine or ingredient I'm obsessing over recently. If I tell him about a new band I like, the next week he'll tell me the songs he listened to off of their new album. He makes me feel like I'm good at the things I like to do. Like the fact that I'm failing nearly every single one of my classes doesn't actually matter. Like I'm meant for bigger things.

Or maybe it's all in my head.

He leaps off the ground again and does another jump before hitting the shore. The afternoon light gleams off his hair. Auburn and beautiful.

Should I have even come out here?

*What else were you going to do, Meadow?* Fox told me to tell Ollie that he's ditched us for a date. Typical of my brother. But Ollie and I have never spent any time alone.

Until now.

I inhale a huge breath. *You got this. Go over there, deliver the message, and then take your butt home.*

Or…I could ask him to help me study? Or, here's a better idea, I can continue hiding behind this giant tree trunk and spend the afternoon watching the way the muscles on the back of his thighs pull taut…

This would be much easier if he were wearing a shirt.

A twig snaps under my foot.

Ollie bats his head over his shoulder, still inches off the ground, shooting me a look laced in curious surprise. "You hiding over there, doe?"

*Doe. That's it. I need to be admitted into a hospital. The Thistlehill Daily* will throw up a headline saying, "Girl Dead from Enormous Crush."

"Uh, no." I throw on my most casual voice and force my feet forward. My arms flail around awkwardly, like I'm a baby giraffe learning to walk.

*Ugh, where should I put my hands?* I settle the small bag of my new cheesy bread recipe on my hips.

"Where's Fox?"

Right. He's only excited to see my brother—like everyone else.

"He decided that he has to take a girl to Inverness today."

Ollie laughs. The sound turns the swarm of nerves in my stomach to a warm simmer. "Who is it this time?"

"There's always someone." I shrug. "The quest for *the one* continues."

My brother's obsession with love has caused him to keep a binder of ideas for his future wedding. Seriously, I've never thought of myself as a wife, but he's been planning to be a husband since he came out of the womb.

"What do ye got there?" Ollie's dreamy brown eyes focus on me advancing toward him.

"Bread!" I shout. "*Cheesy* bread."

"Don't keep it all to yourself. I've been working up an appetite!" He swipes the back of his hand across his forehead, flicking sweat from his brows and locks. Gravel is indented in his large palm, and I want to so badly be the stones leaving their imprint there. He walks to his backpack and pulls out a picnic blanket, laying it on the mossy ground beside the shore. "Come sit, and let's eat together."

He wants me to stay.

"I can just drop this off. Fox isn't here, and if—"

"What are you talking about?" He looks at me as if I've grown a second head.

"I figured since—" I incoherently stumble some more and tug on the hem of my jean shorts.

"Have a seat, Meadow."

I settle down on the blanket, and my knee *accidentally* bumps against his large leg. He smells divine. Actually out of this world. I want to lick his skin. Ollie doesn't seem to notice the explosions happening in my head or the fact that our legs are touching. Our bare legs.

"So, that looks good." He cocks a brow at me.

My pulse steam engines in my veins. "What?" I say through a whisper.

"The cheesy bread."

Of course.

"It's a new recipe." I pass him a slice. "I used fermented garlic, oak honey, and sharp cheddar."

Ollie reaches for it, takes a bite. "Doe," he groans, shaking his head, "you have outdone yourself. *Seriously?*" He chews the mouthful. "You have to make this in a professional kitchen or something."

"Good, yeah?"

Feeding him sparks an unknown joy deep within me. I want to make him smile. It's nothing like cooking for my family, when each meal feels like a way to convince my parents that even though I'm not quite like my brother, I'm also talented. I guess. In my own way.

"Perfect."

I smile giddily, tapping my Converse against a rock at the end of the blanket. My leg shakes his leg as he takes another bite.

"Your rugby training looks like it's going well." I gulp, watching sweat roll down his arm.

"Favorite part of my day, apart from school. When I'm in class, I'm challenged in a way that makes me want to be better and brighter. But in rugby, you have a team; you have a community around you. All of us are just pushing each other to be better."

I hang on to every word. "Maybe you never have to stop playing rugby. You know, because you and Fox are the best on your team."

"Yeah, maybe one day I can even coach my own team," he laughs. The image of him as a coach flashes through my mind, and my chest warms. "But who knows if I'll be any good at that."

"I know you would be." I smile awkwardly.

We sit in silence for a little while, sharing our small lunch. Mom always calls my food a labor of love, but I don't know how anything you love could be labor. Cooking's the opposite of work for me.

It gives me a sense of purpose and peace. It lets me explain to people how I feel about them without having to use words. I struggle in that department plenty as it is.

I shouldn't like him. He's my brother's best friend, and if I can read the room—er, uh, Loch Flora—then it's obvious my feelings are one-sided. But I let my eyes roam over his face anyway.

The smattering of auburn stubble on his chin has been growing this year, and there are nicks in his skin from shaving.

How would it feel to kiss him? What would he taste like?

I'm certain his mouth is covered in the taste of my cheesy bread.

Am I experiencing the same thing as he is? Would we taste the same if we were kissing? We must. Right? If our tongues are tasting the same thing, then it's like we're kissing already.

"So." I shatter the brief pause between us. "Have you started thinking about college yet? Only one year before you two graduate and leave me to tough out sixth year on my own."

"Yeah, I'm actually set on MIT. Hearing all those stories from your da, and the ones you guys talk about from Boston, makes me want to go experience it myself."

Dread washes over me.

"Wow." The enthusiasm in my voice doesn't sound enthusiastic at all. "That's, uh, that's big. Do they have a rugby team there?"

"I don't think so, but maybe there's a local league or something."

"Won't you miss being home?"

I've seen him every day for two years. Part of me was hoping he'd follow Fox to Edinburgh. At least that way I'd get to catch glimpses of him during the holidays. Maybe even see him when I visit my brother.

"Your da said he could write me an alumni recommendation too. Apparently I'd do well in the mathematics program." His excitement is palpable, but I can't bring myself to make the smile stretched across my face feel genuine. "I'll get a finance job right afterward. I'm sure of it."

"Finance is cool," I lie. Math classes will always be the bane of my existence. Even baking is a headache, trying to weigh all the ingredients. Cooking has more expressive freedom, and more room for error. "So grown up."

He laughs, clearly sensing my lack of thrill. "Aye." Ollie bumps my shoulder. "Make fun all you want, but I could make a lot of money and buy all the cool things you and Fox have."

"Is that what you want? To buy cool stuff?"

"Before you and Fox moved here, I didn't know there was an option for anything except this life. Sure, I may come back to Thistlehill when I'm older and have money, like your dad did, but I want more than I can have in Thistlehill. My parents are stuck here. Ma always wishes to go and see the world, but it's just that. A wish. I don't want to dream. After uni, I'd like to fly all over the place. I want to buy whatever I want. Wear cool sneakers and nice clothes. I want to feel like I'm successful."

I swallow. I guess I can't understand what it would be like to go without. My heart crumbles at the idea of going without Ollie. "Won't you miss your family?"

He shrugs. "I don't know. I sometimes feel like I was born into the wrong family. I love my parents, but we're so different. Da wants everything to stay the same, but he's missing out on so much of life by not trying new things. He just cares about that old distillery and nothing else."

I get that. It's as if Ollie would have an easier time living with us than at his own house. That would definitely make my feelings for him so much more complicated. "You help out at the distillery in the summers. I always thought you'd stay and run the family business."

His body tenses, and he scans my face as if he's assessing whether he can trust me or not. He can. *You can*, I tell him through a telepathic gaze.

"Da wants me to, but I don't think it's for me. I have ideas, and he won't listen to them, always rambling about tradition and process. I don't want to work somewhere where I'll be stressed, poor, and can't innovate. Like over the summer, we lost a few barrels due to humidity. I found a monitoring system that could help notify us of excess moisture, but Da wouldn't listen. He just doesn't understand me. Just grumbles about the old way of doing things. That might not make sense to you, I guess."

But it does. I know exactly what it feels like to disappoint your parents, to perceive every choice you make as the wrong one. To be loved through a veil of *Meadow, you need to try harder at school* and *Think about your future, Meadow; you won't be a kid forever.*

I never thought Ollie felt that, not even remotely. He's always so happy and positive.

"You're smart, so I think you can get into MIT, or any of the schools you want to go to. Even University of Edinburgh with Fox." I've seen his grades; he gets higher scores than my brother a lot of the time.

"At least you think I have what it takes." He nudges my shoulder with his bare one. His skin is hot and sticky against mine. I'm never taking a shower again. "What about you? You have two more years to figure it out, but I'm sure your parents already have a whole plan for you."

Couldn't be more true. "Mom and Dad want me to go to college, but my grades are nothing like yours." I kick the rock at my foot again, feeling embarrassed. "Who knows if I'll even get in anywhere. Maybe I'll apply where Fox is going and the admissions team will take pity on me."

Ollie frowns at me. "Edinburgh has a culinary program?"

"Um, I don't know. I don't think so?"

He cocks his head. "I figured you'd want to go somewhere you can learn more about cooking."

The statement feels accusatory, but he can't mean anything bad by it. Sure, when I lie awake at night, I imagine myself as a chef, cooking in big, fancy restaurants around Europe. But that's all it is—a dream.

Cooking is a hobby, not a career, as my dad likes to remind me.

The sun shines brightly in the clear blue sky, casting its warm rays on the sparkling water. I scan the mountains for a while, trying to find a response.

"I doubt my parents would be happy if I went to culinary school."

"What are you talking about? You have the coolest parents in the world. I swear they'd be so cool with it." I bite my tongue, not wishing to burst his bubble. My parents love me, but my dad *loves* Ollie and Fox—two sons to follow in his footsteps. I, on the other hand, can't help feeling like a consolation prize. A Macrae who didn't win the genetic lottery of brilliance. "Have you ever looked into any programs?"

If only he could see the stack of pamphlets beneath my mattress. I've been adding to it each time the career counselor comes by the school.

The other night, when I was out to dinner with my parents, I even got to ask Ramona what she thinks about being a chef. She owns the only restaurant in town, and she didn't even go to culinary school. It was all going well until my dad's face visibly crumpled when she told us that most months, she barely breaks even. He left her an extra-large tip that night.

"There's the CIA," I shrug.

"Okay, now I get why you read all those murder mysteries. You want to be a spy," he teases. "Infiltrating kitchens, poisoning the soups of the enemy."

I laugh. "No, it's called the Culinary Institute of America in New York, or even California. There's also Le Cordon Bleu in France. Apparently, Paris has some incredible restaurants, and I'd get to take trains all over Europe, eat all kinds of cuisines."

"You also want to travel the world?"

"More like eat the world. That was the cool thing about being in Boston, there were so many restaurants there." I smile and tug at the collar of my T-shirt.

Ollie looks out at the ripples in the water. "I guess you'll have to take me to your favorite places when you visit me. If you want."

The offer is casual, but it feels like it could be a bigger proposition. Maybe even a date? Okay, that's too far. This side of Ollie is nice. It's like I have a special little piece of him that only I get to see. The big four-letter word in my mind multiplies each time his eyes skip off the loch and onto mine.

"I will," I promise. Ollie repositions himself. Our legs are more than bumping—they're full-on right on top of each other. Time stills, stretching like hot taffy. He locks eyes with me. I must have cheesy bread all over my face. "What?" I reach for my mouth, swiping at my skin. "Am I covered in crumbs?"

"No," he chuckles, fumbling for his backpack and pulling out the Polaroid camera Fox gifted him a couple weeks ago for his seventeenth birthday. He points the lens at me.

I cover my face with my hands. "What are you doing?"

"Put your hands down." He says the words in a low voice. Conspiratorial, as if we're sharing a secret. I'm compelled to do as he says. In a blink, the camera shutter flicks, and the Polaroid whirs to life, printing a picture. "Here." He hands it to me; the colors slowly develop. "You can use it on one of those television montages when you become a famous chef. The moment

Meadow Macrae was convinced by none other than esteemed Ollie Anderson that she could be a world-renowned chef." He sounds like an announcer at a rugby match, his voice official and deep.

I use my free hand to nudge him on the shoulder. "You're ridiculous."

"Maybe, chef. Maybe you're just really pretty, Meadow."

The world flips over. My heart rollercoasters through my torso and right into my feet. Did he say that? No. He must've said witty? Gritty? Pretty...good at making cheesy bread?

The rocks under the blanket crumble beneath the heavy pressure of my hand. "What?"

Ollie's gaze clips away from me. His cheeks turn red. "I—I shouldn't have said that. Uh, sorry."

I want to scream, *No, say it again. Tell me again. Anything you're thinking, please.*

"You think I'm pretty?" The question sounds pathetic the moment it reaches my ears, but it's the first time I've ever heard a boy say that to me. Most think I'm too tall. Too strange. Too boyish. Too quiet. Too talkative. Too awkward. All the toos that aren't anything to do with too pretty.

"Now you're making me all nervous. Don't be so surprised. Everyone at school thinks so." *No way.* "Fox and I've had to enforce a whole rule—"

"A rule?" I swallow.

"Aye. Your year, ours, and the ones above. Especially for the guys on the rugby team."

"What rule?"

"No going near Meadow Macrae."

My mind short-circuits. "W-why would you do that?"

"To protect you. I want to protect you."

Ollie Anderson wants to protect me. In a sisterly way?

I stare at the photo in my fingers. My smiling face looks back at me even though my eyes were on him. "Oh."

"Forget I said anything. It was silly and—"

"I don't need any protection." What am I even saying?

He puts the camera down. "I know. You don't need anyone. It's one of my favorite things about you. Like if the world suddenly became infested with zombies and we could only rely on other people to survive, I'd be on your team before anyone else's."

Oh, Universe, if you hear this request, I wouldn't be so opposed to flesh-eating zombies taking over the world. "Uh." *Cool, Meadow. Be cool.* "What if that actually happened tomorrow? What would be the first thing you'd do?"

This is how flirting works, right? I knew I should've watched one of those romantic comedies my mom and Riley are always putting on.

"Ask the lass I like if she'd want to kiss me." His whisper is a warm wind.

There's a girl. Of course there's a girl. There's always a girl because that girl is not me.

"Nice. Yeah. That makes sense," I say robotically, gathering my knees to my chest.

"Yeah," he sighs. "Do you want to kiss me, doe?"

I whip my head so hard it almost topples off my shoulders. This can't be happening.

*I do want to kiss you.* The sun dances across his auburn hair. Above, tree branches creak as the birds sing. I stare at my reflection in his brown eyes. "I've never kissed anyone before."

"Me either."

"That can't be true." Fox goes on and on about how all the guys on the rugby team have made out with every single girl in their year.

"Haven't met the right person yet."

"And I'm..." I recross my legs. "The right person?"

Ollie fumbles with the laces of his cleats. "Only if you want me to kiss you. I—I mean, you don't have to kiss me at all. Uh—"

"I want to kiss you, Ollie." I say it with certainty. No more dreaming, no more wishing. He smiles.

"Good." Ollie's fingers brush over my brow, the pad of his thumb pushing my bangs—which I was certain were a mistake right up until this very moment—out of my eyes. I liquefy, morphing into ice cream on a hot day. "Close your eyes, doe, and I'll close mine."

I do as he says, zipping my eyelids. *Oh no—we just ate fermented garlic cheesy bread.* He's going to be so put off. Wait. Maybe not. He's the one who wants to kiss me. The slither of warmth in my veins spreads into my stomach. Silky and smooth. He scoots closer. Heavy legs rest against mine as we sit crisscrossed in front of each other.

Carefully, I let my palm flatten against the muscle of his chest. It's stiff. His skin is warm. I slowly inhale, and his breathing echoes my own. Ollie's nose brushes against the tip of mine. His breath on my lips. My mind is spinning like the Greenway Carousel when it went rogue that one summer.

"You sure this is okay?" he whispers, tracing his fingers up my neck into the back of my hair.

I've never been more sure of anything in my life. "Yes. More than okay."

And then, he kisses me.

Our lips touch. He's softer than I expected. The small prickles of his beard tickle my chin. I part my lips a little, and Ollie does the same until I can taste him.

He tastes like the buttery bread I made for him, salty sweat, and a dash of cinnamon from his toothpaste. I memorize the flavors, as if committing a new favorite recipe to mind—Ollie Anderson.

I've always worried that I would be a bad kisser. There's so much that can go wrong, bumping teeth or laughing in the middle of it. But this feels easy, right. I lean into it.

Our mouths know what to do because every one of his touches amplifies the warmth in my stomach. His racing heart beneath my palm is not something I could ever re-create. My other hand reaches for his hair—one of my favorite parts of him. They're all my favorite parts.

I don't know how long my first kiss lasts, but it feels like we sit at Loch Flora for hours. Ollie is the first to break away, wearing a wide smile on his face.

"That was—"

Then my laughter comes, and he joins me. "Yeah, it was."

Reality doesn't wait to smack me in the face like a hot pan.

I kissed my brother's best friend.

"We can't tell Fox. What if things get weird and we can't hang out together anymore?" I panic and shoot myself to the other side of the blanket.

"I tell him everything." He bites at the edge of his lip.

"Yeah, but this isn't everything. This is his best friend kissing his little sister." The photo Ollie took of me scratches against my thigh, and I leave it on the blanket. Maybe he'll keep it and remember this moment.

This special day that can't ever happen again.

Ollie rolls his eyes. "You're only a year and a half younger than us."

He clearly doesn't see how this can totally fall apart. "In the book I'm reading, *The Broth of Betrayal*, the main character's best friend kisses her brother, and she puts arsenic in both of their pies. The biggest plot twist in the series so far, and not one I wish to re-create."

"Fox doesn't make a very good pie to begin with," he jokes.

"Exactly. So, our last meal would be absolutely dreadful." We laugh for a moment before the serious tone in my voice returns. "Can we have this one secret between us, *please*?" I reach for my swollen lips, wanting to savor the brief moment Ollie was mine before we go back to the way we were before.

"I don't want you to be my secret."

"But we can't kiss again," I say and regret it immediately.

We can't kiss because he's my friend. My brother's best friend. It's always been us three. I can't—no, *we* can't go and muck it all up by kissing.

I want him to protest. I want him to say *To hell with it all, forget about Fox and kiss me again.* But he doesn't.

"If that's what you want, we won't kiss again."

It's not.

But in a year, Ollie will be across an ocean, and I'll be here.

"Promise to not say anything to Fox. Or anyone else, for that matter."

"Okay, Meadow. I promise that this will be our secret."

## Chapter 8
# Meadow

"Ugh, stay on," I groan and struggle to push my rebellious hood back up over my head with my free arm, while balancing precariously on a stepladder outside Fox Den. Rain batters the awning above my head. At least the sign is staying dry.

"Maybe not the best day for that." A voice startles me.

Beside my stepladder, the Cameron twins huddle under a large umbrella, sporting shiny pink and purple trench coats. Their signature matching colors.

"Afternoon, ladies." I smile at them, gripping onto my paintbrush. "I know, Mother Nature's being a real brat today, but it's the last cosmetic change before the opening. It's now or never."

They both smile warmly up at me. "Aye. You've been putting your heart into this place. It's paying off, dear. The color is spectacular. Isn't it, Kenna?"

"Just radiant." Lorna's twin shimmies her shoulders with pleasure.

I've always liked the twins. They add a little bit of color to the town, whether they're rocking the most eclectic clothes or simply hanging out in their bright pink house, which looks like a *Barbie* Dreamhouse.

"Thank you." I bend and dip my paintbrush into the bucket on the step stool beside my ladder, swiping more burnt copper—Fox's favorite color—on the sign. It matches the walls in Fox's room and the faux fur tail he had clipped to his backpack. "What are you two doing out? Not exactly a pleasant day for a walk."

A gust of wind seeps through my jeans and makes my bones tremble.

"Oh, Madame Belle is loose again. Fell asleep on Main Street."

"Our lassie's more free-spirited than we were in our days," Kenna giggles. "She made a few of the teachers late for school. Ms. Lee wasnae pleased with us."

My lips twitch up into a grin. "Klept—uh, Belle's got a mind of her own." The twins are very particular about the accusations that their cow is a thief.

"Don't we all, dear."

Belle, better known as Kleptocow, is Thistlehill's very own troublemaker. At least there's still one of us left. She shows up in the most unexpected places, is always around when something small goes missing, and takes her sweet time moving around. Whenever we catch the cow by our house, Maisie stops to give her a big hug.

"We got her tae move along and clear traffic," Kenna says.

"Wahoo!" Lorna squeals, and I startle, zigzagging my brush into a messy streak. *Deep breath, Meadow. You can fix this.* I hurry to trace over the uneven stroke. "Ah, nearly forgot tae mention that we saw Riley and Seamus's boy with ye at Ramona's last night. Ye ken, he may be a good way for ye tae take some *time* for yerself since ye've been working so hard."

I roll my eyes. This is exactly what I didn't want to happen—the town's rumor mill alight with nonsense. What did my parents think would happen when they set that trap for us at dinner? That

Ollie and I would hug, kiss, and make up? Blow away our history like a sprig of dandelions and skip through the hills hand in hand?

Never going to happen.

At best, he'll have the right sense of mind to wrap up the whisky contract fast. At worst, he'll flash me one of his annoying grins that still manage to unnerve me, make a sly dig about the past, and bring up my brother again.

If that's the case, I'll find a different distiller. Our business partnership doesn't need to cross any boundaries into personal territory.

"Ye two used tae be the bonniest," Kenna coos.

"*Used to* being the key words here." I shoot them a kind enough look to indicate the topic of my first love ends there. "There's nothing going on between us." If the twins see Ollie stop by Fox Den, chaos will ensue. "Belle is probably blocking more roads. You better be on your way," I hint, rushing them along.

Lorna ignores my attempt. "That lad still has eyes for ye. We were takin' bets the whole night on how long he'd keep ogling ye. I had him pegged through the first entrée."

"But I won with dessert." Kenna bumps her sister's shoulder.

Nonsense. It's all nonsense. The town is starving for drama and gossip. Ollie's return is the exact thing to keep people entertained for years to come.

"He must've been drooling over the food on my plate. Ramona's new chef is good." I finish the last swipe of even paint on the letter N and admire my work. It's perfect.

"Can't blame him. I'd be staring at yer plate too if I was such a big lad."

"You wouldn't be talking about me now, would ya?" His voice appears.

I glance at my wristwatch.

1:50. He's early.

I whip around. The stepladder tips forward, and the paint can wobbles, nearly toppling over.

"Ahhh!" the twins yell.

I'm seconds away from my face meeting the pavement. But a heavy hand lands on my hip bone. The heat of his touch seeps through my rain jacket and all the layers underneath.

Deep pools of brown stare up at me. The hint of a grin is hiding in the thicket of his auburn beard. He doesn't try to move away from me.

"I had it," I grumble and unhinge myself from his grasp.

With my luck, *The Thistlehill Daily* will have a headline tomorrow that reads, "Town Golden Boy Saves Struggling Single Mom."

"Glad to help." He sets down the saved paint can and steps away from me.

Good.

Far, far away is the best course of action here.

"This is delectable. We *were* chattin' 'bout ye," Kenna purrs. "What dae ye say, Ollie? Have ye come tae grease the gears of dear Meadow here?"

"My gears don't need any greasing," I snap and make my way down the stepladder to collect my things. "My restaurant, however, needs its whisky. Shall we, Oliver?"

Ollie chuckles as the twins edge their way over to him. "I don't think Meadow wants any of my grease near her."

"Now, I, on the other hand"—Lorna bats her thickly painted lashes at him—"wouldn't mind some grease."

Ollie laughs uncomfortably and retreats from his new fan club. The rain pellets his face, and he gives me a pleading look. "I—uh, Meadow and I have a meeting."

I glance at my watch again and give him my best Hollywood smile. "Actually, we have another eight minutes."

"I only need seven." Lorna reaches for Ollie's jacket and drags her umbrella, along with her sister, over to him.

I do my best to hide the laughter bubbling up in my chest. Alright, maybe throwing him to the Cameron twins is a bit immature, but the farther he is from me, the more this town will forget about an impossible reunion.

I reach for my paint can, secure the lid, and fold up the stepladder.

"Let me help," he calls out.

"No, no, you finish your conversation. I got it." I keep my voice neutral and my eyes away from him.

"Yeah, but—pardon me." He smiles politely at the twins. "I can also get it." He takes the ladder from me, and we play a game of tug-of-war until I give in. "Shall we?"

Working through this contract is going to be a headache.

"Maybe Ollie can come over and shift our ladders later, Kenna," Lorna snickers, winking at me. "See ye two about."

They take off down the cobblestone street toward Betty's Bed & Breakfast, leaving me and Ollie alone.

"So, about this whisky—" he starts.

"Not until we're inside," I cut him off. "I don't need another audience."

Nerves slam in my throat. Ollie Anderson is about to see my restaurant. Why didn't this occur to me before? *Keep your wits. Stay professional. Treat him like you'd treat Seamus.*

Suddenly, a flush of heat lands in my stomach. It's just my period. I swallow, pushing the door open and stepping over the threshold.

Inside, Fox Den is toasty. A crackling fire is roaring in the corner of the main dining room. My custom oak tables and those secondhand chairs are perfectly arranged. The sage paint finished drying last week. Our neutral linens are being dry-cleaned as I stand here.

It's beautiful. Only six more days until the rest of the town can see all of the hard work Fi, Brooke, and I put into this place.

Ollie's eyes spread wide as he surveys the room. "This is exactly how you used to describe it."

*He remembered?* The hairs on my arm prickle. "Huh?"

"The sage walls and oak tables. You had a vivid picture of what you wanted your own place to look like. Clearly, you brought that to life."

"Thanks. I poured every cent I have into this place. It wasn't enough to struggle while putting myself through culinary school, so I thought why not struggle some more? The life of a chef."

A cramp shoots up my leg, and I freeze, inhaling a sharp breath and willing it to stop. My pain medicine needs a re-up.

"You okay?" he asks, coming toward me.

"Only about to give birth to one of my internal organs," I bite.

"I—I didn't realize you still had those wretched bleeds."

"More like they have me. I was diagnosed with fucking fibroids and premenstrual dysphoric disorder."

"Can I—"

"Give me a second." I breathe through the pain.

Another first I got to share with Ollie—though one I would've rather passed up.

We were packing up after one of our trips to the loch, and when I stood up, there was a small stain on the picnic blanket. The one Riley had made for Ollie. I wanted to abandon my body. Vanish forever. But Ollie cracked a joke about something Fox was doing, rolled up the blanket, and asked me if I was okay. Little did I know, my periods were going to worsen over the years. To the point where Ollie even began keeping track of them, especially when we were dating.

He was far too mature for his age.

The cramp finally wanes. I hate that I was weak in front of him.

Ignoring his stare, I drop off the paint can and supplies in the back storage room. When I return, he's still stuck where I left him, at the threshold of the restaurant.

His smile is uneasy as he watches me settle at the four-top table that's doubling as my desk for now. Instead of joining me, he paces, dragging his damp, muddy boots all over my freshly mopped floors. A nerve booms in my forehead.

"Our parents were so obvious last night, huh?" He taps his fingers along the denim hugging his thighs the way he used to do. "Ma gets one glass of wine in her, and she'd try to get me to marry a door." He laughs.

Contract. Whisky.

I pull my notebook in front of me, clicking open the pen. "Did you bring samples of the whisky with you?"

"About that." He hesitates. The walls shrink with his intimidating six-foot-five stature. "I haven't had a chance to go through the casks my da was talking about. I figured we could review the contract terms, and then I'll throw together a selection for you to taste later."

Throw together? What is this, some tasting booth at the Thistlehill Festival?

"If you don't have the samples, what are you doing here?" Annoyance simmers beneath my skin. "I can't dillydally. The contract is pretty much done. You were supposed to bring me options."

"I'm hardly dillydallying, Meadow. Look." He moseys over to me. "Since it's a tight turnaround, I'll guarantee you a cask of Red Label free of charge. Then, when I have time, I can dig through those barrels to find the perfect fit for you. How does that sound?"

I shake my head. "That's not good enough for me. Seamus guaranteed me an exclusive label for Fox Den on opening night."

"I'm running the distillery now—"

"Clearly." I cross my arms over my chest. "I'm not in the mood for this. You're obviously not prepared for this meeting. I have a million things to do, and a rep from Horns Distillery already sent me two options."

"Listen, the On Cloud Nine luxury resort chain will be offering Red Label at fifty of their most prestigious locations. It's good whisky. Used to be your favorite, if I remember correctly." Why does he refuse to get it into his head that we're not familiar like that anymore? Never going to be. "You'll have the best of the best."

A log collapses in the fireplace, and the fire roils. Each raucous crackle matches the agitation building inside me.

"Seamus letting you manage this partnership was a mistake." I push out of my seat, ready to end this meeting.

Ollie straightens and grips the back of a chair, flexing his fingers against the wood, his brown eyes spearing me. "I found out about this contract last night, and I came straight from dropping off my parents at the airport to take this meeting. Forgive me if I'm still trying to get my bearings and find a solution."

"I don't think you're hearing me." I prop a hand on my hip, the other drums against my closed notebook. "I do not have a second to spare while you're getting your bearings. The fact that you haven't come home for almost twenty years isn't my problem. This is my restaurant, my business. It's important to me, and if I'm using your distillery as my supplier, I better be important to you—*for once*."

"Bet you had that jab planned since dinner last night."

Insufferable.

I square my shoulders, peacocking myself to not feel small next to him. An impossible task.

"I will not be disrespected in my own restaurant by a man who clearly has no interest in helping it succeed."

"No—"

"You could've visited or decided to run the distillery for your parents at any other time. Why are you actually in Thistlehill? What did you come back for?" He seems frozen by my question.

"Yeah, I thought so." I shuffle drafts of my menu and some other papers off the table.

"What answer are you looking for? That I came back to help my parents' business because the guilt of being gone for so long kept me up most nights or— " He inhales a sharp breath, and his knuckles turn white. "That not showing up to your brother's funeral has me facing my shame at every corner in this forsaken town? Or what, Meadow?" His voice falters. "Do you want to hear that I came back to see you? Is that what you want? You didn't used to be so disagreeable."

A clasp unlatches in my chest. My body burns like I'm being boiled alive in my anger and shock.

He's mocking me, isn't he? As if I sat around all these years begging for him to come back?

I need him to get out of here.

"This meeting was a mistake. Big fucking mistake. You said so yourself, we meant nothing. We were two silly kids who were way in over their heads. I'm not that same girl you used to know. The fact that you came in here thinking I would be is out of line."

He drags his palms over his face. "I didn't expect you to be her. I'm sorry. I don't want the partnership between Anderson Distillery and Fox Den to start off on the wrong foot. I get it, alright? This is important to you."

"It is." I nod. My tower of defense falters at his devastated expression.

"It's this fucking town. You should understand that better than anyone. We never wanted to be here." He bites out the word *here* as if there's acid burning his mouth. The crack of his sob is washed over with the disgust in his tone. There goes that fleck of empathy he didn't deserve.

"Just because you ran away from home doesn't mean the rest

of us could." I throw my hands up into the air. "I chose to come back and stay in Thistlehill. It's my home. My family's here. Do I need to remind you that I had to bury my brother and raise a child, all before I was thirty?"

His judgmental expression fragments, and another emotion settles onto his face. One I haven't made enough acquaintance with to deduce. "Why did you do that? There's no way Fox would've wanted you to throw your life away."

*Throw my life away...*

There they are.

Those words transform Ollie from the boy I used to know into the arrogant man in front of me now.

A stranger in fancy clothes who has his dream job lined up is making assumptions about my life before he storms out of it again.

It's not enough that I have to deal with the reminder that my parents were left with the wrong child on a weekly basis.

The one who never planned on a family because her life was steel kitchens and late shifts.

The one who almost failed out of school.

The one who didn't end up with the boy next door who they hoped would change her mind about college.

"You have no idea what Fox would've wanted." I struggle to mask the break in my voice. "You burned that bridge from across an ocean."

"I know. I'm aware!" Ollie cups the back of his neck. "I didn't—I'm sorry, I didn't mean to imply that you're throwing your life away. I've been saying all the wrong fucking things since I got here. Please, let me fix this. Let me make it up to you."

"I'm done waiting for you to fix things." I gather my belongings and press them to my chest. "Fox Den will use Horns Distillery."

"Are you serious?"

"Thank you for taking the time to meet with me today. Goodbye." I swing open the front door, gesturing to him to get the hell out. He stares at me in disbelief, but he leaves.

I'll have to throw a fresh coat of paint over the walls to get rid of the memory of him being here.

*Good riddance.*

## Chapter 9
# Ollie

OPERATIONS@ONCLOUDNINERESORTS.COM

Hello Mr. Anderson,

We are thrilled to have the Anderson Red Label Whisky at our resorts for the Spring Season. Kindly keep us apprised of the deliverable dates. We hope to not encounter any delays.

OANDERSON@GMAIL.COM

The shipments will be out on the $1^{st}$ of April. I guarantee it.

I lift another empty oak cask and haul it across the room. My lats burn, and my legs strain with each step, but the laborious afternoon has turned into a meditative practice.

I can't remember the last time I worked with my hands so much. I've missed it, especially because there's nothing else to do in this town besides shoo the damn cow bandit off the road and refresh my delivery apps a million times like a restaurant that delivers food will magically appear. I would do unspeakable things for ten baskets of crab dumplings from the Chinese restaurant down the street from my New York apartment to appear right now.

I set down the cask, wipe sweat off my brow, and inhale the earthy sweetness of the barrel room.

The brick warehouse is filled with racks of aging whisky, and it's only a short walk from the main distillery plant. For the past two hours, I've been searching for the mysterious blends Da swears he has stowed away for Meadow. Not much luck. Apart from the five whiskys we have on the market, I'm only encountering empty casks and spiderwebs.

I stretch out my sore shoulders and return to digging through the dust-covered casks in the dim light overhead.

The whisky-making process involves meticulously malting barley, fermenting it to create wash, distilling it in copper pot stills, and aging the resulting spirit until it achieves optimal maturity before the beautiful amber gold is bottled and shipped.

My lungs fill with the rich scent of oak, wood, earth, and spices as I wrap my hands around another cask and drag it off the ground. When I worked here as a teenager, my clothes would always stain with the smell of the barrel room. I never appreciated all the complexity that my nose is picking up now.

Anderson Distillery does make a fine whisky.

When I return home and start my new position at Viggle, I'll bring my new executive team a few bottles. Earn some of their favor like I had to do with the Silverman Sachs folks.

Only eighty-three days left.

My intestines fiercely knot together again.

I miss my life. I miss my friends—Matthew, Ave, and Robert. What are they up to? Probably getting on with their lives while I'm somehow trapped in my past. They wouldn't have time for me anyway.

Doesn't help that the atmosphere at the distillery has carried the same terse energy as the gloomy clouds outside. Bleak. Callum is still giving me the silent treatment. When I helped Elspeth turn barley in the malting room this morning, I made sure to avoid bringing up the progress I'm making on the distillery. Though it would be great to talk through some of my worries and concerns with someone.

The pressure of getting On Cloud Nine's deliveries out on time continues to weigh on me, especially after the email I got this morning.

I already spoke with Da about building a warehouse on the property, to house the new bottling facility I ordered with the On Cloud Nine account advance. It's set to arrive the last week of March. After Da got all his grumbling about change off his chest, he conceded—as long as I can get approval at Thistlehill's Town Hall meeting.

But that's at the end of the week, which eats into my already tight timeline. The handful of construction companies from the surrounding cities are all out of budget or unavailable. This is rapidly going to turn desperate.

No business moves forward without first updating the council, so whatever the final cost will be, my hands are completely tied for now.

I carefully approach the towering stacks of whisky casks, their presence commanding respect, and drop off another empty barrel. Only a few more before I can get to the rack that's buried in the back of this room. Those have to contain the whisky Da promised Meadow.

*Meadow.*

She's received all the worst parts of me the past couple of days. I cringe at the reminder of yesterday as I navigate through the maze of barrels and pick up another cask.

It's as if I'm finally getting to say all of the things I wanted to say back then. Back when that sapphire ring was stowed in my duffle bag.

It was wrong to tell her that she threw her life away. I'm an absolute fucking nugget. The woman's running her own restaurant like she's always wanted, taking care of a seven-year-old, and had a brilliant career abroad.

I'd do anything for the Viggle position waiting for me in the city. The one promising me the success and money I've always wanted. Can I fault her? Despite the tragedy in her life, she has everything she always wanted.

Sure, I don't belong in Thistlehill, but I shouldn't cling to the mistakes she made as a seventeen-year-old.

I was twenty-eight when her brother died, and I chose to push myself farther away from this place and rot in my grief and shame. While she's managed to take on the impossible and still achieve her dreams, I can barely understand how to keep the employees of my family's distillery from shooting me disappointed glares every time I pass them.

The noose of resentment I've worn for her all these years slackens.

Who am I to judge anyone?

Fuck.

As I carefully set the last of the casks in their designated spot along the far wall of the racks, I take a moment to appreciate the effort I've put in this afternoon. My palms are callused for the first time in years. My neck and back ache in a way that's rewarding. Nothing like the stiffness I feel when I work too long at my computer.

This is real work, like Da used to always say. However much I hate to concede to him, he's right.

I make my way over to the hidden rack and squint in the dim barrel room light to read the inscriptions on the metal plaques. *2005*. The year Meadow and I met. I scan a couple of the neighboring casks, which ascend in sequential order.

These are the ones Da meant for Fox Den.

I bend down for the bottle of water on the dusty floor and take a drink. My hamstrings twitch and burn. *Oft, I'll be sore tomorrow.*

I pat one of the old sherry casks. This is my ticket to mend things with Meadow. The distillery can't afford to lose her business. Truthfully, I can't deal with living right next door to her and bumping into her cold shoulder either.

I'm going to fix this. In a few minutes, I gather all of the necessary equipment to tap the wooden barrels. The task used to be second nature, especially after I worked here in the summers as a boy and during my deferment year, but now each one of my movements is laced with hesitation.

I can do this. It's in my blood, right?

I use the metal bung extractor that looks like a wrench to pop open one of the casks. A loud hiss echoes through the quiet, damp room. I grab the next tool, a bulbous tube that sucks the whisky from the barrel and spits it into a clean tumbler.

The divine scent of fig, hazelnuts, and sulfur fills the air. The deep amber liquid resembles a molten sunset in the glass. Even beneath the pale light above, it's clear to see the true treasure a couple decades of aging produced.

I bring the rim to my lips and sip. A burning symphony rolls over my tongue, leaving behind a lingering sweetness. Perfect. I repeat the tapping on the next two rows, 2006 and 2007, my fingers lit up by muscle memory. One barrel produces an earthy, musky taste, as if the rolling hills around the distillery have been poured into a glass. The other is dense and bold, tasting like fermented honey and molasses.

One of these has to be the perfect match for Meadow.

I grab the clean bottles I pulled from the compact barrel room and fill them to the brim. Only thing left to do is find her and beg for another chance. I'll suck up my pride and get on my knees if I have to. There's no chance I'm going to fuck up another interaction with her.

When we were in love, it was us against the world, against this town, against everyone. There must be some way we can get even a fragment of that back. For both of our businesses, of course.

## Chapter 10
# Ollie
### eighteen years ago

"Ol, I ken yer heart was set on this, but give it a think. Ye'll help me at the distillery for another year like you've done every summer." Da drums his hands on the dining table and beams at me like my letter of deferred admission to MIT is the best thing that's ever happened to him.

To my parents, this is a win. To me, a prison sentence.

I shake my head and pace around the cramped space of our kitchen. "No, there's got to be another way. Maybe I can ask Harris for help."

Da shifts in his chair. The fact that his closest friend was able to do more for me in the application process than he was hasn't quite stopped him from holding a grudge. I'm still not sure against whom.

"I don't know why you're so upset. Ye'll only be in Boston for a couple years, and then you're coming back here to take over the distillery anyways. This year will be a head start."

I grind my molars together. "I'm staying in the States after I graduate," I say for what seems like the hundredth time.

"Seriously, son, ye're just going to leave this all behind?" Da throws his hands up. "Our name is hanging outside that distillery.

I've been training you to be next in line since you were in nappies, and ye want to throw it all away."

"You've never asked me if I wanted to take over. You won't listen to any of my ideas." I inhale a sharp breath, not wanting to have this conversation again. *I don't want to end up like you.* "Whenever I bring up suggestions for the distillery, you shut me down and say I'm ruining tradition." I've been around whisky since I was a boy, but when I make recommendations to my da, about getting better stills, investing in a computer, or maybe sending our product outside of the Highlands to other places in Scotland, even across Europe, he dismisses me.

He doesn't want things to change. But I do.

"I've been working there for fifty years; ye need to put in yer work before we listen to ye about changes to the process."

"I'll put in work at MIT." I glare.

"What's that school going to give you that we can't?"

A way to live a life that's not filled with sacrifice and limitations. "Success," I grumble under my breath, turning to Ma, hoping she can save this from turning into another disaster fight.

Ma's lips are downturned as she narrows her eyes on the deferment notice. "It says here that you've been deferred until Grace Academy sends yer transcripts." She attempts to sound hopeful.

"They had weeks to do that. Clearly, they were late, and I'm stuck waiting until next year because of their mistake."

Sure, I got acceptance letters from other universities in the States and in Scotland, but my heart's been set on MIT for years. I have a plan. Graduate, get a job at Silverman Sachs. Then, when all of that hard work pays off, Harris assured me I'll be able to end up in any role I want, that I'll be rich and successful. Maybe even a director at some international titan of innovation.

*Director.* I like the sound of that far too much to spend another year helping out my da at Anderson Distillery.

"Ol, it'll be okay."

"There's a bank in Inverness. Maybe I can apply there and get some work experience before I move for university, or perhaps the computer store that opened up outside of Thistlehill. I'll need to get a car." I toss the idea out there, but my parents meet me with unenthused looks.

"We dinnae have the money tae buy ye a car." Da's deep set eyes stay focused on the window. It was sunny about an hour ago, but now thick rain clouds roll across the sky.

"Seamus." Ma wraps her hand around his, but he pulls away.

"What, Riley? I cannae sit here and play pretend with our lad and his grand dreams. I've got tae take care of us. Of the business. Because we're not living in some fantasy world filled with silly gadgets and robots."

*Robots are going take over the world* is Da's favorite line. He always recites it while he's sitting in this exact spot, reading *The Thistlehill Daily*. After enough arguments about this, I've learned to let it roll off my shoulders, but that doesn't mean it doesn't hurt.

"If ye work with Da, we'll pay ye some money," Ma chimes in, sensing that the tension in the room is on the verge of a snap. "Save up for a year. It won't be cheap living in a city like Boston." She gives me a kind smile, but I'm shrouded in disappointment.

"Does the distillery even have money to pay me?" I ask. My tone throws a spur of anger into my da's eyes.

An argument is brewing. The last thing I want to do is set them off again. Lately, that's all my ma and da have been doing. Arguing.

This year, two machines had to be replaced at the distillery. The repairs ate into my parents' travel fund and spurred this ongoing pattern of fighting. Ma wants to see the world, while Da just wants to keep the family name successful.

Neither of them is happy. No one's been happy at the Anderson house recently.

"Use our travel savings tae pay him." Ma's eyes burn into his across the table.

My legs quit pacing, and I stand watching them. I can't possibly take my parents' money. Especially not when Ma's been so let down about not getting to go on the honeymoon they never got.

I hate this. Embarrassment and frustration seep into my bones. When I'm older, I will never worry about money. Never fight about it with my family. That's exactly why I need to go to MIT, not any other uni, not take any other path.

My future is the only thing that I can control.

"Ri, if we dae that, we won't be able tae take that trip for years."

A flicker of sadness passes over Ma's face. "Let's help our lad out."

Guilt needles my chest. "Ma—" I plant my hands on the table, facing them.

"Pipe down, Ol. We're yer parents. Ye don't get a say here. When we had ye, we made a promise tae take care of ye, and that's what we'll do. Not our fault yer plans are bigger than ours." Her words drop into the kitchen with the force of a gavel, cold and unmoving. "Ye'll help Da at the distillery and earn a little bit of money to set yerself up at school."

There's no use arguing. Fact of the matter is, I need this money, and I'll have better luck earning it at the distillery than anywhere else. I'll graduate in a few months and be gone in a year. Only five hundred and two days, then I can leave Thistlehill, and this life, behind.

"Thank you." I sigh, avoiding my da's piercing gaze. This is going to turn ugly any second. "I'm going for a run."

I don't hesitate to rush out of the house, leaving behind the bullets of whispers between my parents. Twenty minutes later, the wind whips around me as the last remnants of winter cling to the world. My running shoes pinch my toes, and I shiver from the damp fabric hugging my skin.

I kick around a few frozen pebbles on the loch's shore and look up. The rain stopped halfway through my run, but heavy, leaden clouds remain glued to the sky.

I stare out at the water, the mountains, my family's distillery in the distance.

My damn fate.

"Fuckkkkk!" I scream out. The roar causes the anger pulsing in my veins to double. Tears stream down my face, and I kick the ground beneath me.

There's nothing I want more than to leave this place. Escape Da's expectations and my parents' fighting. To be on my own. To have my own life.

"Ollie?" A soft voice startles me, and I spin on my heels to find *her* standing there. "Are you alright?"

I bat my head away and swipe my palms over my eyes. She can't see me like this. Pathetic and helpless. The last thing I need is pity from Meadow Macrae.

Tossing on a smile, I straighten my spine and face her. "You ever wanna yell at this damn loch?" The words come out with a forced laugh as I try to diffuse the situation.

"Daily." Her lips turn up into a half smile, and she walks down the icy pathway toward me. She's bundled up in a thick jacket, a pair of boots strapped to her feet. She's almost as tall as Fox and me, shy by a handful of inches.

"And what does a girl like you have to yell about, huh?"

The patches of frost on the ground light up the deep blue of her eyes and the chestnut brown of her hair. A tinge of pink coats her cheeks and nose.

My violent heartbeat seems to slow, the way it typically does when she's around. For whatever reason, Meadow always manages to cure all the turmoil in my body.

"You tell me your secrets, and I'll tell you mine." She joins my side at the shore and looks up at me. Her teeth bite down on her crooked smile as she chews her lower lip.

*Secrets.* Our kiss last summer. The only thing that's been occupying my mind besides MIT. The picture I took of her at this very spot and keep tucked in my nightstand doesn't help. Especially when my hands crawl to it most nights, itching for the slice of comfort her smile provides as I'm restlessly kicking around in bed.

It's been torture watching her from a distance all year.

"We're back to sharing secrets now?" I tilt my head.

A rosy bloom spreads across her cheeks. She's so beautiful. The ache in my chest returns, the same one I've fought since I helped bring her luggage up the porch all those years ago.

"Why not?" She shrugs. The cold beneath my windbreaker seems to let up, and heat replaces it. It must be radiating off of her. Or maybe that's just me.

"I got deferred from MIT. I won't be able to attend until next year." I huff, and my breath dances in front of me.

"Ol." Her voice collapses into her throat, and she untucks her hand from her pocket and reaches for mine hanging at my side. "I'm so sorry. I know how important it was for you to go."

Her cold fingers instantly force my breath into a standstill.

The last time we touched was on her sixteenth birthday, five months ago. I bought her these measuring cups that have conversions on them, because she's still struggling with the metric system. For that, she hugged me a second longer than everyone else at her party.

"I'm still going," I say. "In a year."

Meadow nods with understanding, and she doesn't pull her hand away from mine.

"How are you feeling?" The way she's looking at me makes me want to pour my soul out to her. So I do.

"Crushed, doe. I'm crushed." I return her grasp on my hand and trace my pointer over the small, barely visible burn marks on her thumb. The ones she got from testing out water baths in the oven two weeks ago. "Da's thrilled though. I'll be at his disposal at the distillery, which is everything he wants and the last thing I want. I just need to get out of this place, not spend the next year with him ignoring my ideas and hammering me about this being my legacy." Burden straddles my shoulders, and I fight its weight. "I can't struggle. Ma and Da have been saving up to go on a honeymoon since I was born, and they just told me they are going to use the travel fund to pay me to work at the distillery. I don't want to take their money, but I need to save up for MIT. I can't be like them, making ends meet my entire life, not being able to go on trips or buy new shoes or—I'm sorry. I don't know why I'm telling you this."

"No, I'm glad you're telling me. I thought your parents were supportive of you going to MIT," Meadow says.

"They are, but they have this expectation that I'll come back, and I don't know how I could ever run the distillery if Da won't even listen to my ideas," I sigh.

"What ideas?"

"We could take Anderson whisky all over Europe, maybe even the States. There are computers now, but Da thinks if we get one of those things, it'll bring chaos instead of much-needed profit."

"You sound so adult," she giggles, and I blush. Thinking about this is new to me, but I'm smart. I can make things better here, if only my parents would let me.

"Aye."

"What if you go to MIT and come back? Maybe they'll see how much you learn at college, and they'll need your expert opinion," she says hopefully.

"Doubt it. But maybe I will come back to Thistlehill at some point, like your da did. If me and my own da ever get along. I just want it to be my choice. An opportunity to achieve success on my own, far away from this place, especially if my parents don't understand my version of success. Don't you sometimes feel the same way?" I ask, hoping not to be alone in these emotions.

"Yeah, I get what it feels like to have dreams that are totally different from the ones your parents have for you." She sighs and drops her hand from mine. "Especially when you and my brother have everything figured out."

The more time that passes, the more the Macrae house interests me. Meadow's da has been more supportive of my move to the States than my own parents. Harris and Ivy seem to adore their kids, showering them with gifts and trips abroad, but somehow, Meadow still feels like she's on the outside.

I'd trade my own parents for hers any day. I can't imagine them being hard on her or her dreams. Sure, they're different, but that doesn't make them any less important.

"Still no progress with them on your culinary school applications?" I ask.

Her shoulders stiffen, and her gaze falls to a small, white-bellied bird a short distance away from us. "Not really. My parents seem to think they have the summer to convince me to apply to four-year universities. They mean well," she says, but it doesn't sound like she believes it. "Dad doesn't want me to struggle, and Mom wants me to live, not work."

"There are plenty of successful chefs," I remind her.

"True, but I wouldn't be one for a long time. I'd have to put in hours of blood, sweat, and tears to earn my place. But if I can be honest..." She lowers her voice and takes a small step closer to me. "Standing in a kitchen all day sounds like a dream to me, not a nightmare."

"I guess I never asked you why you love cooking so much."

"When I cook, I can make mistakes. It's not like math or the rest of my classes—those things have consequences if I mess them up. But when I'm cooking, the idea of failing isn't all that scary."

"Sounds like it's your true passion."

"I wish my parents understood that."

"I'm sure you can convince them." My mind's far too distracted by the fact that she's only a few inches away from me and I can smell her again.

For all these years, I figured Meadow brought rain with her wherever she went. The smell of petrichor and earth multiplies in her presence. It triggers something instinctual in me. Something only Meadow can rouse.

"I don't know if Fox ever told you, but before we moved to Thistlehill, my parents weren't in a good place. Sure, they're all nausea-inducingly sweet now, but they used to fight. All the time. Dad worked so much he was never home, and Mom would lose her patience with him, and with us."

"Maybe they just don't want you to end up like them." The same can't be said for my own da.

"Isn't that for me to figure out?" Her blue eyes fill with hope and defeat, mirroring the crushed expression on my own face.

I want to make her feel better. Make things right however I can. But what can I do? I can't even get a handle on my own life.

The sad quiver of her bottom lip thrusts a punch into my gut.

"What did you do when they fought?"

She pauses for a moment. Only the sound of the gentle loch waves on the shoreline fills our ears. I hate thinking of her alone in her room at night, listening to her parents argue. She was twelve, thirteen?

"Read mystery books." She smiles. "Fox gave me one that his class was reading, and I've been hooked ever since. He'd stay up with me when their muffled arguments would go through the night and hold my flashlight while I buried myself in the pages."

"He's good like that."

Meadow nods. "Mhm. What do you do?"

"I run," I admit. "Or take pictures, or fiddle with a piece of wood until my Swiss knife manages to get the thing into a recognizable figure."

"I like your little woodworking pieces. Maybe you can make some when you have free time this year."

The reminder strikes a nerve and makes me feel two feet tall. "Doe, I feel like the biggest failure. After graduation, everyone else will be leaving for university, and I'll be stuck here. Alone."

Our eyes meet. "Not actually alone, right? I'll still be here."

Realization hits me like a bag of barley. Fox will be off at the University of Edinburgh. The girl I've been crushing on for the last three years will be finishing up her last year of school.

There won't be any friendships to ruin or best friends to betray. Just Meadow and me.

"You."

I want to thread her fingers back into mine. To hold her. To touch her. "Yeah, Fox will be gone, but we're still friends, right?"

"What about our secret?"

Meadow gives me a mischievous look. The same one she throws on when she's pranking Fox with a new recipe or booing the away teams at our rugby games. "I guess we can be friends who sneak around sometimes and keep secrets."

"Sneaking around? When'd you become such a rebel?" I chuckle to mask the knot of nerves in my chest. The scene in the kitchen feels like a distant memory in her light.

"This year." She tips her head to one side. "You'd know that if you ever noticed me."

I take a step closer to her. The inches between us shrink. I lower my head to her ear and feel her shallow breath on my cheek. "I always notice you."

Meadow swallows heavily. "I notice you too."

"Maybe we don't have to do that in secret while I'm here for the next year."

## Falling for Meadow 115

She pulls her head back and looks right into my eyes. "What do you mean?"

"If I'll be in Thistlehill, we could spend some more time doing *this*." I give in to the visceral urge to touch her again and wrap two of her fingers in my palm. "Or this." I pause by her cheek. My lips are chapped from the brisk air, and I softly connect them with her cold skin. Meadow lets out a breathy sigh. "Is that okay?"

She nods. "I—Ollie—if we—if you do that again, I'm not sure I'll want you to stop."

My hand clasped in hers squeezes harder, and I use my other to gently cup the curve of her jaw and tip her head to mine. "I don't want to stop, Meadow."

"But what do we tell people?"

I shrug. "If you want, we can tell people we're together."

She slips her plump lower lip beneath her teeth. "No. I—I don't want Fox, or our parents, or the whole town, to turn whatever this is into a parade."

She's got a point there. The last thing either of us needs is more expectations. "I guess we'll have to be extra careful then. But I'm going to have to try my hardest to do that."

"Why?"

"Because I haven't stopped thinking about the last time we kissed."

"Me either."

A song bursts in my veins, calling me to her. I pull the tip of her chin closer to mine and whisper against her lips, "Can I?"

"Please."

With that, I kiss Meadow Macrae again.

## Chapter 11
# Ollie

DA'S TRUCK GROWLS AT THE ROUNDABOUT ENTRANCE ON MAIN Street. The heavy afternoon clouds are wringing out rain with the might of Poseidon. Thistlehill's namesake metal statues creak in the rotary. The bleak end of winter always coats the town in a thick, gray smog, but that always signaled the Thistlehill Festival was only a couple short months away.

As I steer the car onto the road, my mind flashes with memories, as if my old camera is firing rogue shots in my head.

In the dog days of summer, the old ice cream parlor on Main Street was an oasis for Fox, Meadow, and me. We'd trudge the half-a-mile-long walk up the hill and into town. Fox would pull out his blue canvas wallet and sift through the colorful notes to pay for all three of our cones.

He'd always been the one kid in our year who had pocket cash. Sometimes when Harris would stop us before we bolted out the door to hand Fox his *just in case you need anything, son* money, he'd slip me a twenty-pound note. I'd feel like a millionaire when I tucked it into the pocket of my belted jeans. Looking back, I wonder if the Macraes understood full well the stress finances caused in my household. They must've. They were my parents' best friends.

A car horn blasts me out of the daydream. Damn. I've looped around the roundabout twice now.

Where is Meadow?

She wasn't at home. If I still remember, Grace Academy's pickup time isn't for another hour. I crane my neck and see the lot behind Fox Den empty of any cars.

I'm starting to cross into stalker territory as I make a third loop and peer into the windows of all the shops on Main Street in search of her. But this can't wait until tonight. The three whisky bottles I prepared for her rattle in the passenger seat.

Tonight, Maisie's at home. At least from what I've been able to gather about her schedule from the way the lights in her house turn on or off in the evenings.

On the fourth circle, I spot her Nissan Leaf in the parking lot of Honeydew Market.

*Jackpot.*

I park the truck beside hers and hurry out of the vehicle, the bottles shielded in my coat as I battle the rain.

*Don't mess this up, Ollie. Apologize for being a complete ass and convince her to try the whisky she was promised.*

Maybe pick up some more of those red apples for that grifting bovine. Kleptocow has taken a liking to interrupting my brief commute to the distillery by acting like a tollbooth employee, demanding payment in the form of fruit to use my own damn road.

The automatic doors swoosh open, and a bell sings through the market.

Fin, the elderly cashier who witnessed me buying an excessive amount of frozen food yesterday, eyes me as I walk in. "Welcome back to Honeydew Market, Ollie. Please leave all outside merchandise on the counter. You can pick it up on the way out."

"But Fin"—I pause and glance down at my bottles—"I need these."

"Aye, mate, we all have those days that only a bottle can fix, but it's store policy." The man shoots me a suggestive wink before nodding to the empty spot on the counter beside him. "Yer ma wouldn't be happy if she knew ye was breaking the rules."

I'm thirty-five years old and the townsfolk are threatening to tell my parents about my behavior? "Are you going to tell my ma on me?" I ask, stunned. Sure, this stuff happened when I was a teenager, but I'm an adult now.

"Riley told me to call her if I noticed you buying *sad people food*." He eyes me with concern. "Told me to throw in some leafy greens with every order. Frozen haggis pies, pizza, and cereal?"

*Sad people food? Wow.* This must be what rock bottom feels like. A man old enough to be my grandfather shaming me because I don't want to cook. I haven't had to in years. I had everything at the tips of my fingers in New York.

"It's called comfort food."

"So comfortable that it's got ye walking in here alone with a whole tavern worth of liquor." He shrugs. I look down at the bottles in my hands. *Right...*

"I—You know what, I don't have time for this." I set the bottles down. "Please do not take your eyes off of them."

"Can't promise anythin'. Saw Kleptocow outside a couple minutes ago. Ye ken things go missing in this town whenever she's around."

My patience is running thin. "Please. Don't give my bottles to that furry, larcenous devil."

"Ye're actin' like this whisky is life or death."

"You have no idea." I rush past him and sprint off into the aisles.

The market is the same as I remember. A little bigger than my New York neighborhood bodega and with about the same selection. White and blue tiles line the floor, graying in the corners. A fluorescent light flickers above me, lighting up the dried goods.

*If I were Meadow, where would I be?*

Instinctively, my legs carry me over to the dairy section. She used to say butter can fix even the biggest cooking mistakes. Maybe that culinary wisdom could be applied here. Yeah, I'll cover myself in melted butter and slip right into her good graces. Brilliant.

The store is empty apart from the cashier up front. This is a good sign. Meadow never liked anyone in her business, and the fewer watchful eyes to witness my pleading, the better.

As anticipated, Meadow stands in front of the rows of milk and yogurt, scrutinizing the list in her notebook. A jumper hugs her waist and abundant hips. Her ass is generous in taut denim. My pulse sings in my veins.

*Keep your head on straight and make this quick.*

"Hey, Meadow, we need to talk," I say, approaching her with the intensity of a starved animal. She looks at me with a bewildered expression. *Okay, maybe cool it a fucking smidge.* "If you have a free second, that is," I add. "Please...and thank you."

*Better.*

Meadow glances at me for a moment, her face not giving away a single emotion, before she sighs and pulls a few sticks of salted butter into her shopping basket. "We already spoke, Oliver. I called Horns today, and I'll be interviewing them to be Fox Den's new supplier. That's that."

The urge to clap back with a petty comment bubbles up to my lips, but I suppress it.

*You're not nineteen anymore, remember? She can send her business wherever she likes. Show her she's a priority.*

That used to come so easily to me.

"You have every right to be upset with me. I acted like a tool at our meeting yesterday. I didn't take your time or the promise Da made to you seriously. I was wrong." I inhale a steady breath and throw on my best puppy-dog eyes, the ones that used to get her to crack every single time I made her upset. Sure, it's a low blow, but it's the only thing in my arsenal.

"You were a tool." She nods. "And wrong."

"Couldn't have said it better myself. That's why—"

"Bit of bawbag too."

I deserve that one. "Sure, but—"

"Maybe *arsepiece* is a better word after the way you handled things at the Den."

A tic splinters my jaw. "Listen, wo—what I'm trying to say…" I huff down the rise in my voice and shake out my wrists. *Don't let her get under your skin.* "I would love it if you could give me another chance. Not for me, but for my family's distillery. We need your business. I'll do anything."

My eyes search her stony expression for a crack. If Da discovers I lost this account because I couldn't work things out with Meadow, he'd never forgive me. Our relationship doesn't need another layer of strain. "Anything?"

A light burns up her blue irises—the crack I was looking for. I grit my teeth. A bead of sweat runs down my neck. "Anything, Meadow."

She briefly smirks, swinging her basket. She is an Amazon of a woman whose looks rival any goddess. Not even rival—absolutely blast them to smithereens. She's too fucking pretty when she's mad.

The petrichor off her skin wafts my way, and my throat dries.

"Give me three reasons why Fox Den should work with Anderson Distillery."

Easy. "We have the best whisky in the Highlands." She shakes her head disapprovingly. "Can't dispute that one. You've had a taste for Red Label since you were sixteen. Tell me you don't have a bottle of it in your kitchen cabinets right now instead of Horns's Single Malt."

Her nostrils flare. *The past, right—dammit.* Why can't I stop digging it up every single time I talk to her? I wince, ready for the counterarguments.

"Fine. That's one. Two more." She crosses her arms over her chest, sending the metal basket into my gut. I don't move, even as the grocery aisles around us feel like they're shrinking.

"You're an incredibly talented chef. Without a doubt, Fox Den will be the best restaurant in all of the Highlands—no, in all of Scotland."

From the small bit of coverage I could find on her, it's obvious that if she'd stayed in France, she'd have her own place and a Michelin star by now. Thistlehill may be the place where my dreams couldn't thrive, but that doesn't mean the same is true for her.

"That's more ass-kissing than an actual reason." Her words throw an image into my mind. Ass-kissing Meadow is off the table. Kissing her ass on a table, now that's—no. *Cut it out.* Fucking hell, her pouty, angry glare is turning me into a caveman.

"Fine. Because your restaurant will be a flaming success, it would be foolish of me not to waive all of our delivery charges for the next year." Fox Den is under a mile away from the distillery. I'll drive the damn whisky to her restaurant for the next eighty-three days if I have to.

"Horns offered me no delivery charges for a four-year contract."

Fucking hell, she's a tough negotiator. The refrigerator hums. "We'll waive delivery charges for the term of the contract and for all renewals. And—" I hesitate. There has to be something I can offer to pique her interest. "I'll make sure that you have the first pick of all the mature casks if you want to switch your signature whisky."

None of our clients have an offer to make any of our whiskys exclusive. Da slashed it out of the On Cloud Nine contract the moment he read their terms.

But I have no doubt in my bones that this partnership can put Anderson Distillery on a global map. Fox Den's Instagram page has over fifty-thousand followers. The search *Fox Den Thistlehill* garners thousands of results online. The distillery needs that kind of attention, and a hot, skilled chef in Scotland can send us across Europe.

Yes, I did more due diligence on her. No, it didn't involve any deep cyberstalking like in the past.

*Ken yer clients*, Da would say, and he's right.

"That's generous." Meadow keeps her voice steady, but I can tell the offer has excited her more than she wants to let on. "Last one. Why should I supply Anderson whisky at my restaurant?"

The answer comes to me faster than a high-speed train. "Because you, Meadow Macrae, are a fucking fighter." I take a small step toward her. The metal edge of her shopping basket digs into my stomach, but I let it. "I've never met someone who made the sacrifices you did. Raising your brother's daughter? Putting yourself through culinary school? Starting your own restaurant? Working under Chef Colette Dubois?" My ramble of reasons almost cuts short as her face splatters with surprise again, but I keep going. "Yes, I did look you up. Okay? Sue me! But I am not going to miss out on the opportunity to have my family's whisky in your restaurant. If there's anyone who's going to succeed in this town, it's you, and I'd be a damn fool to not be on your side when you do."

All the walls she's put up seem to crumble as her shoulders slacken, her lips parting slightly as she inspects me.

"Okay. Those three reasons are sound enough in my book." Meadow bites her lip again. I've made her *nervous*? Can't be. She straightens her spine and nods. "Since you won't take no for an answer, I'll give you one more chance. For your family."

Right. For my family.

A flash of electricity passes through us.

"I have the bottles here, I can—"

Meadow raises a hand to silence me. "Tomorrow, I'll have an hour at lunch. I can stop by the distillery."

"No," I say quickly. I don't want her to see the attitude Callum is giving me and change her mind. "My place. Uh, that'll be easiest. No need to spend any of your limited time shooing that damn Kleptocow out of the way."

Her cerulean eyes give me a once-over. "Fine. But strictly business, Oliver. I don't think you can handle begging for another chance to get this right."

"Just so you know, I was moments away from falling to my knees." I throw on a jovial voice for the joke, but it drops something potent between us. Meadow's cheeks burn a soft shade of pink. It's like spilled watercolor across her pale skin.

"Were ye, aye?" Her voice is all playful sarcasm as she tosses the quintessential teasing phrase at me. "Are you all talk?"

"Seriously?"

She raises a brow, scrutinizing me with expectation. So, right there in the dairy aisle of Honeydew Market, next to the frozen section of the sad people food, I lower onto my left knee in front of Meadow. "I'm not too proud to beg."

"See you tomorrow, Oliver." She walks away, her laughter trailing after her.

I snort. "I'll see you at lunch, Macrae. Right next door."

A second chance. I won't let her slip through my fingers again.

## Chapter 12
# Meadow

Get in. Get out.

A simple business lunch. At the Anderson house. Alone with Ollie.

It's fine. After being back for a week and a half, he's already thrown my entire world off kilter and almost cost me my business.

The reminder of his pleading look as he begged right down on his knees curls the edges of my lips.

Okay. Maybe I was a bit too harsh on him.

Maybe he deserved it.

This whisky will amplify my menu. Everyone has top-shelf spirits and local drafts, but an exclusive blend means I can compete with all the big boys across Scotland. I never got far in any of the jobs I had by playing nice. As a woman in an industry that's flooded with men, making myself heard was the only way to survive.

When I was a sous chef under Colette Dubois at d'Or, my male chefs de partie refused to listen to me. Who could blame them? I was younger, sharper, and female. After one particularly gruesome night in the weeds, I worked up the courage to bring the unshifting dynamic to Colette.

She gave me a sympathetic smile and a squeeze on the shoulder, then said, *Speak louder, chef.*

I did. Until my throat burned raw and my head was bursting at the end of every dinner service.

I stomached their groans and insults, their making fun of me for nagging them when all I asked was for them to do their fucking jobs. I refused to accept anything short of perfection. If things weren't exactly how I demanded them to be, I didn't resist letting them know.

I wasn't going to roll over for Ollie the moment he came to his senses. The soft and tender girl he used to know is long gone. I shake the reminder from my head. Now, I have the best whisky deal on the market, and I'm making sure Seamus and Riley don't get rocked out of the business because of their son. The Andersons have been a second pair of grandparents to Maisie.

Once Ollie is gone, they'll be the people who I have to look after.

I hover my fist beside their weathered door and knock. The act is foreign, as I've let myself into this house so many times before. Silence. I bang harder.

Suddenly, Ollie flings open the door, and my fist rocks right into the white T-shirt stretched across his chest. He's solid and sturdy. I snatch my hand away. My skin is hot, as if I've tossed my palm into a searing pan.

*Universe, you are a cruel beast.*

"You're here." He notes the obvious.

His shoulders are brawny beneath the fabric of his tee, his bulky thighs wrapped in blue and green flannel pajama pants, like a holiday romance logger who's just finished chopping down fresh pine.

I clear my throat. "That's what we agreed on."

Hormones—that's all this is. Out of the corner of my eye, a car barrels down the road. After the Cameron twins' promiscuous assumptions outside of the Den on Monday, I've caught more than a couple of whispers in town.

"Miss Macrae, it is lovely to host you here. Why don't you come in and—"

I push past him, make my way inside, and head toward the kitchen.

I've been in this house as often as my own; it's more of a second home. But it's strange standing here with the man who once occupied these walls.

How he'd sit his large and lanky body at the dining table to my left as I'd watch him try one of my newest concoctions. How we'd watch movies on the couch to the right, holding hands beneath a woolen throw. The same woolen throw he had draped over his bare torso when he spoke to Maisie. The damn sex blanket!

*Maisie. Fox Den. Business.*

No memories.

"Is this the whisky?" I gesture to the unlabeled bottles on the table, each one filled with a rainbow of amber liquid. Beside them, a fresh bouquet of anemones. Their deep blue centers are stark against their bright, silky petals. *Interesting.*

"Yeah, why don't you sit down?" Ollie taps on the dining table and pulls out a seat. "Have you had a chance to eat?"

Not unless you count tasting the four varieties of espagnole Brooke made this morning. Feeding others is part of my DNA. Remembering to feed myself is a different story.

"I only have an hour."

"Can't drink all this whisky on an empty stomach."

I glance around the kitchen. No dishes in the sink. Not a tea towel out of place. Apart from the woody and citrusy scent of the anemones, the house smells clean. *Unusual.* When I was in his room—up thirteen stairs and to the left—as a girl, it looked like a tornado had blown through it.

*He's a grown man, Meadow. What were you expecting? A*

*bachelor pad after his parents have been gone for just three days?*

"Okay," I say and slide into the chair, taking off my coat and keeping a close eye on him as he moves around the kitchen. "Something small. No need to make a fuss."

He walks over to a butcher's block by the sink and pulls off the tea towel covering it. "I made a charcuterie board."

A laugh sneaks out of my throat. "You can't be serious."

"In the city, my team was adamant about having food at meetings. If we're fed, we make our best business decisions." He smiles and sets his creation down in front of me. "I couldn't skimp for the best deal Anderson Distillery has seen in years."

Now he's actually kissing my ass. Almost as much as he was at Honeydew Market.

*Fox Den will be the best restaurant in all of the Highlands— no, in all of Scotland.*

I stare at the three different types of cheeses—Anster, Brie, and Lanark Blue. Blueberry jelly beside a fresh hunk of honeycomb. Dried apricots and figs. Crackers. Sliced, fresh apples and —is that a chili chutney?

My nose confirms it is.

"Where'd you learn to make something like this?" I raise a brow at him.

He shrugs his large shoulders sheepishly, looking almost shy. "One of my friends, and former coworker, Avery, has an insatiable addiction to cheese." He says it so seriously I can't help but chuckle. "When Ave was pregnant, her husband, Luca, would order these elaborate, pregnancy-safe charcuterie boards to the office—they work together—to satisfy her cravings. We all threw her a cheese-themed baby shower. If you ever need a wheel of Brie shaped into a baby, I'm your man."

My ears burn from all of the information. A glimpse into his life, the one he's built across an ocean, filled with friends who have babies and coworkers who throw each other showers. I swallow and rub my palm against my breastbone in an attempt to dull the discomfort that's blooming in my chest.

"It's very pretty." I smile through rolled lips and cut myself a piece of the Anster. The pale, crumbly cheese melts on my tongue, leaving behind an almost mushroomy flavor. Maisie would go bonkers for this spread. Much like Ollie's friend, she has an insatiable cheese addiction. "Thank you for putting it together for our meeting."

"Of course. I can't lose you as our client. Things at the distillery haven't been easy for me."

I figured there would be an adjustment, but given the sorrowful look on his face, it seems there's more to it. "Callum giving you a hard time? I know you never wanted to run the distillery."

"Maybe I wanted to run it in a way that Da didn't. It doesn't matter now; I'll be leaving soon anyway." He shrugs. "It just seems as if the improvements I want to make are too revolutionary."

"What are you changing that has them so upset?"

"All I'm doing is putting in a digital ordering system and getting new bottling equipment."

"That doesn't seem so bad."

"Aye. It'll help us fulfill a big order for a resort conglomerate. Bring in profit for my da and get our whisky into the hands of people all over the world."

A hope dims in his eyes. He truly cares. Maybe more than I realized. "It'll be okay. You know how it is here. Change is a hard thing to grasp your mind around in Thistlehill. But don't let that dissuade you."

"Aye. It's fine. I'll figure it out." Ollie leans over the table, scooting his chair closer to mine.

I fight off the way his oaky smell fogs up my mind.

*What's happening?*

A man in a tee that's far too tight—a man I used to love—is

staring at me with those pleading brown eyes he threw on for me at Honeydew Market yesterday.

"Now, before we begin our formal conversation, can I ask one thing?" His voice is wistful and low.

I clear my throat again and scrape my chair against the floor.

"I think we should stick to the meeting agenda." Especially if my damn cycle is making me sweat out of every orifice in my body. Or maybe it's from being near him.

*Stop giving these weird feelings weight, Meadow.*

He used the past as an excuse to act like a jerk, was under the assumption I threw away my life, and was going to snub me with some second-rate, albeit spectacular, product because he didn't take my business seriously.

But he apologized. Maisie's small voice sings in my head, *Share your feelings and move forward together.*

Fucking hell.

I knew those *Gentle Hearts, Strong Bonds* and *Raising with Kindness* books were going to come back to haunt me.

Ignoring me, he leans in even closer and sends both of his hands beneath the table. Is he trying to touch my leg?

"But I figured we could..." His finger swipes against my knee, and I nearly jolt out of my seat.

"What are you doing?" My voice shoots up.

To my surprise, Ollie bounces back up in his seat and produces a baguette from underneath the table like some sort of magician.

"Breaking bread," he explains, batting the loaf at me as if it's a sword. "Before we dive into the tasting? We could break some bread. Is this absolutely ridiculous?"

Reluctantly, I laugh again. "Do you have a basket of petticoat tails under there too?"

"Maybe next time. What do you say, Macrae? Truce?"

I take the fresh baguette from him and rip off the tip, slathering it in the chili chutney and Brie before taking a bite.

I eye him for a moment. Those damn round eyes. He obviously regrets the things he said. As much as I'd enjoy channeling all of the stress from the opening into being angry at him—I can't. My heart's already forgiven him, whether I like it or not.

"Truce." I nod, and his mouth stretches into a wide smile beneath the thicket of his auburn beard.

"Good." Ollie reaches for the Lanark Blue and chutney.

"Uh, don't—never mind."

"What? Is this a bad combination?" He looks at the board and back up at me. "I trust your instincts here. I may make a mean board, but flavor's always been your strong suit."

"Go for the apples. The earthy flavor pairs better with some crisp sweetness."

"Yes, chef."

He does as I say and chews, closing his eyes and letting out the faintest moan.

A fleck of warmth lands in my stomach, gliding lower and lower along my abdomen as my gaze remains sternly locked in on his handsome face.

"Having someone with your skill set around is an underrated luxury." He beams, taking no notice of my frigid posture or uncouth ogling. "Shall we?" I nod. "I can offer you three whiskys. Each one has been aged in sherry oak casks and has a distinct flavor." A vein in his forearm bulges as he uncaps one of the bottles, pours a dram of the medium-amber liquid into a tumbler, and slides it over to me. "Since you like the Red Label, I'm going to bet this will be your favorite."

I pick up the glass and bring it beneath my nose. When I inhale, goosebumps spread along the back of my neck.

"Fig?" I take a careful sip, letting the whisky roll over my tongue. "And hazelnuts. That hint of sweetness in the aftertaste is phenomenal. Seamus knows his stuff." I drain my glass. Heat lights up my chest. A satisfied grin appears as Ollie uncaps the other two bottles. He carefully fills two more clear tumblers and slides them over. I pick up the darkest of the liquids and repeat the same procedure. "This one has sherry cask all over it. Honey? No, maybe even molasses. It's indulgent."

"I thought the same thing," he laughs and takes a sip of the whisky. "Good, innit? We have about twenty barrels of each of these. Here, let me know what you think of this one. I couldn't quite place it."

I take a bigger swig of the third dram than I should, but my hands refuse to stop tingling. "Like taking a bite of earth."

"Right?"

"It's the geosmin. Almost as if you've swum to the bottom of Loch Flora and licked the lake bed."

He shakes his head and stares at me in awe. Is that what it is? Can't be. I hastily toss the rest of the drink down my throat. My lungs and nose burn from the taste. Three drams of whisky and my mind's fucking with my perception of reality.

"I forgot how damn good you are at this."

I set down the empty tumbler and smile. "Years of practice." A silence unfurls between us like a block of chocolate left out on a hot day. Not uncomfortable or awkward. Just quiet. The howling of the wind outside makes a brief appearance. "I don't remember the last time I drank in the middle of the day. Can't exactly find the time to savor whisky at lunch when you're a mother."

In France, Brooke and I would stay out partying into dawn and swindle gorgeous French men out of free drinks before our shifts. I was free-spirited then, without a seven-year-old to care for or a whole business on my shoulders.

That girl feels impossibly far away.

"Maisie seems like a great kid. You're obviously a wonderful parent."

"Yeah," I nod. "Thanks. I try my best with her."

My brother would've given his little girl the world, and I promised that I'd do the same.

"Trust me, sharing drinks with a beautiful woman isn't how I thought I'd spend my lunch hour either." My lower lip drops open. The whisky-induced redness on his face deepens. "I only meant—"

"It's fine." I shake my head reassuringly. No need to make this awkward. Even though I hate to admit it, it's nice to still be thought of as beautiful by the one person who made me feel it the most. "When was this one barreled?" I eye the whisky he thought I'd favor the most. He was right.

"The year we met," he whispers, avoiding my gaze. Unexpectedly, he laughs. "Do you remember when we—actually, forget it."

I yearn for him to finish speaking. Bringing up the past is probably not the wisest thing to do, but I want to know what he's thinking about. What memory flooded his mind? Was it one that I can recall?

"No." I slide my hand over the table and reach toward him. When my fingers are a lick away from his skin, I stop myself. The drinks are loosening my inhibitions too much. "You can tell me. One story can't hurt."

Ollie pours another dram of my favorite whisky and sets it in front of me. My foot drums against the floor. I shouldn't have downed those other three so fast, but I was desperate to quench my fried nerves.

"I was thinking about one of the first nights we snuck into the distillery. We must've been, what? Fifteen? Sixteen years old?"

The vivid picture of the cold December day swoops into my mind. "It was a week after my sixteenth birthday."

"Right." He scrunches his nose together and slices off a bit of Brie before popping it into his mouth. "You had decided it was time for you to try the liquid gold we'd all been talking about. Didn't give in when Fox and I tried to push you to take even the smallest sip the year before."

The mention of my brother doesn't strike a nerve this time. Instead, the sweet recollection of the moment nestles a comfort into my belly. Right beside the escalating warmth from watching his fingers trace the outer rim of his tumbler.

"You guys were terrible influences."

"Aye, but you'd always done things on your own terms."

"It wasn't that." I smile, remembering what was going through my mind all those years ago. "I'd seen my mom frown and squirm with every sip when she was trying her best to get your parents to like her. I had no interest in whatever that horrendous liquor was going to do to my poor taste buds."

He chortles and claps his palm against the table. Heat drops in my stomach, right in between my thighs.

"Must have been why you downed your first glass in one gulp."

Those early years of our relationship were filled with sneaking around and secrets. Hushed whispers and footsie beneath the dinner table when our families ate together on Sundays. Our relationship was as sacred as the pages of my old diary, filled with scribbles and kisses that were kept under lock and key.

It was amazing when we were young. I never found that same rush between other people's sheets. You never really do forget your first. At least, I didn't.

"Remember Fiona? She was a year or two above you at Grace Academy," I say, giving myself permission to share something about my life too. Because however much I try to resist letting him in, I also have an urge to share a sliver of my life. So he can see who I became, who I am now.

"Fiona Walker?"

"Yeah, she's my business partner and chef de patisserie." I roll the tumbler of whisky between my fingers and palm, keeping my eyes away from his—because I'm concerned that if I look up into them for too long, I'll see Ollie. The one I fell in love with, not the one who's brokering a partnership between my restaurant and his family's distillery. "She'd be able to use this in a damn good caramel sauce."

"You mentioned another name at that setup dinner a few nights ago. Brooke, was it?"

He listened. He remembered. The fact sends a shiver up each vertebra. "My sous chef. She's from Florida. We were at Le Cordon Bleu together." I say the words with a hushed whisper, afraid of what they might make him feel. When I finally give in and glance up into his eyes, the resentment I expected is gone. Instead, he tips his head, urging me to go on. "Worked in kitchens all over France. They're my best friends."

"Nothing beats running a business with your mates."

The stress that's been coiled around me like a boa constrictor since I stepped foot in this house is slowly unwinding. Time slips by as we nosh on his pretty charcuterie board, do another round of whisky tasting, and parse through the contract terms without a single argument. It feels easy.

Intimate and comfortable.

"This was nice, Oliver; thank you for putting it together," I say, polishing off the last drink and glancing at my watch. Our hour-long meeting ended thirty minutes ago. *Crap.* "I have to go." I push up from my seat, and the alcohol rushes to my head. Driving like this is out of the question.

"Let me walk you home," he offers, leaping out of his seat and moving the charcuterie board off the table.

I take a step, stumbling forward.

One moment, Ollie is standing across the kitchen from me. The next, his hands grip my shoulders. His skin is a roaring fire burning my fingertips. That familiar woodsy smell permeates my senses and imprints itself into every cell of my body.

Neither of us moves, afraid to break this moment.

"Meadow," he whispers in a voice that's no longer hiding behind a barricade of friendliness or business.

It's a voice I remember.

"We're drunk," I whisper.

*Don't look up. Walk home.* The pleas are useless, as my legs remain bolted into the kitchen floor.

My fingers spread over his shoulders, exploring the firmness of his body. Is it possible for something to feel the same but be completely different? I know it's him in there, because I'm in here too.

I swallow. I don't want to care about the man in front of me. The same one who didn't pick up any of my calls, who set fire to the friendship he had with my brother, who didn't come to Fox's funeral, who disregarded people's emotions.

But a part of me does.

Care? Or maybe crave?

A piece of me is seeking something I haven't shined a light on in a long time.

Closure?

No. That can't be it. We both bolted shut that part of our lives long, long ago.

"Doe." He speaks again, and the nickname settles over my body like the first bite of a meal that's just been pulled from the oven.

I drag my eyes up to his.

*Don't breathe. Or do, but don't breathe so deep that you'll let him fill up your lungs.*

A wisp of pine tingles my nose, and temptation wins as I inhale the smoky fragrance of whisky on his lips. Every neuron in my brain is flustered, as if someone's pouring hot oil into my skull.

I'm her again.

The girl I was before all the cuts, burns, and sorrow.

Before the pressure and responsibility. Before motherhood, endless bills, and a town full of people who count on her.

The girl who had a brother.

The same girl who was in love with his best friend—the boy standing in front of her who would hold her in his arms like he'd never let her go.

*That's a fantasy.* This entire moment is a twisted game of make-believe. Maybe if I close my eyes, it'll vanish like a bad dream.

Because he did let me go. He drowned me out with a fortress of silence.

But I was no better for letting him go too.

"Ollie," I manage in a quiet voice.

His name is alien on my tongue, but my mouth welcomes the shape. I used to say, laugh, moan, and scream it seventeen years ago. My heart beats in my throat so fiercely it must be obvious.

Minutes tick by as he runs his fingers over my arms, taking my hands off his shoulders and into his. His touch is so soft in comparison to my working hands. My thumbs trace the deep lines in his palms and the barely formed calluses on his skin.

With each stroke, I inch closer, as if I'm searching for something. *But what?*

He mirrors me and wades closer.

It's bad—a terrible, awful idea.

But I've turned into a flightless bird who's stumbled across shelter. A familiar reprieve from reality. I want this moment to last a little longer.

A chance to be that girl one more time.

To feel alive and carefree.

Instead of running out of this house and boarding up my front door, I press myself into the warmth of his chest, close my eyes, and for the first time in over six-thousand days, I kiss Ollie Anderson.

It's nothing like the first or second kiss we shared. Nothing like the tenth or the fiftieth. I counted each one meticulously, until the number became so inflated I could hardly keep track of it in my journal. Until the idea of tallying up something that was supposed to last forever seemed pointless.

His beard is surprisingly soft as it caresses my chin. Nothing like the scratchy patches of hair that used to sprout up along his jaw. He's got whisky on his breath, the acid dancing across a faint taste of peppermint.

And then there's him.

Sweet Ollie on my tongue.

Our mouths meld together, a reuniting of old lovers who found each other after years apart.

We can't be that.

*We won't be that!* I yell into the crevices of my sizzling mind, but the voice is snuffed out as Ollie's hands run down my body with familiarity. He traces over the ripples of my curves, my back, my hips.

*Make yourself heard.*

I don't want to be heard.

I don't want to stop.

The tendrils in my stomach flambé. My veins wring into knots as his arms fall around me, sling across my waist, and drag me even closer to his chest, as if he's trying to bury me there.

I've kissed so many people since we've been apart, anyone and everyone who may have helped me erase him from my mind.

But nothing compares to this.

The goodbye I never gave us.

*Is that what's happening?*

I don't know. I can't think straight. The alcohol has turned every teaspoon of common sense left in me into a barrel of mashed grain.

So when Ollie kisses me like it's the last time, I do the same.

"Doe," he breathes against my lips in a plea, repairing the fissures in my heart. Deep, wounded cracks I never thought would heal. And I can't let him be responsible for that. For fixing any part of me that may still be broken, lost, or afraid.

"Don't," I beg unconvincingly, not wanting him to stop, but also not wanting to give him the power to bring me back there. To my old life. It's too late for that, as sanity escapes me when his tongue glides over the seam of my lips. We spin and push and pull, as if fighting the moment we're both recklessly collapsing into.

I shuffle back without breaking our connection, and Ollie follows me like I'm a northern star, a place he knows, a place he can navigate too easily.

That's not right. For almost twenty years, he had lost the internal compass that used to lead him home to me. A sorrowful well splits open my chest as a sting pricks my eyes. *No. Not this.*

*Ignore it.*

I tug at his neck and the collar of his T-shirt. Ollie unbuttons my cardigan and strips it off my shoulders. It falls to the floor. My feet are swept off the ground as he lifts me with ease and sets me on the edge of the kitchen table.

"I've missed—" he rasps through a heavy voice.

I shake my head no. "Not now."

I can't bear to hear the end of that sentence. A potential sobering blow to end this high.

"Come closer." He nods against me, and I let myself melt beneath the exploring touch of his fingers. He takes my lower lip into his teeth, the way he used to do when our sarcastic sparring turned a playful fight into more. His beard scratches against my soft cheeks.

"Closer," he demands.

I do as he says.

My own hands refuse to stop their journey over his large shoulders, the muscle beneath the thick skin and soft dimples of his arms, until my fingers wind between his auburn waves.

My heart jackhammers against my chest like a violent anvil.

I need him.

One more time.

One time to forget all of the times before.

*Yeah. That's sound logic.*

I graze my knuckles over his flannel pants, inching up his inner thigh until I'm close to his erection. He wants this as much as I do. Ollie inhales a sharp breath, his body stiffening, and stares down at me.

"We shouldn't." I shake my head, but it's no use. Even he knows I'm lying.

"We shouldn't have done a lot of things, and we most definitely shouldn't do this." He attempts to keep us from diving headfirst into endless temptation. We heave against each other, foreheads connecting. The brown caramel of his eyes is glazed over in darkness. "But you, doe, you've been on my mind since—"

I kiss the words off his lips.

He was my first. I was his.

We weren't meant to be each other's last.

But we were young, naive, and foolish.

Obviously, we still are. I thought age was supposed to make me wiser, but at thirty-four, I'm still a lovestruck teenager losing all my senses around him. An obsession I could never replace.

*He's leaving.*

This is temporary. A fantasy.

Continuing to ignore all of my own pointless warnings, I kiss him deeper, trying to erase the words from my mind. Ollie runs his warm breath over my neck, his teeth and tongue gliding down my throat.

I yank down his flannel pajamas. Excitement burns in my veins as his fingers unclasp the top button of my jeans.

His hands run over my breasts, and I moan. The table bucks as he closes in on me, cementing his palms on the outsides of my thighs and grinding his hips in between my legs.

"Fuck," he growls.

Then a cascade of splintering wood groans beneath me, leaving me suspended for a breath before we crash to the floor. A loud clatter echoes through the kitchen. My body tumbles backward, and I grab for Ollie's collar as we slam hard onto the broken table now shattered on the kitchen floor.

I sober instantly.

I shouldn't be here. I let myself indulge too much.

"Are you hurt?" Ollie rushes onto his forearms, his face potent with panic. The weight of his large body numbs my legs.

"No," I say quickly. "But I need to go."

He wraps his arm around my lower back and hoists us out of the rubble. That table's been in his family for decades.

*What the fuck did I do?* This is exactly why I can't cut loose. I can't just jet off on a trip down memory lane. A mistake. What a huge and irresponsible mistake.

I'm a mom. A business owner whose restaurant opens in four days.

"Right." Ollie tugs up his pajama pants. The hardness I felt in his boxers persists. "Why don't I give you a ride?"

"I live next door." I swoop my cardigan off the floor, shaking out the splinters of wood stuck in the fibers, and fish my jacket off the chair.

"Duh. Um, wait," he stutters and reaches for me. I sidestep his outstretched hand. That hand is what got us into this mess in the first place. "Wait, Meadow."

"No, this was a mistake. Big, big mistake." I point at the broken table on the floor. "That was enough of a sign from the universe to confirm that what we were doing was wrong."

"Or it was an old table." His face is laced with disappointment. *Was the kiss bad?* I slap my palm to my forehead. *Leave. Go home!*

I hurry toward the door, but before I leave, I spin my head back. "Do the terms of our contract still stand?"

"Of course. Why wouldn't they?"

"Today was the first time we've been able to remain cordial since you've come back. Then we did whatever that was—"

"Kiss?"

"I have the biggest moment in my career happening on Saturday. My daughter is counting on me, my family, everyone in this town. This is the last thing I need on my plate."

A frown deepens beneath his beard. "Bu—"

I don't hear him as I pull open the door and bolt out into the cold spring air.

## Chapter 13
# Ollie

**HR@VIGGLE.COM**
Oliver Anderson, please find your welcome packet attached. We look forward to your June 1st start date.

THE STARK SOUND of a dropped gavel bounces through the room.

"We'll be addressing new business today," Jody, the town provost, stands behind the podium at the front of the hall. "The annual Thistlehill Festival is scheduled to commence on the First of May, like usual. The sign-ups for the caber toss can be found on the bulletin by the front door. Let's try to win this year, aye? We've had a three-year losing streak to out-of-towners."

My knees dig into my chest as I shuffle around in one of the tiny chairs supplied for the hundred attendees.

Thistlehill's Town Hall meeting is held in a small, stone building a short walk away from Main Street. Traditionally, all the town's business owners meet here to share announcements and vote on town-related business.

# Falling for Meadow   143

"Now, first order of business...ah, yes." Jody smiles and steps aside. "Miss Macrae, the floor is yours."

Meadow makes her way toward the wooden podium. If I hadn't walked in late, I would've said hello and tried to clear the air between us after what happened two days ago.

That damn kiss. Who even started it? Me or her? Does it even matter? It's only natural that we'd get along. Maybe the whole thing can be chalked up to a slipup.

A slipup that left me hard for hours after she was gone. No amount of freezing water in the shower managed to lift the heat her touch left on my skin.

"Hi, everyone. Just wanted to remind all of you that Fox Den is officially opening its doors tomorrow. Brooke, Fi, and I are thrilled to see you at dinner service." Her voice is amplified by the microphone, and my heartbeat unsteadies—the same way it's been struggling to keep a normal pace since the slipup.

I can still feel the ghost of her soft mouth on mine. The supple and lush curves taking up the full breadth of my hands. Her scent still circulates in my lungs. The tender graze of her fingers up my thighs.

No point in pretending it wasn't the best damn kiss I've had in twenty years.

"We're all so proud of ya." Lorna claps her hands together from the row behind me. "Thistlehill's very own Chef Meadow."

"That's our daughter," Ivy sings from the chair beside Meadow's empty one in the front row at the other side of the hall. Maisie and Harris are in the seats beside her.

"I'm closing up shop so we can all go enjoy your big night," Ramona's scratchy voice calls out from somewhere in the back.

The entire room fills with applause and cheers. The town loves her. Why wouldn't they? She said it herself: this is her home. My fingers tap the denim holstering my legs. Hopefully everyone will give me even a fraction of this warmth.

"If that's all, Lorna and Kenna, you had something you wanted to share?" Jody takes back her podium, fixing the collar of her emerald pantsuit.

Meadow works her way back to her seat. I steal the briefest glance and flash her a smile; she returns a tight-lipped one before sitting down.

Should I go over there and sit with the Macraes?

No. She wanted to be cordial. We're business partners. That wouldn't be appropriate. Callum's voice rings in my ears, *Our customers like a personalized touch.*

Touch.

Meadow's scarred hands in mine. The coarse stroke of her fingertips in my hair. Her teeth and tongue. Wednesday's meeting projects itself behind my lids, the reminder heating my blood.

Cordial. Nothing about the growing hardness in my jeans is cordial.

Neither was her peering from behind the curtains in her living room as I hauled wood from the old shed behind my house and onto the front lawn at the break of dawn.

After a sleepless night of resisting wrapping my fist around myself and blowing off the pent-up steam I couldn't shake after our kiss, I had to do something. And we needed a new kitchen table.

I haven't used my hands for building since I was a boy, but after the labor I put in at the distillery, I needed the same feeling that kept my mind clear before.

*Stay focused, Ollie.* Coming to this meeting has nothing to do with Meadow. I came with a purpose—improve my family's distillery. That goal hasn't changed because she's here and the blue jeans she's wearing crease around her thighs in a way that makes me want to drag her out of here and finish what we started.

*No.*

Coming back to Thistlehill was meant to be an easy in and out. And it will be. The Director of Sustainable Innovation position is waiting for me in the city.

The Cameron twins take the podium dressed in glittering jumpers that shine beneath the dim light of the hall. When Kenna spots me, she shoots me a suggestive wink. My face burns red, and I bat my head away only to find Meadow suppressing a smile at the interaction.

At least I can still make her laugh.

"We're here to discuss the Thistlehill ghost," Lorna begins.

Muffled voices groan from the back of the room.

"Not this again, ladies." Jody shuffles her heels across the floor and reaches for the microphone. "We spent thirty minutes on the supposed Thistlehill ghost last month."

"And yet things are still going missing!" Kenna huffs, yanking the microphone out of the provost's grasp. "The scarves we made at Ivy's knitting club, the red ones, have disappeared."

"We all ken it's that cow of yours. Took two of my garden gnomes—Perry and Jerry are nowhere to be found," Betty chimes in. The owner of the only bed and breakfast in town has a yard decorated with hundreds of those creepy dolls.

*How does she even keep track of them?*

"It's not Madame Belle—"

"You mean Kleptocow?"

"Stop calling her that! She's a lady!" Lorna protests. "Where would she even be taking the stuff?"

"Probably to some secret lair. Or it's you two who are thieving and selling our stuff on eBay." Betty points in accusation.

"Nobody wants yer gnomes."

"Aye—"

"We'll continue investigating the disappearances." Jody claps her gavel against the podium again, quieting the ruckus in the room. "Unless anyone has any other new business, I say we call it an early night."

"Wait!" I leap out of my chair, nearly knocking it over. The elderly couple beside me looks bewildered as they clutch onto each other. "Sorry," I say and steady the chair before straightening myself. "I'm here on behalf of Anderson Distillery."

All the eyes in the room target me. A string of whispers weaves around the hall.

*Is that Ollie?*

*Can't be, lad's in America.*

*No, I think it's him.*

*I saw him outside of Fox Den a few days ago.*

"Alright, come on up here." Jody adjusts the microphone and steps aside. "But make it quick. I'd like to get home as soon as possible. There's a new episode of *Love Island* tonight."

Nerves pinch at my skin as I make my way to the front of the room. My boots get heavier with each step.

*Don't be nervous.*

*You know these people. They know you and your family.*

*Stop sweating as if their approval will make or break the distillery.*

The pep talk doesn't work. Without their okay, I can't guarantee that On Cloud Nine's orders will be bottled and shipped out in two weeks' time. I'll lose the account. The entire plan to come back here and set my parents up for their retirement would be a failure.

I scan the hall as I take my spot at the podium. Despite towering over the stand, I feel small.

"We're waiting, Ol," Jody whispers.

*Focus.*

I clear my throat and address the room. "Right. Some of you may already know, but I'm helping my parents by updating the distillery." My gaze skips from the crowd of blank faces to the

Macrae family. Harris nods. *I can do this.* At least I have one person on my team, someone who always understood me. "I will be building a new bottling facility on the land to keep up with orders. That's why I'm here today, to request your approval in a town vote."

"Doesn't the distillery already have that?" someone I don't recognize calls out from the fourth row.

"Yes, but the new bottling equipment I'm installing needs more space. Only an acre to house the machinery that'll bring Anderson Distillery into the future."

"Aye, the last thing good whisky needs is to rush into the future." Callum's voice is easily recognizable across the room. He's been avoiding me this week and not being shy about it. When I asked him for construction crew recommendations for the build, he threw a cold shoulder at me and pretended to take a call.

I spot him sitting cross-armed and stony a few seats behind Meadow. I drop my eyes back to her.

God, she's beautiful. A real sight for sore eyes.

She gives me a look I can't quite read. Pity? Sympathy? Disappointment? This announcement is going as bad as the meeting I had with her in Fox Den.

The room is bleak with silence as the townsfolk blink at me with uninterested expressions. Didn't exactly expect them to whip out sparklers in celebration, but any kind of reaction is better than this.

"How long will this take?" Jody asks from beside me.

Typically, a project like this would take two months, but I don't have that kind of time. I rub my palms together nervously. "Needs to be done in two weeks."

The hall scurries to life. Townsfolk break out into not-so-hushed whispers as their questions and suspicions pellet the room.

"Two weeks?" Jody exclaims.

"Acre right beside our Loch Flora? Seems like a disaster," someone in the crowd calls out.

Sweat slicks down my neck as I nervously latch my hands onto the podium. I take it back. This reaction is most definitely not better than no reaction.

"Are Callum and Elspeth going to lose their jobs?" Betty cries with the same fervor she had for her gnomes.

"Of course not." I white-knuckle the wooden podium in front of me. Callum's glare burns into my forehead. He's going to tell Da all about this. "The current process wastes product and creates CO2 emissions, which are hurting the loch and polluting the town. The new machines will only need to be used once a week and can bottle about two hundred bottles per minute."

"Sounds like Anderson whisky will no longer be the Highlands' own with updates like that."

"Aye, next thing ye ken they'll be selling blends instead of single malt," Fin from Honeydew chimes in.

Callum decides to weigh in again. "Just like Macallan and Walker is what he said."

"No, not all," I call out, a headache forming behind my eyes. I'm losing control of the situation. "The numbers show that the distillery could use less and bring in even more profit—and my da, along with Callum and Elspeth, could work fewer hours."

*Because they'll be replaced with robots.*

*It's unnatural.*

*That's all these city folk want. More profit!*

Annoyance flares deep in my chest. This is why I hate goddamn small towns. Are they all seriously intent on keeping my family's distillery in the nineteen hundreds? Why can't they see these are good things? Fighting for more pollution for the sake of avoiding change isn't exactly reasonable.

Commotion breaks out in the hall as people drone on about the importance of tradition. Booing simmers through the pitchfork audience. Actual booing. *Fuck.* I'll never be able to sway them now.

Panicked, I glance over at Meadow again. The same look as before sits on her face. Doesn't matter. I'm an absolute tool standing up here, getting rejected by my own town. How am I going to help my parents if I can't manage to get approval to build a warehouse on our own property?

Jody's gavel snaps me out of my spiral. "Order, order! I said settle down." Town Hall quiets. "You've all made your position on the distillery construction very clear. Sorry, Ol, but this clearly means—"

"Surely this needs a vote," Harris's voice interrupts. "Ollie's a Thistlehill man, aren't you, son?" *Son.* He called me that at dinner over a week ago. Shame prickles my chest the same way it did then. I give him a tepid nod. "That means his proposal gets the same treatment as the rest of the businesses in this town."

Jody hesitates for a second before throwing on a plastic smile. "Alright, all in favor of allowing Anderson Distillery to build a new bottling facility, raise your hand."

My pulse halts as everyone's arms remain firmly at their side.

After a breath, Harris raises his hand. Ivy follows him, then Maisie. My heart melts at the sweet smile on her face as she tries her hardest to reach for the roof.

Meadow picks up her hand and turns back, searching the crowd for someone. Once she makes eye contact with two women standing by the door, she tips her head at them.

Is that Fiona? Must be. Her green eyes and pointed nose are still the same. She raises her hand into the air. Beside her, a curly-haired blonde woman throws her hand up as well. A few younger faces I don't recall lift their hands, but it's barely a fraction of the room.

"Guess that settles it—" A chair scrapes against the floor.

Meadow stands tall in the crowd. "Did you have something you wanted to say, Miss Macrae?"

"Yes." *What is she doing?* "Oliver here forgot to mention the most important part of this project."

"I did?" She scolds me with her gaze before surveying the crowd. "I did. Right."

"What's he gonna do? Give our cows engines and put them tae work?" a stranger shouts from the back of the room, making everyone laugh. My molars grind together.

"Don't give Lorna and Kenna any ideas on how to improve their thieving cow."

"Leave Belle out of this!" one of the twins cries.

"Yeah, leave her alone," Maisie says.

"Are you going to fight against that adorable face?" Meadow quirks a brow at the crowd. The tension diffuses instantly. She's saving my arse. "Now, before you all go get your torches and set poor Anderson here on fire"—she tips her head in my direction—"you should know that he'll be using Blair and Brothers construction company to do the work. Our guys did a great job at Fox Den, didn't they?"

A few people nod. Others turn to their neighbor and whisper behind the palms of their hands.

"Is that true?" Jody asks me.

I have no idea who Meadow's talking about, but if this is my chance out of this mess, then I'll take it. "Yes. A local company makes the most sense."

This can't go over budget, but at this point I'll pay anything. Can't possibly be more than the quotes I already got. "Doesn't sound like he's taking away anyone's jobs," Lorna sings.

"Alright, in light of this information, all in favor of the proposal?" Jody addresses the room again.

More hands shoot up. Surely this is more than half now—barely, but it must be enough.

"Hands up where I can see them," Jody tells the room before she starts counting.

I feel light-headed, then I realize I'm holding my breath. I let it out in a choked rush, and Meadow glances up at me with a concerned look in her eyes.

I give her a terse nod. *I'm okay*, I silently tell her.

She nods back. Guess seventeen years didn't damage the Ollie and Meadow telepathic phone line. My heart might explode.

"Then it's settled. Anderson Distillery will build a new bottling facility."

## Chapter 14
# Meadow

OUTSIDE OF TOWN HALL, PEOPLE HUDDLE IN SMALL GROUPS. The night air is unseasonably warm, but it beats the tirade of cold and rain the past couple of weeks.

Tension wraps itself around my forehead in a suffocating band. Did I have to go and involve myself in Ollie's mess? Especially after what happened at his house yesterday? Surely what I did is the opposite of keeping my distance.

But he had that look on his face—sad and scared. The same one he wore when he shared his worries about the distillery.

When did I get so mushy over a man's feelings? *Ugh.* That kiss. This damn ovulation cycle.

"Mommy, Cece invited me to a sleepover tonight. Please oh please can I go?" Maisie tugs at my hand and pouts her little lip at me.

Without a doubt, she's the one person in my life I'll always have a soft spot for.

"Sure, plum, that's fine. I can take you home to get your things and then we can drive over to the Mackenzie house."

"We can do that," my mom says quickly. Gray strands fall

around the deep lines etching her hopeful face. "Bet it'll be nice to have a night to yourself before the big day."

"No, it's fine. I can take care of Maisie," I assure her.

"Of course you can, sweetheart. I didn't mean—"

A shard of guilt stabs my chest. There's so much unsavory history between us that we never talk about, but lately, each interaction feels marinated in words unsaid.

Dad swings his arm around her shoulder. "We want to help take some things off your plate."

"Maybe you can take the night and…" Mom pauses and stares at something over my shoulder. Ollie walks toward us. "We'll leave you two to say hello. I'm sure he wants to thank you for saving his butt in there."

"That was nothing."

My parents ignore me and follow Maisie over to where she's jumping up and down with her friend Cece.

"I truly appreciate what you did for me." Ollie's voice sends a ripple of warmth up my spine. He smells so good. I inhale and let him fill up my lungs. *You're a wreck, Meadow.* "They were going to eat me alive."

"Don't worry about it," I say in a curt and professional manner. My body, however, is improper and unscrupulous. My stomach tightens as the smell of his skin rolls over me. "You should've seen the picketing that almost happened when I asked to put a new lamppost and flower beds outside of Fox Den."

Ollie smiles. A big and genuine smile.

"Meadow." Neil's voice snags my attention. *Fuck.* He's going to be so pissed that I roped him into this fiasco. "Apparently, my favorite client is eager to give out referrals. If Fox Den doesn't work out, we could use someone with your sales skills."

The joke scatters salt across a worried wound. The restaurant failing isn't a reality I can laugh about.

"Favorite, huh?" I raise a brow at him. "Doubt you felt that way when I had you redo my floors four times because the hardwood planks didn't have the right grain pattern."

"Ye and that meticulous eye. Worth every second to get yer place into the shape ye wanted it." He winks. Neil's the opposite to all of Ollie's mass and manliness. His fair hair is neatly swept back, and his pale-gray eyes are warm. Nothing like the unsettling darkness I see every time I look into Ollie's.

"Thanks, Neil. Hopefully I didn't impose too much here. Thought you two would work well together. I'm sure Anderson won't be the stickler I was." I grin and turn to Ollie. "Neil has all the best connections for labor in the area. If you need a job done, he's your guy."

"You're Blair and Brothers? Last I heard, you were at Oxford." Ollie ruffles his fingers through his messy waves.

"Ye say that like it's a bad thing." Neil gives him a nudge. "I was, then I graduated and worked in Edinburgh for a few years until I realized I missed home. Missed my family. Missed the town. But you were always set on a different life than the rest of us. You and Meadow here."

"Oh, no, I didn't—I only meant that you haven't changed one bit. You look as bonnie as I remember you," Ollie says, attempting to recover.

*He's making a real ass of himself again.*

Neil snorts with amusement. "Aye, can say the same thing about you. What is this, Patagucci?" He pinches the navy fabric of Ollie's fleece, making him wince. Has he not been showing his face around town because of interactions like this? "Listen, only a bit of craic; I'm happy for the work. It's the off-season, so business has been slow after Fox Den. If the weather's right, two weeks for a two-month job is difficult, but it's nothing my lads can't handle. They are good and fast."

"Thank you, Neil," Ollie says.

"But how about I sweeten the deal a bit? A trade of sorts."

"A trade?" Ollie clears his throat.

Maisie's little footsteps rush over to us. "Coach Neil!" She hugs his leg.

"Ah, my best fullback." Neil pats her head. "Meadow, have you told her about how Ollie here used to play with her da?"

"Really?" Maisie's voice is quiet, hopeful.

I should've excused myself from the conversation the moment Neil walked over here. But now, because I couldn't stop getting a whiff of Ollie's skin, my little girl's expecting an answer.

"That he did, plum." If it wasn't for the sleepover tonight, I'd be under her magnifying glass all over again.

"Anderson was one of the best blindside flankers on our team. Had a mean follow-through. Always landed those high kicks with your da, just like the ones we're practicing now." He turns to Ollie and lowers his voice. "Been coaching the Thistlehill Tacklers since the season started. That's what I wanted to ask you about. For a discount on the job, I'd love some help on the pitch."

"I've never coached rugby before—"

"Aye, not that hard. Promise. My assistant coach quit, and I was going to pay him. If you have the time and don't mind chasing around two handfuls of sugar-fueled kids, then the job is yours. I save money on a coach's salary; you get a discount."

My posture stiffens, as if the temperature has dropped a few degrees. Ollie steals a glance at me before answering, "Uh—I'm only here for two and a half more months."

Neil frowns. "The season ends before June, so it would be perfect. We practice on Tuesdays and Thursdays at the pitch by Grace Academy."

"Oh, please?" Maisie sings and presses her hands together. Great, now she's putting those doe eyes to use on Ollie.

"I'll think about it," he says politely.

"You can start now and help me with my high kick." She thrusts her palms onto her hips. "You have to convince him to do it, Mommy. I want to practice my high kick. We have our first game next week."

I go to speak, but Ollie interrupts me. "I'm sure you two ladies have a whole evening planned."

He's honoring my boundaries. The most basic respect one can grant another person, truly the bare minimum, and my little heart's all fired up from it.

"No, I'm going to a sleepover with my best friend. She can wait." Maisie rocks back and forth on her heels. "Please, Mommy?"

I guess one kick wouldn't hurt. "Sure, if Mr. Anderson doesn't mind."

Neil lights up and gives Ollie another bump with his fist. "I got a footie in my truck. We'll say this is your tryout for assistant coach."

"Thank you." Maisie reaches for my face, and when I bend to her eye level, she smacks a big, damp kiss on my cheek. "Thank you so much."

"Don't make Gran and Grandpa wait for too long," I call after her as she trails on Neil's heels.

The moment they're out of earshot, Ollie leans down. My senses go into overdrive as his warmth spreads across my skin like a blanket on a cold morning. "I can look for other workers in the area. The discount would be a big help, but I don't want to overstep or make you uncomfortable in any way. You're still my most important client."

*Client.* The reminder cools every speck of heat twirling through my blood. What am I getting sour over when this is what I demanded? A cordial, professional relationship. "No. If you need the discount, then take the position. Neil's crew is the best. He uses guys from the local rugby clubs who need the extra cash. I just—I can't have Maisie getting too attached to you since you'll be leaving."

He strokes his beard. "I promise, it'll be strictly coaching. No mentions of Fox. If you want me to stop at any point, I'll quit the team and find a new construction company to work with."

My memory returns to last night. The way Ollie tasted like whisky. The way his hands touched me, as if I would vanish if he didn't embed his fingerprints onto my skin. The way his teeth ground against my lips like the skid of tires on a freshly laid tarmac.

I swallow.

"Ollie?" Maisie calls out, waving at him on her tippy toes. "Are you coming?"

"On my way," he replies.

I STAND off to the side as Ollie, Maisie, and Neil settle onto the grass in the small park beside Town Hall. The flicker of stars shines down on them. "When you're kicking toward the goal, it's important to position the ball correctly," Ollie says with confidence and wisdom. My knees feel like freshly set souffles. "Most kickers like to angle it slightly forward on the kicking tee. This allows them to kick through it instead of under."

Maisie nods along. "That's what I want to do."

"Let's give it a go, okay?"

"Okay."

He bends, and the taut fabric of his jeans hugs his thick thighs. He places the ball down in front of her, and Maisie gets her game face on. "Remember, right through it."

I know he said he'd never coached before, but he's good at this. I'm ready to skip over to the middle of the park and send my foot through that footie.

"Through it, not under," she repeats and focuses on the ball. A small crowd gathers on the edge of the park, and their attention shifts to my little girl getting ready for her kick. My breath stills.

Ollie bobs his head, and Maisie sets off. Her small legs speed through the grass. She shifts her hips and sends her right foot through the middle of the footie. It spirals off the ground, anchoring through the air several feet away.

I tug at the golden thistle around my neck. *She definitely got her athletic abilities from you, Fox.*

The few folks beside me cheer, and I join them.

"Mom, Mom, Mom!" Maisie skips toward me, spinning and giggling on her way. "Did you see!? I got it, I did it!"

"You're a natural." I hug her. The crowd around us disperses.

"Ollie helped," she reminds me. "He's a good coach."

His eyes are firmly set on Maisie and me. His body is frozen in a tentative lock, as if he's debating walking over or staying alone in the grass a few feet away. Some deep part of me wants him to risk the trek, wrap his arms around me and her, and hold us until the town melts away.

A bad part, one I need to muffle.

"He is." I smile. "Remember, he'll only be your coach for this season." Breaking her heart is the last thing I want to do. I know firsthand how hard it is to recover from losing Ollie Anderson.

"That's okay. We can still be friends right now. Maybe he'll love teaching my team so much that he'll stay around to do it forever. And if not, at least I have the best high kick on the team."

It'll never fail to amaze me how much hope and pragmatism is wrapped up in this girl.

"We gotta get going, little one." Dad outstretches his hand to Maisie.

"Bye, Mommy." She reaches for my face again.

I throw my fingers into a tickling dance along her side and smother her face with kisses. Maisie shrieks and howls with laughter. "Love you, Mais, so, so much. Be on your best behavior, okay?"

"Always am." She giggles and runs to my dad.

My chest tightens. Town Hall is already empty and pitch black. It's late. I turn and find Ollie standing beside me. "Oh, hey." Apart from us, there's only a handful of people chatting outside of their parked cars on the street.

"I wanted to say thank you for helping me back there."

"You already did, remember?"

His pale skin glows under the streetlights. He looks at me expectantly, and curiosity creeps beneath my skin. "Right. I figured if you ever needed anything or—"

"Mommy?" Maisie's voice pulls my attention, and I turn away from him. "Gram said she forgot the keys to the house, and my jammies are there."

"No problem," I say, retrieving the keys out of my purse. "Don't stay up too late, okay? And promise to not eat all of Cece's Nutella like last time."

"I can't promise things like that," she laughs. "Okay, bye."

"Bye, plum."

"Sorry about that," I say, but he's gone.

He left without saying goodbye. My chest sinks. After what happened yesterday, it's obvious we shouldn't be spending any more time around each other—especially not alone. Regardless, I search for a glimpse of him in the darkness.

Under a streetlight, the faintest shadow of his frame flickers into view. There's a bottle of whisky in his hand. I check the parking lot again. He left his truck here. Where is he going? He turns off the cobblestone road and onto the one leading to the loch.

Since I ran out of his door, a feeling I've missed has been simmering beneath my skin.

Excitement? Thrill? A moment of being that girl again? The one who wasn't just a thirty-four-year-old mother full of rugby schedules, snack prep, homework, and tap dancing routines.

The girl I was when I was with him. The woman I got to be in his arms.

Temptation surges in my blood. I try to resist, but it's useless. My feet are already following him through the streets.

Maybe one more night couldn't hurt. It's like Maisie said: when he leaves, at least she'll have the best high kick on the team.

Maybe I'll have a small part of who I used to be. Or an excellent lesson in why following men through the shadows is a horrible idea.

Guess there's only one way to find out.

---

THE MOONLIGHT SHINES along the loch, making it look like a marble basin.

"I've missed the stars," Ollie says, sensing my presence as I settle next to him on a large stone by the shoreline. He takes a sip of whisky from the bottle and passes it to me. "In New York, you're lucky to catch a handful of them on a clear night. But when I was in Gaya Island for an ocean-cleaning mission, I'd lie outside for hours, even if it meant getting eaten alive by mosquitoes."

The small collections of his life have felt like grains of sand through my fingers. I want to investigate each one, look closer and find out more about them.

"I missed the stars when I was in France too. Nothing like the Highlands. They're beautiful here."

His gaze turns to me. "Aye, very beautiful." My cheeks heat a degree. Thank goodness we're shrouded by the darkness, otherwise I'd probably resemble a boiled beet. "You frequently stalk lonely men in the dark?"

"You looked like a danger to yourself—a bottle of whisky in

your hand as you carelessly wandered nowhere," I say defensively. The reason sounds terribly unconvincing.

He smiles cheekily. "And you thought to come to my rescue for a second time tonight?"

I shrug. Following him was instinctual, but I can't tell him that. "You clearly need the help."

"Thank you," he says sincerely. "I've been out of my element here, and if you hadn't helped calm the crowd at Town Hall, I would've been in deep shit."

"In Thistlehill, being in deep shit isn't exactly an unusual occurrence."

His laugh is hearty and warm. "Aye."

"What's going on at the distillery? Callum didn't seem happy when you made that announcement about the bottling facility."

"It's the same thing that happened when I was a boy," he explains. "Da wasn't interested in my big ideas for the distillery, and Callum's as traditional as he is. Apparently, one new ordering system and a more efficient way to bottle our product means I'm ruining the legacy."

I scoff. "That's nonsense."

"It's fine. Hopefully once I make the improvements, it'll convince them. If not, at least it'll set my parents up for their retirement."

The weight of that responsibility feels as large as the pressure I've felt to repay my parents' loan.

"Have you at least enjoyed any of it, despite the stuff with Callum? I remember you used to love running around the distillery. You taught me about the smells and processes all of the years you worked there."

He looks at me for a long while before he nods. "Honestly, yeah. In the city, I spent so much time in front of the computer, I forgot what it was like to use my body. To move barrels, touch the grain. Even to smell fresh air, to see the stars." He smiles and looks up at the sky. "If my da was suddenly on board and Callum didn't give me a hard time, I don't know. Maybe things would be different."

I'm not sure what he means, but I'm too afraid to ask. Would he give up his dream job to come back here and work at the distillery? I doubt it. But there's something in his voice. An air of possibility that I used to be able to hear. Surely the whisky is tainting my mind.

Silence simmers as we pass the bottle back and forth. A lump forms in my throat.

"Have you been out here since you've been back?" I ask.

"No, have you?" The lines on his face slacken.

"Took Maisie here once, but it didn't feel the same."

"I hear that." He stares off into the distance. I want to ask him if he's thinking about Fox, but not tonight.

So instead, I admit, "I read up on your company."

"Did ye, aye?" A flicker of amusement lights up his face, and he bumps me with his shoulder.

I roll my eyes playfully. "What? You're allowed to keep tabs, but if I do, it's a problem?"

"Can picture you now, crouched over your laptop, searching variations of my name and scanning each article—"

I pick up a stone and toss it at him. "Shut up."

His laughter pours over the rolling hills in the distance, forcing the night's insects to stop chirping. "What'd you find on me, doe?"

"That you cleaned up the Great Pacific Garbage Patch. Never heard you talk about conservation when we were younger."

"A friend of mine at MIT, Matthew Hudson, came up with the idea. He's always been a save-the-planet kind of guy, and he needed a team to build the technology. Your da was right—at some point, Silverman Sachs wasn't a way of life anymore. I felt like I lost myself there, like I looked up one day and my soul was gone."

"So you found yourself in trash?" My breath dances in the air in front of me.

He kicks up the rocks beneath his boots. "Tease all you want, but it's fulfilling work. I loved my coworkers and the impact I was making. I had a chance to help people—more than one person—and make a change that would last."

Just like he always wanted.

"Sounds like teenage Ollie would be proud of you," I say, setting the whisky bottle on the rocky ground.

"Hmm?"

Clearing my throat, I do my best to throw on his heavy voice. "Esteemed Ollie Anderson, traveling the world."

"You have the memory of an elephant." Or maybe it's just always been easy to remember things about him. If there had been a class on him at Grace Academy, I'd have actually passed for once. "The real dream is the one I have lined up in New York. It's the one that will make my career worth it."

A sobering reminder that he's leaving in June.

"I hope it makes you happy," I whisper, and I realize I mean it.

"Even if it doesn't, at least I'll be well off."

"That was always important to you."

Despite all the bad blood between us, I know our jobs mean the world to us. As a kid, Ollie always wanted to have more than his family could provide. He seems well-off. How much more could he want?

I gaze into the distance. The silhouette of the distillery stands monumental on the hillside. I wrap my windbreaker tighter around me, feeling the chill seep into my bones.

"Can I ask you a question?" Ollie breaks the spell of nature-filled silence. "But I don't want you to take it the wrong way."

"We're back to tolerating each other, and you want to ruin that?"

"Tough audience, huh?" A genuine concern seems to brim his eyes.

My lips curl at the edges. "Go ahead."

"What was it like when you moved back here? As kids we talked about leaving this place because it felt like a prison most days." The question rolls around my mind like a kiwano. Though it doesn't taste nearly as mild and sweet.

"I know it felt that way for you, but I was always happy in Thistlehill. That last year, after Fox went off to college, is when I think I lost my love for it. You know how my parents were," I explain, and he nods in understanding. "When they refused to pay for culinary school, I swore I was done with this town and with them. But I was away for a decade, and the homesickness had no cure." I reach for the bottle and pass it to him.

He shakes his head. "I'm good, thank you."

"Sure." I take another sip and set it down. The blistering burn of the whisky keeps me warm, and I tuck my hands back into my pockets. My heart begs to share more with him, and whether it's the liquor or the fact that he's known a version of me that no one else ever has, I don't resist. "I thought about taking Maisie back to Lyon, but my life didn't make sense there anymore."

"If you were given the choice again, would you have taken her to France?"

I observe him awhile, mulling over the question. Finally, I say, "No. This is our home. I know what you're thinking, that I threw away my career when I—"

"No," he interrupts. "Not at all, Meadow. I'm in awe of you. Your resilience, your thick skin, and the way you simply are. I— I'm sorry that I couldn't have been here."

"The past is a lesson, not a home."

"I'm just learning that," he admits. A sadness passes over him again. One that's been flickering in and out of his brown eyes since he got back. "Anything you miss from before?"

There are hundreds of things. Of course I have interests and wants and needs and desires. I'm a human being—a woman. But with the way my life is now, there's no room for those things. Can he understand that?

"I miss being able to make mistakes." I let the truth splinter through my lips. "Being reckless and not having consequences for my actions. Is that irresponsible and totally terrible?"

I hoped after the first years, the feelings of inadequacy and self-doubt would go away, but they never did. Mommy guilt was a harsh reality to wrap my head around.

Not only do I feel like I'm not doing enough, I feel like no matter how much I try to protect Maisie, to give her everything she needs and wants, to help build a world around her that is filled with love, it won't be right.

And that's a feeling you can't share with people.

Motherhood is about being brave, strong, caring, supportive, understanding, vulnerable, strict but not too strict, and kind—but not so kind that your kid walks all over you. There's no award for your sacrifices.

Everyone feels entitled to an opinion on your parenting. *Maisie looks a little thin, are you feeding her enough? She was tired today, are you sure you're putting her to bed on time?*

Any shift in her temperament is on me. Not the fact that she's a tiny, living, breathing human being who has imperfect days like the rest of us.

"Oh, Meadow." He sits up and drops his forearms onto his knees. "Everyone's allowed to make mistakes. You may be a chef and a mother, but you're still a person."

"Yeah, but—"

"No buts. You deserve to live your life as if it's the first time you're doing it too."

He used to be my biggest champion. As if cheering me on came natural to him. That's what he's doing now, and effortlessly. But can he truly understand what my life is like?

My nose sneaks up into a sniffle. "I guess." I force a smile.

"What haven't you done in years? And give me something good and juicy, okay? I want to be able to use it the next time I shove my foot in my mouth and piss you off."

"Hey." I lean over and swat his knees with my hand.

"C'mon. Tell me." There's a flicker of challenge in his eyes.

My mind shuffles through the long list of things. Take risks. Cook for myself. Make mistakes. Run around naked in my own house.

"Date." The word slips out, but it's too late to take it back.

"That's not that exciting, Meadow. I haven't dated for who knows how long."

I scoff. "I find that impossible to believe."

"Hey, I did my dating, especially in New York. Everyone's on the apps. They make it easy to meet people, and some dates were fascinating, but it got old after a while." I did my fair share of living in my twenties, but my gut twists thinking about Ollie doing the same thing. "You're not missing much," he finishes. "Besides, if you wanted to, you could catch anyone you wanted."

"I doubt catching people was ever an issue for you. You're six-foot-five, built like a mountain, and have a Scottish accent. The ladies must've been all over you."

His lip curls into a smirk beneath his beard. "Oh yeah? And you've got legs that go for miles, an arse that makes my mouth water, and that goddamn face."

"What about my face?" I gasp.

"Don't pretend you don't know. You're doing it now. That little frown, the crease right between your brows, your round eyes getting all narrow like you're about to pounce."

"That's attractive?"

"You have no idea," he laughs. The wind rustles through the trees, and an owl hoots nearby. We're flirting and it's…nice. So freaking wonderful to not worry about bedtimes and the to-do lists at the restaurant. To feel pretty for a moment. "You know what we should do?" His voice is laced with excitement. *Finish what we started when we broke your table?*

"What?" I settle on instead.

"Let's get in the water." He tips his head at the loch.

My head shoots back at the suggestion. "Are you out of your mind?"

"Come on, didn't you say you missed feeling alive?"

"I didn't mean I wanted to experience hypothermia."

"I *dare* you." He pulls off his Patagonia vest and drops it on the ground.

"You're not serious, are you? You want to skinny-dip in the loch? It must be like ten degrees Celsius out here."

"It'll be quick. A cold plunge." He kicks off his boots.

"Are you trying to see me naked?"

"I already have." He claps a wink my way that makes my heart race.

"Not in almost twenty years."

"I doubt much has changed. You're as gorgeous as you've ever been." He reads the hesitation on my face. "Meadow, I *double* dare you."

"Stop saying that, we're not fifteen anymore." But a part of me wants to. I must have had too much whisky.

As if he is reading my mind, he says, "This is the safest, most reckless thing you can do right now. What do you have to lose? I'll carry you home, even drop off some soup for the hypothermia. No one would even know Meadow Macrae stripped down to her birthday suit and went streaking through the loch."

"You're impossible," I say, but my body responds for me, and I stand.

"You want to do it. I can see it in your eyes."

Hell, I'm only thirty-four, but I act older than my parents most days. No one's waiting for me tonight. There are no expectations to get things right. *Fuck it.* I take off my boots and yank off the socks.

"You're doing it? Oh my god, you're going to do it." His voice booms around the loch. "Yes!"

"Don't make me change my mind." I fight off the windbreaker that's keeping all of my heat clinging to my skin. My feet are already frozen as I stand beside the shoreline. "And no funny business."

"This is very funny business, if you ask me," he says. I glare at him before spinning around and slinking out of the rest of my clothes. "There she is. Unnerving glare." As we undress, I sneak a glance at him stripping off his shirt. His large chest glows under the moonlight, unruly and firmly built. Arms with stretch marks and dimples.

"Shut up," I scowl, but my ovaries do a little happy dance. Seriously? All week, my uterus has been doing a jig in stilettos, spearing pain through me, but now, we're friends?

I hate being a woman.

"Better not catch you looking at my arse, doe," he says with a gruff laugh from only a few feet beside me on the shore.

"I'm not!" I totally am. My chin remains glued to my shoulder. His butt is round and sculpted. It's the nicest ass I've ever seen on a man. My teeth ache to sink themselves into his pale flesh.

Ollie catches my slack-jawed expression, wiggles his back end, and says, "You can slap it if you want."

"You may enjoy that more than you think."

"I dare—" he begins.

"Turn around, and no peeking," I say. Then I strip off the rest of my clothes, tossing them onto the ground until I'm stark naked in my birthday suit.

"I like when you give me orders," he chuckles.

There's no going back now.

"Double dare!" I shriek, wrapping my hands around my chest and bolting into the water. The moment the surface of the loch slams into my stomach, the breath is thrusted out of my lungs.

"Fuck!" I yell. "Oh my fuck. Shit balls. It's so cold." My teeth chatter. "What a mistake!"

"Don't be a wuss."

"How'd I let you talk me into this?"

The frigid water seeps into every crevice, stealing away any warmth that remains. My chest tightens with shock. My senses feel like they're rolling across jagged rocks from the biting cold that surrounds me.

"Breathe." Ollie's voice comes from beside me. I didn't even hear him get in. I battle the numbing sensation with each second.

Fucking hell. It's freezing.

"I can't!" I shriek.

"I got you." Under the water, his hands find my lower back. On pure instinct, I wade toward his warmth and cling to him. Our naked bodies press together for the first time in years. My soft against his rough. I want to be a lady, one who utilizes distance and slyness to maintain even a smidge of decorum. But I'm freezing. I wrap my legs around his torso, and my arms stretch over his neck. He's so warm. My body hums as he pulls me closer, cradling my lower back. "Inhale then exhale, slowly."

I do as he says, trembling as the adrenaline fries my brain. "How are you not cold?"

"No such thing as being cold around you, Meadow."

Seventeen years have passed, but it feels like a blip. His soft hands trace soothing circles along my lower back. His touch feels comforting, like it always used to, but it's slow. As if he's lingering through every stroke. As if each small brush of his fingertips on my skin is a way to remember me.

No different from the way my rapid heartbeat rushes against his chest as I remember him. I fight through the chatter of my teeth and the rattling in my brain and look into his eyes.

His gaze is as dark as the night above us. Ringlets of damp waves are glued to his face. Creases around the outside of his eyes. Lines on his forehead. A very small dash of gray in his beard and brows, as if the stars simply left them there after they kissed his face.

Behind his handsome yet rugged appearance, I see the boy I fell in love with. The same one who has swum with me in this loch many times before. Whose laughter would strum in my heart like a song I could never get out of my head.

*Ollie.* My heart beats his name as if she knows where I am. As if it were possible for my heart to even understand how I got back here, to him. My screeching pulse slowly settles.

"See, this ain't so bad," he says, noticing my shivering draw to a close.

Despite being dangerously close to losing my fingers and toes, I don't feel like Meadow Macrae, mother and chef, anymore. I feel the way I did all those years ago.

I'm still in here.

I scrutinize the man I was meant to grow old with. The one who's lived in my mind, helplessly shining light onto the darkest parts of me. The parts I'd always been ashamed of or afraid to scream about—the messy, the reckless, the hard to understand.

What is happening to us? I can't answer that, and I don't want to either.

My decision fatigue has crashed in on me, and I simply need to be present. To be held by him.

"Ollie," I whisper into the narrow space between us.

"Yeah, doe?"

"Do you want to come to my opening tomorrow?" My voice hits my ears in a way it hasn't before.

The voice of a girl from long, long ago.

"Meadow Macrae, it would be my honor."

# Chapter 15
# Meadow

OPENING NIGHT IS FINALLY HERE, AND THE KITCHEN IS A symphony of coordinated chaos.

Chopping knives. Sizzling pans. Flames spurting off the used Molteni range I scouted online—in far better condition than the price I paid for it. Our refrigerator is at a perfect 0°C. Titanium cookware has been searing lamb, frying fondant potatoes, and wilting the first greens of the cusp of spring—chives and parsley.

A classic menu, but it's just right. The town is going to like it.

"What do we have on deck?" Brooke's rhythmic knife doesn't break pace on her garlic as she yells over at Isla, our aboyeur. She's a sprightly grad from Edinburgh who recently moved back to a neighboring town to take care of her folks. She's been on top of her game, throwing out orders into the kitchen.

"Two more of the lamb," Isla reads off an order ticket.

The heart of my team has been here since dawn. Now we're at the end of dinner service, but the rush still feels like it's booming. Brooke and I ran through the recipes and adjusted the temperatures of the grills for the hundredth time. Fi's been singing Hozier under her breath after finding a fresh crop of rhubarb in our local farm delivery.

"What'd I say, Grace?" I yell over my shoulder to the grill master while I inspect the steak. "We want these steaks medium rare." Grace was recommended to Fi by a classmate at her Glasgow pastry school. She's a tough woman who's got about ten years on us, a brooding glare, and a heck of an attitude.

"Chef." Brooke rushes to my side. "This is fine. We're not in the weeds."

"I'm not presenting *fine*, chef."

Grace looks between Brooke and me, not knowing what to say. "I'll grab a thermometer."

"Please do," I say at the same time Brooke shouts, "No need."

She shoots me a glare. "What's gotten into you? That steak was perfect."

Grace returns with the thermometer before I have a chance to respond. We pierce the seared meat—59.8 Celsius. "It needs to be over sixty. Flash it and get it on a plate. Now."

"Heard," Grace nods.

Brooke shakes her head at me. I don't have time for her judgment today. It's the fourth plate my cooks have butchered tonight.

Perfection is the only thing we're allowed to serve—nothing less.

"Get back to work, chef," I bark and return to plating an order for table five. Three orders of garlic-crusted lamb chops. One carraway salmon. One scotch beef with baby vegetables. One crab ravioli.

"Ready?" Alba says, grabbing the plates. Alba is a local lady who needed extra cash to pay for rugby equipment for her four boys—no one works harder than a mother.

"Run these and get back here for table nine," I say to Alba.

Grace presents the steak again. This time, the temp reads 61.3°C. "Better. Keep it up." I pull the towel off my shoulder and give the plate a wipe.

Around the kitchen, the line cooks work tirelessly at their designated stations. Fi flambés the plums for her dessert tarts. Steam rises from pots of boiling water and sauces. The air is sticky and humid. Paradise. I've missed this—the rush, the control. It never felt like this when I was cooking at Ramona's. I forgot how alive a bustling kitchen can make you feel.

The kitchen doors swing open, and Davina, our front of house hostess, rockets through them. Davina gave up her primary teaching gig at Grace Academy. Apparently, an all-woman operation excited her more than a bunch of sniffling tots. "Someone's asking for you."

"I'll tap tables later on in the evening." I wave her off. "We close in an hour anyway."

"She insisted," Davina says nervously.

"Who?"

"A Colette Dubois."

My nerves circumvent my focus. I can't wait for Colette to see what I've accomplished on my own. Maybe she'll offer some of her hard-earned praise, or even a granule of advice.

I turn to Brooke, who taps her left shoulder twice, our old sign for *I got this*. I tap back and follow Davina out of the kitchen.

The front of the house erupts with laughter and forks clinking against plates. Bouquets of pale hyacinths and daffodils decorate the tables. A warm fire roars in the corner of the room. Scottish linen tablecloths. Ceramic dinnerware sourced from regional materials. Custom, amber candleholders sit among half-empty glasses of wine and cocktails.

I inhale a breath, weaving through the tables, soaking in all of my hard work.

"Compliments to the chef," Kenna calls out as jus drips from her chin. Lorna sits opposite her, wearing a glittering orange sweater.

"Thanks, guys. I'll be back 'round in a sec, okay?"

As I pass the crowd of seated patrons, Ollie sits alone at table nine—he came. His smile makes my heart stop as he lifts his dram of whisky and mouths the words, *I'm proud of you.*

*Thanks*, I mouth back.

I flush. The jacket he let me borrow last night after we went skinny-dipping sits on my bed at home. The smell of him was like a lullaby singing me to sleep last night. I needed that. A new secret.

*Kind of like old times.* Nerves tremble beneath my skin, reminding me that I can't get too close.

My mentor spots me across the room. The corner of her meticulously painted red lip lifts.

"Mom!" Maisie's voice drifts through the noisy restaurant.

I hold up a finger to Colette and navigate to my family. "Hi, everyone. Enjoying yourselves?"

"Chef Mommy," Maisie sings, lifting a spoonful of risotto to her lips.

"What's your favorite thing so far?"

"The mushroom *rosieoootto*," she giggles.

"Mushrooms were always your dad's favorite too." He used to steal them off my plate at every single meal. I touch the golden thistle around my neck. *Miss you, big brother.*

Mom and Dad join in on her laughter. "The salmon was something else, dear. Truly amazing."

"The best investment your father and I've ever made is you."

*Investment.* That's all this is. A guilt-ridden financial exchange. My hands tingle. Tonight is a step toward becoming that daughter they can be proud of. "Thanks, Mom. I don't want to let you down."

She pats my nicked and scarred imperfect hands. "You could never do that. You make us and Fox so proud."

The memory of my brother is always a safe topic. We can all connect when we talk about his ugly, old flat in Edinburgh or how Maisie is his carbon copy, from her confident walk to the goofy faces she likes to pull behind our backs. It's the one piece that managed to repair some of the dents in our relationship.

"Be sure to save room for dessert; Fi's working on something extra special."

"Will do. I love you, Mommy."

"I love you too, plum. Don't wait for me tonight." I kiss her head and face my parents. "I'll be there around midnight to pick her up."

"You can always get her in the morning."

"I'll be there tonight." I nod curtly and walk away. My daughter will not be spending six nights a week with my parents. They do too much for us already. I'll have to figure out how to be a present parent and business owner on my own.

Colette is a commanding presence. Square jaw. Pale white bob, perfectly cut around her chin. She's a heavily decorated chef. Seven restaurants across the world. Three Michelin stars for eight consecutive years in a row. Stars I made sure she kept.

As I proceed toward her, I feel like that twenty-year-old girl who cried in her kitchen because I'd lost my lucky paring knife. She replaced it the following day without an explanation. The rest of the kitchen joked that she was made of stone. But with me, Colette acted differently. She pushed me harder, rewarded me more, and forced me to test my own limits.

I never took her teachings for granted. She's made a huge impact on my career, in France, and now, hopefully here, at my own restaurant.

"Colette, I'm so happy you could make it."

"Meadow." She stands, hugging me and placing a small kiss on each cheek. At her table, an empty wineglass sits beside three neatly arranged plates, only a bite missing from each one—carraway salmon, filet mignon, and Cullen skink. I'll need to tell Davina to crack open a bottle of Cristal and bring it over here stat. "Take a seat."

I hesitate. I need to get back to the kitchen to ensure no more meat is undercooked, but Brooke can hold down the fort for a few more moments. Colette flew all the way out to the Highlands.

"How was everything?" I slide into the seat opposite her.

"The restaurant is magnificent," she says in her heavy French accent. "The dinnerware, cutlery, ambiance. You've taken great care with my advice and made it your own."

"I'm so glad you like it."

"*Oui.*" She bites her lip. "Like it, I do. That may be the problem?"

"Problem?" My forehead creases, and I nervously reach for my necklace, fumbling with the chain. Colette's flat expression melts as she watches the nervous tic she's seen hundreds of times before.

"There's no easy way to say this, but your food is missing something."

My ears must be full of wax. "Missing something?"

"You. I can't find where *you* are on this plate."

The words slap me hard. "I—" I'm speechless, wrapping my hands around myself in an attempt to hide. This is a nightmare.

*How could this happen?* I know I played it safe, but not *that* safe.

"Meadow, when you worked for me, there is one thing that always kept you going more than the others in my kitchen. It was this, this place, this restaurant that I know you wanted." Her eyes drop to the plates in disappointment. "You could always elevate a recipe, execute my menu to perfection, but the thing you had that the others didn't was creativity. A deeper understanding of flavors and technique. This right here..." She pokes at the steak in front of her. "This is perfect execution, yes. No one is doubting that. But there's no heart here."

"Oh." I've let her down. My throat dries, and tears claw at my eyes.

*Don't cry now. You're not a helpless child.*

"I came here today to extend something to you," she says quietly. "But I may have been over my head with the decision."

"Extend what?"

Colette reaches one of her deeply callused, worn hands toward mine and holds it. "Two weeks ago, a gentleman stopped by d'Or. At first, the name didn't ring much of a bell, but as he was leaving, I put together the connection. Does 'Adair Grant' mean something to you?"

It does. "One of the Best of Scotland critics?"

She nods. "I may have overstepped when I mentioned how a protégé of mine was opening a new restaurant in the Highlands. His curiosity was piqued after I sang your praises, and he immediately added you to his tour. On the thirteenth of May, Fox Den is his last stop."

A wave of shock rumbles through me. Best of Scotland wasn't in the cards for us for another year or two. It's an impossibly hard guide to get on, especially when your restaurant is as far north as mine.

Wait, May thirteenth? I may not be good at math, but that's soon. *Too soon.*

"That's only two months away."

"When you were at d'Or, you'd stay late after closing to use the kitchen. I never understood how you'd come in the following morning with more energy than any of us. A chef with roots in America, Scotland, and France, creating things that were far beyond our comprehension," she says, and my mouth drops open. "Yes, even my own. Don't think I didn't add that caramelized veal sweetbread to my menu after you left."

The compliment isn't enough. My tears come undammed.

*Don't panic.* I'm crying in front of my mentor. My food is lacking. I haven't lived up to my potential. This is mortifying.

"What do I do?" I croak. My voice sounds small and shameful. "Colette, I—I just opened. How am I supposed to *elevate* everything in two months?"

It took three months to finalize the menu we're serving tonight. A perfect Thistlehill-approved menu. One that was easy to learn, straightforward.

My hands tremble. I can't even imagine curating an entirely different upscale dining experience in such a short amount of time. A tasting menu would require multiple courses. We'd have to retrain the kitchen staff and the servers.

There would need to be balance, equilibrium, a spark of some kind.

What does she even mean I'm missing from my food? I'm right here. Clearly, I'm not good enough.

Her eyes narrow on me, not a hint of sympathy on her face. "I always liked you because you could take advice and figure out how to implement it. Do you want to get Best of Scotland?"

Swallowing my nerves and wiping away my tears with my chef's coat, I say, "Of course I do, but—"

"Work on a tasting menu," Colette hisses. "I don't have to explain how that works. This was once your passion, if I recall correctly. You've got the ingredients and the team. Cook like it."

Winning Best of Scotland would be life-changing. More press, money, accolades. I'd be able to pay my parents back faster. I'd make them proud.

Them and Maisie.

"Yes, chef."

*How did I not anticipate this?* I should've listened to Brooke. I should've pushed myself harder. Why was I so afraid to get creative?

Ridiculous question. I didn't want to risk failure. I've been on safe, reliable autopilot for the past seven years, and I lost myself. *Autopilot.* That's where my hands, my taste, my mind have been.

I used to be creative.

I used to have a promising career.

*Used to.*

Nausea squelches in my gut. I need to find the chef I once was, or this restaurant and everything that's riding on it will fall apart. Because of me.

I need to do more. I have to fix this.

## Chapter 16
# Meadow

***Fox Den: A Lackluster Culinary Déjà Vu from Not-So-Rising Star***

With high expectations for Colette Dubois's protégé, we anticipated more from Fox Den, helmed by chef Meadow Macrae. Macrae's background in Michelin-starred kitchens is evident, with solid execution and attention to detail.

However, the menu largely emulates the old favorites of local staple Ramona's, leaving us wondering where the thrill is and if all those years at d'Or sucked the creativity out of this seasoned chef. Fox Den delivers comfort and consistency, but there's a palpable absence of innovation and excitement. While the restaurant may not redefine Thistlehill's dining scene, it offers a reliable and enjoyable experience for those seeking familiarity in an elegant setting.

Execution 10/10. Excitement 5/10.

By Food Critic Nigel Young

"Are you fucking kidding me?" I groan as I scan the *Inverness News* article on my phone.

Who the hell is Nigel Young? His name was nowhere to be found on our reservations list. Was he a walk-in?

Doesn't matter. His review echoes everything Colette said to me on Saturday.

My mentor believes my recipes were boring and stale. Now this damn article. The first ever review of a restaurant I've dreamed about opening since I was a little girl.

*Leaving us wondering where the thrill is*, I read again. *Excitement 5/10.*

Exhaustion spreads like tar over my body.

Of all the things to go wrong on opening night, this was the worst. My brother's name is above the door.

What would Fox think of me now?

I failed him. I failed my staff and my business partners. I failed my parents.

I failed Maisie.

My seatbelt feels like a choking snare. I yank it off and push back the driver's seat. I've been parked outside of my house for a half hour, deep-diving into internet searches about Fox Den. No other disappointing comments have come up, but this will be the first thing people read when they search my restaurant.

*May not redefine Thistlehill's dining scene.*

*Sucked the creativity out of this seasoned chef.*

After dinner service on Saturday, I could barely get through last night's service. Thank god the kitchen is closed on Mondays. I haven't slept. The house is a wreck; two-day-old dishes await me in the sink. Dirty pans. A stack of laundry I have to do or else Maisie won't have her rugby uniform for practice tomorrow and Thursday. Groceries have to get picked up.

Not only am I failing as a chef, I'm also failing as a mother.

The arteries in my heart have split open.

My options are limited. Work tirelessly to save Fox Den, or seal my fate as the chef of a restaurant with missed opportunities.

Maybe the latter makes the most sense. I'm clearly not good enough. Nothing I served was going to be good enough. I should've seen this coming. My own sous chef did, and I couldn't even hear her through my own fears. The thing my dad was always so adamant about—how I'd have the slimmest chance of succeeding—has been proven true.

Clearly, he was right. The money I owe them was blown on a ridiculous pipe dream.

The world around me starts to blur, my vision narrowing with tunnel-like focus on the phone. I blink, and warm tears roll down my cheeks.

Just pathetic.

Playing it safe. Quitting my job, borrowing money from my parents, and starting a restaurant in the middle of the Highlands is *safe*?

Two months until I can throw myself in front of another critic —Adair Grant, who may say the same thing as Colette and Nigel Young.

Panic washes over me in relentless waves. My neck is sore from two nights of full-house service, my hands dry and cracked. Each of my breaths are shallow and insufficient. The small trek to the front door feels impossible.

A soft rap against the window startles me. Ollie peers into the passenger window, the rain pelting down on him. Mud splatters the top of his brow, and his eyes are flooded with concern.

No. Not now.

"Meadow?" His voice is muffled. "Are you alright in there?"

"I'm fine." I can't have him see me like this. I swipe the sleeves of my sweater under my eyes. "I'm fine. Can you leave?"

He loops around the car and catches my attention from the driver's window. "Doesn't look like you're fine."

My heart hammers in my chest like a wild beast desperate for escape. The car around me shrinks. I can't breathe.

"Please," I cry and swat my hand at him. My own body has turned against me, ready to burst on the spot.

*This was once your passion.* Colette's tone landed heavy on the *once*, like cooking is no longer my everything.

The driver's door opens. "Meadow, I'm going to get you inside, is that okay?"

His voice barely makes it past the ringing in my ears. The rain outside slams onto the car. My hands shake, and I sew my eyes together.

If I keep them closed, maybe he'll go away. Maybe this will all be one bad dream.

A warmth snakes behind my neck and under my arms. Another under my legs.

"Duck your head. I got you." I have no energy to resist. "You're sleepin' in your parents' old room, right?" His words are muggy and escape my mind. I don't know if I respond.

Time is liquid as the sound of the rain stops and the cold no longer bites my cheeks. Stairs creak. Heavy grunting. I open my eyes. We're in my bedroom. I'm in bed. Ollie has my legs propped up on his thighs. I jolt.

"You shouldn't be here," I weep, but his hands tighten around my calves, rubbing the tension in my legs incessantly. A small prick of relief tingles through me.

"Aye, but I'm not going anywhere."

I stitch my eyes together again, shaking the entire weekend out of my head. My mind floods with Fox. He and Penelope are standing on the sidelines of Maisie's game. My parents are beside them. They laugh and cheer her on. They're a family, and I'm not there.

I don't belong there.

Adrenaline surges through my body, causing my hands to shake uncontrollably. Tears refuse to stop. I'm so small. Helpless. "I failed." The words choke out of me. I wish they didn't, but there's nothing I can do to stop them. "Fox Den is a failure. What was I thinking?"

"That's not true," Ollie's voice says. "Stay present, doe. Feel my hands on you."

*No heart here.*

My body is numb. Stars explode, tunneling my vision. The panic is a tsunami wave, suffocating me, ripping me through a perilous, never-ending torture.

Flashes of Fox, my family, my staff.

I've let them all down. Every single one.

"Fox," I wail, razor blades cutting through my throat. "I'm sorry. It should've been me. I should've been the one in that car and not you."

I'm spinning out of control. A squeeze comes from somewhere on my body. I focus on it. My gasps sync with the kneading. On my thigh? No, my calf.

A heavy weight clings to me, and his voice finally comes. "Breathe. Keep breathing. It's just a panic attack." *An angel?* The scent of wood brushes up against my nose. Ollie. He's here. He shouldn't be. But for the first time since I parked the car, I manage a breath, and the world disappears. "I got you, doe. I got you."

## Chapter 17
# Meadow
### eighteen years ago

"I'm never going to be good enough for you." I slam my bedroom door, tears streaming down my face. In the living room, my parents' hushed voices manage to break through the walls.

"If we don't pay for it, then she'll have no choice but to go to a four-year university," Dad says.

Anger coats my throat like a vat of fondue.

Ha! They're vastly underestimating me if they think I won't find a way to put myself through culinary school. I pace around, avoiding the mess of books and clothes sprawled out on the rug. I'll figure it out all by myself. I must. Cooking is the thing I love most in this world. Right next to Ollie Anderson.

"We can't push her away." Mom's footsteps drum up the stairs. "Maybe we can find a compromise."

My hands shake at my sides.

"Not once did we have to worry about Fox. But with Meadow, a chef?" My dad's voice is muffled as he follows after her. "The chances of her succeeding are slim."

*Fox, Fox, Fox.*

I love my brother, but I'm over being compared to him by

my teachers and my parents. Can't they see that we're two different people? It's not my fault I didn't inherit the smart gene.

Nothing I ever do will be good enough for them. No amount of cooking or pleading about my passion will sway their opinion.

"Maybe Fox can change her mind?" The ground beneath my feet shakes. Unlike my parents, my brother supports my dreams, but there's only so much he can do to convince them. "We saved up money for the both of them to go to any college of their choice."

"She doesn't have the grades for University of Edinburgh or MIT." Dad's flat voice is the final straw. "Ivy, I just don't want our daughter to struggle. The life of a chef is nothing like the one she's used to."

No more of this. I cannot take it.

I throw on the radio before diving into bed. I screech into my mattress. I hate this. I hate them. No. The thought feels wrong. I only wish they could see me for who I am and accept me as such. I wish they could genuinely be proud of the fact that I'm different from them and not see it as some kind of problem they need to solve.

Ever since Fox left for college, every ounce of their attention has been focused on what I'll do after graduation. Once-beloved family dinners are now opportunities to lecture me about the quadratic formula. Our Sunday mornings in Inverness have turned into poorly executed commercials for a four-year degree.

Numbers and letters don't make sense in my head. They become a jumbled mess of nonsense. All I want to do is cook. To be in a kitchen where I can make mistakes without disappointing my parents.

The familiar pattern of knocks on my bedroom window pulls me off my bed.

Ollie.

It's as if he knew I needed him.

I wipe the tears from my face, lock my bedroom door, and pull back my blinds. Ollie stands outside my window, a smile on his lips. A kiss from him will make this all better. It'll calm the anxiety in my veins like it always does. The cool night air wafts in as he climbs in, the way he has most nights since our first time in the back of his da's truck.

Some nights we spend listening to music. Other nights, we explore each other beneath my sheets or stay up whispering through the night. A few times, we've snuck out to skinny-dip in the loch under the stars and share sips of the Anderson whisky he sometimes steals from the distillery.

Two rebellious teenagers, never good enough for our parents, but perfect for each other.

"Need a distraction?"

He doesn't ask me if I'm okay because he knows I'm not. Sometimes, I think he knows everything about my soul. That she speaks to him in their own special language.

"Please," I croak.

He lifts each of my knuckles to his lips. "Stay present, remember? I'm here now. Stay with me."

Ollie massages my hands, rubbing his thumbs into the webs of my fingers. At least I can count on him to always be a second home—my safety.

"That's nice. Thank you." I lean into his entire body, taking a whiff of his familiar rugby sweatshirt. My blood cools a degree.

"Want me to do your legs?"

"Maybe later," I whisper.

The panic attacks aren't exactly new. The first one I had was a few months ago, between second and third period, after I found out I got another F, this time on my chemistry midterm. I'd begged my parents to let me drop the class and take Conservation and Farming instead, but they refused. Ollie found me huddled beneath the metal seats on the rugby pitch, my eyes burning red, my hands shaking.

He didn't run or shame me for it. He just held on to me and rubbed my hands until I stopped crying.

He kept me present. That's all I have to do when I panic; try to stay present.

"Are you parents at it again?" he asks, surveying my room. I should've cleaned up, but my nerves have been fried. Embarrassment tickles my cheeks.

"Yeah." I sit on the bed, moving away the clutter on my duvet. "They officially decided that they won't pay for culinary school. Apparently, they're totally fine with me going later in life, but I need to get a real university degree first."

He watches me for a long while—with pity or understanding, I can't tell. Ollie knows better than anyone what it's like to have parents who don't accept you. Despite that, he's still going to MIT. I must be able to figure out how to chase my dreams as well.

"Would you ever want to come to Boston with me?" he asks.

"What?" Did I hear him right? I sit up on the bed, pressing my back against the wall. "You want me to go to Boston with you?"

"I know we've only been together for five months, but Meadow, I—I've loved you since the first day I saw you."

My heart expands in my chest. He loves me? Ollie Anderson actually loves me. "I love you too."

The panic in my gut diminishes in an instant. I've never heard sweeter or better words from his lips before. We love each other. But moving back to America? We're so young.

"With the stuff that happened with my parents there, I—I never thought about going back to Boston," I admit.

"I know you don't have the best memories there, but we can make new ones. Just us, doe. If your parents refuse to pay for culinary school, then we can figure it out instead. Together."

Shouldn't this be something I solve for myself? If it's my

dream? My throat feels dry as I try to find the words. "Ollie—I can't do that," I say.

"Yes, you can. I know it's fast." He nods, as if reading my mind. "But maybe it isn't at all. I've known you for three years, Meadow. I know you better than the back of my own hand. I get that Harris and Ivy don't want you to go to culinary school, but we can be our own family together." Ollie takes a seat on the edge of the bed and runs his hand over my own.

Of course I want to be with him. In my most vivid dreams, I picture what it would be like to see his hair go gray and for us to have little babies running around. The home would be filled with laughter and the smell of something delicious on the stove.

But that's so far in the distance. I'm only sixteen—seventeen in two months.

My mind spins with the possibilities. "Where would we even live?"

"Somewhere between MIT and a place that lets you become a better chef. I'd always keep *Beck* on the TV, and I'd build you a bookshelf to house all those mystery novels you love."

"You've given this a lot of thought." I smile nervously.

"Because I—I fucking adore you, Meadow. But I'm serious. I'm serious about you, about our life together, about how good it can be. But I'd never pressure you to do something you don't want to, doe. I want it to be your choice."

Ollie kicks off his shoes and rises from the bed. He begins picking up the clothes on the floor. The future spirals around my head. I pull my knees to my chest. "Leave it, I'll clean up later."

"Aye, I know you will, but why not let me do it?"

I bite my lower lip. "You want to clean my room?"

"Doe, you may not want to admit it, but when you're stressed, you can't focus on anything else. If I can take care of a few things for you, then that makes me happy. Besides, if we live together, your mess will be as good as mine."

Our mess. Together. A life that's ours. No parents to make

decisions for us. No disapproval, and no fights. It could work. It may just work.

"If my parents won't pay for culinary school, I doubt they'll let me move abroad." But do I even care about what they will or will not allow me to do? I'd be on my own. No. Better. I'd be with Ollie.

Ollie thinks for a moment before he says, "We can warm your parents up to the idea. You know, after we tell them about us." He smiles, but the hesitation on my face must be obvious. For the past five months now, our relationship has been a secret. Maybe it is time to start being brave and taking control of my life. "Look, there's no way they'd be against this. Your da loves me, your ma too. If they know that I'll be there to support you, maybe they'll worry less."

"Support me?" I frown. "I don't need anyone to support me."

"I only meant like this," he says, pointing to the neat stack of books he shuffled into my bookcase. "I've already been looking at jobs, and I found one on campus that'll let me work in the tech lab."

"I could get a job too, or maybe there are work-study programs available." I join in on the planning, feeling myself shed an old skin.

"Between the scholarship I got and the money I've saved up from the distillery, you wouldn't need to pay much in rent."

"Wait, does Boston even have a culinary school?"

Ollie nods. "The Cambridge School of Culinary Arts. But you can still apply to the CIA and Le Cordon Bleu. If you get into those, we can still find some way to be together."

My dream schools. Ones that have GPA requirements I don't even know if I can meet. Sure, we could try out long distance if I got into the CIA, but Le Cordon Bleu is in France. Ollie can't possibly give up his dream school to go with me to Paris. No. I won't let that happen.

I'll look into the Cambridge School of Culinary Arts. It'll be good enough.

"What if we never see each other? Between your school schedule and mine, and both of us working part time?" My voice shakes with panic. Nerves sprout in my veins.

He joins me back on the bed, squeezing my knee, the indicator to stretch my legs out beside him, and he starts rubbing my calves. Ugh. I love it when he does that. All my worries start to melt away. His arms are roped with veins and muscle from the labor he's put in at the distillery.

"Even a second with you is better than no time at all."

I giggle into my hands. "You're such a romantic mush."

"I know what I want, Meadow, and I can give you what you want too," he promises. "The hard years will pass in a blink. Then I'll be at my finance job, and you'll have your own restaurant."

"With the sage walls and oak tables?"

"Yes, chef, and we'll stay up late to watch reruns of *Beck*."

"And we'll eat lobster rolls and try out new restaurants," I say, feeling myself ignite again.

"And maybe you can finally teach me about baseball at Fenway Park. Doubt it's as fun as rugby though." Ollie plants a kiss on my lips. For the first time all night, I relax.

And I stay there, in our daydream, where there are no parents to disapprove of us. A place where my dreams are real, and so are his. I'll have my own restaurant, and Ollie would come to the opening, with Fox flying in to celebrate. Maybe by then my parents will even come around because they'll see how successful I've become.

They'll finally believe in me.

"I love you, Ollie. I'm ready. I think I want to go to Boston with you."

Sparks light up his eyes in the darkness of my room. "I love you, doe. Forever and always."

"Forever and always."

## Chapter 18
# Meadow

I PUSH THE DUVET OFF OF MY HEAD, PEEL OPEN MY EYES, AND turn to the clock on my nightstand.

14:00.

I shoot up onto my forearm. My jeans and long-sleeved tee are wrinkled from sleep. Where did the morning go? I have to clean the house and meal prep for Maisie. The tasting menu. My stomach growls as the day comes back to me all at once.

I had a panic attack in front of Ollie. Cried and wailed like a helpless girl when he carried me up the stairs to my bedroom.

Downstairs, there's a clatter.

*Ollie?*

Quietly, I slip a cardigan over my shoulders and descend the stairs. When I enter the kitchen, shock hits me like a frying pan.

Instead of the disaster of a mess I made the last two nights, the kitchen counters are wiped clean. Not a single plate or pan in the sink. A small bouquet of flowers sits on the windowsill. My eyes roam over the living room—not a cushion out of place.

A fire crackles in the fireplace. On the couch across from it, Ollie stares into the flames, his fingers fumbling with a paring knife and a piece of wood.

I clear my throat. "Ollie?"

He startles. "Oh," he sighs with relief. "Meadow. How are you feeling? Do you need anything?" His eyes scan me fiercely from head to toe, like a spotlight dragging over my body.

"I—About before, I—" I stumble through my words, scared to be vulnerable. He's seen me like that before, but still my hands wring together nervously.

He ignores my attempted apology. "You look a lot better, doe. Thank god, because I was worried. I wish you'd told me you still had those panic attacks, but I guess…never mind that."

"I don't get them that often anymore. Barely ever now, and I know how to take care of them. It's just…I was exhausted, and I forgot to do what I needed to do to bring myself back to the present moment. I'm sorry."

He shakes his head. "No, don't you dare. No apologizing for something like that. You didn't do anything wrong. Look, if you're okay right now, then are you hungry?"

I hesitate at the bottom of the stairs. "Did you stay here? What about the distillery?"

Ollie stands, looking as big in my house as he did the first night he stumbled in. His jeans are covered in dirt, and the Aran sweater stretching over his torso has flecks of mud on it. "Aye, Neil's crew and I began laying the foundation for the new bottling facility, but within two hours the rain got too brutal, and we had to stop. We'll try again tomorrow."

"Um, thank you for helping me inside and staying with me," I say around a dry throat. "I have to be honest, I'm pretty embarrassed that you saw me like that."

He shakes his head as he approaches me. "Don't be. I sort of put together what happened." Ollie squares his shoulders. "That dickwad at the *Inverness News* has no idea what he's talking about."

The reminder surges my pulse.

The review. Colette's words. A tasting menu. My chest shakes as I try to breathe.

"I—uh—" I glance at the clock in the kitchen. "I need to pick up Maisie in an hour and drive her to tap class."

Thank goodness Fox Den is closed tonight and Maisie has tap. It'll give me an evening to put together a plan for this tasting menu.

He frowns. "It's not my place to say anything, but could you maybe take the day for yourself? Can your parents handle Maisie?"

Guilt swings like a pendulum through my weak body. "No, she's my daughter. I can do it. I just had a rough morning."

"Of course you can, Meadow. But you need to put on your own oxygen mask before you put on someone else's."

It's the same spiel my parents, my business partners, and everyone else in town always gives me.

*You're doing too much.*

*Take a break.*

*Look after yourself.*

Clearly, I haven't spent enough energy on my restaurant and my menu. My lids are still heavy with exhaustion, but the last thing I need to fail at today is taking care of Maisie. She's counting on me to be there for her.

My stomach rumbles loudly.

"Why don't we get some food in you and you can think about it?" Ollie walks to my used Viking stove, where my Dutch oven sits above a low flame. The scent of thyme and garlic wades through the air.

"Did you make soup?" I examine my spotless kitchen. The marble countertops are wiped down and dust-free. "And clean my house?"

"Aye. Do you still take your coffee black?" he asks casually, grabbing my moka pot off the stove and pouring the freshly brewed liquid into a cup.

"You remember how I take my coffee?" I blink. My ears must be deceiving me.

"Hard thing to forget a sixteen-year-old asking for a coffee without sugar so she could taste the notes."

"Hey, good coffee doesn't need sugar."

"You're telling me my da's coffee was *good*?"

"It was coffee." I shrug, taking the steaming mug from his hand.

"Have a seat and drink a sip while I serve you some soup." I do as he says and watch him as he retrieves two bowls, ladles some golden liquid into them, and places them on the kitchen island. There's no fight left in me. I need food. My throat warms as I inhale the chicken, herbs, and vegetables in front of me. Ollie sits across from me.

"Thank you." *When was the last time someone took care of me?* As I slurp, my eyes find the fridge, where the never-ending list of chores, reminders, due dates, and Maisie's schedule all hang on display. All of the tasks have been scratched out in black ink. Sweep the porch. Mop the floors. Laundry. Groceries. My brows knit together as I stare at it in disbelief. "Did you…?"

He notices me staring and says, "I had the energy and time. You needed the rest, and after what happened, I didn't want to leave you."

Over the years, I've stayed away from men. Anything long term always felt like it would lead to a situation where I'd be parenting two children rather than one.

The last thing I need is to remind someone to take out the trash or pick up their clothes.

I never had it in me to teach another partner how to fit into my life, to keep up with my needs and goals. How to care for Maisie. How to choose what to prioritize, because, truthfully, it's not my place to decide that for someone else.

I always handled it on my own.

"So, you thought you'd mop my floors?"

"It only took a few minutes." He winks.

"I don't understand."

"Meadow, you saved my arse back at Town Hall. Got me an incredible crew, at a discount, and helped me get approval for the bottling facility. The least I could do is thank you for that."

"By cleaning?"

"Yes." He palms the back of his neck. "Actually, never mind the chores. We need to talk about what happened."

My nerves, like tangled wires, pulsate beneath my skin. "Was there another article?"

His shoulders lift as his chest fills with a heavy sigh. "No. Nothing like that. But in the middle of your panic, you said something." He swallows. "Something about Fox."

I bite down on my lower lip. "I—I had no idea what I was saying."

"Meadow." Ollie places a hand on my thigh. Its calming weight eases the swirling soup in my gut. "I think, maybe, you thought I was Fox for a second. You said that you wished you were the one in that car. It sounded like you believed that you should've died instead of him."

The world around me fades into the background. *There's no way*. Not even at my most vulnerable have I ever said those words aloud. My biggest fear that I've kept nestled in the bedrock of my mind.

"I—" The words scrape against my throat. He can't know this part of me. No one can. It's always been my secret.

"Look, I won't push you about it, okay? But I'm here if you want to talk. I promise."

Those words strike a nerve. One that wants to drape me in a protective force. *Keep him out. Keep yourself from getting hurt and losing someone you already lost once.*

"For now," I say coldly.

He shakes his head, letting out a heavy huff. "Right. Well,

I'll leave you to your soup." He pushes out of his seat and starts toward the door.

My stomach sinks. I want to call after him. When he turns the handle, he stops and whips back toward me.

"You know what? Enough. If you won't tell me your secrets, that's fine. But here's mine. I spent years of my life beating myself up over the way I handled Fox's death." He winces. "I— I'd never lost anyone before. Except it wasn't just Fox, was it? It was you too. You were both my best friends; your parents were like my own."

"I spent years regretting how I handled things," I admit.

He swipes a palm over his face. "I'm sorry that I never picked up your calls. I told you that I got a new number. I always felt like an outcast with my da, and you were the first person who made me feel like all my dreams for the future weren't outlandish. So, when you backed out on the plans we made, I felt heartbroken, lost, and abandoned. I've held on to that as my token of pain, let my mind use it against you when I'd feel the hurt of losing my closest friends." His eyes search my face. "Losing the woman I loved."

My heart cracks at his admission. Tears pinch my eyes, and I allow them to roll down my cheeks. There's no point in playing strong.

Hearing this hurts. The whole day has hurt.

"You made me feel seen too. When everyone else told me to apply for universities, you encouraged me to become a chef. Ol, the day of our flight, I should have shown up, or at least called, but I was scared. I didn't know how to tell you that I applied to Le Cordon Bleu on a whim. That I figured there was no way I was getting in." I take a breath and Ollie returns to the seat opposite me. "I fucked up; I knew it as soon as I sent that text. But you were always the person I could make mistakes around. I was seventeen. I thought I could say, *Hey, Ollie, I messed up by not telling you that I applied,* and you'd understand." I nervously chew my bottom lip. "I wish you had let me make it right, because even if you could never forgive me, my brother was in your life too. Fox shouldn't have been punished because of me. He lost a friend over something that had nothing to do with him."

Ollie frowns. Something else skips across his face, but I can't make out what it is. "I wish I had too. My ego was so hurt that by the time I heard about the accident, I was so far into my stubbornness that I couldn't see the forest for the trees." His warm fingers nervously tap my thigh, and I spread my own hand on top of his. "I drowned my twenties working fifteen-hour days until I'd drained myself into exhaustion. That's how I coped with you leaving and Fox dying. It was easier to ignore the ache inside of me when my body was numb."

I know a thing or two about that.

"Your mom said she called you when he passed. What happened after you answered?" The question trembles in my throat.

I've never heard this before. Riley told me that she reached out to Ollie, and he'd been busy.

He nods. "When she told me, I had nothing to say. I was so angry at her—wrongfully so—for bothering me with the news. I tried to convince myself that Fox and I weren't friends since we hadn't spoken for ten years. That it was pointless to share in what was going on in Scotland when I'd already made a life in New York." The confession splinters him. The whites of his eyes turn red. "I was so fucking foolish, Meadow. So fucking ashamed that I didn't even let myself process his death. *Whatever*, I kept saying. *They didn't care about me anyway*."

I squeeze his hand with reassurance. "Neither of us ever stopped caring about you—"

"Aye, and I cared about my ego more. I couldn't bring myself back home. I wanted to stay to prove a point, that I could be successful without anyone from my past. The longer I kept away from this place, the easier it was to pretend that all those years we shared didn't happen."

As much as I want to hold on to the hurt he caused me, I can't bring myself to do it. Can't bring myself to stay angry at him, because then I'd let what happened with us be a chip on my shoulder. My own defense in the grief I carry for my brother. The one thing I can hold on to. In a way, Ollie not showing up to Fox's funeral was keeping me close to my brother.

"I'm sorry, Ollie," I say, because I'm at a loss for any other words.

"I'm sorry, doe." Our fingers spin together, entwining like they used to. There's no hesitation, no tentativeness in the touch. It's natural. "I still think you should talk about what you said with someone. It doesn't have to be me. I don't deserve that. At least, not now."

"When? When would you deserve that, or how?" I desperately want to know if this thing between us is actually something, or if we're just two kids who have seventeen years of age on their skin.

We both know he's leaving soon. That's not changing. Are we digging ourselves too deep by getting close, by healing this wound we both wear?

"I don't know," he sighs. "What I do know is that I've never stopped caring about you, and when you said that about Fox, I felt myself shatter to pieces. The same way I broke when I got that call from my ma, or that text from you at the airport."

And I believe him. I do. Because between all of this, the ocean of distance and hurt, he's the same boy I fell in love with. He was everything to me. And the most painful truth of all: he's my last bit of Fox, one I don't know if I can ever let go of.

"My brother, you know, he was perfect," I say around the weight in my throat. My free hand wraps around the chain of my necklace. "Smart. He figured out the wife and kid thing. A few months before everything happened, he told me that he was going to buy this house from my parents and set them up real good. The golden boy." I'd never been jealous of my brother, but I'd also never been naive to the fact that Fox was the better of my parents' children. The one they were most proud of.

"And you—"

"And I was the outcast. Every family has one. I was pursuing a risky career that paid absolutely nothing like my parents said it would. I was in France, no kids or partner to bring home. I—" My emotions overwhelm me. This next confession is risky, but Ollie has shared a piece of himself too. *Be brave. For Fox.* "I know that if I'd been the one who passed, people would've cried, they would've grieved me, but they'd move on. When Fox died, it was like a piece of everyone evaporated."

"Meadow, that's not true."

"It is, Ollie," I assure him. "You see how they all still talk about him, and they should. Fox was one of the best people in the world, the kindest and most loving. He'd never have left you at the airport. He'd never have run from home or let my parents down."

"But your parents, this entire town, they're so proud of you. They rely on you. I see it, so fucking plainly. Everyone needs you here."

When Fox passed, I knew in my bones that I had to come back and take Maisie. I wasn't going to be that girl who let people down anymore. That's the price I agreed to pay for the universe's sick joke of taking Fox instead of me. "You don't understand."

"I want to." He reaches for my face, swiping away the tears I've let fall freely. "I want to try and understand. I don't want to be a distant guest in your life. I don't want to be a memory, Meadow."

My eyes trail over the beard along his jaw and the lines in his face.

Behind him, the stove reads 14:40.

I need to leave, but I can't will myself to move. My oxygen mask has clearly slipped.

"Did you grab my phone out of the car?"

He nods to the counter, where I keep my charger, and I yank my phone off the cord. I swipe up to close out of the *Inverness News* article and the notifications on my home screen. Then I send my mom a text.

> MEADOW
> 
> can u please take maisie today. not feeling well

> MOM
> 
> Of course, honey.
> 
> Not a problem at all.

Surely they've already read the review. Brooke and Fi too, if the missed calls are any indication. I click off my phone and return it to the counter.

"I asked my parents to take Maisie tonight," I explain. "You were right. I'm in no place to take care of her."

"Good. There's nothing wrong with asking for help."

Isn't there?

Guilt hangs heavy over me. I almost yank my phone back and text Mom that I sent that message by mistake. But I notice my trembling hands. The pit of pain clawing my gut. My eyes burn.

*Stop.* I try to stay present. I get one day. One day until I return to work. Return to my life and be strong and brave again.

My body aches to be close to Ollie. To touch the spot behind his left ear that always made him melt.

*Thank you.* I glance into his brown eyes.

*No need.* The corner of his lips lifts into a sad smile.

*I've missed this.*

He doesn't stop mapping out all the lines in my knuckles, my palms, my wrist. *I've missed you so much.*

We sit between the silent confession for a while. I want the most innate part of me to take the lead. No thoughts. No feelings. Just me and the man who used to make me feel like it was us against the world.

Can it be that simple?

Worry continues to fade in and out of my heart.

It feels foreign to take a day for myself, to not be in my car, bussing Maisie around, or on my feet in the kitchen.

The girl with no responsibilities and a whole afternoon. She's been coming around when Ollie's here. I've missed her too.

Ollie's fingers stroke up the inside of my arm until they're in the crevice of my neck. The knots of guilt in my stomach loosen for the first time, turning the pit in my stomach warm.

I lean forward, hushing the warnings in my mind. Our noses touch; our foreheads press together. The smell of him engulfs me, blowing away my hesitation.

"I want you to take me upstairs," I whisper against his mouth. Then I pull back and look into his eyes, committing each new freckle and dent to memory, learning the path of his skin.

The old. The new.

"Are you sure?"

I nod and bring my lips to his.

The warmth of his mouth is like that first sip of coffee on a cold winter morning. We kiss so tenderly. His coarse beard tickles my chin. Rough against my soft.

His tongue breaks past the seam of my lips. He doesn't linger. Ollie stops his own exploration and swipes his hand under my thighs, lifting me off the chair.

He always made me feel weightless. Never like I took up too much space, like I was too heavy in his hands. With him, it always felt like this. Like I fit in a way I never had before.

Our lips don't separate the entire trip up to my bedroom. The kisses feel so right, yet sometimes Ollie groans in a way I've never heard before. Or touches me with more confidence than I've known from him.

To think I gave this up once, that I let him go. That he never came back. That we'd both been stubborn enough to turn our back on this familiar intimacy, the kind you could only have with the person you'd started this part of your life with.

Ollie carefully sets me down on my bed.

I'm sixteen again, nerves humming through my bones as Ollie and I take our time fumbling with each other's clothes.

This isn't anything like the kiss in his house or the skinny-dipping at the loch. The urge to wipe him from my memory is completely gone.

Instead, I want to embrace him, keep him close.

I pull off his sweater and take my time unbuttoning the flannel underneath. When I shake it off his shoulders, desire corkscrews through me.

I spread a palm over his pecs; the coarse auburn hair bristles against my skin.

"You look nice," I say through a shy grin. "I like all the..." I pause. "The chest hair."

He smiles. "Oh yeah? Time will do that."

"Time's been good to you."

"Here I was thinking the gray in my beard would scare you off." He laughs, bracketing my jaw in his hand, and I lean my cheek into his touch. "Can I help you out of that?" He eyes my cardigan.

I nod. "Please."

He undresses me carefully, soaking up my bare skin. From my neck to the stretch marks on my breasts and the rolls on my belly. I flush as his brown gaze turns hungry.

"Honestly, doe, you've never looked better." He runs his free hand over my curves, stroking the skin of my stomach, which would normally send me into a nervous spiral. "Such a beautiful woman. All these curves, your waist, your hips. There's so much beauty here for me to take care of and worship."

"Not *too* much?" I whisper. The voice of my sixteen-year-old self who hopes that I am enough. I've never been insecure about my body before. Especially not around Ollie. I like the space I take up. But I can't help but crave to be right for him.

"Meadow, you're flawless."

And for the first time since my mentor's voice drowned me in an ocean of doubt, I feel like I may be enough simply as I am.

I reach for the waist of his jeans and tug down the denim, and he does the same to me until he's in his boxer briefs and I'm in my panties.

He sucks his teeth. "Man, am I fucking lucky." The heat between my thighs multiplies. "Is it okay if I touch you here?" He hovers over my breast, and I nod, arching my back. He cups my skin slowly, tenderly, as if he's savoring the moment.

I let myself be held like I matter. Like I always have.

He runs his fingertips over my hardened nipples, circling them until they start to sting with pleasure. The hardness in his boxer briefs presses against me.

But Ollie doesn't rush. It's how he'd always been. Treating my body like a gift.

I run my knuckles over his strong biceps and forearms. Each touch is concentrated and tender. The scent of him grows stronger with each passing second. Musk and wood and sweat.

*Ollie.* My heart beats his name.

To be loved is to be known. That's what he does. He knows me. Ollie understands me, sees me for every broken part, and still wants me.

When I climb my hands up to his neck and spin the auburn waves at his nape around my finger, his breath goes ragged.

Mine does the same as his caresses sink along the top of my stomach and below my belly button. The strokes are butterfly-soft. As if he's thinking the same thing I am.

The knowing of each other. Not the discovery. But simply the awareness and recognition of who each of us is at our core.

That's not something you can experience with just anyone.

His warmth slinks around my waist and lower as he pulls me into him. My body presses into the full mass of his. I kiss him, my senses erupting at the familiarity of his lips and tongue.

He groans against my teeth. My pulse escalates. I want more of him. I trace the cotton fabric that envelops his hardness. Ollie drags me closer and thrusts his hips into me.

"You've been driving me mad, woman. That's what I've been. So mad, so out of my mind, all because of you. I want you, doe. I want to take care of every single one of your needs. Of you."

My head bobs up and down, and I sprawl out onto the bed behind me. Ollie follows me, kissing along my neck.

"There are condoms in the drawer," I say in a small voice.

He doesn't take his mouth off of me as he fumbles through my bedside drawer and pulls out a silver wrapper. I can't even remember when I bought those. At least I take my birth control as often as I can remember.

Ollie's lips leave tingles along my jaw and neck. Breathy moans dislodge themselves from my throat. The kisses follow a path down my chest, and his tongue rolls over each of my nipples before he works down the slope of my belly.

He tears the condom wrapper with his teeth before spitting the edge of it out to the side. God, that was hot seventeen years ago, and it's sure as hell hot now.

"Can I?" I reach for the rubber, and he hands it over. I want to touch the man he's become. Get familiar with him and the way his body has changed over the years. Notice the things I can only witness when we're together.

"Of course." Ollie keeps one knee on the bed and his other leg on the floor as I yank down his boxer briefs and work the latex over his considerable length. He's large. Very large. My chest constricts with nerves. He was always sizable, but this is… well, another way time has been generous to him. I pause and feel his veins ripple beneath my palm.

Curse him for still having one of the best cocks I've ever seen.

He steps back and out of his boxer briefs. He's monumental in front of me. Hard and eager. Strong. There are nicks and bumps on his arms I've never seen before. A scar above his right knee. More hair. More muscle. More of him. The same way there's more of me.

A treasure trove across his skin that my fingers itch to touch.

When my explorative glance finally finds his eyes, I catch him watching me with the same awe that I'm seeing him with. A spotlight almost shines on me as I realize I'm splayed out across the bed. Served up to him on a platter.

"Are you planning on watching me from all the way over there?" I whisper.

A sardonic chuckle rolls out of his chest. Seductive and manly. Another new piece of him. An almost carnal reaction. *Grown.* "I'm going to take these off"—Ollie's fingers tug at my wet panties—"and have you."

I want to be had by him so badly.

"Good." I lick my lips, taking another breath as I give up control. *Safe*, my body sighs. *You're safe.*

I am.

Carefully, he parts my knees, and the heavy weight of his body returns as he centers his cock at my entrance. His veiny forearm cradles my head. His warmth feels right and comforting.

My guarded heart lifts from my chest, handing itself over to the home in his rib cage.

"I'm looking forward to feeling you wrapped around me," he whispers against my lips. "I think I've been looking forward to it for a long fucking time, doe."

*Me too.* As scary as that is to admit. I feel like I've been waiting for this without even realizing it.

"Please," I breathe. Not only am I feeling like I haven't felt in a long time, but I truly can't remember when I was ever so polite. Maybe this is all part of the cordial relationship we promised we'd have. Though there's nothing affable about the head of his cock at my entrance.

Our eyes stay on each other as he gently pushes himself inside of me. The pleasure is mind-splintering.

Perfect.

"You feel—" I swallow my breath as he inches deeper and deeper. He throbs inside of me. A pillar of strength between my thighs. With another thrust of his hips, he's all the way inside. My walls clasp around him. I groan, finding his lips. Needing to taste him on my tongue. To breathe in his air.

It's visceral.

My hands rotate between his chest, his shoulders, his neck, as Ollie slowly works himself in and out of me.

"Fuck," he whimpers. "Just right, isn't it?" He smiles widely, as if piecing together the same thing that I am. "Feels so fucking right."

Overwhelming euphoria swarms through my body. His hips slap against my thighs, taking and giving everything that he has over to me. As if we are reuniting pieces of a puzzle that have been lodged under an old shelf, finally finding themselves in the frame they belonged in.

I fumble with the curls at the nape of his neck as a slow sweat breaks out across his face. The aching need in the pit of my stomach continues to build as I take everything he gives me.

However much I want this to be nothing, we're doing the one thing that always came naturally to us—we're making love. Why wouldn't we? We learned it with each other.

"Ol." I bite his lower lip. "I need more. So much more."

He lifts his arm and uses his hand to hike up my leg, bringing my knee between our chests, and plunges deeper inside of me. His movements are confident. As if he's learned his way around a woman's body from someone who isn't just me.

The thought slips from my mind as he hits the end of me. Somehow, we're suddenly one person in a way I've never been able to share with anyone else.

I almost wince or cry or scream or laugh. It's overwhelming.

Ollie senses the turbulent emotions playing out in my head and nudges his nose against mine. "Like that?" he groans. I nod. "Yeah, doe, I know you need it just like that."

I keep nodding furiously as he drives himself over the spot buried deep inside of me.

Ollie lifts slightly, hiking up onto one of his arms and releasing my thigh. "Keep this gorgeous leg right here," he instructs, and I do as he says. He brings his fingers to my lips. "Lick." I obey again.

I've been dishing out so many orders for the past few months that the idea of being under his control should make me panic. But it doesn't. I like it. I need it. Sometimes it's hard to admit that being as independent as I am isn't always so fucking great. Sometimes I don't want to be in charge of everything.

"Precious woman." He smiles before lowering his fingers to my clit. "I want to feel this perfect pussy tighten around me. Can you give me that, Meadow?"

Wouldn't be hard. "Mhm." I swallow. "I can."

He works his fingers into circles over my swollen center and doesn't let up his strokes. Doesn't break pace as my mattress creaks, the bed frame shaking against the wall.

With each thrust, he gets harder and bigger. As if that's even possible. A flame passes through his gaze. I know that one. That isn't new at all. That's mine. That's Ollie. He's close. I recognize that pulsating inside my body as if it were my own. That same excitement that used to overwhelm me comes again. The sheer desire to make him finish inside of me.

"Keep going," I assure him, and I pull my leg up higher, wanting him deeper. He keeps thrusting above me, working my center until the heat in my spine turns into flames. "Don't—ah—don't stop, please." A primal switch in my brain urges me to take more. To yank at all the selfish needs inside of me. To be reckless.

Every time the darkness in his eyes finds mine, I give in. Release myself to the fact that this isn't fucking. That this isn't casual or a one-time thing. This is sex with Ollie Anderson.

This is familiar.

This is right. *He was right.*

This is so fucking right.

"I'm sorry, Meadow," he says in a breath. "I—taking you like this…I don't have a lot of patience left in me."

The recklessness takes over, and I move without even knowing what I'm doing. One hand stretches to the back of his neck, wrapping his hair in my fingers, and the other presses me up off the bed. Ollie doesn't stop his pounding as I shift my weight to the side. He moves with me until we roll over and switch spots. Me on top. Him beneath me.

"Doe." He catches his breath for a moment, settling on the pillows behind him. "You're an actual goddess."

I feel like one from up here. After some struggle to adjust to the generous size of him, I begin rocking my hips, savoring each new sensation that he pierces through me. "How's that patience doing?" I whisper with a laugh.

"Hanging on by a thread," he says and squeezes my curves with both of his hands, guiding each roll of my hips with his firm grip.

I press both of my palms into his chest and work myself over him without mercy. I want to get him there. I want to make him finish the way I always knew how to. It doesn't take long before his grasp starts to slacken, and he begins to match my pace with punching thrusts.

"Together?" I say with panic as the flood of pleasure starts to teeter me on the edge.

"Together." He whispers the word like a promise, carrying both of us over the finish line. In a few vicious upward thrusts, the nerves and hesitation in my body fall apart, and I fall with him, as release avalanches through me with a loud cry. My thighs shake above him. My nails digging into chest hair that's all brand new to me.

Ollie ruptures beneath me with a heavy groan. I collapse my forehead onto his, holding myself up.

"Let go," he whispers, pulling my palms into his, entwining our fingers together, and letting my face fall onto his chest. His hair spreads across my pillow. Auburn locks against my white sheets. I don't rush to pull him out of me. Breathing in the musk of his skin, I close my eyes and let myself be for a moment.

"What now?" I ask after what feels like an eternity of suspended time.

"Let's rest."

---

Wͪᴏ ᴋɴᴇᴡ I was one orgasm away from feeling relaxed? It can't be that simple. After we had sex or made love—I'm not quite ready to address which one it was—we fell asleep.

Two naps in one day. Who am I?

Maybe I'm the person Colette told me to serve up on a plate.

When I woke up, the kitchen called to me the way it always does when I have to process something, be alone in my thoughts, or spend a little time with myself.

But instead of mess and anxiety, there's a sense of calm. Like I'm connecting with a part of myself that has been a little dormant.

Fire flickers beneath a pan on the stovetop, filling my kitchen with the sweet smell of fennel seeds. I open the fridge, not yet used to it being stocked to the brim without having done the work myself.

Not only stocked, but processed.

The man who's currently asleep in my bed stored escarole and watercress in sealed containers. Trimmed herbs into clean jars with water and covered them with plastic. Cut the tops off my carrots. Organized my crisper drawer.

I shake my head in disbelief and pluck a handful of parsley from a jar, setting it back on my cutting board and chopping it finely.

How'd he get all this done in six hours?

The blood orange zest and spiced marinated veal strips lie in a ceramic dish beside the board. Carefully, I lay thinly sliced prosciutto slices on top of the plastic wrap that clings to my clean counters.

Veal porchetta, with a little twist. A favorite of Ollie's. At least, it used to be.

"You move around the kitchen like a maestro," his sleepy voice laughs from the bottom of the stairs. His flannel is loosely unbuttoned at the neck.

"How long have you been standing there?"

"Long enough." He stretches his arms overhead in a lion-sized yawn. "I have to be honest, I've been squashed into my old twin-sized bed for days, and our nap might be the best sleep I've gotten since I set foot in this town."

"It's the only good sleep I've had in a while too." I overlap the strips of veal across the prosciutto.

"That smells divine." He takes a seat on one of the stools, watching me.

*So do you*, I almost reply, but I settle on "Porchetta."

"With veal?"

"Still like it?"

"Sure do, chef. Smells way better than the lunch I cooked for you."

"Nobody ever cooks for me," I admit. "I appreciated it." My hesitation around him evaporates. There's no urge to run or snap or hide. Maybe things between us don't need to turn into something serious.

Maybe it's possible for it to be this easy. For it to feel simple, even for a little while. Especially if getting to be with him again sparks up my joy of cooking like it did all those years ago.

"Happy to do it." He doesn't take his eyes off my hands as I vacuum seal the veal and place it carefully into the sous vide machine. When you work in a professional kitchen for long enough, being under a scrutinizing eye stops feeling scary. Now, however, I want to impress him more than anyone else.

"Can you tell me about Paris?"

His question surprises me. "What about it?" I cut the limes for the citrus chimichurri.

"Anything."

So, while I cook, I tell him about Le Cordon Bleu. My favorite cafe in Montmartre. The foot-numbing hours in the Paris kitchens and getting a job at d'Or. The time I got to run a pop-up in Versailles and how Brooke and I spent a few months on the coast of Normandy, scaling fish and drinking wine.

He asks all the right questions, listens to every word, and shares stories from his own life. By the time the hour timer goes off for the veal, it's like I've shed a new skin.

"I wish I could've seen it, heard about it in real time." He stands, pulling plates out of the cabinets as I heat up my cast iron, pouring a generous amount of oil onto the pan. "At least I can be here to see you run Fox Den."

The reminder of Colette's words on opening night turns my palate sour. "I guess."

"Why guess? Your opening night was incredibly successful. Fuck what that review said. It doesn't matter."

I pull the porchetta from its wrapping, pat it dry, and carefully lay it on the pan, listening to the sizzle of meat. "It's not only the review. My mentor was there, the chef who owns d'Or."

"That's who you were talking to," he muses.

"You do like to keep an eye on me, don't you?"

"Aye." He shrugs. "Hard not to." After I brown the porchetta I slice it, revealing a beautiful mosaic of herbs and meat inside. "What did she say?"

I serve two rounds on each plate, topping them with the chimichurri and adding a garnish of microgreens and delicate slices of blood orange. "She said the same thing the reviewer did. That I played the menu too safe. Apparently my food lacked one key ingredient."

"What's that?"

"Me."

He tsks. "That's impossible—"

"No, Ollie, they were right." I set the plate down in front of him on the kitchen island and hand him a fork. "My menu was safe. I cooked for the town because I was so terrified of taking too big of a risk. So much is riding on Fox Den being a success that I didn't even consider doing an inventive menu."

"Okay. So, what does that mean? What are you going to do?"

"I have two months to create a degustation menu, which consists of several bite-sized dishes that are served as a single meal. A tasting format that will require me to retrain my staff and come up with new recipes."

Ollie cuts into the veal with his fork. It melts beneath the silverware, and he takes a bite. Anticipation strums in my chest.

He groans, the way he did only a few hours ago when we were together, rolling his eyes far back into his head. "Fucking hell."

"Good?"

"Amazing." He goes in for another bite. "You should put this on the new menu."

I shrug. "It needs to be something special if I'm going to impress the critic from Best of Scotland. Colette pulled a favor and convinced the great Adair Grant to make Fox Den one of the last stops on his Highland tour."

"It sounds like a lot, but who am I to doubt you?" he says, finishing off the veal on his plate and using his pointer finger to lick up the sauce.

"I have no other choice," I sigh. "If I'm ever going to get on that list, which could be life-changing, then I can't fail—"

"You won't," he says firmly. The way he used to when I'd second-guess my dishes or get worried I'd been too ambitious with a new recipe. The way he did when we were younger. That tone was the reason I took a risk on myself in the first place. "Meadow Macrae doesn't fail."

I hope that's true.

"I don't know where to begin," I confide. "I feel overwhelmed having to refind myself and then cook myself into a recipe."

"I have it on good authority that you taste delicious."

"Shut up." I blush.

"The most important thing is that you're not alone. You have Brooke and Fi and an incredible team, from what I saw on Saturday." He's right. "You have me now too."

"You got any mind-blowing and unique recipes up your sleeve?" I tease.

"No." He shakes his head. "But the last two times we were together, we had fun. I know we did. You said so yourself—you miss having a little bit of freedom and recklessness in your life. Maybe I can help you there?"

"I can't exactly drop all of my responsibilities to skinny-dip in the loch or waste a day hanging around the house."

"Why not?"

I raise a brow at him. "I'm not sure you remember a little girl, about yay high?" I raise my hand to my hip. "Then there's the house and, well, the restaurant. It's called Fox Den; have you heard of it?"

He reaches around and grabs a mean handful of my ass. "You're a handful; has anyone ever told you that?" I squeal and skip away from him, laughing. "Of course I'm aware of all of those things. But look around your house now. Doesn't seem out of order, does it?"

"What do you want me to do, hire the Anderson cleaning service every Monday?"

"Why not?" I roll my eyes. "No, listen to me, Meadow? Why not?"

"Because that's ridiculous."

He shakes his head. "What if all I want to do is you and your dishes?"

"Stop," I scold.

"Doe, I already told you, it's the least I could do after you saved my ass at Town Hall and connected me with Neil."

"I would have done that for anyone."

"I'm serious. I've been lonely since I arrived. And look, this may be selfish, but being with you actually makes me remember why I liked this place. Maybe this is the do-over we needed. We can put all our expectations out on the table so no one gets hurt," he offers. "We can try to figure out if we even make good friends as adults."

"You'll be leaving in June."

The ease between us collapses under the landslide of reality. "Aye, and your life is here."

A part of me, a part that's big enough it's become a grating weight on my chest, wants to be back in it with him. To feel that sense of life lighting up in my body. To talk to him, laugh with him, share the things I haven't been able to share with anyone else.

Fuck or make love. Kiss and yell and laugh.

I don't know where we're going to end up after this, but what good would it do to end it so soon? When I'm with him, I get brazen, take risks. He makes me feel strong enough to do those things because he believes in me, in my abilities.

Probably plenty of good would come from calling it quits right now. A sterile and safe goodbye.

My heart flashes my brain the finger. Clearly the two aren't getting along.

"So, since your time to craft an argument or a witty insult has expired, when are you free?"

I can't help but chuckle. "You're eager."

"No point in wasting any time. You have a tasting menu to make, and there are dishes in the sink."

"This isn't a relationship." The reminder and the distance I need. "I want to be careful that Maisie doesn't get the wrong idea and start seeing you as a stand-in dad. There's a reason why I never dated over the years."

"That makes sense. I wouldn't want to give her the wrong impression either."

"And whatever happens, I need to be certain that we'll end on good, clear terms. No more blocking each other out. No itchy fingers skipping around the web, searching for proof of life."

"We end it clean. Maybe even remain real friends this time around?"

I nod. "Yes."

"So, when do we start?"

"The only evenings I have free are Mondays, like today. That's when Maisie is at her tap class."

"Perfect. What should we call this? A business collaboration? We already signed one contract." He raises a brow at me, taunting me. "I'm a great business partner. I have testimonials if you need them. Trust me, I've got a whole perks and benefits package you can look into."

"Be serious." I nudge him.

"We kept our relationship a secret for six months the first

time. Can't see why it'd be a problem now. If I remember, you used to love all the sneaking around anyway. It'll be fun."

Maybe we could try it. Something casual. "Fine, but this is just that—fun. You could even see other people."

"Other people?" His eyebrows knot with a frown.

"Absolutely. If we're not getting too attached, then I don't see why not. We're adults; this isn't going to end badly, right? We agreed." Though the thought of Ollie with someone else makes the porchetta in my belly turn over.

"Aye. No ending badly," he says uneasily. "Sure. Whatever you want, doe. Two months of fun. You find a bit of yourself, and I fall back in love with Thistlehill."

"And after we're done, we go back to a different normal."

"I like that."

"Me too."

Maybe it can work. Maybe it will.

## Chapter 19
# Meadow

BROOKE, FI, AND I SIT AT A TABLE BY THE FIREPLACE, WATCHING the waning flames. A kettle of lavender Earl Grey sits in the middle, along with a few shortbreads Fi prepared.

Tuesday dinner service won't begin for another seven hours, but after the review, we all agreed to come to Fox Den this morning for a debrief and to sketch out a plan for moving forward. I filled them in on Colette's impression of our menu on opening night.

"Who even is this Nigel person?" Fi furrows her brows, pulling out her phone and probably looking up the reporter's social media pages. "The entire town loved the food, and they're our customers. Just because Ramona's has crab doesn't mean we can't have crab. Does Ramona source crab from Oban?"

One fact can't be disputed: Ramona's ingredients are no match for ours. Clearly, the only thing I'm doing is failing at using them because I'm on autopilot. The hint of panic is still pulling itself out of my veins. No point in comparing the two—Fox Den is its own restaurant.

"The article is already out there. Nothing we can do about it now," I remind her. "If we're going to be a raving success, we're going to need more than kindness and word of mouth to get us there. And Brooke—" Nerves catch in my throat, but I swallow my ego down. "I'm sorry I didn't listen to you when you suggested we should do something a little more inventive with the appetizers. Your instinct was right, and I sort of bulldozed my way through that meeting."

"Thanks, chef." Brooke gives me a soft smile. "I'm still a little worried though; it seems like such a short time to prepare an entirely new menu—a tasting menu, at that. We just started to hit a rhythm with the crew."

"I know." I hesitate. If I'm going to reconnect with myself, then being a little more vulnerable with my friends is a start. "I'm anxious about how we're going to get it done and the work that it'll take. But I know we can't pass up this opportunity."

My mind has been ingredients and ideas since Ollie left yesterday, the gears finally starting to turn in a way they hadn't in a while. Guess I did need my gears greased. Ugh.

"Can't Colette ask the critic to come later in the season? If he's here on May thirteenth, then everything should be finalized by the sixth, which leaves us seven weeks." Brooke's face is laced with concern.

"She believes we can get it done." I drum my fingers on the linen tablecloth. My notebook is torn up with scribbles and menu ideas. The pages stare back at me. "Adair Grant is already going out of his way to make the trek up here. This is our chance to become a must-see stop on the North Coast 500. We'd be able to drum up enough business to break even on our initial investment, and we'd be on the road to getting a Michelin star."

"Not if we lose our head chef in the process," Fi grumbles under her breath and tosses her hair back from her forehead. "You haven't had a panic attack in ages, and this seems like the perfect way to welcome them back."

Guilt needles beneath my skin. "That won't happen. I'm fine, I promise."

"Meadow." Fi's snap turns into sympathy. "The restaurant is important to us, but we'll have other opportunities. We won't get another you."

I want to assure them that I can handle it, but it doesn't even sound convincing in my own head. "You're right," I say, ready to declare defeat. "But I can't let it go without at least trying."

They pass another glance back and forth. When did they get so good at having silent conversations that I can't understand?

"What if we compromise?" Brooke offers across the table, her golden waves glowing from the fire. "We can scale back weeknight dinner service."

My mouth drops open to protest, but Fi interrupts me. "Only for the next month, before tourist season starts."

The fireplace heat licks up my spine. My insides quiver like I'm on a sadistic rollercoaster whose sole purpose is to scare me shitless. If we cut back now and this whole thing fails, it could set us back months. "We've only been open for two nights. What will people think if we start scaling back already?"

Brooke cocks a brow at me, her lips flatlining. "The Meadow I know couldn't give less of a fuck what the people in town think about her. It's our damn restaurant; we could rip all this gorgeous decor out and turn it into a hot dog stand if we wanted."

The vivid image forces a small laugh of relief into my chest. "Fi, is this what you want to do?"

"Not sure about the hot dog stand." She nudges Brooke. "But if we have more time to dedicate to experimenting with a new menu without reaching our wit's end, then it makes sense. We'll take a loss, but make it back in the summer—especially if we win that spot on Best of Scotland's guide."

Brooke and Fi have far better boundaries around their commitment to our work and their obligations than I do. The idea of taking time away from the restaurant feels unnatural, but if this is the only way to try and make the tasting menu happen, then I have to concede.

"Okay, I can agree to that. We can stay open Wednesday through Sunday," I resolve. Only two days off instead of one. I swallow the concern lodged in my throat. *See, Meadow, that wasn't so scary.*

"Thursday through Sunday," Brooke counters.

Fi nods in agreement.

The invisible weight I felt yesterday morning begins to crush my chest like a metal compressor smashing old cars. Okay, this is terrifying.

*Tell them that. They're not going to judge you.*

I hesitate. "I gotta be frank with you both, that terrifies me."

Fi offers me a reassuring smile and reaches her hand across the table to envelop mine. "Rest days are as important as work days."

I roll my eyes. "I know." Logically, everything they're saying makes sense. If a person doesn't recharge, how can they give their full energy to something? But I'd always worked without rest. I always gave every last bit of myself to everything I did. Is that why there's very little of me left?

Brooke mirrors Fi until the three of us have our arms stretched around the table like we're performing a summoning. "Let's say it together."

"You can't be serious."

Fi nods. "Rest days are as important as work days," they say together. "Now, your turn."

This must be what Maisie felt like in her toddler years when I had to sit her down and explain that biting her friends wasn't nice. *Ha!* My friends are gentle parenting me.

"Rest days," I pause and glance away from their expectant faces. "Areasimportantasworkdays," I say without a breath.

"Meadow." Brooke's brow shoots up in disapproval.

"This is starting to feel condescending," I snap.

"We don't love you because you're this powerhouse mama who never takes a break. It's not because of everything you do for others and us. It's because *you*, on your own, without Fox Den, without all the things you've managed to achieve, are a wonderful person, Meadow."

But am I if I'm not using that wonderfulness to help others?

Fi can obviously tell where my thoughts are going. "Even if you decided to do nothing for the rest of your life, we'd still love you. You'd always have so much worth."

I slide my eyes between their satisfied faces. "You two have been doing a lot of agreeing lately."

"We found something in common," Fi shrugs.

"What?"

"How much we care about you."

A smile breaks out across my face. I'd be lost without them. But this is officially turning into a therapy session that I did not sign up for. "Fine. We'll be closed for dinner on Monday, Tuesday, and Wednesday." I hope they can't feel my hands trembling in theirs. "And thank you for caring about me, guys. Honestly. It means a lot. And thank you for trying to take on this new menu with me."

"Any time. But now can we finally talk about the elephant in the room?" Brooke pulls her hand out of my grasp and sets it under her chin.

"What's up?" I nervously flip through the pages of my notebook.

Fi taps her finger on the table. "All these ideas pouring out of you, agreeing to cut back on work, not doing your usual panic cooking. Something happened."

"You had sex!" Brooke squeals.

*Stay cool and act casual.* "Huh? No clue what you're talking about."

"You're a terrible liar, don't even bother," Fi laughs.

"Did a certain six-foot-five Scot finally come over to borrow some sugar yesterday?" Brooke sits back in her chair, stretching her legs onto the stone ledge of the fireplace. "Get you all nice and caramelized with his blowtorch?"

I shudder at how uncomfortably on the nose her metaphor is. "Fine. We had sex. We're not telling anyone it happened. End of conversation."

Brooke's mouth hangs open in disbelief. "End of conversation? How did it happen? Did he spread you out on your kitchen counter? No—the porch! Are you going to do it again? You must."

"Can't wait to use some of that wild imagination on the tasting menu." I wave her off. "It's nothing serious. He's an old friend. Plus, he's got good whisky. Maybe we can coax him into giving us two house exclusives. It may give us a leg up."

"Did he give you a leg up too?" Brooke snickers like an overly excited kid who's discovered something naughty.

Ignoring her, I say, "He could be a good resource to help me connect with my roots again and take Colette's advice about putting *me* on a plate."

"I'm sure he'd love to eat you off a plate."

"That's cannibalism," Fi deadpans before the dining room fills with laughter.

When we settle down, I explain, "We agreed to have fun. I have Maisie to think about, and I'm far too busy to manage a man."

"With all this time off, maybe he can manage you a bit."

"As long as he manages not to hurt you, it may be good for you," Fi chimes in. Of anyone, she's been the biggest campaigner against any kind of relationship with Ollie. She was there to see how I handled becoming a mother with loss in my heart and the disappointment of Ollie not coming to my brother's funeral.

This isn't like that now. The expectations are set and clear. Ollie's leaving, I'm here. A little dive into the past could be a good thing. A way to bring my creativity back. A foolproof, no-heartbreak-guaranteed plan. Getting hurt is not an option.

"Can we get back to work and run through some of these menu ideas together?" They give me a reluctant nod, and I thumb through my notes. "Standard tasting menus are six courses. Two starters, seafood, vegetarian, meat, finished off with a dessert."

"Can I have one of the starters? I've been playing around with parsnips, and there's a foam that may be perfect," Brooke suggests.

"I trust your instincts. Go all out," I nod, scribbling her name next to the first starter.

"I'll be on dessert." Fi taps the course on my notebook.

"Wouldn't have it any other way. That leaves us with four dishes. We can do the seafood course together. We're all from places where seafood plays a huge role—me with New England, Fi with Scotland, and Brooke with Florida. A way to showcase our skills together."

"Love that," Brooke nods.

"Me too."

I finish jotting down my notes and look up at them. "I'll take the other three. We'll post the new schedule on the door tomorrow, and I'll have Davina work on managing all of the reservations for the next few weeks."

We all push out of our seats. "Sounds like a plan," Brooke says.

As she and Fi work their way into the kitchen and toward our lockers, I get a text.

> **UNKNOWN**
> Are you dropping Maisie off at practice tonight?

> **MEADOW**
> who is this

> **UNKNOWN**
> I thought we moved past that question

*Ollie.* I smile as I save his number in my phone.

> **MEADOW**
> did my mom give you this number? that's low of her

> **OLLIE NEW NUMBER**
> All the rugby coaches have access to parents numbers

> **MEADOW**
> u havent even had ur first practice & ur already violating rugby coach integrity to text me

> **OLLIE NEW NUMBER**
> I'm allowed to use them in case of emergencies

> **MEADOW**
> and my driving her to practice is an emergency?

> **OLLIE NEW NUMBER**
> It is if it means I get to see you again

My heart leaps in my chest as the chat bubble appears on the screen.

> **MEADOW**
> tuesdays are the only days i can make it

> **OLLIE NEW NUMBER**
> Not the Thursday practices?

> **MEADOW**
> gotta open Den at 5
> tuesday only works cz they start at 3

But now I guess I'll be free every Tuesday night with Fox Den's new schedule.

**OLLIE NEW NUMBER**
Sounds like I'll only get to see you twice a week.

As long as you haven't changed your mind about Monday night.

**MEADOW**
not yet

**OLLIE NEW NUMBER**
I guess it'll be more often if I catch you spying on me working in my woodshed

**MEADOW**
i don't spy

**OLLIE NEW NUMBER**
Whatever you say

By the way, I left you something at your place

**MEADOW**
we need to discuss this obsession with breaking into my home

**OLLIE NEW NUMBER**
They're just flowers I picked at the loch today. And don't worry, I left them on the porch

My phone chimes with a picture of the loch and the distillery in the background. Ollie's thick fingers hold an array of wildflowers in his fist. Our old place. The memory of his ass glistening in the moonlight the other night makes the edges of my mouth curl.

**MEADOW**
looking 4 another skinny dip partner already?

heard kleptocow likes swimming

> **OLLIE NEW NUMBER**
> You're the only skinny dipping partner for me

> **MEADOW**
> thx in advance for the flwrs

> **OLLIE NEW NUMBER**
> Anytime
>
> The least I can do after spending all day thinking about you

> **MEADOW**
> did u mean my food?

> **OLLIE NEW NUMBER**
> No. I meant you.

---

THE LATE AFTERNOON sun fights for its place amid the thick, gray clouds above. After the rain yesterday, the ground is more mud than grass. Fi, Brooke, and I spent the rest of the morning at Fox Den, brainstorming—although nothing came of it.

For the time being, we are keeping the menu the same.

Surrounded by lush greenery and mountains, the field is already a hub of energy as the Thistlehill Tacklers' team colors—soft blue and navy—spill out onto the pitch.

I navigate the sidelines with my folding chair slung over my shoulder and follow the sturdy white lines that mark the boundaries of the field. The tall goalposts stand like beacons at each end.

I spot Maisie on the outskirts. Her eyes are fixed on a fierce scrum, with bodies locked in a battle for dominance. *Kid rugby is so intense.* She waves, and I take my seat beside the other parents.

Slowly, I scan the sidelines, and my pulse shoots up. Ollie stands on the edge of the field. His incredibly muscular thighs tease the fabric of his five-inch-inseam shorts. They're tiny on him and fucking irresistible. Someone should give the person who invented micro shorts a fucking Nobel Peace Prize—they can cure even the worst of days.

His strong arms are raised above his head. That charming smile hugs his face like a beam of sun lighting up the gloomy afternoon. He shoots me a heart-stopping wink before his attention hops back to the practice.

*Fuck me.* Heat ricochets through my body and straight into the base of my spine.

I shake the memory of our afternoon out of my mind and focus on the pitch.

"Bloody freezing today," Catherine, Cece's mom, sighs, uncapping her thermos and taking a long sip. Catherine was in my year in school. She's a petite woman with sleek black hair that cascades down to her shoulders, framing her porcelain-like complexion. Today, she's bundled up in a cozy, bulky jacket that shields her from the chilly air.

"Save your complaints; we have a whole season of this to go," I remind her.

"Hey, ladies." Reina slings her folding chair off her shoulder and sets up to my right.

Neil's sister has a habit of coming to all rugby games and practices, not-so-secretly hoping to catch the eye of a visiting scout or a substitute coach or any of the single dads in town. I don't blame her. The dating pool in Thistlehill isn't exactly chock-full of eligible bachelors.

"Hey," Catherine and I say in unison.

Reina adds another swipe of glittering gloss to her lips and takes a seat.

"Did you two hear that Elspeth's band is playing at Tavern on Saturday night?" Reina asks.

"Fi mentioned it today, but we don't close up until eleven, so I probably won't make it."

"They don't even start until midnight—you should totally come. I just wish I had a date." Reina frowns and unrolls a fleece blanket over her legs. "I'm tired of third-wheeling with Neil and Josie."

"Speaking of dates." Catherine leans over my left and lowers her voice. "Where's your mind been with Ollie coming back to Thistlehill?"

"Haven't really thought about it," I lie. No fueling the rumor mill today. Not on my watch.

"So, he's single?" Reina's voice carries a level of excitement that forces an unease into my chest.

On the pitch, Ollie's muscles flex as he demonstrates a move, and his eyes light up when he sees a player mimic it.

"I think so?" *Yes* was the answer I should've given her. I'm the one who said we can see other people and stay casual. What's up with this hesitation?

"You have to set us up, Meadow. Please set us up. I've had such a dry spell that I'm going to need to douse myself in Vaseline before even making eye contact with a living, breathing man again."

Catherine snorts up her coffee, coughing through her laughter.

Reina's request is perfectly normal. Of course she'd be interested in Ollie—it's impossible to ignore the fact that he is *fine*. Tall and imposing on the field, with his auburn hair and a thick beard. The same one I moaned against as he was thrusting into me only yesterday.

"Reina," Catherine scolds, "there's a history here. Maybe Mama Bear still has feelings for him."

"I do not!" I snap loud enough to force a few heads to turn our way. "He's a friend of the family. And I'm sure your brother would have a better in with him than me. They're coaches together, after all."

Catherine raises her brows at me. My mind replays the sound

of his heavy breathing against my cheek as he kissed me. His coarse chest gliding along my breasts. His thick fingers running over every inch of my skin.

*Snap out of it, Meadow.*

"If it's not a problem with you, Meadow, I'm going to go for it." Reina nods. "I promise you gals that by the end of this practice, that man will be on his knees begging for a date with me."

The image of Ollie in the dairy aisle of Honeydew Market flashes in my head.

"Milk him for all he's worth," I giggle, but a pinch of bitterness flavors my tone.

My eyes focus back on the huddled commotion of players and coaches. They're surrounding someone. Not just someone. *My* someone. Maisie is sprawled out on the ground. My heart leaps into my rubber boots.

"Maisie!" I yell, rushing out of my chair. Ollie towers over her, waving his arms for people to stay back. *She's okay.* My ears ring with panic. I focus on the sound of my steps squelching in the mud. *She's going to be okay.*

When I reach her, Ollie's pouring water over a bloody scrape on her knee, a plastic first aid kit open at his feet. Maisie grits her teeth and winces.

"This is going to hurt a little bit, Mais, but you're tough, right?"

Her round blue eyes are red. Her entire uniform is covered in thick globs of mud and grass. There's dirt on her face and in the cracks of her little knuckles.

"Let me help," I insist.

"Hold her hand."

I cup Maisie's cold hands as Ollie uncaps the bottle of alcohol. "This is like that time outside the house, remember? We were playing tag," I say. "You got caught on that little stone and we had to get you all bandaged up."

"We used the Elsa Band-Aids then."

"We sure did, plum."

Ollie pours the alcohol over her skin, and Maisie winces. "I don't like how that feels."

"I know, but it'll be over in a sec," I comfort her as Ollie expertly cleans her wound. He's so calm and good with her. "Almost there."

"Am I going to get a cute plaster?" she asks.

"You're in luck—there's a sparkly one in here. Couldn't patch up our star player with some plain old plaster." Maisie laughs, and Ollie winks before carefully rolling the bandage over her wound. "There, all set. Like it never happened."

"You're okay, Mais?"

I release her hands, and she stands, stretching out her freshly bandaged leg. "All good. Coach Ollie fixed it!"

"You can sit this one out. I have some hot cocoa back at my seat."

"No way." She shakes her head. "I have to finish practice."

Ollie places a hand on her shoulder and turns to face me. "She's fine. Took a tumble, and a loose stick grazed her."

"Okay."

It's over. Maisie's not hurt. Ollie took care of her. I scamper off the pitch and back to my seat. That was so heroic. My damn ovaries are operating in overdrive.

"And he's good with kids!" Reina sings from her seat. There's a gleam in her eyes. "Gosh, that was hot. Makes me want to jump on the field and roll around in mud just so he can patch me up."

Catherine tips her head at me, but I ignore it. Whatever. Reina's interest in Ollie has nothing to do with me. And the way my lower belly is lighting up with fireworks is temporary.

For the rest of practice, I keep a close eye on the pitch and spend less time talking to the other parents. When the whistle blows, Maisie runs toward me, her arms outstretched.

"Mom, did you see that? My high kick put pressure on the other team."

I hop out of my chair and lift her into a spinning hug. "Best one yet, plum. I'm so proud of you. Now we're both going to need a shower." I laugh at the mud clinging to my clothes from her uniform. "How's the leg?"

"Can't even feel it." Her feet meet the ground. "Look at this." She shows me a small ribbon tied to her uniform sleeve. "Coach Ollie gave a ribbon to everyone on the team. Apparently it used to be his good luck charm when he played with Dad as a kid."

The silk tie is barely noticeable on her dirty shirt, but it opens up the ground beneath my feet.

It's the same little ribbon I used to tie into Fox and Ollie's shirts before they played. A way for them to find each other in pile-ups or on the field.

It never meant anything outside of a practical advantage, yet now it's causing my knees to weaken.

He remembered.

And he wants the Thistlehill Tacklers to have that tradition too. He is trying to fall back in love with this town.

"That's lovely, Mais." I hand her a pack of orange slices and begin packing up my chair.

"Coach Neil said we have a real shot at the playoffs."

These guys and their sports. It's only the third practice of the season, and they are already planning for playoffs.

"How could you not? You were amazing out there." I ruffle her hair and swing my folding chair over my shoulder. "Go say bye to your teammates, grab your bag, and let's get going."

She places a sweaty kiss on my cheek before sprinting off to the benches. Her friends shower her with high fives as she passes. I helplessly search the field again, wanting to say bye to Ollie and thank him for helping with Maisie, but when I spot him, my excitement withers like an old onion.

Reina's already talking to Ollie, her neatly manicured fingers stroking the whistle around his neck.

I suck in cool air through my teeth.

It doesn't matter. We agreed we could see other people.

Doesn't mean I have to see him with those *other* people.

## Chapter 20
# Ollie

"I'm not buying it," Avery's serious executive voice chimes over the video call. It's the same tone she uses when fundraising or talking to her husband, Luca.

*I'm in trouble.*

I called Ave to thank her for her help in putting together the design layout for the new ordering system. She's a genius at stuff like this. When we brought her on to work on Plastech, she redid all our marketing materials and raised us hundreds of thousands of dollars in her first few months.

But now that the ordering system is done, her questions are pointed at me.

"What do you mean?" I squint at her in my kitchen and tap my fingers against my thigh.

"You haven't been home in almost two decades. How are you actually feeling about being back? Aside from all of the distillery stress." Avery's from a small town in Vermont. She, much like me, left her life behind to make it big in the city, following her father's dreams of creating a sustainable world for generations to come.

"It's not all bad." I tap my finger on my chin. "I've forgotten how much I like being outside, away from the computer."

"Ha! I could have told you that. You never liked sitting still."

"That's because the chairs were always too small," I chuckle. "But yeah, even with the rain and cold, it's nice being outside. I never told you, but when I was a kid, I used to do woodworking. This week, I built my parents a new kitchen table." Every time I eat breakfast, I can't help but think about Meadow.

"A table! That's so badass. Lumberjack Ollie."

I rub the new calluses that are forming on my skin. My back aches, but not from sitting all day in front of my computer until my arse atrophies, but with a tiredness that can only come from manually crafting something.

I've missed the thrill of tangible achievements, slowly cutting and carving a slab of wood until it takes an entirely new shape. The smell of the sawdust and varnish is nostalgic, shocking me back to when I was sixteen and would spend hours sitting by the loch, whittling away on a stick, dreaming about the future.

"I'll send you a picture of it when we hang up." I pause, shooting her a half smile.

"It sounds like you're really enjoying being back there."

"In some way, I am…" I hesitate.

"I have a feeling you're still not giving me the whole story," Ave probes. She's always been able to read people.

"Everything's the same, and yet I feel like I don't belong the way I used to. I'm coaching rugby with a lad I went to school with, and he has this group of guys that are working on the new building at the distillery. There are years of jokes between them, and I'm an outsider. I guess I thought the loneliness I felt in New York wouldn't follow me here?"

On top of my lack of admission to the boy's club, Callum's still throwing grunts and glares my way. My folks lost cell service somewhere around Cyprus, and Meadow's been busy.

Doubt curdles in my chest. I stretch my legs out beneath the kitchen table I finished restoring this week. The seal on the wood is nearly dry.

"You felt lonely in the city?"

"Aye. You and Mattie are married now, and Bobbie has that online girl he's been seeing. To be honest, the last couple of months, I sort of felt like I was getting left behind."

"We'd never leave you behind, Ol."

"No, I know. Maybe more in the family sense. You all have your village, your kids, your new ventures and futures. What do I have that could measure up? My new position at Viggle? Can't exactly snuggle up to that in bed."

"What about that picture you carry in your wallet? The girl you left behind?" she asks wistfully.

"It's complicated. We have a lot of difficult history. And besides, I have to go back to New York."

"Even though you said you felt lonely here?"

She's got me there. "It's the career move of a lifetime."

"Alright, let's say you can stomach the loneliness—which I don't think is a good thing, Ol. But you told me yourself you hated being behind a computer screen all day. You love the outdoors, and you love being around people."

"I can put up with screens for a few years. The money and the perks are worth it. I'd be a real success." I try to convince her, but the words don't feel believable.

"Do you really want to go through life putting up with things?" Avery rests her chin in her palm as her free hand fumbles with the watch on her wrist. "After my dad died, I forced my head down and checked off the elaborate list of things I *needed* to achieve—as a way to feel closer to him. Looking back, I was using work to cope with my grief. I thought if I had the right job, made the right career moves, I would fill whatever that hole inside of me was."

My chest strains, a tightness that constricts my breath,

making it hard to inhale. "Remember when we first started working in the ORO offices and I told you about my old job? How that one asshole called me a screw-up and it was the reason I finally snapped out of my corporate haze?"

"Mhm." She nods.

"There's more to it than that." I wince, admitting something I hid through the years. "Before I left Thistlehill and started at MIT, I had a best friend here. Barely the word to describe him—he was like a brother to me."

"What was his name?"

"Fox Macrae." My eyes sting as tears well up. "Hell, that must be the first time I've said his full name out loud in years." My muscles tense, as if preparing for a fight-or-flight response.

"Oh, Ol." Avery's lip trembles.

The story pours out of me; there's no way to contain it. I tell her everything, not leaving a single stone unturned. How Meadow left me at the airport the day we were going to start a new life together in America. The fight with Fox weeks after I settled in at MIT. His car accident. The year I spent hating myself, the one after that, and another. Why I'd never come back here. How there's a kid now, my best friend's daughter that the first and only love of my life is raising. How Meadow's as incredible as I remembered her.

By the time I finish speaking, a heavy chain has loosened.

"Grief alters reality. Even if you're simply grieving your old self." Except I'm not grieving my old self. I'm facing the grief I never processed. "I'm so sorry that you had to go through all of that on your own." Concern fills her eyes. "It sounds like you still have some unresolved feelings. You didn't just lose your best friend—you lost this girl, this first love, and she's there now. You have a chance to know her in a different way. Maybe even learn things about yourself and the goals you had set up for your life. Of course, this is rich coming from a workaholic who's married to another workaholic, but sometimes, love and family are more important than work."

Could that be true? Is that why Ma and Da stayed together all these years despite never being truly comfortable? Because they loved each other? Could I even love Meadow that way again after everything that's happened?

"You're smart, you know?" I laugh, trying to push the strain out of my chest.

"I miss you."

"I miss you too."

"Let's circle back to something. You're coaching Meadow's daughter's rugby team?"

"Started off as a way to get workers for the new bottling facility." I attempt a lazy explanation. It's become so much more than that. On the pitch, seeing Maisie run around with the other kids has been a kind of fun I've never experienced. It has reconnected me with old memories of games with Fox. The things I loved as a boy before this town became too small for me. Meadow cheering in the stands. A community formed from a team.

"The Highlands are brimming with things to do, and you chose to be around her little girl instead."

She's not wrong. I could've hired Blair and Brothers at full price, even if it would cut deep into our budget.

"Maybe, Ave. But I'm leaving, remember? The job of my dreams." There's no excitement in my voice.

Nagging doubts have been sprouting inside me like nasty weeds. Rationally, becoming the Director of Sustainable Innovation at the leading tech giant would give me all of the money and success I've wanted since I was a boy.

But that same boy wanted Meadow.

Being there for her on Monday, helping out, felt easy.

What do I even know about being someone's *more*? I've had a taste of her once, and my mind's already gone. It's foolish.

When the Viggle offer came in January, I was thrilled. It was going to be my solution to everything that wasn't quite right. No—I am *still* thrilled. But I didn't expect to feel something about my priorities shift after I spoke with Meadow about Fox. All of that grief clouded my ability to see how much older my parents have gotten. How little time I may still have with them because I stayed away.

The seventy-three days I have left now loom over me.

"You have two months to figure out what's important to you. No need to make any decisions now—but listen to your heart, not that brain of yours. You're always good at knowing what your gut and heart are feeling. And if you want to come back to the city, all of us will be here, welcoming you with open arms," she says. My friends have the best intentions, but their open arms will soon be wrapped around their own families. The loneliness will creep back in. My career and success will be the only totems to keep me company.

"Thanks, Ave."

"And you can always stay in Scotland. Maybe you had a good reason to leave before, but I was young and foolish once. I thought I knew what I wanted," she says. "It took meeting Luca to realize that my life was missing a partner, someone at my side to fight with me and challenge me on a daily basis."

I chuckle. "I think you and my girl would get along on that fact alone." *My girl*. Meadow. In the video, Avery's eyes soften. "Uh—I just mean you're right. I obviously have some thinking to do."

"The Highlands are on our destination list. Kaia would love it. Try to enjoy the time you have there. And think about why you left in the first place. Was it because of your parents? The distillery? Or the girl?"

"Mommy," a small voice sings in the background.

"That's gonna be Kaia." Avery smiles, getting out of her chair. "Are you going to be alright?"

"Yes," I promise. "Go, I'll talk to you later."

"You better. And, I don't know, try to hang out with those guys at the distillery outside of work—our team grew closer at those trivia nights."

"Good advice. Bye, Ave."

Making peace with Thistlehill and the history here could be the thing that rocks the unsettled feeling that's haunted me all these years. If I'm to truly make peace with the past, enjoy my job at Viggle, and not return to New York feeling lonely and empty, then I have to give my home a *real* chance.

---

"WILL YE KEEP IT DOWN? Some of us are tryin' to work." Steam comes out of Callum's flared nostrils as he stomps across the freshly laid foundation for the bottling facility. *Shit.* He's in one of his moods again.

"Sorry about the noise, Callum." I drop my brick trowel into the bucket of mortar and slap my hands together. "This'll all be over next week."

"No' soon enough," he groans under his breath. "Doubt yer da would appreciate ye disruptin' the peace."

Annoyance slices through my chest. Enough's enough. All ten of Neil's guys are red in the face, sweat drenching their clothes after they finished laying the bricks for the four outer walls of the warehouse. At the rate we're working, we have a real chance at wrapping up without a second to spare.

The roof goes up tomorrow. Electricity wired on Tuesday. The rinser, bottling and capping machine, and the labeler all arrive on Thursday.

I've been enjoying putting this all together and managing the project. The changes I'm making are like the ones I thought of as a boy—they'll get Anderson whisky out into the world. As they should. We have a damn good product.

Callum's grouchy attitude isn't going to put a stop to any of that.

"Da will be fine. He left me in charge," I remind him as sternly as possible.

"Fine, have it yer way." Callum stares daggers at me, muttering as he storms off. "The prodigal lad with all his bright notions."

I return to work, hauling the remainder of the masonry tools out of the way. The entire place needs to be cleared out before the crane arrives in the morning. My arms strain as I carry two buckets full of excess mortar.

In spite of Callum's grumblings, the best part about throwing myself into this construction is getting to reconnect with the part of myself that loved the outdoors. We've been working from sunrise to sunset. My muscles have been pummeled with relentless work.

It's the most present I've felt in years. The way I used to feel on my runs as a boy, or when I played rugby. It's just me and the pounding of my heart in my ears.

The way I felt with Meadow when we made love.

Maybe she's not the only one in need of reconnecting with herself.

I used to love being active, using my body like a tool and not a house for my brain.

"Callum's always been a hard one to crack," Neil says sympathetically, a plank of scaffolding on his right shoulder.

"Aye."

"You work as if you've done it your whole life. I could use a big guy like you on our team." Neil sends a fist into my shoulder, and I wince. The buckets I'm carrying almost collapse onto the ground.

Alright, maybe between the rugby coaching and the manual labor, I'm a bit spent.

"I'd only slow you down. But if we're talking about poker

tonight, then you all better stay sharp," I call out to the guys. Thanks to Ave's advice, I'm hosting everyone. Great way to put the stability of my new kitchen table to the test.

"Bletherin' skite! Ye never even played with us before. Ye'll be eatin' yer words soon, lad, tremblin' like you was a few days ago," Ewan shouts across the large space, a giant smile on his scraped-up face. He's the shortest among us, but what he lacks in height, he makes up by having more teeth than the rest of the crew.

They're all part of the Thistlehill rugby club, and when they rolled into work a few days ago with split lips, black eyes, and missing teeth, I nearly had a heart attack. They all got a real laugh out of my reaction. Sure, maybe I'm the butt of a new joke, but it's one I'm a part of now.

"Means you won't know any of my tells."

"Clyde over here rubs his beard anytime he has good cards." Neil nods toward the skinny lad collecting the fans around the warehouse. He's fresh out of school, working to save up for his own business in town.

"Shut it," Clyde snaps at him. "Or I'll tell Ol here all about yer itchin' nose."

A hearty chuckle rips out of my chest. "Look at you clucking like two old hens."

"Wait 'til we get some of Anderson's Black Label in us. Won't be able to keep our mouths shut 'bout the damn best whisky in Scotland." Andie's gruff voice lights up the room. He lugs four large rubbish bags and follows the rest of the crew out of the facility.

"Good, innit? Da knew what he was doing when he made that one," I say.

The Black Label was Da's first blend on the market. However much we may disagree on the process, it's hard not to be impressed with how much he's managed to achieve without a hoard of new-age tech. Part of me wishes I'd paid a little more attention to his lessons about choosing the right grains and sourcing the best casks.

Maybe I could put a whisky to maturity while I'm here. Sure, I wouldn't be able to try it for at least three years, but maybe that'll be the excuse I need to start visiting more. To check on the whisky. To check on my new friends. On a certain someone else.

"Oi, Ol, you all there?" Clyde shouts, his thick mustache moving as he speaks. "Maybe the lad doesn't want to go with us."

"Go where?" I ask, coming out of my reverie.

Neil shakes his head. "Elspeth's band is playin' at Tavern. Ye got any plans on Saturday night?"

That must've been what Reina was talking about after rugby practice.

"Aye, come with us. Lad's night. Long as we get a round off yer fancy arse." Ewan shakes the dust off his hands and swipes the sweat on his brow with the collar of his shirt.

"You've convinced me." Anything to pass the time before I get to see Meadow. Monday can't come soon enough. I could invite her to Tavern on Saturday, but I doubt she'll come. A public outing with me is the last thing she'll want.

The early night brings with it a warm breeze, but in the distance, the clouds are starting to roll in. We did hit a long stretch of time there. Luck and hard work sure do pay off. I set down my buckets and stretch out my shoulder blades. Gravel crunches beneath my feet as I shake out each of my limbs.

"Thanks, Neil, for all of this." I glance up at the almost-finished warehouse. "Still can't believe we got it up so fast."

"Your da may have the best whisky, and you may have your wits about ya, but I got the best crew," Neil boasts, clapping a wink my way. "The good weather helps. Once that roof goes up, we'll need to get a tarp over the whole thing."

"Right."

"Ol, we'll see you at yours." Ewan revs his engine with

Andie in the passenger seat. "We won't start dealin' without the rest of you."

"Given the caber toss sign-ups any thought? You used to compete as a boy. After all the back breaking you've done, may be worth representing Thistlehill," Neil says, setting down his scaffolding remains.

The whole point of a caber toss is to launch a wooden pole as far from you as you can. The Thistlehill Festival is built around the competition. The crowd used to go wild for each contestant. As kids, we'd watch from beneath the bleachers while we snuck beer from the local vendors. In my later teens, I competed in the young division. One of the three times my da ever said he was proud of me was when I got second place.

Guess it wouldn't hurt to try again. Maybe go for first? As part of my falling back in love with Thistlehill. Plus, Meadow and Maisie are likely going to be there.

"Count me in."

"Got the right attire?"

"Worrying about my fashion again?" I tsk. "I'll borrow one of Da's kilts."

We walk to our cars, which are parked beside each other. Neil opens his door, then pokes his head over the roof of his sedan. "I host weekly practice down the road from my house. Stop by if you want. I bring the beers, and you can bring along a bottle of your whisky—or three."

"Sounds like more drinking than practicing."

He shrugs. "How do you think poker's gonna go tonight? See ye at yours."

We laugh, and I get in the truck, starting up the engine. My phone rests on the dash, and I grab it to check if there are any texts from her. None since Tuesday. It's barely been a handful of days, and I miss her terribly. More than I did when I let myself believe she was a distant memory.

I'm like a dog at her door with a bird in my teeth.

# Falling for Meadow 245

I check the time. 18:00. She's definitely at the start of dinner service. Maybe something casual couldn't hurt. Just to see how she's doing.

We never got to text as teenagers. My first phone followed me on that plane to Boston.

> **OLLIE**
> Break an egg tonight.

That was incredibly cheesy. I run my dusty palm over my face.

No way she's answering. I go to shut off my phone, but the chat bubble blooms to life.

> **DOE**
> violating rugby coach integrity again

> **OLLIE**
> Pesky emergencies keep coming up

> **DOE**
> what is it this time

*I can't stop thinking about you.*

> **OLLIE**
> Elspeth's band playing at Tavern on Saturday
> The lads and I are going to go

> **DOE**
> neils crew?

> **OLLIE**
> Yeah

When she doesn't respond, I reach for some kind of lifeline.

> **OLLIE**
> How's the star player's leg?

DOE
like it never even happened

thx again

OLLIE
Don't worry about it

She doesn't text back.

## Chapter 21
# Meadow

"I'M ONLY GOING TO ASK YOU ONE FINAL TIME, CHEF." Brooke throws on her authoritative tone and tosses a dish towel over her shoulder. "Can we please go celebrate? The Den has been open for an entire week, and despite what that one review said, it's been a success. In the name of rest, please, let's get fucked up."

"And your idea of rest is to get blasted drunk at Tavern?"

She huffs and paces around the kitchen. We closed out our final customer thirty minutes ago when Brooke decided to spring this on me. "Obviously. Fi, help me here."

Low blow to use my other best friend against me. I interject before Fi can get a word in. "We have dinner service tomorrow, and we still need to clean this kitchen."

"Meadow, we have a whole team to help us do that."

I wipe the stainless-steel counters clean and glance at the clock. 00:03. "Or we can get a good night's sleep."

Fi laughs, pulling her apron overhead and hanging it up in her locker. "Okay, now I have to agree with Brooke. You're being a bit stubborn. When's the last time you actually slept?"

With Ollie on Monday. But she has a point.

I spent the entire week working. Not quite sticking to our

resting plan, but sue me—it's hard to sit down and stop doing all the things I have to do. It makes me feel useless. *Helpless.* When my head hasn't been failing through flavor combinations at home, searching for whoever I am through aromatics and sauces, I've been working at the Den or taking care of Mais.

Ollie's been pummeled with work as well. I caught his sweat-drenched clothes and tired body working out in his woodshed on more than one occasion.

"Getting our lady juices revved up isn't just for our rest, chef! We have to wing-woman for Fi." Brooke throws another argument at me, then turns to our pastry chef. "Fi, what instrument does Elspeth play again?"

A pink blush spreads over Fi's cheeks. "Bass."

My lower back stings, as if a colossal rhino has mercilessly trampled upon it. Seriously, in what universe is it natural to have a week of normalcy before my raging hormones throw me on edge again?

"Fine, but only to stop your nagging. Maisie is having a sleepover at Cece's again." I set down my cleaning supplies. "We can go. I just need to get home and change, maybe even take a shower. My hands smell like fermented garlic."

"What's wrong with that?"

"At least we'll keep away all the vampires. C'mon, we'll get ready at mine." Brooke strips off her apron. She and Fi are practically neighbors. They live in town, a short five-minute walk from the restaurant. "A real girl's night. This is exactly what we've been needing. Prowl the town. Suck the blood of innocents. Catch some man meat."

"Suck blood?" Fi squirms.

"Who knows, maybe a sacrifice is in order tonight." Brooke devilishly rubs her hands together.

I raise a brow at her. "I thought my garlic fingers were keeping the vampires away…"

"Right, I fucked up my analogy. See, look, I'm already plastered out of my mind, and I've been sober all week! We're going to have so much fun," she cheers.

The tickle of nervous butterfly wings grazes my stomach. I forgot Ollie will be there with Neil and his friends. But that doesn't matter. We're keeping things between us on the down low. I won't interrupt his guys' night or sacrifice my girls' night.

"Elspeth mentioned Ollie will be there." Fi shoots me a look from across the kitchen.

"He will, but there won't be any prowling, blood sucking, man meat eating, or garlic fingers around him. Our little…*whatever* is a secret, remember?"

They both share a look like they don't believe me. "If he just so happens to be at the only bar in town while you are too, then there's nothing wrong with saying hello," Brooke resolves and zips up her coat.

I pull out my phone.

> MEADOW
> u up?

OLLIE NEW NUMBER
I'm sorry, did Meadow Macrae just hit me with the classic booty call text?

> MEADOW
> no

*Maybe?*

> MEADOW
> r u still going to tavern 2nite

OLLIE NEW NUMBER
A booty call and a date in one night. I am a lucky man

> **MEADOW**
> im going with brooke and fi
> will u be there

> **OLLIE NEW NUMBER**
> Sounds like you want to go to Tavern with me

> **MEADOW**
> ur the worst
> nvm

> **OLLIE NEW NUMBER**
> I'm already here
> Are we allowed to talk to each other in public?

My fingers pause. It's probably best that we don't. Especially when strange feelings have been coming up after I saw Ollie with Maisie on the rugby pitch. They range from out-of-my mind horniness over his sexy caretaking—I blame the PMDD for that particular mood swing—to a profound sense of admiration for him. He's as gentle as I always knew him to be. Kind and thoughtful.

Ugh! I'm blushing like a schoolgirl again.

Besides, Catherine and a few of the other moms gossiped about how good he was with my plum and how he was meant to come back for me. I can't deal with that.

Childhood ex-lovers turned…casual hookups on Monday nights so I can come up with a tasting menu that can impress Adair Grant and he can fall back in love with this town before he goes home in June.

Maybe it's easier to say we're just friends.

But friends can say hello to each other in town without things getting strange. Can't they?

> **MEADOW**
> hvnt decided yet

> **OLLIE NEW NUMBER**
> Do you remember the last school dance before I graduated? We snuck out the back together and onto the rugby pitch?

Where we proceeded to roll around in the muddy grass, taking our time holding each other. It was one of the first times he made me come—a place he took me to effortlessly on Monday.

> **MEADOW**
> my mom was not happy w my ripped dress

> **OLLIE NEW NUMBER**
> Maybe you can wear another one tonight

> **MEADOW**
> c u

Thirty minutes later, I strategically adjust my bra as we strut the short, cobblestoned walk from Brooke's house to Tavern. After pregaming with three shots of Jäger—fine, four—Brooke convinced me to squeeze into a burgundy wrap dress while she curled my hair, painted my face, and stuck me into a pair of her heels.

I do look good though. Feel good. Even if this is the allotment of my chest exposure for the entire year.

After my texts with Ollie, a dress was an easy choice. We can't exactly touch tonight or linger around each other for too long, but I like the temptation.

All week, I watched his swollen muscles unpack construction supplies from the back of his truck or lug wood into the backyard. He deserves to have a little forbidden fruit dangled in front of him.

"I gotta be honest, I haven't been out to a bar at night...probably since I was in Lyon."

"Seven years is far too long to go without shaking your ass at a bar. We love this new Meadow. Hot mama taking on the town!" Brooke's laugh carries through the almost empty Main Street.

"I doubt my ass is going to be doing any shaking tonight."

"Elspeth could make even my pa shake his booty." We all laugh at Fi's joke as she loops her arm through mine and squeezes me close. She always gets a little touchier when we drink. "Can I just say red is your color?"

"The lip and wrap combo is chef's kiss," Brooke squeals.

"Speaking of kisses." I throw on my most conspiratorial voice and nudge Fi's side. "Will you finally make a move tonight?"

Brooke joins in. "Surely after you see Elspeth up there, *fingering* that bass, the thick gleam of strobe lights on her milky blonde hair..."

Under the streetlights, Fi's blush is obvious. "You're disgusting."

My pastry chef's crush on Elspeth has been long lasting. After Elspeth went through a divorce two years ago, Fi did the neighborly thing and dropped off some of her best pecan and caramel muffins as a consolation. Ever since, Fi blushes every time Elspeth's name comes up.

"Yeah, but you guys love me. If growing up in Florida taught me anything, it was to be the life of the party," Brooke sings. "That, and never feed a gator your leftover turkey carcass at Thanksgiving."

Fi looks positively shocked. "A gator?"

"You heard me," Brooke laughs. "Swamp puppies."

"Like my tits in the heat of August," I chortle, not able to resist the terrible joke. "Did your party manual include a chapter on how to wear these things?" I look down at my heels. My ankles wobble. Our kitchen clogs aren't high fashion, but they sure are comfortable.

Brooke rolls her eyes at me over her shoulder, strutting in stilettos. "Stop bitching; those aren't even my knock-'em dead pair. There's barely an inch of heel on those! Beauty is pain."

"A man must've come up with that one," Fi chimes in.

I rub the scars on my hands. "Agreed."

We push through the heavy, creaking door of the pub. The air is saturated with the sour smell of alcohol, musk, and cigar smoke.

Wooden plaques hang on the wooden walls, and dim light filters through the tight space. At the entrance, a pair of pool tables stand beside each other. The bar top is filled with people, all in jeans and sweaters, and a few booths on the opposite wall are still empty.

"I'm overdressed," I whisper to my friend.

"That might not be a bad thing tonight." Fi nudges to the end of the bar.

Ollie is slung over a stool. After all this time, my body still lights up around him, as if it's that very first time I saw him outside my house.

A neatly pressed shirt hugs his body. Those typically unruly waves are slicked back. He looks damn fine.

My mouth dries.

He doesn't notice us.

I glance at the person beside him—Reina. One of those beautifully painted fingernails drawing circles along the lip of her martini glass. I wring my own hands together, embarrassed by the marks and dents along my skin.

"Is he on a date with her?" Brooke says through her teeth.

I shrug a shoulder and shake my head. "Doesn't matter."

If he wants to talk to Reina, then I'm not going to put a stop to that. She's a great girl. Sweet and kind. *Young.* I'm sure they have stuff in common.

"I'll get us a booth," Fi says, transfixed by the band—by one particular member. Elspeth's rocking a fishnet tee, a shimmery bralette visible beneath it.

"I got drinks," I offer.

"I'll come with you."

Brooke and I approach the mahogany bar a few stools away from Ollie. *Don't look at him yet.* Play it cool. I haven't flirted with a man since my days in Lyon.

My lessons with Brooke come floating back. Her number one tip—act like the most confident person in the room.

I roll my shoulders back. *This man wants you, Meadow.*

Sure, it's silly to play a game of jealousy, but it used to be fun back in our day. What's happening between us now is supposed to be fun. I want to feel wanted. I want to make him want me, even if I'm using dirty tactics to make it happen.

"Hey, Frank, three highballs, please—use the *Johnnie Walker.*" I speak loudly to the bartender, enunciating each syllable.

I've never had a problem with Brooke's second flirting tip—be a little mean to them.

Out of the corner of my eye, Ollie stares at me.

*Bait taken.*

The warmth in my cheeks smokes down my neck, through my shoulders.

"Your gentle giant will not stop looking at you," Brooke whispers into my side, but my eyes stay on Frank.

Ollie clears his throat. "Frank, throw those on my tab, will you? Give you an extra twenty if you make 'em all with my Red Label." *His* Red Label. My, oh my. Frank's brows raise as he checks if that's alright. I subtly nod. "Hey, Meadow." Ollie's deep voice wraps itself around me.

Brooke pinches my left side.

Third tip—make him work for eye contact.

"Lovely to see you, Oliver." I glance at him briefly. His grin is bright and delicious. I want to nab his lips between my teeth and bite down until his hands are fighting to pull me away, a groan clipping out of his throat.

Those pregame shots and my hormones have created a cocktail I can't sober from.

"Hey, girls." Reina peeks out from his side with a beautiful cat eye. "So glad you could make it! My brother's over there." She tilts her head to the bathroom line in the corner. "Couldn't resist crashing his boys' night and saying hello to Thistlehill's most impressive assistant rugby coach." She brushes Ollie's bicep. He leans away from her.

"We're just having a night on the town," Brooke says.

Ollie's gaze roams over my face and chest. I refuse to lock eyes with him.

"Fun!" Reina laughs. "Don't let me keep you; the dance floor is calling me." She turns to Ollie. "Maybe you can join me there later, big man?"

He tugs the collar of his shirt and replies, "Not much of a dancer."

"Don't worry, I'm a bonnie teacher." Reina winks and abandons his side, swinging away toward the band.

The tic in my jaw eases.

"You must be Brooke," Ollie says, extending his hand to her. That wicked sear from his eyes won't let up.

Brooke giggles and shakes his hand. "The one and only. And you're Ollie; I've heard *loads* about you. Thanks for the drinks."

"Charge up my tab, if you'd like."

Drinks at Tavern aren't exactly the prices he must be used to in New York City, but offering to pay for my friends? Why is that so sickeningly attractive?

"We're not going to say no to that, are we, Meadow?" She bumps my arm. "We love some good hospitality."

Frank timely sets down three tall glasses down. "Anything else?"

I hesitate, then lock eyes with Ollie. Those brown rings hug his wide pupils like crescent moons. I want to drag him to the back of this loud bar and find out if he's as worked up as I am. He's right—I really do love my secrets.

The small privacy of what we are is like a flame under my feet. But tonight's about my friends. I slide my gaze to the band as their music fills the bar.

"Get a round of these for the band as well, will you? Let 'em know Oliver sent them on behalf of Fi." I wink.

Brooke's mouth drops open.

"Do as the lady wants, Frank," Ollie says in a deep voice. His lips curl into a one-sided smirk.

I grab my drink off the bar, and Brooke sweeps up the other two in her fists.

Before he can get in the last word, I say, "Enjoy your date." Then I strut off, putting an extra swing into my hips as we weave through the crowd of dancing bodies. My mind is barely focused on the sound of the guitar and the singing in the room.

"That was so hot, Meadow. The mama's still got it."

"Honestly, I think I fucking blacked out for a second."

"He couldn't tell at all, I promise. The girls"—she looks at my cleavage—"kept him well distracted."

"All thanks to your flirting tips and this dress." I bump her hip, and she squeals. "My palms are so sweaty, I'm about to drop my glass," I confess through a nervous giggle.

"Hold on tighter; he's still ogling you," she says.

In a few more steps, we slide into the booth Fi snagged for us. I strategically position myself in Ollie's line of sight and return to my very controlled game of resistance. I would've paid to see the look on his face as he watched me saunter away.

Brooke leans over to Fi. "Meadow is going to fuck the mountain man." The guitar riffs and pulsating bass lines drown out her recap. My phone buzzes in my pocket.

**OLLIE NEW NUMBER**
You look fucking incredible

MEADOW
ik

**OLLIE NEW NUMBER**
I'm coming over to sit with you

MEADOW
no

2 suspicious

stay over there with reina

**OLLIE NEW NUMBER**
Jealous?

MEADOW
u wish

**OLLIE NEW NUMBER**
I'm here with Neil and the guys, like I said I would be

MEADOW
no need to explain

all good

**OLLIE NEW NUMBER**
Sounds like you may be a little jealous

MEADOW
a lil but we're keeping things a secret

**OLLIE NEW NUMBER**
We don't have to. I can come over there right now and we can break the news to everyone

MEADOW
we agreed

pls pretend ur here with smn or alone

**OLLIE NEW NUMBER**
You're right

Guess I'll enjoy secretly flirting with you

And making you jealous

I tuck my phone away and send the highball down my throat. My pulse matches the music. Neil's back in the seat beside Ollie, and a couple of the guys from Blair and Brothers slam their glasses together around the bar. Okay, I'm a little jealous. Not of Reina or the lads, but of his attention and the fact that I want it all to myself.

A kaleidoscope of colors flickers off of people's raised hands on the dance floor as they move to the upbeat melody. Vibrations from the drums shoot up my heels and into my legs.

"Meadow? Is that you, or do my eyes deceive me?" Harry Pears's hand lands on our table. Harry owns a coffee shop on the outskirts of Thistlehill. He has a nephew in the same year as Maisie. He asked me out a few years ago, and despite the gentle rejection, he hasn't let up in his pursuit.

"Hey, Harry." I smile and steal a look across the room. Ollie's darkened stare is all up in flames now, his veiny forearms flexing as he taps his fist on his thigh. *Oh. Now who's jealous?*

"Ye ladies got room for one more in here?" Harry asks. He's got that quintessential pretty-boy look. Well-defined cheekbones and a strong jawline. Caramel-colored hair trimmed close to his skull.

Is it a little childish to let him sit with us just to make Ollie jealous? Absolutely.

Is that going to be enough to stop me? No.

I scoot over. "We do. Have a seat."

This night is about to get a lot more exhilarating.

## Chapter 22
# Ollie

"And that's how I ended up in London at three in the morning on a Tuesday. Isn't it, Neil?" Reina's singing laughter creeps into my right ear. Her brother joins in on the chatter, but my vision is tunneled on Meadow.

The mouth on her. Plump lips smothered in red. I bet she tastes so fucking good right now. I can still recall her gasps and moans and spit on my lips from our afternoon together. Thick curls tumble around that damn wicked dress, hugging her lush and plentiful curves in all of the right places.

Maddening. That's what she is. Making me absolutely mad.

Her head tips back in a laugh, exposing the pearly skin of her chest.

The hair on my neck stiffens, and I recross my legs in front of me. I've been hard since the moment she walked into this bar, and now some other fucker has her attention.

Harry's saucer eyes are locked firmly on her breasts. *Prick.* Tension strains my neck. What gives him the right to look at her perfect tits anyway? Not like he'd have a clue what to do with them. Or her.

He was in her form at school and clearly stuck around. He's

not a terrible fella. Was never rude to any of us back in school. But he's not right for Meadow—or Maisie, for that matter. Just by the looks of him, I doubt he can even throw together a decent load of laundry. Let alone take care of my two girls.

*Fuck.* What am I even thinking? I'm clearly drunk, because they are not mine.

Something in my stomach flickers like a deficient lightbulb.

I recross my legs again, my hand curling into a fist as it beats against my thigh. The free one fumbles with the drink menu on the bar top in front of me. I check my phone again. My five messages to Meadow since Harry sat down still don't have a response. Fucking hell, it's like I'm sixteen again and watching lads flirt with her at school.

No matter how much I'd rough up the lads on the rugby team when they'd get particularly close to her, it was never enough to keep them from risking my tackle just to talk to her.

I clear my throat, the sound like a tire scraping against asphalt.

Harry stretches his arm behind her and scoots closer in the leather booth. Alright. He's got one second to take his hand off of her or I'll march over there and remove it. Apart from the pitch, I've never been prone to violence, but since coming back to town, I've been experiencing lots of changes.

"Ol," Neil says, dragging me out of my mind. "Got something against that menu?"

"Huh?" The laminated list of cocktails is crumpled in my fist. "Oh, uh, can't decide on the next round."

I set the menu down on the bar top and smooth it with both hands. Frank shoots me a disappointed stare.

I'm being ridiculous.

"I, for one, am going to have another Anderson Black Label." Reina bats her eyelashes, patting my thigh. "Neat."

I nearly topple off the barstool. "Right." I gather myself and stand straight.

She hasn't stopped flirting with me even though I've made it clear that I'm not interested.

There's nothing wrong with Reina. She's a beautiful girl. Neil's blonde hair. A dazzling smile that looks the same way it did in school—pearly white. But when Meadow's in the room, no one else can compete with the hold she has over my attention.

Meadow's laugh lights up her corner of the bar. Even over the deep, muddy sound of Elspeth's bass, it's impossible to miss.

Harry's fingers hover at her cheek before swiping a strand of hair behind her ear.

Enough's enough. I would rather pluck out every one of my beard hairs than watch him spend another second talking to her. We can still keep things between us a secret while I put an end to this one-upmanship.

On their table, empty glasses sit. She can't stay parched any longer. That's all this is—a friend getting his casual, out-of-this-world beautiful, bloody-minded, delectable *friend* a drink. I spin toward the bar, nearly knocking over my glass, and wave to Frank.

"Another four highballs, please." I nod, then turn to Neil. "Gonna go say hi to Fiona at the booths." I point to Meadow's booth. Harry has moved closer to her. My nostrils flare. Can Frank pour those drinks any faster? "Haven't seen her since we were in school."

Neil meets me with a shit-eating grin. "Sure, pass along our hellos to *Fiona*."

I fist the drinks off the bar top and thrust myself into the crowd of dancing bodies. Heavy clouds of smoke brush up against my skin as I walk.

"Hey, everyone, having a good time?" I smile like a blubbering buffoon and try to sound as cool as possible.

"Better now." Brooke distributes the drinks around the table. "You sure do know how to make an excellent impression."

"Fiona, long time no see!" I say.

"Thanks, yeah, it's Fi now, by the way," she says impatiently. "Mind just scooting a bit that way?" She swipes me to the side, and I take a step to the right. Much closer to Meadow.

I glance behind me to the band. "Right, sure, sorry. Congrats on the first week at Fox Den."

"Thank you." Brooke smiles, her eyes widening at Meadow. *What are they saying to each other?*

"Look, Harry, isn't it so thoughtful of Ollie to get you a drink?" Meadow slides the glass in front of me over to the poor bloke.

Guess we're both acting like teenagers tonight. No worries. If Meadow wants me to work for it, if she wants me down on my damn knees and begging—or with my fist in Harry's face if he touches her one more time—fine. I haven't felt this pumped up with visceral desire in years.

I want her. I want to show her how much I want her.

"Hey, big lad." Harry stands from his seat at the edge of the booth and extends his hand. I grasp it extra tightly.

"Harry," I bleat, and he flinches. He drags his hand out of mine, shaking out his fingers. "Let's have a game of pool?"

"Guid grip there," he laughs awkwardly, his eyes bouncing to Meadow, who's got that smart fucking smirk on her beautiful lips. The same ones I've held in my teeth. The same damn mouth I've imagined wrapped around my cock. "Och, maybe another time."

My hand smacks against the table. I've lost all sense of rationale and patience.

Brooke's gaze bounces between us as if she's moments away from ordering popcorn for the table.

"Aye, alright," Harry says reluctantly. He shoots Meadow a wink. "I'll be back. I'll be back just for ye."

I hang my arm over his shoulders and drag him from the table to the back of the bar like a hooded crow hoarding away its treasure. The pool tables are only a few steps away from Meadow's booth.

Out of my peripheral vision, I can tell she's watching. I chalk a pool cue as Harry racks the table.

"So, you and Meadow." I fail at sounding nonchalant. "How long has that been going on?"

Harry laughs a deep-throated chuckle. "More like how long have I been begging that lass tae take a chance on me." He nods for me to have the break shot.

Satisfaction rolls through my blood like warm steam. There's nothing there. At least, not yet. *What about after I leave? When I can't throw myself between her and every other drooling fool who wants to get their hands on her?* I push the thought from my mind and lean over the pool table. The balls clack and spin off in different directions before the solid yellow and maroon sink into the pockets.

"You're stripes," I call, missing my next shot.

"Doubt I even have a chance; she's practically untouchable. Full-on career woman, that lass, and a single maw." Harry shrugs, lines up his cue, and misses. "Might be a bit over my head wi' that one."

His comment stings. "What do you mean?"

"Ye ken, single maws," he drones.

"No, I have no idea what you're talking about."

Why's Meadow entertaining a fool like this? She's the full fucking package, not some kind of consolation prize.

"Loads o' responsibility, is all. It's yer shot."

"Aye, sounds like a job for a *real* man," I bite, positioning myself behind the cue ball. Meadow's mouth hangs open as she stares at me—not Harry. Ha! I don't take my eyes off of her as I lean forward, take a deep breath, and draw the stick back smoothly and deliberately.

I strike the cue ball. It clangs against the side of the table, spins around, and sinks the green ball into the exact pocket I planned.

"Och, lad, ye're guid," Harry slurs.

Ignoring him, I raise a brow at Meadow. *You can do better.*

She rolls her eyes at me. *You're peacocking.*

*This next one's for you.*

I hit the cue ball, pocketing another shot.

*Show-off.* Her brow arches; the hint of a smile dances on her lips.

I shrug, stroking my hand up and down the cue. *Enjoy watching me.*

Ten minutes later, I'm left with a blue number two. The same deep color of Meadow's eyes. A small crowd of onlookers holds their breath as I line up my shot and pocket it smoothly.

Sure, I'm peacocking. But I'd hop around in a bird suit if it meant keeping her attention on me for a moment longer.

*Still a show-off?* I flash her a playful glance.

Meadow bites her lip, nodding in response. I lean over the table again, setting up to sink the eight ball. Thank fuck it's dark in here, or my raging hard-on would be the one on display. With a final, decisive shot, I get the last ball into its designated pocket. The sound of victory fills the room as the people around me cheer.

"Guid job, mate." Harry pats me on the back, but I couldn't care less about the win.

My real prize is whispering to Brooke. Meadow catches my eye and tips her head to the door. *Have a good night.* She slides out of the booth and exits Tavern. I drop my stick, grab my jacket off the barstool, and follow her like a loyal dog.

After the display tonight, Meadow could tell me to sit and I'd be on the ground before she took another breath.

Outside the pub, the cool air laps through her hair as she slides into the back of a Tipsy Taxi. The golf cart whirs to life.

No one's out here, which means fair game. I jog over to the cart and slide in right beside her.

"Trying to leave without me?"

"You're here, aren't you?" Whisky dances on her breath. The familiar scent still drives me wild. I lean over and inhale the warmth radiating off of her skin. The petrichor sizzles through my lungs and brain. If I was a goner before, now there's no telling how far I'm willing to go for her attention. My cock throbs against my jeans.

I want to break her apart for spending the entire night driving me out of my mind, and then I'll reassemble her, just as a reminder of how perfect I make her feel. Worshiping her body has always been second nature.

"Is this okay, Mrs. Macrae?" The teenage driver tilts the rearview mirror, eyeing me nervously.

I didn't even see him when I got in.

"It's *Miss*, Brian," she corrects him. "And yes, it's fine. Mr. Anderson can ride with us. We're neighbors, and there's no point in wasting any petrol."

"Yes, the petrol is very important," I whisper, scooting close to her until our legs are pressed together.

"Okay, just buckle up." Brian takes off in the golf cart. The town center is lit up by the soft glow of streetlights. We pass Fox Den, charming stores with stone exteriors, and the giant thistle statue. A small crowd of locals strolls along the sidewalks, leaving Ramona's. Laughter and the echo of music from Tavern fill the air.

But she's the only thing that matters.

I swing an arm around her, pressing her round shoulder right into the crook, and graze my nose against her ear. Keeping my voice low, I say, "Did you put on this dress for me tonight, doe?"

"Seatbelt, Oliver." She straps the belt across her lap. "And, no, I wore it for myself." She narrows her eyes and pretends to be sick of my nonsense, but I'm actually an irritatingly entertaining game she can't stop playing.

"Well, it's fucking sexy." I buckle my seatbelt.

Brian clears his throat from the front seat.

"Eyes on the road, Brian," Meadow snaps before whispering through her teeth, "You were almost green in the face after your little match with Harry."

"Of course I was jealous. I don't like to share." Her pretty eyes splatter with shock, that heavy bottom lip scrimmaging between her teeth. My pulse spikes.

"Shouldn't you have learned to share in grade school?"

"Not when it comes to my favorite things." As we leave the town center behind, the houses become more spread out, giving way to the start of our quiet road. Brian turns the corner, hitting a pothole and causing Meadow and I to jump closer together. "Did what happened back there turn you on?"

"You playing with all those balls?"

"Seemed you liked the way I handled my stick."

"Clearly you've had a lot of practice, but maybe there's room for improvement," she snorts. I've missed being able to so freely toss around jabs and jokes without fear of being hurt. She gets me, and she understands how far we can push each other while keeping the other safe.

"I'm great at feedback," I wink. "Especially when it's you telling me what to do. You love doing that, don't you?"

"A little," she admits.

I lean closer and trace my tongue over her earlobe and down her neck. Meadow's eyes close as she cranes her face. "I want to kiss you."

"You're drunk," she whispers under her breath, but the resistance she's trying for is unconvincing. "And we're in public."

Brian's face is locked firmly on the road in front of him. "That boy doesn't know me."

"He knows me," she counters. Meadow's tongue runs along

her bottom lip, tantalizing me. I want those lips to stain every inch of my skin while I thank her for it. She knows what she's doing as she glances at me beneath those thick, dark lashes and plays coy. "Must be hard for you."

*Very fucking hard.* "Hmm?"

I stretch out my other hand, gripping the leather passenger seat in front of me in an attempt to ignore the ache of desire in my balls.

"Not getting what you want." Meadow grazes her thumb up my jeans.

A gruff laugh tickles my chest. Fine. If she wants to tease, two can play that game.

"No, I have you right where you want to be," I say. I drag my jacket over her lap, covering her legs, and then pull her closer. My fingers slip beneath my coat, coaxing the hem of her dress.

"What are you doing?" she says breathlessly, frozen beneath my touch.

"One word. Just tell me to stop, and I'll behave like a perfect gentleman the entire ride home." I explore the soft skin above her knees.

"Oh, well, after seeing you at those rugby practices, I was hoping for the man on the field and not a gentleman."

"My whistle gets you going? I'll let you blow it next time."

The offer lights up something in her eyes. She gulps, her chest shaking on her exhale. "What are you planning on doing with your hand right now?"

"Taking care of your needs." My hand climbs higher, to the hot skin of her thighs, until my fingers graze something damp. A wicked smirk crests my face. "Oh, doe, making a mess for me already?"

"Shut up," she scoffs. The deep blue of her irises matches the speckled night sky above us.

"Don't be shy, beautiful. I want you just as much as you want me." I grab the hand resting on my jeans and spread her palm against the denim. "Like that, huh?" I return to my explorative touches. She parts her knees as she palms my cock. A spiral of heat jerks itself into my lower spine. "All night I've thought about how good you taste. How I could be sending my tongue over your jaw, down your neck, until my teeth are grinding into the skin of your perfect tits."

Meadow gasps as my fingers push her panties to the side. Her grip on my cock tightens. "Then what would you do?"

"Touch this pretty pussy," I say. I do as promised, pressing my pointer and middle fingers along the hot, wet center of her precious cunt. "Suck at your clit until you're writhing in my arms, begging for release."

She bucks her hips and spreads her knees a little wider in the cramped cart. My fingers trace circles along her swollen clit. A bead of sweat drips from her forehead. With my thumb, I swipe at it, tasting her, before bracketing her jaw and turning her face toward me.

"Ah," Meadow moans against my mouth. Her eyes close as I increase my pace on her clit.

"Quiet," I remind her. "We wouldn't want to scare the poor kid."

"I hate you." Her nostrils flare.

"Sure. As much as you hate this, huh?" I cover my mouth with hers before she can respond, tasting the sour whisky on her tongue and sending my already unsteady heart into atrophy. I resume the circles on her clit with my thumb and slide two fingers into her scorching pussy.

"Good god, woman. You're so tight and wet because of me. Aren't you?" Meadow squirms; her pace on my cock turns ragged, and I force her steady with the arm slung around her. "Don't resist it, doe."

I continue the punishing thrusts of my fingers into her cunt, skimming the rough spot buried deep inside. Meadow groans against my mouth. Her walls tighten around my fingers.

"The moment I saw those pretty curves of yours strut around the bar, I knew I had to have you tonight. Take you. Make every inch of your body mine." The O of her lips creases into a smile, and her eyes remain locked on me. "And when you played your little game like you used to, making me jealous like that—fuck. You know how to push all of my buttons so well. Made me want to splay you right over my lap, get that gorgeous ass up in the air, and remind you who knows how to worship you the way you like. Yeah, baby." I push myself deeper, coaxing her orgasm as it starts to hit its precipice. "You make me feel like a starved animal just waiting to get his fill."

"Ollie," she cries, and I smother the sound with my tongue against hers.

"Give it to me, Meadow. Show me how much I deserve this pretty cunt."

As the flood of heat starts to coat my fingers, the golf cart rattles to a stop.

"We're here, Miss Meadow," Brian says tentatively. Dammit, why is the ride only five minutes? I need longer. Hours longer. We were just getting started. "That'll be ten pounds."

Meadow sobers quickly, the fire in her eyes extinguished as she shucks my jacket off her legs and pulls herself off of me.

"One second, Brian," she says, digging for her wallet.

I drop my hand on top of hers. "Absolutely not."

"I can pay for my own taxi home."

"Of course you can, but why should you?" I hand Brian a red note, covering far more than the fare and a tip.

"Such a gentleman," Meadow laughs with her syrupy voice and climbs out of the cart. I hurry after her, draping my jacket over my hard-on. The cart spurts off, leaving us in the dark. Crisp air dances along my skin, breezing through her hair and carrying the smell of her skin up to me.

I need to finish what we started.

No lights are glowing in her windows. "Maisie home tonight?"

"Sleeping over at Cece's. They've been practicing a new tap routine."

"Care to invite me inside? I don't believe I got to give you what I wanted to give you."

A flash of mischief glows in her eyes. "Just as you started being a gentleman again?"

"Doe, I promise, what I'm going to do to you will not be anywhere near polite."

She laughs. "Shame. I was hoping I could teach you some manners."

I take a step closer, and she doesn't shy away. My hand works its way to the nape of her neck, clutching the hair there and tugging gently. "I promise to be an excellent student."

Meadow tips her head up to mine and plants the softest, most mind-numbing kiss on my lips. A far cry from how our lips exchanged delirious and desire-drunk whispers in the golf cart.

"Then go to your room, Oliver."

The heat in my chest dampens. "Really?"

"I'll see you later."

She leaves me in her wake, disappearing behind the front door. The taste of her is a stain on my mind.

I'm fucking obsessed with her.

I sprint home and up the stairs to my room, where I pull back the curtains.

Across the way, a light flicks on in the upstairs room opposite mine. Her bedroom has had the blinds drawn since I returned to town. Now they're open.

*Is she going to let me watch?*

I swallow the dryness in my mouth. She appears, her back facing me. The small orange glow of a bedside lamp dances across her skin. In the mirror in the corner of her room, I can make out the outline of her front.

Mercy. *Please.*
My phone vibrates.

> DOE
> impolite to stare

> OLLIE
> I thought you didn't want polite

Slowly, she unties the belt of her dress. It comes loose. Her movements are achingly languid as she traces a finger over her shoulders, causing the fabric to lazily drape off her back and around her arms until the wretched dress falls to the ground, leaving behind only lingerie.

> OLLIE
> This is torture

I dial her number. She ignores the call. Fucking hell. I try again. No luck.

> OLLIE
> I am seconds from breaking down the door
> And chasing you around the whole damn house if I have to
> I need to touch you

> DOE
> take ur eyes off me and the night is over

A brief smile, lit up by her phone, shimmers on her face in the reflection of the mirror. My patience grows thin.

When we first learned about pleasure together, Meadow knew how to tattoo herself into my skin with every graze and kiss. On Monday, that was no different. If I went over there now, she'd do it again.

The distance between us is punishment. Torment. The second

circle of hell.

In the mirror, her face is a blur, and her ample curves flicker in and out of view. Full breasts. Strong thighs. Soft stomach.

On instinct, I palm my stiff cock through my jeans. She languidly tips her bra strap off her round shoulder. My movements get faster as need multiplies in my veins.

Fuck. I'm practically howling out of my window.

What I'd give to touch her, to kiss her soft lips again, to take them between my teeth until she groans and bites back. Yes, I want to gnaw on every inch of that woman. I can't help it. Every lick and bite and kiss fills me with lust. Out of my mind, that's what comes most naturally. I can only think of her and nothing else.

The silvery night sky streams into her window. She pulls the second strap off and reaches behind her, unclasping the damn thing. Her bra falls off, revealing the swells of her breasts.

Fuck me.

I unbuckle my belt and strip off my jeans before I stroke my cock again.

Meadow comes toward her window. My heart drums so loudly in my ears, it sounds like Armageddon has come to bury me in the mere vision of her.

She exhales onto the glass and draws on the condensation.

My forehead collapses against my window. My strokes grow hungrier as warmth spills along my spine. Does she know what hell she's putting me through?

I think the message spells out, *Sleep well*. Or, *Go to hell*.

She spins; her voluptuous arse swings. She bends low, giving me the full view of her small panties and dimpled skin, and opens the drawer.

*No fucking way.*

My body reels with yearning. She stops digging in her drawer, and suddenly the lights turn off. She escapes from view.

"No," I groan desperately. "Fuck no."

I laugh helplessly, dialing her phone. She ignores it. My eyes blur as I call over and over again.

Finally, she picks up. "Who is this?" Her coy voice is labored.

"You love torturing me, don't you, doe?" I manage the words through my own heavy breathing. My cock throbs in my palm.

"Oh, Coach Ollie. You're breaking rules again? What is the council going to say about this?"

I pause. "The council?

"Just go with it. I haven't done this in a while." She chuckles, and I embrace the story she's weaving for us. Whatever. I'd give Meadow any fantasy she wants.

"Fuck the rugby council." We both laugh at that one.

"Yeah, fuck them and whoever put you into those micro shorts. Fucking driving me out of my mind!" Glad to know those pesky things did more for her than they managed to do for my leg coverage. The thought of her getting turned on by me on the field makes my cock even harder.

"I'd put them on for you right now. All you have to do is invite me over there."

"But torturing you from all the way over here is so easy."

"Let me make another thing easy," I say. "Let me make you feel good."

"I've already got something to do that."

"There's no chance that blue, vibrating, TV-fixing rabbit of yours could replicate how my fingers worked your pussy only moments ago."

"Is that right?" A soft moan escapes her lips.

"I need you. I want you. So fucking desperately."

"Tell me what you're doing."

"I haven't stopped touching myself since I saw you turn on that lamp. Thinking about how you felt wrapped around my fingers, the way you moaned into my beard, palmed my cock... how much I want to be on my knees in front of you, savoring every taste." She rasps on the other end of the line. In the background, I hear the low hum of her vibrator as her mattress creaks. "That make you want to touch yourself?"

"Mhm," she moans.

"Say it, Meadow. Say how much you enjoy knowing you have control over me."

"I—ah, enjoy knowing how desperate you are."

The heavy confession forces a chuckle out of me. "Hit that speaker button for me, will ya?" I do the same. "You're going to do exactly what I say, got it?"

"Mhm."

"Meadow," I scold.

"Yes. I'll do what you say."

"Take one of your hands and run it across those beautiful breasts. How does that feel?"

"Lovely."

"Gonna need a little bit more than that."

"My skin is soft." She swallows. "My nipples are hard against my fingers."

"Give them a tug, then do the same on the other breast." The image of her lying in her bed, in the next house over, only forty-seven steps away, is no match for the fantasies I've had about her. Knowing that she's touching herself, letting me take the lead…it's a sense of control I'd never felt before. A task that's more like a duty. Wanting to please her, take care of her. "How's that feel?"

"Splendid."

"Good. It should. I want you to feel the way you're making me feel—so fucking fantastic."

"Really?"

"Yes," I assure her as I stroke my cock. The heavy weight of need begs for release, but I follow her. Keep the lock on myself until she's there too. "I'm doing everything I can to keep myself together, but the sound of you moaning is splitting my mind in half."

"What next?"

"Are you nice and wet for me?"

"Mhm."

"Working that toy in and out of your gorgeous cunt?"

"This entire time."

"Fuck," I huff. "I love to hear that. Close your eyes; listen to my voice, okay?" She flashes me a lazy, obedient agreement. "Run your fingers over your chest and up your neck. Keep that vibrator turned on. I want to hear it on the other end."

"It feels terrific."

"More, doe."

"I—" She pauses. "My vibrator is making me wetter. My clit is so swollen. I—I'm thrusting it deeper."

I want to insert myself, but not yet.

"God, I love hearing you work that needy cunt for me," I whisper, keeping up with her escalating moans. "Don't turn that thing off, not even when it gets to be too much, when you think you can't take it anymore, okay? I want to hear how desperate you are to get close with me."

"A-are you?"

"Right here with you. I'm right here with you."

Then she does something that sends an even deeper shock into my system. "I—I can't stop thinking about your chest, the muscles in your back, how you picked me up like I was—weightless."

Her play into the fantasy may push me over the edge. *Keep it together.* "Been thinking about how it felt to be in my arms? I haven't been able to get it out of my mind. How fucking perfect your curves felt in my fingers. The smell of your hair. Those little sounds you make." Her giggle turns into a moan. "Yeah, just like that one. You're fucking angelic, Meadow. Could make any man lose his mind with just a look."

"That's what happened tonight. You jealous, jealous man," she mewls.

"Yes, woman, you turn me into an animal. Starved for your attention. Knowing your pussy is soaking wet because of me, because of how marvelous of a listener you are. I've never felt more deserving of your spell on me than I do now."

"Are you—are you almost—?"

"So close," I promise. Closer than she realizes. Not just the inevitable release fighting its way out of my body. Not the short distance between my bed and hers. But in a deeper way, a way that's been humming in my veins since I saw her for the first time in seventeen years.

How terribly it made me want to throw myself back at her doorway. Show her the ugliest parts of me, learn the ugliest parts of her. Memorize the moments I've missed. Turn her into my vice, a need I can't break from.

"Keep doing that." I keep us both present. "Keep fucking that pussy with your vibrator for me. Fuck. Remember how good it felt to have me inside of you?"

"Exceptional."

"My cock's so fucking hard, like it was then," I say with more force than I intend. "I want to give you all of it, give you every last drop I have."

"*Please.*"

Oh, dammit. There's no way I can last a second longer.

"Come with me," I demand. A pleasurable pain ripples in my balls. "Come right now."

As if on cue, the sound of her orgasm pierces through my speaker, followed by my own. We're moans and groans for what feels like hours, until only our shallow breathing remains.

I want to reach through my phone and over to her. Stroke her face. Feel the heat coming off her body.

"Meadow," I whisper.

"Come over," she says, and the call ends.

## Chapter 23
# Ollie

ON MEADOW'S KITCHEN ISLAND, EMPTY TUMBLERS SIT BESIDE stoneware plates. There's a bottle of her Fox Den whisky between us. For the past hour, we've been flirting, drinking, and eating. Meadow cooked while I cleaned. Our first official Monday night date. Or, as she insisted on calling it, a night of *fun*.

To me, it's a date. But I reached a certain age and realized you need to pick your battles.

"Just how I remember it." My last bite of her walnut-crusted lamb leg practically melts in my mouth. Memories of my eighteenth birthday dance on my tongue. "It never fails to shock me how wonderful you are at this."

"Are you sure you like it? Something about the nuts wasn't sitting right with me. Maybe I should've tried hazelnuts." She sighs, rubbing the crease out of her forehead and adjusting the apron around her neck. "Definitely would've complemented the chard better."

"I wouldn't have had two helpings if I didn't like it," I assure her. "I also really like a woman in uniform."

"Uniform?"

"Your chef's apron is doing it for me. Like my shorts do it for you."

She sighs. "You're such a flirt. I'm being serious. I need this dish to be perfect. I've lost count of how many recipes have already ended up in the trash with nothing to show for it. Three dishes are my responsibility, and I'm butchering each one."

I frown. "Why does it need to be perfect?" She shoots me a look. "No, of course I understand why you want this to come out right, but I don't remember you wanting things to go perfectly all the time."

She shrinks, and I hate that I even brought it up, but she used to feel so much freedom in this exact kitchen—her one domain. When things were good, Meadow would try new recipes. When things were bad, she'd fill the house with smoke and try again. It was only when Meadow couldn't cook, didn't have the opportunity to fail with ease, that everything around her started to crumble.

I still remember the mess her room would turn into when she'd fight with her parents about culinary school. Just like her house did right after Fox Den opened.

"When I came back to Thistlehill, my freedom to make mistakes didn't come with me. I had to be responsible and serious; I didn't want to fail at that."

I want to pry more, understand what happened that day she didn't come with me to Boston, ask her why she never told me that she'd applied to Le Cordon Bleu, but I don't.

"Remember those lobster rolls you made when we were younger? Think you spent the first week of summer break in the kitchen, trying to perfect your mayonnaise dressing."

"*Aioli*," she laughs.

"Aye, chef, and when you got it right, we begged you to make them all summer."

She taps her fingers on the island. "True. It's easy to forget how much trial and error cooking can be. Under Colette, I strived for perfection and spent the rest of my energy on inventing new recipes when my shift was done. But once I started at Ramona's, I went into autopilot—a chef's biggest mistake."

"But the freedom to make mistakes is why you fell in love with cooking in the first place, isn't it? Our fun and adventures could help you reconnect with that forgotten part of yourself." Her blue eyes twinkle, like they used to when an idea would start to brew. "What's going on in that head of yours?"

She leans forward across the island. "Not a bad idea. Colette wants to see me on a plate, and there was nothing more *me* than when we were younger. My mom missed the lobster rolls from Boston; we used to get them on weekends as a family. I wanted to replicate the memory through food, even if I had to fail a bunch to get it right."

"The way you're making me relive my eighteenth birthday with this lamb." I tap my fork against my empty plate.

"I wanted to impress you that day," she admits. "It was the first time we got to play house."

Our parents went to a whisky conference in Edinburgh and left us alone for the night. Ma was endlessly apologetic for missing my eighteenth, but I couldn't get her out of the house fast enough. We wanted to see what it would be like when we left Thistlehill.

She made me a lamb leg roast, nearly burning down the house in the process, and I dug through the charred crust to the tender meat near the bone. We snuggled up on the couch, watching *Beck* reruns, until our eyes were on each other, her lips on mine.

"You still impress me, doe. Much like this lamb does."

She sits down on the counter stool beside me, tucking her shoulder-length hair behind her ears. Her low-cut jumper shifts, revealing an inch more of skin. "That's the tasting menu. Each dish can have a core memory attached to it."

"Brilliant." I smile, ignoring the small prick of something unsettling in my chest.

"Thank you, Ol, for helping me figure this whole thing out. And for making me laugh. This was fun." Her thumb rubs across the rough skin on my palms that wasn't there when I arrived in Scotland. "These pretty hands of yours are toughening up."

Construction on the bottling facility hasn't hit any snags. Our roof went up without an issue. The electrician comes tomorrow. Everything is as it should be.

The discomfort beneath my rib cage tightens. Ignoring the unnerved feeling, I take Meadow's hand in mine and trace the marks. There's a raw, bright red one that runs down her index finger.

"How'd you get this one?" I ask.

"I accidentally peeled my hand instead of a carrot."

"*No way*. Ouch."

"I had to bandage my hand, throw out the entire blood-covered vat of carrots, and start peeling again. It still hurts sometimes when I'm out in the cold for too long."

"Here, let me help." I knead her joints with my thumbs. Her eyes flutter closed.

"That feels so nice." I move down to her palm, carefully massaging the skin until I reach her wrist. "Ugh, you're spoiling me."

"That's a bad thing?" I repeat the tender grazes on her other hand.

"I'm not used to someone taking care of me." She pauses. "But I also don't go skinny-dipping, get fingered in a golf cart, or have phone sex. My plan to be a little more reckless is working."

"If you'd like, I can go get my rugby shorts from next door and we can drive over to the pitch," I tease and work my way up her arm, stroking my fingers over her forearm and strong bicep.

"Will you bring the whistle?" Her gaze is playful, but I can tell that she'd want the little fantasy to come to life.

"If you ask really nicely."

"Should I keep my apron on?" She tugs at the strings around her waist.

"Don't tease me, doe. If I had my way, that'd be the only thing you had on." I trail my free hand along the cotton fabric of the apron near her nape, imagining how good her skin would feel.

"And what would you do if it was?"

The flirtatious song in her voice sends a spell of heat below my belt. "Pay my compliments to the chef."

"Time to prove you're not all talk," she winks and darts for the stairs. "Stay here; I'll be right back."

"Where are you going?"

"Behave, Oliver. I need to fetch dessert."

"Aye, chef."

Meadow slinks out of my grasp and tiptoes upstairs. While she's gone, I clean the rest of the kitchen, washing her plate and then my own. In the rack, Maisie's Thistlehill Tacklers glass has a small stain at the bottom of it. I pull it beneath the hot stream and give it another wash. *Spick-and-span.*

"Alright, I hope you're hungry." Meadow's voice comes from behind me.

When I turn, my eyes bulge out of my head. Surely my tongue is hanging out of my mouth, like one of those cartoon dogs. She stands in the kitchen wearing an apron and nothing else. Not a damn thing.

"Is this for me?" I take her in. "Forget about dessert—you're the whole damn meal."

The tie around her neck. Those round curves bursting out of the neckline. The small hint of her bare ass as she shimmies around in place, shyly pressing her knees and feet together. And those legs. *Christ.*

"A little something fun. You like it? No one's ever seen me naked under one of these before."

"I'm glad I'm your first." I don't test my resistance any longer and walk toward her. I put one hand in her hair, the other around her waist. She kisses me for the first time tonight, and she's anything but soft about it. There's no tenderness translating from her tongue to mine; it's as if she's staking a claim on me. I do the same in return.

I squeeze her bare ass, digging my fingers into her flesh and scooting her closer to me.

"Is this little apron really as good as my dress the other night?"

"Better. So much fucking better," I whisper against her teeth. "Especially since you wore it just for me."

"The dress was for you too."

"I knew it."

She rolls her eyes, and I connect her lips with mine. My fingers slide up to her neck. The bulge in my jeans grinds into her.

We swallow and relish in the taste of us.

I need her. More of her. So much fucking more. Meadow is heaven in my hands. I'm sky-bound with her. I find the tie at the back of her waist and yank it loose. "I'm desperate for you."

She glides her tongue against mine and sinks a canine into the corner of my lip. *Zero mercy.* "How desperate?"

I let out a sardonic laugh, savoring the burn she imprinted into my skin. "Fucking besotted."

Her hands ripple over the muscles in my arms, down to the waist of my jeans. Every touch ignites me. I tug, pinch, choke, and squeeze every inch of her skin.

Anything to get her to empty a groan into my throat.

Once she gets my belt buckle loose, Meadow slips the leather off my waist.

"You're a fucking dream, doe." I shake my head in disbelief, caressing her full breasts and delicious ass. There'll never be enough of her for me to handle. "*Un-fucking-believable.*"

"You going to keep tossing around compliments or..."

"Toss you around?"

Her brow curves in defiance, but the smirk on her lips tells me just how much she wants that exact thing to happen. I pull the belt from her hand, and her pupils dilate.

"What are you doing with that?" she sings with curiosity.

"Nothing just yet." I let out a hearty laugh. My cock aches at the curious look on her face. "But I'll keep that intrigued reaction in mind for another time."

"Oh, hush." She rolls her eyes.

That I can do. "How badly do you want me to be quiet? To stop telling you how out of my mind you make me?"

"So badly." She digs her fingers into my chest. "I hate that smart fucking mouth of yours."

"Then we're gonna need to keep it occupied now, aren't we?" I wrap an arm around her and spin her around, pushing her hips and waist against her kitchen island. "Can you do that, doe? Can you keep my tongue from running off about you?"

Meadow groans as I bend her over the marble countertop. I take in the gorgeous, deep dimples and creases in her thighs. Her voluptuous, full curves. My cock almost claws at my zipper. *Patience.*

"You knew how much fun your little presentation here would be for us, didn't you?"

"We are having fun, aren't we?"

The comment sparks a challenge in me to break down the little boundary she's putting between us. But there's no point. This *is* fun. Meadow wants to have fun, and that's something I can do for her. Keep my promise. "Did you know how much it was going to make me want to reward you?"

"Yes." She nods her head.

This woman makes me feral with a simple yes. My fingers

slide down to the warmth between her thighs, eager for the wetness awaiting me.

"I'm going to work this pretty cunt until all you can feel is my tongue thrusting in and out of it, Meadow." I lasciviously trace my fingertips over the backs of her thighs. My other hand remains on the soft curve of her arse. She arches her spine, legs trembling as she spreads her feet wider. "Gonna show you how thankful I am for the meal you made me."

"You better," she grits through her teeth, chasing after my caresses.

I stop my teasing strokes, sling my arm across her waist, and turn her toward me.

Her gaze is drunk with desire. Mine must be too, because she gives me that smile. The one that says this night will end with both of us losing our minds for each other.

I yank loose the tie on the back of her apron. It falls to the ground. Her gorgeous skin glows in the dim light of the kitchen. Perfect tits, so round and full, press into me. Her full figure is plump to the touch. The tall, strong girl I knew is all fucking woman, and I can't get over it.

All woman, and in my possession.

"Meadow, I gotta admit, I haven't stopped thinking about these curves since we were upstairs in your bedroom. Since my fingers stroked between your legs on Saturday night. Honestly, I haven't once been able to stop thinking about how delectable you are."

"You picked up a lot of ass-kissing in the States," she teases.

"Aye, wait until you see what I have in store for you." I bend at the knees and lower myself, ready to hike her up on the counter.

"I—" Her voice is suddenly panicked as she tries to scoot back. "Ol, I—I can do it."

I glance up at her. That girlish shyness all over her face. No, that won't do. My woman doesn't feel timid when she's in my arms. "What did you just say?"

"It's just—you don't have to lift me up, I can—" She looks uneasy, still trying to wrestle out of my grasp. *Absolutely not.*

"Shut the fuck up, chef." I hike her up onto the island and kiss away the utter shock on her face. "I'm trying to pay my compliments here."

My lips work a path down her neck, over her breasts. I lap my tongue over every nook on her skin until I settle on my knees before her.

I look up at her. A goddess with perfect thighs spread out before me.

"I don't think you understand how fucking lucky I am."

Her pink cheeks deepen into that familiar deep purple color. "Honestly, you look good down there, all on your knees again—"

"And ready to please?"

"Finishing all my sentences today, aren't you?"

I shrug a shoulder at her. "It's easy when I know you like the back of my own hand."

"Sounds like it may be your turn to shut the fuck up." She laughs, and without hesitating, takes her hand behind my head and drags me to the heat between her legs. The sweet smell of her intoxicates me. *A drug.*

"I'm going to make you come, doe. Fast and fucking hard. Then I'm going to do it again, and again, until it feels like you drank a cask full of my whisky."

"Don't make promises you can't keep." Her lips curl into a devilish grin.

I clasp my teeth over the hood of her clit, gently tugging at the skin. Meadow's wails reverberate through the house. I release my bite and suck her clit hard.

"Fuck, Ollie." She yanks at my strands, pulling my head

back and revealing a blissfully beseeched look on her face. "What the fuck was that? You bit me."

"I did," I smile. "Want me to do it again?"

The veins in her forearm flex. Strong and beautiful. Those gorgeous hands clasp onto me so hard, I'll have no fucking hair left by the time she's done with me.

I trail my fingers over her thigh, down to her needy cunt, and slip a finger into her hot entrance. Meadow's mouth drops open as she parts her thighs even more.

"Mmm," she moans when I add in a second finger. Her gaze is stuck to me as I breathe on her clit.

"You always did like watching me eat. Now keep your eyes on me as I feast on you." She does as I command. "Good girl."

I make no effort to be gentle. I made a promise, and I'm intent on keeping it. My tongue laps against her clit, my fingers working in and out of her at a steady pace. The salty taste of her cunt mixed with the meal she made me still clinging to the back of my throat is perfect.

Meadow struggles above me, tossing her legs around as if she has nowhere to put them. I grasp her thigh, toss it over my shoulder, and angle myself in a way that lets her ass come closer to the edge.

She tenses up.

"Relax," I growl. "I got you, doe. Let me have you."

This time, she doesn't put up an argument full of useless concerns. *Smart.*

My pulse increases, keeping up with the pace inside her cunt as my tongue glides over her clit in steady circles. Her pussy soaks my beard. I devour her like she deserves. My balls ache, desperate to get free. I latch on to her, letting my breath go slow, and focus on the way her gasps turn heavy, keeping a steady rhythm.

"Let go, sweetheart. I'm right here." Her walls tighten around my fingers. The same way they did in that Tipsy Taxi. I deepen my thrusts inside of her, finding that spot with ease again.

I work her pussy like my life depends on it. *Fuck.* If I die right here, I'd be the happiest man alive.

As another wave of warmth slips out onto my palm, she lets go. An unhinged wail pierces my ears, and I relish in her legs crushing my skull as she rides out her orgasm. When her convulsions finally stop, my cheeks ache from smiling so big.

"That the kind of fun you had in mind?" I pull my head out of the embrace of her thighs and hike her back up onto the counter.

She leans back on her forearms on the kitchen island. Hair a beautiful mess. Pink cheeks against her pale skin. The valleys of curves across her body. *Ethereal.*

"That's definitely the kind of spoiling I was talking about before," she laughs while I walk into the laundry room and grab a towel to clean her up. I run it under some warm water, turn the tap cold, and fill up a glass for her before returning myself between her thighs and taking care of the mess I made.

Meadow downs the water. "Thank you."

"We're not done yet." I pick her up, and she squeals.

"Where are you taking me?"

"So many questions." I carry her to the living room and gently place her onto the couch in front of the fire. I grab the throw and cover her before stripping down to my underwear and sitting on the floor beside her. "Comfortable?"

"This really is like your eighteenth birthday now," she laughs and rests her cool cheek on my shoulder.

"Hopefully I've improved a ton since then," I tease.

"Plenty, but you always knew how to get me *there.* How to take your time. I never realized how much I was going to miss that."

The ache returns to my chest, sagging down on my heart. I'm going to miss this when I leave in June. Our temporary little life together. I force the thoughts from my mind. "Now you're just flattering me."

She climbs up onto her arms, wraps the blanket around her body, and slinks onto the rug beside me. "I'm serious, Ol. I forgot what sex should feel like. Thank you for reminding me."

*I want to remind you daily.*

But I can't, can I?

Would our life look like tonight if I don't go back to New York? If I give up the job? The logs crackle at our feet, sparks twirling in the fireplace.

"Never thank me for something like that, Meadow. We taught each other." Unlocked a piece that I had buried and avoided. "On my birthday, all those years ago, we spent the entire time in front of this fire, remember? My lips were so sore from kissing you that I was sure they were going to fall off."

"Your scruff made my mouth feel the same way. Now, all this bushy beard…" She reaches for my jaw and strokes the hair there. "It's all nice and soft."

"I started using beard oil. Learned a thing or two about keeping all of this in good condition."

"Manscaping, huh?" She chuckles.

"Just want to be nice for you."

"You were nice then also." She stares at the crackling wood. "Those were the easy days."

I chew on the corner of my lip. There's so much about Meadow I don't know, years I've missed. Whatever this is between us can be a restoration of the past, or it can be cultivated into something new, better.

A relationship that could transcend what we were when we were young. That starts with both of us attempting vulnerability, however much it makes my muscles twist beneath my skin. However much I am afraid of what it might mean to get closer—will it feel like closure or the beginning of the end?

"I want to know about the hard days too. If you don't mind

sharing with me. What happened when you decided to take care of Maisie?" I ask in a quiet voice as I put my arm around her, scooting her closer to me.

"Those years feel like such a blur. I was only twenty-seven; I still felt like a child myself."

Each memory she gives me is a gift.

"I can't imagine it."

"No. I wouldn't wish it on anyone, not even in their imagination." Her foot taps against mine, and I rub the knot in her right shoulder. "I never talk about this. But I was Fox's emergency contact, after Penelope, and the hospital must've called me at around two or three in the morning as I was finishing my shift. I knew they were coming to visit my parents from Edinburgh. Maisie had finally gotten over a cold, so it felt like the right time to make the drive to Thistlehill." Her voice chokes up, and I rub her shoulder.

"It's horrible that we were both at work when we found out the news."

She shrugs. "That's all I did in my twenties." Me too. "Anyway, the snow was thick, and a drunk driver came out of nowhere, taking Fox and Penelope with them on impact. Maisie was strapped into her car seat. A seatbelt saved her, but not her parents. I was the one who had to call my mom and dad and let them know." A tear rolls down her cheek, and it breaks me up inside. "Dad wailed. Mom was inconsolable. I barely remember what happened after that. Brooke helped me pack. I told Colette I was quitting d'Or. At the time, it felt like an easy decision."

"It couldn't have been though—I mean, to give up your whole life just like that?"

"Sometimes, you don't have a choice. I did, however, have a chance at something else. I had an opportunity to step up and be the person Fox would've been if it were me who'd died in that accident. Penelope didn't have any family, so custody of Maisie was left to me or my parents. But their will said that I was the first pick."

A small tremor goes through her body, and I run my palms over her arms. "I'm so sorry."

"I think I just realized that I still had a family who loved me, whatever our differences were. Even if I was not quite as impressive as I may have dreamt of being. Even if my parents didn't pay for culinary school. The day of his funeral, my parents were so hollow, I was concerned that when they lowered his casket they were going to jump in after him. I almost did. I can still feel the dirt in my palm, how mealy and cruddy it felt. But Maisie was on my hip, oblivious to what was going on as we put both of her parents in the ground. I think that's what kept me from collapsing, just the weight of her."

"I should've been there." An abrupt feebleness enters my limbs as she fights through every word she says.

"I catered his funeral, you know?" She lets out a devastated laugh. "I thought if I stood still for even a second, if I wasn't useful, I'd simply fall apart. *That* wasn't an option at all."

"You would've had every right to fall apart, doe."

She shrugs but doesn't pull away from me. "I couldn't. I had to deal with all of the logistics. My parents couldn't pack up this house or even touch Fox's room. I took care of all of that. His room is still sitting empty." She inhales sharply. "In France, I was saving up for my own restaurant. But I used the money to buy this house from my parents." She looks at the brass light fixtures above us, then the same hardwood floors that have always been in this house. "I swore Maisie would have a good life, one that would measure up to even a fraction of what Fox and Penelope would've given her."

My heart aches to join hers in her chest. To take the weight of what the world has given her off of her shoulders, even a little bit. I want to understand more. Gather up more pieces of her in my hands and hold her as if she were water. "What was becoming a parent like?"

Meadow's bright smile splits her face, illuminated by the fire. "It's the most extreme measure of being alive. Maisie's given me so many days. Ones where I feel like I've become a goddess, where the success of my career barely holds a candle, where the mere having her, being with her, seeing her happy is more rewarding than anything I'd ever experience. Then there are days where I cry as loud as she does, where I wish I could just hit pause and leave the life I chose." She glances at me, worry in her eyes. "I know that's a terrible thing to say, but it's true. Maisie's given me every emotion a person can experience, and she stretched and twisted them, pushed them past limits, but I'd still choose her a million times over."

I'd always let myself keep a small fantasy in the back of my mind, an amateur sketch of a life I planned to have with Meadow. After years of being buried and creased, the image unfolds in my thoughts.

The piercing wail of a child. The first time they'd cry in my arms. Meadow, exhausted and powerful, watching us. My family. The life we would've had in America if we'd made it there together. The one we would've come back to here.

The picture flashes in my mind, and I let myself indulge a moment longer. Maisie as an older sister. Floaties at the loch. Diaper changes. Sleepless nights with Meadow in bed beside me.

I drop the weaving thread of something that isn't real from my mind. Sagging back against the couch, I struggle to force some life back into my lungs. *I'm leaving*, I remind myself. That life is still just a dream.

"Sounds life-altering."

"She makes it easy," Meadow says lightly, clearly sensing that I've run off for a moment in my own mind. "Maisie's probably the smartest, most independent, and kindest seven-year-old ever."

"Much like her ma." I smile.

Meadow wrinkles her nose, sliding her head onto my pec.

"What about you?" She looks up, and her eyes scan my own. "Have you ever wanted kids? I'm sure you had plenty of opportunities in the States. Especially with a face like that."

A corner of my lips lifts. "What exactly does my face look like? I'm going to need you to be specific. Paint me the full picture."

"Covered in me, it looks pretty good." Meadow's cheeks redden, and she strokes my beard again. "Now, answer the damn question, Anderson."

That adorable glare she does when she's pretending to be upset blooms over her face. Waggled brows and lips fixed in a quivering, disappointed line. It's so fucking perfect.

"Of course I've thought about it, the way any thirty-something man thinks about it, in a distant part of his life. I was a bachelor along with my best friends in New York. Then Mattie went and got married. Bobbie has some online girlfriend. It was easy being single when there was a group of us, and then it was suddenly just me."

"I get that. Brooke and Fi are a long way from motherhood, but that's never stopped them from being a part of my life."

"And it shouldn't. I think I mentioned a few friends of mine before, Avery and Luca—you'd love them. Workaholics just like you," I tease, and she rolls her eyes. "They had a little girl not too long ago. I love that kid. But, for me, it just seemed too far in the future to be real. And, to be honest, I couldn't picture being a parent with anyone I met." Except Meadow.

At nineteen, I wanted her to be my wife, to carry our children. I wanted to give her a future that would make her happy.

"Try and look closer for a bit." Those beautiful doe eyes stare up at me. "Apart from that dream job in New York, is a family in the future for you? I'm sure you've had daydreams, like any other thirty-something man," she teases.

Can I tell her that it's her? That she's in the distance, waiting for me, with Maisie standing right by her side? No. Not when it's just a fantasy. However real it feels.

"As a kid, I always liked it when there were three of us," I hedge. "You, me, and Fox."

"Three's a good number." She smiles.

It is. "What about you? Do you want more kids?"

Her hand runs through my chest hair. "It's not that simple."

"Why not?"

"I'm thirty-four, which makes me high risk. But on top of that, I have fibroids. So even if I find myself with someone I can tolerate, let alone spend my life with, I don't know if I can have kids."

My lips purse together as something latches in the back of my throat. Uneasiness? Sadness?

Helplessness.

"Fibroids?" I ask for clarification.

"They're in my uterus. It's one of the reasons I have heavy periods, which are made way worse by my PMDD. They're not a cause for infertility, but my gyno always told me that it may be hard to conceive. I take birth control to help with the hormone imbalance, but it doesn't do much."

That explains a lot. Meadow had always had bleeds that seemed different than any of the ladies we grew up with. Hers would leave her on her back, unable to move for days at a time.

"You mentioned the PMDD before. I looked it up online, but there aren't that many articles about it."

She sits up, looking at me. "Premenstrual dysphoric disorder. There's no treatment, just a fun cocktail of chaos that I have to deal with." She attempts a joke, but I can tell it bothers her. "All of that is to say, I've never tried getting pregnant, but I'm not holding my breath."

A few years back, I panic tested myself after Matthew shared that he was infertile. I figured it was better to know than be surprised, but my tests came back normal. I never thought it would matter.

But even if Meadow can't have kids, she and Maisie are enough.

*Fuck.* What is in my head tonight?

"How does that make you feel?" I try to distract myself.

After a long pause, she says, "I don't know. I love Maisie. She's my girl. I guess if the right person came along, maybe I'd want to try? I haven't thought about having kids with anyone since we were together." Shadows dance across her face. "When we were younger, I mean. Remember how Fox had those elaborate ideas of what we'd be like as adults?"

"Aye, I do. He was always a hopeless romantic."

The first dance we attended at fourteen, he made me stay up late into the wee hours of the morning, practicing the appropriate amount of swaying. Apparently, I was a terrible dancing partner, but I was a head taller than him, which I'm sure didn't help.

"Nothing like us."

"I miss him."

"Me too," I admit.

Meadow's words brim along the memories smoking up my heart. *The past is a lesson, not a home.* Remembering Fox, the before, is nice, but if I open the gates to those memories, I may fall apart.

So I do what I do best when I spend too long considering a future with her in it.

Deflect.

"What do you have going on this week?"

Meadow doesn't seem to mind the change of subject. "I'm busy tomorrow."

"Don't you have two more full days off?" I'm going to need

to give Brooke and Fi a standing ovation for managing to encourage her to take more time off.

"I do, but I also have that list of chores, remember? And I have Maisie's practice." She lifts a brow at me. "That reminds me, whose decision was it to make all the Thursday practices at three now? I'm not complaining, because I can finally come see the little plum play, but I can't imagine the rest of the parents were happy."

I play it cool. "A club decision. You know how rugby is," I say, leaving out how I spent the week dishing out bribes, making incessant phone calls to the other parents. The act was purely selfish, because the more practices Meadow attends, the more I get to see her. "The council is only good for one thing: the micro shorts."

Meadow bites her lip. The embers from earlier still flicker in her eyes. She checks her watch. "Our night isn't over for another twenty minutes."

I kiss each of her knuckles before saying, "Then I better make every second count."

# Chapter 24
# Ollie

"Blasted machines," Callum curses as he stands in front of the main digital control panel, his brow furrowed and eyes narrowed. I've been trying—more like failing miserably—to teach him how to use the new bottling equipment since early this morning. Elspeth picked it up an hour ago and now stands at the end of the capping conveyor belt, dipping the freshly filled bottles of Red Label into green wax.

At this rate, the first shipment for On Cloud Nine will be ready by tonight. I'll call the delivery truck this afternoon to double-check they'll be here Monday.

"Callum, why don't we give it a break for today and try again tomorrow?"

"No, ye'll not replace me with this clattering beast." The unfamiliar buttons and screens seem to intimidate him, and he repeatedly presses the wrong ones. With each failed attempt, he becomes more exasperated, his face turning red with agitation. The sanitizing machine screeches loudly, the steam turning the warehouse into a sauna. "Far too bloody loud in here," he groans. "I'm leaving. I don't need this, lad. Ye've barged into this place and stripped it of its integrity and tradition."

"This place? That's my name above the door, Callum." My temper rises, but I keep my voice steady. "This new facility is good for everyone. I guarantee it."

"Do ye, aye?" Sarcasm slaps his bushy brows higher up on his face. "I need to check the stills." He abandons the spot beside me, yanks his jacket off the metal railing, and storms out of the warehouse.

I close my eyes for a moment. It's fine. He'll come around. I hope. When I open them, I find Elspeth staring at me with a sympathetic expression.

"I'm sorry I lost my patience with him, and I'm sorry you had to see it," I say over the grumbling machinery. This thing is excessively loud, but it'll only run once a week. That's gotta be a suitable enough compromise.

"Pa just doesn't like change." Elspeth shrugs and fumbles with the sleeve of her tattered Grace Academy sweatshirt. The same one I have hanging in a closet at the house. "He's got a good heart. To be honest, I reckon he's mourning the fact that we won't be sharin' our Sundays slappin' on labels together."

I'm a damn bawbag, just like Meadow said. Of course Callum wasn't just upset about me coming here and making changes—I'm disrupting something in his routine. A piece of his life that he clearly values. Why couldn't he just tell me that?

"With the free time these machines will give you both, you can do other things together," I offer as a terrible suggestion.

"The distillery's all Pa's got, but I'll talk to him," she assures me. "I like the new contraptions, by the way. I've had more time to play bass and...spend time with a lady."

"Thank you, El." I smile. "You were amazing last weekend, by the way. Next time your band plays, I'll be sure to come and support."

She spins the frayed edge of her blonde hair around her finger. "Appreciate that. I don't want to say anything out of line, but it's obvious that coming back here was a lot for you. You know, being from the big city and all."

"I was from here once," I remind her, and myself. "But it was hard back then too. My da never cared for my ideas for the distillery. So, I just decided to focus all my energy on getting out of here."

"But your ideas are actually good for this place." She smiles.

"At least you think so."

"Pa will too—yours and mine. They're just stubborn fellas. My pa didn't have an easy time with the fact that I wanted to play bass in a rock band."

"How did you get him to come around?"

"I was happy," she admits. "I think after enough time passed, he saw that I wasn't going to give it up, and, well, he gave in."

Is that how Da's going to feel about these machines? "I don't have that much time."

Elspeth frowns, clearly understanding the delicacy of this subject. "Aye. Look, Ol, I don't know anything about how your life was in the States, or how you and your da were at the distillery when you were a boy, but you seem content here."

"Thistlehill isn't so bad."

"Even if it were," she laughs and nudges me, "you wouldn't be putting in this work if you didn't care about the distillery. You could've easily sat back and let Neil and his crew do all the work, but you jumped in. You built this place." She looks around our new bottling facility. "You chose to leave a mark here. That must mean some part of you loves this place."

*I do.* The answer comes before I can even process it. The distillery does mean a lot to me, because she's right—I am leaving a mark of my own here. "You're wise, kid."

"I'm just calling it how I see it. Now I got to get back to work; we have orders to ship out, aye?"

"That's right."

I check the flashing green light on the control panel. Everything's going smoothly. This is good. I push away the nerves in my chest and go to join Elspeth by the wax, but a buzzing comes from my pocket—Da.

I exit the loud facility and rush down the path headed toward the loch. Sunlight filters through the tranquil mountains and the dense canopy of trees. The scent of fresh dew is in the air as small flowers sprout along the path. It sure is beautiful out here.

"Hi, Da, I've been trying to get ahold of you for days." I keep a steady pace down the trail. "How's your trip? How was the Cyprus stop?"

"What's goin' on over there? I've had an earful from Callum about how ye're ruining the place." Anger piques his voice and blasts it through the receiver.

This is low. To not see eye to eye with me is one thing, but to go blabbering to my da is crossing a line. Couldn't we have talked about this together?

"We're using the new bottling facility for the first time today. Those On Cloud Nine shipments are going out on schedule," I reply calmly.

"Then why's Callum saying ye're tryin' tae give him the boot?"

"I'm not firing him; I would never do that. He snapped when I tried to train him on the new machine. It's not my fault he doesn't care about the betterment of this distillery." The edge in my voice slips through all the control I could muster.

Is Da really siding with Callum against his own son?

"If he cannae figure out how to use it, do ye think I can manage? Ye're gonna leave, and then naebody's gettin' their shipments. Ye should've just fixed up the ol' one."

Ah, finally, we've gotten to the bottom of the reason for his call. My insides twist and knot as the familiar feeling of his doubt snakes its way into my body. The expectations I'm not meeting. The ones I've set for myself that he won't even try to understand. Much like Callum won't try to understand the new machine.

"The old one was wasting us nearly a quarter of each cask. I sent you the specs on this new—"

"It's always new, new, new with ye. Money fixes everything in your eyes," he snaps, and in the background I hear my ma's voice. Frustration cuts down the guilt that's boiling my blood. I kick a rock on the stone path, then another, and another, until my chest settles. "Nay, Ri, we're goin' home. I made a mistake leavin' our boy in charge."

Absolutely not. "Do not come home. I have everything handled."

"Callum and Elspeth are family; they aren't some employees ye can trot over with yer Grenson boots."

Wow. They're all in the mood for some low digs today. "I'm your family too," I remind him. "Doesn't that matter? Can't you trust me?" The phone line crackles. "Hello? Da?"

His voice returns full force. "Ye're leavin' me with more trouble than when ye started."

"No, I'm setting you up for your future retirement."

"No one asked ye tae do that."

His words hurt. I'm only trying to help, but it seems I steamrolled my way back home like some guilt-driven Prince Charming. Meadow said that when I arrived.

"Da, we have a good whisky here. Even if it isn't about the money, more people will get to enjoy what our family has worked on for generations."

My boots stain the ground with their tracks. He's never going to understand where I'm coming from. Doesn't matter. This nonsense won't stop me from making amends for all the years I've been gone. Even if Da can't get on board. The updates I've made will serve Anderson Distillery for centuries—they're good for Da and for my damn distillery too. Callum's just another project I have to manage. There has to be something else making him tick, outside of what Elspeth shared about me shaking up his normal.

"I'm going to fix things with Callum," I promise. "He hasn't been shy about how unhappy he is to have me here, not for a damn minute."

The line crackles again. "In the nursing home in London." His voice comes in gravelly.

"What? I can't hear you."

"Callum's sister—she's sick." *He has a sister?* The receiver screeches again. "Hard time already taking care of her—with the bit of wages we have at the distillery. Do not make it any harder on them."

A lightbulb flicks on in my head. Callum's afraid of being replaced by the machines because his money's tied up with helping his sister. That's fixable. We'll have more revenue once we get the second payment from On Cloud Nine next month. A promotion could be what fixes this whole thing.

Money softened me when I had to deal with the grueling bosses at Silverman Sachs. Maybe it'll help with Callum too.

"I'll make amends and train him. I'll sort this out, Da. I will."

"If ye don't, I'm on the next flight out of here."

*Click.* The line goes silent.

The entire exchange is an example of why moving back to Thistlehill could never be in the cards for me. It isn't. The money I'll be making at Viggle means too much anyway. But if something—or someone—were to ever keep me here, it wouldn't be my da. There's been too much distrust built up over the years, clogging up our already distant relationship.

When my annoyance finally settles, I realize I've walked all the way down to the stony shore of the loch.

Soft leaves rustle in the air. The gentle sunlight sparkles along the loch, making it look like a milky way. The surrounding hills hold it all together, and I gaze up at them. Their sheer magnitude makes me feel infinitesimal.

A small speck. A minuscule part of something larger.

My chest expands with another hefty inhale. Sweetness and the fermentation from the distillery strike my senses. The fight with Callum and the phone call with my da is trivial in comparison to the feeling of standing here.

A good reminder that this will all have a conclusion, and a good one if I don't run from it. My hands flex. There was only ever one person I'd want to talk to after a fight with my parents. I glance down at my phone again and find her name.

> **OLLIE**
> Are you in for another late one tonight?
> Can we talk after your shift?

> **DOE**
> done at midnight
> r u ok?

> **OLLIE**
> Could use a friend

> **DOE**
> ill b there

---

DOWN THE ROAD, Meadow's car comes bobbing toward me before turning into her driveway.

For the past hour, I've sat on my porch, waiting for her to be near me again. It's only been a month, but it's like we were never apart.

I stand, swiping the shards of wood from my newest project from my lap, and walk the forty-seven steps over to her house.

"Hey," she whispers, quietly ducking out of her car and nodding to the back seat. Maisie is strapped into her car seat, head lolled to the side and mouth wide open as she sleeps.

Adorable. "I gotta get her in bed, then I'll meet you on the porch?"

Moonlight dances over her skin. Her hair is in a messy bun atop her head. She looks exhausted. How could she not be? She's been on her feet for the past eight hours.

"Can I help?" I pocket my small knife and wood carving and reach for the car door handle. Instead of protesting, she nods. I pull the kiddo out of the back, handling her with extra care, and follow Meadow inside.

Maisie's soft breath brushes against my shirt. Her body weighs barely more than a feather as I carry her through the house to Meadow's old room. She's so much smaller than I realized. On the pitch, Maisie's some kind of Viking incarnate, throwing elbows and knees at kids without care. But her small head leaning against my arm makes me understand why Meadow always calls her plum.

"Set her down here," Meadow whispers and pulls back the *Frozen*-themed duvet on the small pink bed.

Instinctively, I give Maisie a small squeeze and set her down. Meadow places a kiss on her forehead and pulls the blankets over her before ushering me out of the room and closing the door behind her.

We walk back outside and sit down on the porch swing. "She's so small."

"And yet, somehow, she's getting bigger by the day." Meadow smiles. For the first time, it truly hits me—I won't get to see Maisie grow up. I won't get to help carry her out of the car as she sprouts a few more inches. Can't bandage up scraped skin in New York. "Thanks for doing that."

I swallow the unease in my throat, take out my carving, and fidget with the wood. "You know, I could watch her sometime. So you wouldn't have to pick her up from your parents' house after work."

Her eyes dart toward the front yard, and she scans the darkness as if looking for something. "I don't know. She won't stop talking about her rugby practices already. I'm trying to keep you, and this, at a safe distance from her."

"Right, of course." The glimmer of hope wilts in my chest like grocery store roses. Meadow's only protecting her daughter from the downfall of our time together. But, selfishly, I want to spend more time with her. With both of them.

"What happened today?"

"Da blew his lid at me. Thanks to Callum, he thinks I'm firing his two employees and running the distillery into the ground." After Elspeth and I finalized the first of many shipments for On Cloud Nine, I searched the entire property for Callum so I could mend the bad blood between us. I looked for over an hour, but he was nowhere to be found.

Come Monday, we'll get to have our talk, and I'll fix things.

"That can't be possible. You're only trying to modernize things; it's not like you're changing the distilling process. But what do I know? I was too afraid to get inventive with my menu because of what everyone in Thistlehill would think of it."

How could a town that helped us come up with such big ideas be so limiting now?

"Nothing's changed from when I was here as a kid. If Da can't understand it, he'd rather stick with what he knows. Callum's the same. Even if I am doing our family legacy a good service."

She frowns. "I support you. When you came back, you seemed overwhelmed and lost here. Fish out of water. But I can see that this is important to you."

It is. For more reasons than just setting up my parents. I'm reconnecting with a part of myself I haven't touched in a long time. "Working there has given me a different purpose. Rugby has helped too. I don't know. Maybe I'm exaggerating. It's just been nice to use my hands and help get Anderson whisky out into the world."

"Like you always wanted."

I shrug. "Aye, but Da didn't. He should be proud of his product, of the years he sacrificed to ensure its integrity. I want other people to enjoy our good whisky too."

"I'm sorry, Ol. People around here do take a long time to warm up to things."

"It's hard when I only have two more months left." Meadow stiffens beside me. My grip on the small knife tightens. She hasn't asked me anything about Viggle, but I think both of us are trying not to think about the future. I'm failing miserably. "I've been wrestling with the guilt of not coming back home for so long, and now guilt for changing things here before I leave again." She slides her hand onto my knee, and I settle beneath her touch.

"Maybe this time you don't have to stay away for so long."

She's right. "I had a mindset in my twenties—money and prestige would help me cope with not being accepted by my parents." Cope with how Meadow broke things off with me, and cope with how I left things with Fox. "I think I had it all wrong. All that brought me is a big paycheck and a lot of loneliness." *Fucking capitalism.*

"Trust me," she sighs and stretches out her legs, rolling her ankles. Her feet must be killing her. "I was sure if I proved my parents wrong and succeeded as a chef, then I'd have won something over them. But you see how Fox Den's opening turned out."

She always understood me better than anyone. "You'll figure out this tasting menu, Meadow, and you're going to succeed at it. The way you've succeeded at anything you set your mind to."

"I hope so." She pauses, looking nervous. "A lot is riding on the restaurant."

"I can't imagine the pressure of wanting to get your dream the way you always imagined it."

She frowns. "It's nothing like I imagined it. My dream was to have a restaurant in Paris."

"When we were kids and you'd describe your own place, it looked exactly like Fox Den looks now. Doesn't matter where your dreams happen, doe. You succeeded at making them happen."

That's something I need to ruminate on. Ave brought up the question that hasn't left my mind. Why did I truly leave Thistlehill and never come back? Did I achieve everything I desired in the States? I have substantial savings, a seven-figure sum. Here, that amount means that I would never experience discomfort. I could have any material good I wanted. I'd only give up the title, *Director*. It doesn't sound as fulfilling as Dad or Meadow's husband.

"Yeah, but in my dream, I didn't have to take a loan from my parents for my third of the business." She winces. "Brooke and Fi also invested, but as the owner, I have to carry the heavier financial burden."

"I had no idea." The panic attack in her car, the stress of the past couple of weeks, her emotions being fried…it all makes so much more sense now. The pressure must be crushing her. Especially after what she and her parents have been through.

"I promise, I know a thing or two about family guilt," she says.

*Oh, doe.*

"Come here." I set down my wood carving and tap her knee. "Give me your legs. You've been on your feet all day."

She turns in the porch swing, her back against the armrest, and stretches her legs across my thighs. I pull off her clogs and massage her ankles. "Mmm," she moans, then lets out a massive yawn. "Ugh, sorry, just a long day."

"Don't apologize; I gotcha. That feel good?" I press my thumbs into the arches of her feet, and she gives me a soft smile.

"Great." She yawns again. "Have you taken some time to

redefine *your* version of success? I mean, you just reminded me that I still have my dream restaurant, even if it's not where I initially planned to open it, or it didn't go exactly how I planned."

*Every time I'm with you, all I'm doing is redefining the damn word.* My mind's a jumble of what-ifs. I've lost track of how many days need to pass before I leave for New York City. The Viggle benefits package they sent me at the beginning of this month is still sitting in my email, unopened.

I can't explain why I'm putting off opening it. The lure of the half-a-million-dollar salary, company shares, and my own office used to feel like it would satisfy my desire for something more. That the work and the title would help plug up the tinge of loneliness inside of my heart. And it will. I think.

That was the answer I had before coming back here, and now, I'm not so sure.

"I'm working on it. For now, I have to fix things at the distillery and break bread with Callum. Hopefully, that'll be enough to smooth things out with my da. This time, I want to leave and not be riddled with twenty more years of guilt."

Her round eyes fill with sympathy. "Did you ever wrestle with any of that guilt when we were making plans to leave? Honestly, I was afraid of what leaving Thistlehill would be like."

"Not really." I pause. "We always said we'd come back here after we achieved all of our big dreams. When we broke up, I just saw Thistlehill as a part of my past."

I reach for her other foot, rubbing circles into the soles with my fingers. "Would you ever come back for good?" Her voice is small, and I can tell she's hiding the words I've been thinking for days.

Could I move back to Thistlehill if what's happening between us turns serious?

How could I when my parents and I still can't get along? When I can't even make my own family legacy proud? "How did you make things right with your parents?" I answer her question with one of my own.

"Honestly, we never moved past them not paying for culinary school. After Fox died, they sort of glossed over our history of fighting about my life choices. We never talk about that." She lets out a bitter laugh. "It's funny because everything they said would happen came true. I was so stubborn about figuring it out for myself. Now, I'm working constantly and not making any real money. I'm struggling, just like they said I would be. I'm the one who had to tuck my tail between my legs and ask them to help me with a dream they never even supported."

The wind squalls around us, tossing up the pieces of hair around my face. I want to convince her that it isn't true—I used to be able to do that—but I'm helpless sitting beside her. "Maybe their loan was a way to help repair their mistakes?" I can relate to using money as a way to deal with unspoken feelings. I'm doing that exact same thing at the distillery.

"I only wanted to hear them say they were proud of me and genuinely believe it. The way they were with Fox. Now that they have one kid left, it's like they're pretending and trying their best to think of my dreams as good enough."

She's holding the whole world in her hands, and apart from some kind words, I can't become the ground underneath her feet. I'm leaving. I won't be here to lean on, to catch her if she falls.

"Doe." My nose and eyes sting. "You're their kid. I know it may not feel like they truly care, but they must. They love you. My da has only ever told me he was proud of me three times in my life, but, deep down, I know he still wishes I was here."

"This is what happens when two rebellious teenagers try and make their childish dreams come alive, isn't it? A lot of complicated feelings and new definitions of success?" She laughs, swiping away her tears.

"Aye, it's not easy getting older." I built my life around a superficial pipe dream. My career did good for the world. I made an impact at the Oceanic Research Organization. I paid my dues at Silverman Sachs. But can I truly spend the rest of my life prioritizing the rush that accolades give me?

I glance over at Meadow. Maybe I've been afraid of coming back here because I knew she'd help me see my reflection—the one that got older—and send me into a landslide of questions.

Ones I'd been afraid to ask myself.

Is the dream I had for myself almost two decades ago still the one I have now? Or can I build my life around something—someone—else?

"No, your dreams don't get any protection as an adult," she sighs. "You have to fight for them all on your own."

"You, Meadow Macrae, are still my first choice in a zombie apocalypse." I smile, hoping to edge one out of her too.

It works, and her chest rumbles with a quiet laugh. "You still remember that?"

"How could I ever forget my first kiss?" The sky above us is a mesmerizing canvas of stars. You can really see the whole universe from here. "Can we sit here for a while longer and do nothing?"

"I'd love that." She repositions herself on the swing, swinging her legs to the other side and leaning her body into my chest. "What's that?" She points to the wood I've been fiddling with since I got home.

I lean down, careful of her weight on me, and pick up the small carving. "Something small for you."

Meadow takes the small fox in her hand and runs her fingers over it. The tail swings around its body. Small ears at the top of its head. She traces her thumb over the snout and looks up at me. "Ollie," she breathes.

"It's nothing."

"It's everything." She travels the familiar path between her lips and mine. We kiss until stars start to fill my own eyes.

Am I a fool for still wanting to leave?

## Chapter 25
# Meadow

Since I picked up Maisie from school, we've done homework, which thankfully had zero math assignments. Even second-grade math is hell—numbers give me hives.

We threw together a living room obstacle course, tossing around pillows and blankets to avoid all the floor lava. We blasted Maisie's Greatest Hits: "Fearless" by Taylor Swift, "Heat Waves" by Glass Animals, "Pompeii" by Bastille, "Let It Go" from *Frozen*, and her favorite BTS songs.

She braided ribbons into my hair, and I painted our nails with the periwinkle color we found at Honeydew Market when we picked up snacks.

"Okay, best night ever." Maisie smiles, pulling her knees into her chest as she snuggles up to me on the couch. *Beck* is projected onto the screen in front of us. "Wednesdays should always be Mommy and Maisie nights."

I hadn't realized how much I missed my girl. Between troubleshooting new recipes, failing and trying again, running Fox Den, and trying to keep my head above water, I forgot to prioritize spending time with my best friend.

Guilt waits by the door of my mind. *I'm doing my best*, I remind myself. *She's happy. We're here together.*

"They will be, at least for the next month. Then, when the restaurant gets back to its normal schedule, we'll figure out a new day that's just for us."

She springs her round blue eyes to me. "Yes. Oh, and maybe we can invite Gran."

"I'm sure she'd love that," I give her little body a squeeze, readjusting my heating pad. My cramps are extra rude this cycle. "Maybe I can ask her to join us next week."

After my conversation with Ollie on Sunday, I realized that ignoring my past with my parents is causing so much unnecessary stress. The desire to do everything on my own to prove to them that I'm okay is overwhelming.

I need to talk to them. Is it selfish to rehash the past, to bring up the raw moments of Fox's death? Or do I want to carry the burden of thinking that I'm not the child they would've wanted to keep around? Maisie deserves a good relationship with her grandparents, and that'll only be possible if this roadblock between us is cleared.

"Oh no, Detective Beck is on their trail!"

"He's that good."

I yank the heavy blanket off the back of the couch and tug it over us. His smell hits me in an instant. Whisky and smoke. Ollie.

The smell must've bled into the yarn after our second Monday night dinner. My teenage self would have been screaming if she knew I was eating lamb, naked, once again, at the kitchen table with Ollie Anderson.

One thing is the same: in the mornings, I trace over the ghost of his touch on my skin, wishing he was in my bed.

Spending the night is off-limits. My body can't get used to having him around. He'll be leaving two months from today. This is all simply pretend.

"Wouldn't it be super if we could bring Belle into the house with us so she can watch TV?" Maisie giggles at the screen.

"Cow Belle?"

She nods her head into my side. "What do you think she'd have to say?"

"Probably that we're all annoying for trying to get her out of the way when we're driving. Or she'd steal your toys."

"I'd share with Belle. It's not her fault she likes pretty things."

I join her little laughter. The image of the Cameron twins' hairy cow playing tea party with Maisie and her dolls is too ridiculous.

"I bet she could be my best friend," she muses. Maisie has always had a fascination with the town cow, but who could blame her? The sweet beast is harmless. A little slow on the draw, but she's a diva. It's her cow world, and we're just living in it.

"I don't see why not; you're my best friend."

She sits up, giving me a serious look. "Am I *reaalllyyyy*?"

"*Reaaallly*." I mimic her exaggerated pronunciation.

"I thought Coach Ollie was your best friend again." Maisie's eyes narrow on me, and she purses her lips.

Of course the little detective of the house is aware that something is going on with me and Ollie. This is what I was afraid of. "He hasn't been my best friend in a long time, plum. Remember?"

"You could use another best friend, like I have you and Cece."

"I have Brooke and Fi," I remind her.

Maisie waves her hand at me. "They're different."

The smell of Ollie is suffocating, and I rip the blanket off of us and toss it to the floor. "How so?"

"They keep you busy. You need a best friend to watch movies with, or the episodes of *Beck* that I can't watch."

My mouth drops in surprise and sarcastically, I ask, "What kind of episodes can't we watch together?"

"You know, the ones with all the"—she leans in close, her breath tickling my cheek—"*muuuuuurder.*"

Yeah, the Worst Parent of the Year award goes to Meadow Macrae. Gather around, folks, and watch a clueless mother figure out how to deal with the fact that she's let her seven-year-old know about her obsession with murder mysteries.

"But the episodes we watch are my favorite."

"Because Ollie's in them," Maisie declares.

"Ollie isn't in *Beck.*"

She crosses her little arms over each other, bringing them right up to her chin. "Are you sure?"

"Positive." My comfort television show and Ollie Anderson have nothing to do with each other. Sure, Kristofer Hivju and Ollie bear the smallest, faintest resemblance to each other. Both have that auburn hair that looks like flames in the sun. Bushy brows. Strong arms. But it's barely even noticeable. That's definitely not why I watch it. "You getting hungry yet?" I switch topics. The last thing Maisie and I need is a man taking up space in our girls night. No matter how much I miss him.

My daughter's stomach growls loudly in response. "I am!" She sits up on her knees, sticking out her tummy. "A grilled cheese?"

"The cheesiest," I nod and reach for her belly, giving her a tickle. She squirms into a ball, kicking and giggling.

"Hurry, Mom, Detective Beck is waiting for us," Maisie says through labored pants, tears of laughter streaming down her cheeks.

"I'm hurrying!" I pop off the couch and make a scene of rushing to the kitchen, Maisie on my heels. We pull all the cheese out of the fridge—cheddar, Asiago, mozzarella, Parmesan, provolone, and goat Gouda—and I set up a cutting board and a grater before I slice up the sourdough and heat a pan. She crawls up onto a stool, surveying the array of cheese. "Alright, chef, tonight's special blend is all yours."

Her eyes flood with surprise. "Really?"

"That's right," I encourage her. "Remember the special trick?"

"Soft, stretchy, and a base."

"Smart girl."

Maisie lifts up a jalapeño goat cheese I whipped up. "This for the soft." Next, she scrutinizes the mozzarella and the provolone, sniffing both before choosing to slide over the fresh ball of mozzarella. "The stretchy. And finally..." She taps her finger on her head, her eyes bouncing between the sharp cheddar and the goat Gouda. "The cheddar."

"Heard." I grate the cheddar while she shreds the mozzarella with her fingers before we spread the goat cheese onto the slices of sourdough. "Feeling like a little kick tonight?"

"I like it spicy."

"Your dad did too." I touch the necklace around my throat. A sharp pain radiates from my uterus to my leg, causing me to grip the counter.

"You okay, Mommy? Need another pain medicine?"

"I'm okay, baby." I breathe through my nose, willing the cramps to leave me, at least until I have to put Maisie to bed.

Maisie sets her forearms on the counter and lays her cheek onto them. "Can you tell me the story again? The one with Dad and my other mommy?"

For years, the only way Maisie would go to sleep was if I shared a memory about Penelope and Fox. This particular one was always my favorite.

"As you know," I say, dropping the first side of the grilled cheese onto the pan and listening to it sizzle, "your dad was a big, soppy romantic—*huge*. He'd cry at all the love movies and write sweet letters." Maisie hangs on to every single word. "On the night before their wedding, your mom told Fox that she had a craving for a grilled cheese. He got it into his head that getting her one was the most important thing in the world, even though they both had to be up in just a couple of hours for the big day."

"And Daddy knew just who to call," she joins in.

Colette gave me forty-eight hours off for the nuptial celebrations before she needed her sous chef back in Lyon. "That he did. He banged on my bedroom door—the one you're in now—until I got out of bed. Pretty soon, Gran and Grandpa were up, trying to figure out what all the noise was about."

"Then what happened?"

I flip the sourdough in the pan, satisfied at the beautifully browned crust. Just like the lamb I made for Ollie on Monday, this one is second nature. The other ones I worked on during the week have been less innate. "I got to cooking, making grilled cheese sandwiches for the whole family. We sat and ate them right at this kitchen island as the sun started to wake up for the day."

Little did we know that Maisie would be conceived that night. Forty weeks later, I was flying back home to meet this precious little girl.

"That's why I love grilled cheese so much. All three of my parents love them too."

She may not know it, but the words almost bring me to my knees. *All three of her parents*. My heart sings.

"Don't think there's a better explanation than that." I plate our sandwiches, cutting them in half.

She picks hers up and pulls the cheese apart, letting it hang in the air. "This is yummy!"

I bite into mine, my tongue exploding with the flavors of Maisie's cheese choices. *Damn, this is good.* "Mais, you're onto something here."

"Really?"

"My compliments to the chef." I raise half of a sandwich to her in a salute before diving back in.

I remember Dad coming home late and making us sandwiches. Or after school, on weekend mornings, through winter storms and hot summer days. Sitting at this kitchen island, sharing the small joy of crusty bread and salty cheese.

Now they're a staple in my life with Maisie.

But not just with her.

I made the same sandwiches with Fi after long nights at Ramona's, when we were too lazy to make anything else. The honey-drenched goat cheese Brooke and I would grill between baguettes.

Comfort. Warmth. Safety.

A version of this has to be on the tasting menu. I fish my notebook from the drawer in the island and start scribbling.

*Romano, Asiago, and kimchi? Mushrooms, burrata, and truffle? Goat cheddar with a smoked duck?*

When I look up, Maisie is watching me, half a sandwich on her plate. "You don't want to finish that?"

"I'm saving it."

"For who, plum?"

Maisie spins her plate around. "Coach Ollie."

"I think he's having dinner at his house tonight."

"I know." She shrugs as though it were obvious. "But maybe we can save it for him."

She's a sweetheart, caring for others. "You like him so much that you'd share your delicious creation with him?" I zip it up into a plastic bag and set it on the counter.

"I like him a lot. He's a good coach. He bandages up the team's boo-boos, puts up our hair, and always cleans my cleats and no one else's on the team." Now that's the kind of favoritism I can get behind. "And I like that he makes you happy."

"Does he now?"

"Don't be silly, Mommy. The only other time I see you that happy is when you watch me play rugby or you're cooking."

*Don't get too attached. Don't let Maisie get too attached.*

It's pointless. Ollie is weaseling his way into my life, and it's both exhilarating and terrifying. It's like a page-turner I can sink into and can't put down. Whatever chapter we opened here, I don't know how it's going to end.

The comfort of mystery and romance novels is that you can always predict the ending—death or love, sometimes both.

Here, I don't have any idea what will happen.

"Go cue up the next episode, Mais. I'll finish up here."

She dashes off to the living room, filtering through the *Beck* episodes she's allowed to watch. I grab my phone off the counter and open my messages. I pause for a moment. What would tonight look like if Ollie wasn't a text away, but here, in my house, with us?

Would he put away the dishes or join Maisie in the living room? Would he make her laugh until she cried? How late would we stay up, or would we crash together on the couch? How would we split the bills? There's no point in denying that Ollie has more than I do. Would he become the one who gets to spoil Maisie? Would he hold her when she cries through *Shrek* or be patient with her when she has a temper? What did he eat at home in New York? Would there be nights when he'd make dinner? Apart from the soup, I have no idea what else he can cook.

Would he buy the groceries? Would I have to remind him all the time, or is that something he'd just do? Would he text me from the store, asking if a recipe needs an ingredient I may have forgotten to write down, or would he just pick it up?

My heart thrums, and I force it to slow.

*Slow down.*

Where is my mind even going?

Half a grilled cheese sandwich, and I'm suddenly spiraling out of control.

MEADOW

u hungry?

> OLLIE NEW NUMBER
> For you, always

>> MEADOW
>> 4 cheese

> OLLIE NEW NUMBER
> On you? I guess we can try it

>> MEADOW
>> no, on a sandwich

> OLLIE NEW NUMBER
> Be there in two minutes

>> MEADOW
>> l8r

> OLLIE NEW NUMBER
> Missing me, Macrae?

*Yes.*

>> MEADOW
>> found out my daughter is a culinary genius

> OLLIE NEW NUMBER
> Takes after her ma

>> MEADOW
>> got a new dish for the menu

> OLLIE NEW NUMBER
> Now you have my attention
>
> Let me know when you're ready for me and we'll meet on the porch like last time?
>
> I have something for you anyway

>> MEADOW
>> fiddling w ur wood again?

**OLLIE NEW NUMBER**
No, I'll save that for you

**MEADOW**
lol

The small fox carving he gave me the other night has sat at my finishing station in Fox Den's service area. A small piece of my brother and his friend with me.

**OLLIE NEW NUMBER**
Btw, I started rewatching Beck.

Be honest, do you only watch the 13 episodes that have Kristofer Hivju in them?

Because it seems like it

**MEADOW**
did mais put u up to this?

**OLLIE NEW NUMBER**
What?

**MEADOW**
nvm

peter haber is dreamy + fun plot twists

**OLLIE NEW NUMBER**
Sure

I'm on season 6 episode 4 and all I've seen is Hivju smolder

**MEADOW**
best smolder in the biz

**OLLIE NEW NUMBER**
Are your cramps any better today?

**MEADOW**
not as bad as yesterday

### Kels & Denise Stone

OLLIE NEW NUMBER

Hate that I can't take them from you

MEADOW

ur back rub on mon helped

c u in a bit

## Chapter 26
# Meadow
### seventeen years ago

"I didn't get in." A raw sob wrenches out of me.

I burrow my face deeper into the comfort of Ollie's chest as he holds his arms around me on the bed. It's no use. However much I try to suffocate the panic swirling in my chest, my mind sings like a choir.

*Failure.* That's all I am.

I knew when my dad handed me the envelope with the Cambridge School of Culinary Arts logo—it was so small. Apparently, my GPA was far too low.

My parents' disappointed faces were worse than the letters themselves. It's bad enough that I'm not going to college, but now I can't even get into culinary school. Each rejection felt as if I'd stabbed their hearts with a dull knife. Their failure of a daughter. Fox got into every single school he applied to, and I couldn't even get into one.

First it was the CIA. Now the school that was meant to be the stepping-stone for the life Ollie and I were going to build together in Boston. All because of my grades.

Wasn't the entire point of going to culinary school not needing to show them my transcripts?

"It'll be okay, doe," Ollie repeats for the hundredth time tonight. My body shakes, and tears pour out. A pain stabs me in my uterus. This period is worse than the last few. My stomach is in knots. I can't even remember the last time I ate. "It'll be okay."

"Of course this is happening right when Fox is visiting for winter break." Of course it had to come a week before my birthday. The whole day, I poured all my shame and humiliation into the Cullen skink that's finishing on the stove. "You must think—"

"That you're the most talented, beautiful, generous person and that those culinary schools are going to be kicking themselves when you become the most famous chef in the world." He brushes back my hair, wet with tears, from my face and runs his thumbs under my eyes. "I still have that Polaroid I took of you at the loch when you kissed me. I'm saving it for your big day in the spotlight."

"I want that so badly." I melt beneath his touch, letting myself be cradled by him. "What am I going to do?"

"What about Le Cordon Bleu? You can still apply there," he offers.

"That's in France."

"And?" He raises a brow at me.

"We agreed that we're going to Boston, Ollie," I remind him. I glance over at my desk. The brochure for Le Cordon Bleu sits on top of a scattered pile of papers. They offer a work-study program as well, but if the past two rejections are any indication of how that application would go, I can't stomach it.

"I could come with you. There must be a good university I can apply to," he says. Deep down, I know that Ollie would follow me to Paris if I asked. If I got in and told him that it was my only shot. He would decline MIT and come with me to France.

"Absolutely not. MIT has always been your dream, Ollie." I can't be the reason he gives up on the future he's wanted since I've known him.

"Your dreams are just as important as mine. We'll figure it out."

My chest becomes a pit of guilt.

He would sacrifice his biggest dreams for a chance at mine? My heart splinters. Despite the fact that I've been rejected from two culinary schools, some small hope still lives within me. But I need to be honest with myself. "Le Cordon Bleu is one of the best culinary schools in the world. A total pipe dream. I doubt I'd get in if my GPA was too low for those other schools." It's pointless to speculate. "I want to go with you to Boston," I say with certainty.

"Meadow, I want you to be happy." He kisses me. "We can make Boston work. You can reapply to the Cambridge school next year. They won't turn you down if you have more experience."

"In the meantime, maybe I can work as a line cook," I offer, but the words aren't full of hope and excitement the way they were when we planned our future together over two months ago, in this very room.

A compromise. It's an amendment to our dream, but I'd be with him.

"Look, doe, I hated that I got deferred from MIT, but this turned out to be the best year of my life."

"You're right," I nod into his chest.

I'm moving to Boston with Ollie. Sure, I won't be able to get started on my dreams straight away, but I can still cook at home. In our little apartment. While he lives out his dream and I fall behind on mine.

I told my parents that college was out of the cards for me and I was going to go to America with Ollie to figure out culinary school for myself. The past couple of months haven't been easy at the Macrae household, but at least they've stopped trying to change my mind.

Some part of me can't help but wonder if my parents have decided that Ollie will take care of me. But they don't know anything about our relationship.

We take care of each other, and I'm fully capable of taking care of myself. My heart sinks further into my chest. At least, I want to be able to take care of myself.

Downstairs, the front door slams shut.

"Hello? I'm home," Fox's voice sings through the house. He's early.

"I don't want him to see me like this," I whisper.

My brother has always been supportive of my dreams, but that never stopped my parents from roping him into a conversation behind closed doors, trying to get him to make me change my mind. It hurts that they'd use my love for him against me like that.

"You need a few minutes?"

"More like a hundred." I reluctantly unglue myself from Ollie's warm chest and walk to my vanity, swiping the tears off my face. My cheeks are red and splotchy. Hair in tangles. "I can't go out there looking like a mess."

"You could never look like a mess." Ollie walks over to me, grabs my hairbrush, and runs it through my hair. He takes his time, slowly brushing out the knots. Gently raking the bristles through each tangled strand before sweeping them over my shoulder.

His thumbs find that one spot in my neck that's always like a tough cut of meat, growing tighter when I'm stressed, and kneads it softly.

"Thank you." Despite all my insufficiencies, Ollie looks at me like he loves me. Every broken bit.

"I love you. We'll figure this out."

"I love you too."

In a few breaths, my heart rate calms. I drink the water on my nightstand and throw my hair into a braid. *I got this.*

Ollie and I walk hand in hand to the kitchen. It's still strange to be touching in public.

It was unnerving when we drove back up to Edinburgh in November to tell Fox about us. My brother feigned giving us a hard time even though he was completely joking. He loves that Ollie and I are together—everyone does.

My parents laughed when we told them, said they knew for months and expressed how happy they were. We told them that we were going to go to America together if our plan worked out. Dad gave Ollie a big hug and said, *You'll take care of her, won't you?* And Ollie promised that he would.

Then the news spread outside of our little houses. Customers at Honeydew Market congratulated us. At the monthly Town Hall, Jody, the town's provost, even decided to announce that we were dating. Sure, it was the most embarrassing thing in the world, but I like not having to sneak around anymore.

When we reach the kitchen, my mom's arms are wrapped around a girl. She's stunning. Long, light brown hair, curvy waist, and eyes that reminded me of black truffles. That must be Penelope. Fox's *the one*.

"There's my favorite happy couple," Fox sings, running over and pulling us into a group hug.

"What is on your face?" I yank at the mustache curling above my brother's lip while his long arms and Ollie's strong ones suffocate me between their embrace.

"See, I knew we'd get along." My brother's girlfriend joins us, smiling so brightly. She's golden like him. Has that peculiar quality that Fox always had, as if he would glimmer in the light whenever you talked to him. "I told him to shave it weeks ago, but apparently it's sticking around."

"Coach at the rugby club swears we're winning games

because none of us have shaved. Can't let the green shirts down." Fox shrugs.

"You must be Penelope." I have to lean down to hug her because of our height difference. I'm closer in height to my brother than I am to her. Her skin smells of vanilla. "It's nice to finally meet you."

"I am so excited to be here. Fox tells me you're going to spoil us with dinner?"

"Just some Cullen skink. He's always talking me up."

"You're one of my favorite people, sis. Of course I'm going to brag about you."

Penelope's head tilts almost straight up to look at Ollie. "And you're Ollie?"

He nods. Fox slings his arms around all three of us. "Now all my favorite people are here together."

We had an uneventful dinner that consisted of my parents fawning over my brother and me trying to stay small on my side of the table. Thankfully, they didn't bring up my newest rejection and put it up for group discussion.

Fox scrubs dishes at the sink beside me while I dry them. Penelope, Ollie, and my parents went to drop off leftovers at the Andersons' and sample Seamus's new whisky.

"I like Penelope a lot, but I have to be honest—sharing your first kiss after you got your midterm grades? You've always been such a nerd," I tease and whip his arm with the hand towel. Some of my anxiety from earlier has eased.

"Hey!" He splashes me with soapy water, and I shriek with laughter. "What did you expect me to do, Meadow? She got a higher score than me. Not just looks, that one. She's actually perfect, you know?"

"She ate two helpings of my smoked haddock, so I like her."

"I love her," he says confidently. Fox has been waiting to start his life with *the one* since he was a little kid.

"Finally, that wedding binder can get put to good use."

He sends a heavy nudge into my shoulder. "Make fun all you want; you'll be borrowing it when you and Ollie get married."

I laugh. "Don't make too many plans for me. Clearly, whatever I set my mind to falls through the cracks."

Fox continues scrubbing the pan with a soft-bristle brush, the way I taught him. "What do you mean?"

"My GPA was too low for the CIA, and the Cambridge program thought the same."

"Meadow, that's their fucking loss." He leans over and whispers, "What about the big LCB?"

Another rush of guilt torrents my stomach. My cramps physically punish me with a blow. "I haven't applied."

Fox gives me an understanding frown. Of course he gets that it's more complicated than it seems. If Ollie wasn't in the picture, the application would've already been on its way. But I'm choosing between my first love—Ollie—and my other first love—cooking.

"You still have time," he assures me.

I hold fast. "No, Fox. Ollie and I are going to Boston together."

"But you didn't get into the Cambridge school?"

"I'll find work at some kind of restaurant until I can reapply." I try to seem upbeat about the decision, but my excitement falters.

"Why don't you see what Le Cordon Bleu has to say first?" I hesitate, and he can tell that the suggestion is making me uncomfortable. "Look, Meadow, I know Ollie is my best friend, but you're my sister. I want you to be happy—"

"I'll be happy with Ollie."

Fox frowns. "College is really time-consuming, especially if you'll both be working. It'll be harder to enjoy the little bit of time you'll have together if you're not doing something you want to be doing." He says my biggest fear out loud. That love may not be enough to help me endure a year of waiting to go to culinary school. My one chance to learn everything I can about food. To become a better cook. "Let's say you get into LCB. What happens?"

"I hurt Ollie."

"He'll understand. Even if it means you have to put your plans to be together on hold. Don't let your fear of how this will affect Ollie stop you from applying. You'll regret it if you don't."

"I know," I sigh. Ollie was so supportive tonight, but I can't tell him I'm still thinking about applying. "What about Mom and Dad? If, in some weird twist of fate, I get into LCB and don't go to Boston with Ollie, I'll just disappoint them again. It's bad enough that they're still refusing to pay for culinary school."

"So, fuck 'em."

I gasp. "Did you just say that about Mom and Dad?"

"Look, I know they're our parents, okay? But they shouldn't get in the way of your dreams. No one fucking should. You're Meadow—Chef Meadow. You're tougher than all of us put together."

"Fox…" Sobs claw their way up my chest.

Fox hands me the pan, and I take it from him and dry it off with the rag. "They'll come around, I promise. And you'll figure it out. I'll help however I can. Time heals all things, right?"

Boots pound on the steps outside. I glance out the window and see my dad with his arm around Ollie, Penelope and my mom huddled close together. *A family.* A sinking feeling goes down my throat and into my stomach.

"It doesn't feel like that."

"I know, sis. But your dreams are as important as anyone's. Take a chance on yourself. You never know where life may lead you."

Could I apply to Le Cordon Bleu and give up my life with Ollie? Would our paths even cross again? The front door unlatches, and the love of my life walks through, smiling right at me.

It couldn't hurt to try. I'm sure whatever happens, Ollie would understand.

He loves me, and I love him. Things will have to work out.

## Chapter 27
# Ollie

"Guess Madame *Moo-dini* is happy that it's finally spring." Up on the hill, between new blossoms of bluebells and primrose, the big fluffy hustler frolics along a mossy path.

"What did you call her?" Meadow laughs. A glint of sunlight rustles through the chestnut color of her hair. The blue sky above us is no match for her eyes.

"*Moo-dini*," I huff. "You know, like Harry Houdini, because she makes things disappear?"

"You and your bad puns." She shakes her head, and I nudge her side.

"You liked my bad puns when we were younger."

"Or I just tolerated them because I liked you."

"Liked me?"

"Don't let it go to your head, or I'll tell Belle that your fancy clothes are worth stealing."

I snort. "That damn cow's put me out a hundred pounds' worth of apples."

"A few weeks ago, on the night I gave you that grilled cheese, actually, Maisie thought it would be prudent to invite the lady cow to watch *Beck* with us."

"You didn't tell me that." I return her grin. The familiar ache that's been gnawing at me for the past month returns. I'm missing memories. Small moments you can't capture with photos or stories. And instead of filling up with shame or guilt, I just feel sad.

"Must've slipped my mind," she says. A basket drapes from her forearm.

We've been meeting up on Mondays. I tease her with my shorts at practice, and we hang out on the porch more nights than not, whenever Meadow is done with work and I can't sleep. It's been nice having a normal routine together.

"That's okay." I force a smile.

For the past two hours, we've been strolling through the forest between our houses and the loch. Meadow stopped by the distillery to drop off some lobster rolls for Callum, Elspeth, and me before inviting me to join her while she foraged for spring mushrooms for the tasting menu.

Callum and I have come close to making amends. This weekend, we all worked on bottling the next shipment for On Cloud Nine together—the first shipment went so well that the hotel conglomerate already wants to increase their monthly order. And there wasn't a single argument or grumble between us.

The raise I gave them both probably didn't hurt either. Callum is too proud to have asked my da for it, but I think he and Elspeth deserve the bump in pay, especially after having to learn the new technology.

"How's Maisie feeling about her game this week?"

"Nervous, I think? You probably know better than I do." She shrugs. "At night, I can hear her in her room, practicing her high kick."

"She's the most committed player on our team. I can't imagine how good she'll be when she's older."

"Do you like coaching the kiddos? I know you loved rugby as a kid; I have no idea if you even played in the States."

The team relies on me. So does Neil, and it's nice. I want every one of them to do well, and knowing that I can contribute to that, even a little bit, has felt as good as some of the work I did in the States. "Honestly, it's really fun. It feels rewarding to be a role model because of something I was good at in the past. It reminds me of Fox too, of the summers we spent training at the loch, of how good it felt to have teammates in school."

"When you put it that way, I think it's really sweet." She smiles.

"I regret not joining a league in the States. I thought rugby would bring up bad memories, but it's only made me reconnect with the boy I was in Thistlehill. Not the lonely workaholic I became in America," I admit. "It's funny, because I felt this intuition when I was abroad. Like I was too big for the concrete buildings I worked in."

"Why did you ignore it?"

I was afraid of what it would force me to face—the fact that, despite not getting along with my da and my fear of living a life filled with sacrifice, I didn't hate Thistlehill as much as I'd convinced myself I did. I had a best friend here. The girl of my dreams. Life could've gone very differently if I'd come back after university. "Because I was stubborn."

"Still, it clearly helped you achieve the life you always wanted."

Did it? The doubts have been curdling in my mind since I've been back. Sure, I have friends in the States, and the job at Viggle, with its money and prestige, but I was nowhere close to having a life like the one I've been living here. A life with Maisie, Meadow, and the people who knew me as a little boy. Even if small-town life is irritating at times, I feel bigger here than I did in New York.

We walk along the path, spotting mushrooms and footprints of wildlife in the mud that clings to my hiking boots. The air is crisp and filled with the smell of fresh ferns.

"Oh, look, those are plump oyster mushrooms." She points to a gathering of birch trees and walks toward them. She hands me her basket as she kneels down and inspects the treasure, gently popping them off the bark and breathing them in. Her eyes close. The corners of her lips gently turn up.

The last couple of weeks have flown by without any mention of the future. Perhaps because it's impossible for us to talk about one together.

Could I visit for her birthday in December and spend Christmas here? New Year's too? Viggle doesn't offer that many vacation days, especially not for a director. My life will be work all the time. But maybe I could figure something out? Besides, even if Da and I aren't exactly on the best terms, they may still need my help somehow. I'm determined to not waste more time avoiding home—er, Thistlehill.

"I'm going to give these a try tonight." She holds up the shell-like cluster of gray mushrooms. I take them from her, using the soft rag in the basket to swipe off any excess dirt before setting them down beside the rest of our collection.

"Can't wait." We stroll ahead, and I step over a birch tree blocking our path, the second one today. A huge storm blew through town last Saturday. Or was it the Saturday before? Time has been slipping away from us. I'm not sure I'll be ready to leave. "Look under here." I nod toward the fallen white trunk. "Some nice pickings."

She sinks to her knees again, trying to roll the tree trunk over. "I think those belong to this tree; I can't move this thing."

I hand her the basket. "I got it." I squat down, wrap my hands around the thin white trunk, and lift it up, heaving it off the trail and turning it so that Meadow can see the mushrooms hiding underneath.

Her brow curves up mischievously. "Those caber toss practices are more than a bunch of guys passing around a whisky bottle and gossiping, huh?"

"You offend me! Are these muscles not a good enough indicator of how much wood I've been moving around?" The waxed Barbour jacket I bought for my trip barely fits around my shoulders anymore.

"If anyone's been moving wood around, it's me." She smiles and narrows her eyes, shaking her head. We've had a lot of fun times together over the past few weeks.

"I guess I'll have to show you how strong I've gotten." I take two large steps toward her, yank her off the ground, and toss her over my shoulder. Her shriek fills the forest.

"No! My mushrooms!" She kicks her feet, bashing her basket against my back. "Put me down."

"Can't," I say, bracing her with one arm and sending the other right into the firm curve of her ass. One spank, then two. "Gotta see how far I can throw you since my muscles aren't that impressive to my woman."

"Ollie!" She laughs before the sound cuts short and a stinging bite sinks into the flesh of my lower back.

"Ouch!" I shout and gently return Meadow to the ground. "What was that?"

"Retaliation. You roughed up my oyster mushrooms," she huffs.

I bracket her jaw, pull her nose to mine, and kiss her. "Guess you can let me make it up to you later tonight."

"You're the worst," she whispers against my beard.

"Really, Meadow? Not even going to threaten me with a knife for that? You're losing your tough side."

The playful look on her face spins into annoyance, and she smacks the back of my head. "Keep talking and you might just learn how much I know about mushrooms. There's a bundle in here that is poisonous."

"I was wondering what you were going to do with that Galerina." I point to the medium-sized, yellow-capped mushrooms in her basket.

"That's sheathed woodtuft," she explains plainly and starts walking ahead of me. When I join her side, she looks up at me. "Or is it?"

I laugh, a hearty one from the depths of my chest. The same one I get when Maisie sasses a kid like her own ma on the field. Or when Meadow and I spend nights on the porch, flipping through memories together. Even the kind of laughter I have when I stop by Fox Den for dinner.

"I'll let you surprise me." I wink. "Seventeen-year-old Meadow would be so impressed with you right now. Identifying poisonous mushrooms to sneak into my dinner later? Can't imagine all of the things you learned in culinary school."

She opens her mouth to speak but hesitates, staring down at the mossy ground. "I'm sorry I never told you that I applied to Le Cordon Bleu."

The school she insisted was a pipe dream for her. The one I encouraged her to apply to.

"I don't actually know what happened the day you sent me that text." I wince. "I—I've been avoiding asking you because I'm sure it's going to hurt."

"The day we were meant to fly to Boston, I got the letter from Le Cordon Bleu." Meadow swallows, and my chest constricts. This is a piece of her life she hasn't shared with me. "It looked nothing like the rejections I received from the other schools. This was a thick, glistening blue envelope. I opened it surrounded by the packed suitcases my parents were ready to load into Fox's car before he dropped me off at the airport."

The pain of our abrupt ending comes back like a sorrowful melody in my body. "Why didn't you ever tell me that you applied in the first place? We talked about it, Meadow, and you said it wasn't in the cards for you."

"I didn't want to hurt you. I thought that in some distant future, maybe the achieving our dreams together portion of our plan would happen separately and we'd find each other again. Fox actually put that into my head."

"He knew?" I try to keep my hands steady, but a tremor runs through them. The fight we had all those years ago flashes through my head. His screams. My own.

I wonder if Fox ever told Meadow that he came to visit me. I doubt it. We were not the best versions of ourselves that night. There's no need to tell her now and perhaps tarnish the memory of her brother—that mess was between Fox and me.

Meadow shrugs a shoulder. "He encouraged me to apply, and I didn't for the longest time. But I felt so scared that I would spend a year compromising my own dreams."

Looking back, the idea of her living in Boston, a place that didn't come with the best memories, while I buried myself in textbooks, wasn't ever going to make her happy. "I wish I'd known. Your dreams were always just as important as mine."

"I loved you so much, Ollie, and you loved me. One of us would have had to sacrifice our future, and I couldn't let you do that."

She does know me to my core. "It would've been my choice to make."

"I didn't want to make you choose. So, I made the choice myself. For both of us. For our careers." She keeps her eyes on her muddy boots, but I can tell they're turning red. "I promise, it wasn't an easy decision."

I'm sure it wasn't, having to decide between love and your career at seventeen. Love. That's what I feel for her so plainly, I never even had to redefine it, and I never fell into it again. I've always loved her. And now I'm in her shoes, needing to choose between staying in Scotland with Meadow or returning to New York. Viggle is starting to look less like a dream job and just another gateway to a paycheck with a lonely life.

Can Meadow and I have a second chance at this?

"I was going to propose to you." I wince as I say the words

out loud for the first time. "I had a ring with me at the airport. A sapphire thing, to match your eyes." She looks at me, and my heart stops. "Uh, barely even a ring to be honest, but when we got the keys to our flat, I was going to pop the question."

"Ah, fuck." She lets out the burden of a sigh in her chest. "Ol, I had no clue."

"Aye," I shrug. "What would you have said?"

"Huh?"

I kick a rogue twig out of our path and stride ahead. "If I'd asked you to marry me?"

Meadow stops and pulls my gaze to hers. "Yes. I would've said yes." Her response sets the hairs on my arm on edge. "But if I got into Le Cordon Bleu and didn't go, I may have woken up one morning, five, ten, twenty years down the road and realized that I resented you."

The way I resented her all these years. But it was unfounded. Yeah, Meadow didn't come with me, and yeah, I was a lovestruck teenager who believed our relationship could conquer anything. But we both lived our lives. Now we are here together. Like Fox told her we would be. "Timing just wasn't on our side."

"It wasn't."

"I'm glad your brother encouraged you to apply."

She smiles. "Me too. He flew out for the first day of orientation and helped me with LCB's work-study program. My parents and I weren't on great terms—they were steadfast in their assumption that I'd come back to Thistlehill faster than I left. But he promised me that I would succeed."

"And you lived up to his promise."

She touches the small, gold thistle that always hangs around her neck. "And he gave me this, just in case I ever got homesick, so I had a small part of home with me all the time."

I pull her hand into mine, holding it close. "It sounds like you should make a dish for Fox, doe."

Meadow brings our clasped fingers to her lips. "Already

ahead of you." She grins and sidesteps me, walking to a decayed elm tree in our path. "Velvet shanks. His favorite." She squats down and plucks off a stack of bright orange mushrooms. "Want to join me at Fox Den and see what I can make with all of these?"

I have a little over a month left with her. I'm done living in the past. I look at her sun-kissed cheeks and beautiful smile. The present is much sweeter. "I'd love to."

## Chapter 28
# Meadow

"Do you actually want me here? In your sacred space? I know a chef's kitchen is special, rituals and all."

"You had a mouthful of my sacred space on Saturday."

His laughter fills the front seat. The sound warms up every cell in my body. "Touché."

"So, there's your answer."

"Alright, let's go, chef."

Ollie steps out of the truck, swings around the front, opens my door, and takes the basket of mushrooms out of my lap before helping me out of the vehicle. He follows me as I unlock the back entrance and flip on the lights. I strip off my coat, leaving on my denim shirt. The stainless-steel countertops are spotless. The prep areas and the sinks are glimmering. White tiled floors without a mark or stain.

Just how I like it.

"Can you set the mushrooms down by the sink?" I call out, already headed for the fridge to pick up butter, shallots, a few aromatics, and a bulb of garlic. Start with the classics.

"What are we cooking?" He smiles at me as I set my ingredients beside the basket and throw on an apron before finding a spare one that might fit him. "Please tell me we're having you in an apron again." He tugs on the apron, but it looks like a baby tee on a lumberjack. It hits the top of his thighs and barely stretches over his torso. "Or maybe we're having me…"

"You're insatiable," I laugh.

He shrugs and gives me one of those irresistible smiles that briefly lights up the nerves in my tummy. *Focus*. These damn ovulation hormones. "Are you going to put me to work?"

I pass him the white peppercorn and fennel seeds. "Grab the mortar and pestle from the top rack two stations down and put those strong arms of yours to use."

He quirks a brow at me. "Strong arms?"

"If you're in my kitchen and I'm giving orders, it's *yes, chef*."

"Yes, chef," he smirks.

As Ollie locates the mortar and gets to work, I begin brushing the fresh dirt off the mushrooms. "When Fox and I were kids, we stumbled onto some velvet shanks just like these." I pause, watching Ollie's hands begin to work the pestle against the peppercorns. Veins bulge in his forearms. Biceps flexing. As he picks up the fennel seeds, my attention slips. "Actually, hold off on those fennel seeds. Too much licorice."

"Aye, chef," he winks.

I roll my eyes. "Anyway, we took them home. I got the skillet hot with a mix of butter and oil—that's the secret—while he cleaned them off." The memory is like a warm hug. "I made the mushrooms nice and crispy with just a little bit of salt and pepper before we piled them onto toasted bread and doused them in maple syrup."

"Maple syrup?"

"It needed something rich and sweet. Couldn't exactly crack into my parents' bar for sherry." The sound of the pestle ceases, and I look over at him. Those brown eyes are gliding over me with aching slowness. "What are you gawking at?"

"You're beautiful when you're in your space, in your element. It's hard to not spare a second to watch you." My cheeks heat. I grab one of my chef's knives and pull out the butcher block. "Woah, woah, woah, I was only paying you a compliment!" He steps back, eyes wide on the knife.

I can't help but laugh at his imposing stature in my kitchen. "When you're meant to be working," I tease. My nose tingles. Something briny. "Here." I hand him the dried fish mint we imported a few weeks ago. *Is that the wrong thing to use?* Can't hurt to give it a try. "Set the peppercorns aside and grind these."

"Yes, chef." He does as I say while I chop the mushrooms and prepare my skillet. A prickling runs along my neck. "Keep going, I want to hear how your brain works."

"Velvet shanks are sweet and a little mealy. Fox would say that they tasted like the forest and loch were in his mouth." It was a gift to live surrounded by nature, to get to explore the different tastes and smells of things when I was just a kid. Boston always smelled like smoke, burnt rubber, and low tide. Thistlehill smells like home. "I'm thinking of somehow putting that feeling onto a plate. In some cultures, mushrooms symbolize rebirth. It would be a way to honor his memory."

"That's lovely, doe—uh, chef. That's very lovely, chef."

I ignore the soft flames stoking inside my stomach and return to the real ones in front of me. *Is frying even the right move? Should I roast them?* "That's why this needs to be perfect."

"Your herbs are ground." He sets them beside me.

"Good. Mince the garlic?"

"Yes, chef." He walks over to my prep station and gets to work, breaking off cloves and using the flat side of my chef's knife to gently press down and loosen the skin. He finely minces them, sending the pungent, sharp smell right into the kitchen. "How's this?"

"Not bad, chef." I return to my hot pan, adding oil and butter, but as I go to drop in the mushrooms, I hesitate. Something's not right. "I feel like I'm losing the recipe. I had it in my head, the earth, the briny loch, all dressed on a cerulean blue plate but..." I look around at the aromatics, my hand on my hip. Shallots. Ginger. Thyme. *No.* I search my thoughts, grasping at ghosts of memories. "Fuck. I lost it."

I turn off the stovetop and toss my pan on a cool rack. It clatters loudly through the kitchen.

There's about a month left until Adair Grant arrives at Fox Den, and I can't even throw a basic fucking mushroom dish together.

I stare at the orange caps, waiting for them to say something to me, but nothing comes.

"Chef?" Ollie's hands land on my shoulders.

I jerk beneath his touch and spin around to face him. "I almost forgot you were here."

"You're going to figure it out," he assures me, but the familiar fear of failing returns. I hate this.

"I feel out of touch with my own senses, is that even reasonable? As a chef, your intuition, smell, and taste are the most important things in your tool kit, and after all these years on autopilot, mine are practically numb." All the old standards are failing me now.

So counterintuitive! *Ugh.*

He rubs my shoulders with his thumbs, the way he always does when I get tense. My body relaxes a bit. "Guess we need to help you get back in touch with your senses."

"How?" I cross my arms over my chest and look up at him.

"I can think of a few different ways," he says in that low, core-tingling voice of his.

My eyes dart around the kitchen. "Here?" Ollie nods and doesn't give me a chance to protest. He picks me up and sets me down on one of the stainless-steel counters. The metal is cool, even through my jeans. "This is violating all kinds of health and safety regulations," I scold him, but I make no effort to hop down.

"I'll scrub it clean after we're done." He smirks and pulls a dish towel off the stack of freshly pressed laundry we keep by the staff lockers. He hands it to me. "Put this on."

I eye the thing. "I got naked under an apron once, and now this? You should know there's no way *that* can fit around any part of me."

He laughs. Warm and hearty. "Around your eyes, doe. We want to dull out some of your senses to heighten the others. Trust me."

Without hesitating, I tie the towel around my eyes. The bright fluorescent light fades from view. His heavy boots stomp around my kitchen, and I listen carefully to him rustling around. Then the room quiets, and an icy sensation runs over my fingertips.

"Ah!" I wince, jerking away.

"How's that feel?"

"Cold." He carefully rolls up one sleeve of my shirt, exposing my forearm and running the damp, icy hardness over the tender skin. Goosebumps rush up my arm and over the slope of my shoulders. "Very cold."

"I can fix that," he whispers. Ollie's fingers trail up my arm, warming me up as he goes.

"Okay, that's nice."

"Not sure if you've noticed, but making you feel nice has always been a bit of an obsession for me."

My lips curl. I probably look like a fool with the towel around my eyes and the biggest grin on my face. "I hadn't noticed," I say sarcastically.

The coarse hair of his beard tickles my chin and jaw; I inhale his woodsy scent. He breathes along my lips. "You're going to have to keep that smart mouth under wraps and focus on guessing."

"Or what?"

"Or I'll keep those lips busy some other way."

My core heats at his threatening words. I tip my head up, ready for the impact of his mouth on mine, but it doesn't come. Instead, clattering fills the kitchen again, and I anxiously wait.

Suddenly, his fingers glide against my lips, dragging something thick and sticky along the seam of my mouth. My breathing slows as he dips his thumb into my mouth, and I stick out my tongue, licking off the sugary taste.

"Honey?"

He pulls away. "Yes, sweetheart?"

"No," I smirk. "I meant that's honey."

"What kind?"

I let my tastebuds soak up the sweetness. Caramelized, malty, and bitter all at once.

"Heather? We picked up a batch at the Inverness farmers market not long ago."

"Good girl." The praise stokes the flames in my belly. A whisking sound comes before his finger is back on my lips. I don't play coy, just wrap my mouth around it and suck off the taste. He exhales roughly. "How about now?"

Succulent, rich flavors explode in my mouth. Thick and creamy. A smoky aftertaste. I'd know that anywhere. "That's honey and whisky. My Anderson blend. Make these harder, won't you?"

"So bossy."

"It's my kitchen," I remind him.

"And yet, you're at my whim."

A blush creeps up into my cheeks. My brain sparks like water on hot oil, and before I have a chance to respond, something rough and prickly tickles my other arm. I lift it to my nose and inhale.

"Rosemary?"

"And?" I inhale again, but I'm struggling to focus as my feet brush up against his legs. He's so close and so far. "I'm waiting, chef."

I will all of my instincts to work and find the lingering scent of peppermint between the pungent rosemary oil. "Water mint."

He chuckles. The sound races my heartbeat into a sprint. "You're impressive."

I straighten on the counter and tap my fingers on the steel with anticipation as Ollie leaves my side again and makes his way around my domain. More glass touching metal. The familiar sound of the stovetop flicking on.

"You better not be messing up my kitchen too much," I tease.

"What did I say about that mouth?"

He doesn't let me retort as his lips close on mine. The taste of him, the feel, steals the air from my lungs. So familiar. So sweet? A hint of cinnamon and taffy.

"You taste yummy," I whisper.

"Like what?"

"Candy."

His nose brushes against mine. I scoot closer to the edge of the counter, trying to steal another small touch, but he pulls away. "Be specific."

"Reed's Cinnamon Candy?"

"Try again."

"I may need another taste." The words leave me desperately.

Ollie grants my request and traces his tongue along the seam of my lips. As he moves away, my upper half follows him. Ugh. This is starting to feel like torture.

"Where did you get Lucky Tatties?"

"Saw them around." I can hear the smile in his voice. "Want to keep going?"

I do. "Yes."

He serves me slices of blood oranges, the citrus flavor

lighting up my tastebuds. Valerian on my fingertips. A whiff of toasted nutmeg. Fresh strawberries. This is the most fun I've had in the kitchen since I made Ollie his lamb. Any time my two loves are together, I'm alive.

*Love?* I swallow. But there's no point in pretending I don't feel that for him—I always have.

After some more fumbling around, Ollie's low whisper returns to my ears. "I'm going to take off your shirt, okay?"

"Okay."

Nerves tiptoe across my chest as he sets each button free. A kiss follows each clasp that comes loose until my denim shirt falls somewhere on the floor. My heart beats against my ears, teeth grinding together with need.

A cold, sharp object digs into my upper arm. It's surely steel. My eyes widen beneath the towel.

"How's that?"

"Is that a knife?" I shy away, but Ollie doesn't let up.

"Which one?" I can just about hear the smile in his voice. Adrenaline works overtime in my body.

"Is this payback for threatening you?"

"Now that you mention it." He drags the dull side of the blade along my skin, stinging it with pleasure. The heat between my legs multiplies. What is wrong with me? I've been caught under a blade before, burned skin and nearly sliced to my bones, but this is something else. "I'm waiting, chef."

"This is impossible."

He tsks. "I don't believe that. Try."

The blade flips onto its side, and the texture of hammered steel glides along my arm. The cold, stinging pleasure makes me lose my breath.

"Uh…" I sew my eyes shut, thinking. "The blue steel Gyuto?"

"Is that a question?"

"The Gyuto with a walnut handle," I say with more certainty.

"You're something else, you know that?" A warm wetness appears on my chest, followed by the coarse hair of his beard. A moan sneaks out of my throat as his tongue traces the slopes of my breasts. Something hot follows, shocking my system—not burning, but not just warm either. The heat dulls the moment one of his hands cups my tits and his teeth pinch my hardened nipple through the fabric of my bralette.

"Ah." I suck in air through my lips.

"Waiting for an answer." His voice is muffled.

"Your teeth."

"What else?" I focus on the warmth along my breast, losing concentration as he moves to the other, stroking and biting. "I'm waiting, chef."

Heat drips down my skin and coats my bralette. "Hot oil?"

"Mhm." He licks the warm path and unsnaps the back of my bra, carefully pulling it off. The cool air makes my skin pebble. Ollie kisses all of me.

"That's all you."

"How do I feel?"

"Rough and tender at the same time," I say. "You smell like whisky—you always did—and wood."

He grabs a handful of my waist and pulls me closer, until his body is imposing between my thighs. He reaches for the button of my jeans. "May I take these off of you?"

"Yes." I nod as he slowly works the zipper.

"To me, you smell like rain. I love it."

I attempt to peek through the towel over my eyes. "I do?"

"You do," Ollie confirms, as if it's a fact. "Sometimes, when it used to rain in Boston, or even in the city, I'd have to lock myself in my apartment just to keep my body from reacting to that smell of petrichor."

His words shock me, and I yank off the towel. The fluorescent light of the kitchen burns my eyes. "I had no idea. Did I always smell like rain?"

"Yes, doe. Back then and now. It's like you'd know when to come and wash off the world so I'd never really be able to forget you. A lot of things reminded me of you. Anytime I was in a kitchen, pulling out my pans, I'd get a pang in my chest," he admits, his pupils swallowing his irises.

At that, I kiss him, my heart reaching for his. My body is compelled to embrace him. We exchange panting breaths and moans. The counter is unsteady beneath me.

"I want you," I whisper.

"I want you too."

I help him take off my jeans, scooting around before my behind sits on the steel and Ollie is on his knees in front of me, pulling off my boots and then the denim. He kisses up my legs—blistering and consuming.

"Meadow, I could literally devour you," he laughs, biting his knuckles. "Just—*fuuuuck*." His warm palms move up my legs, over my stomach. "Open these up for me?" He taps my knees.

I do as he says.

He doesn't hesitate, just starts kissing and biting along my legs. He glides his pointer finger along the seam of my panties. His hot breath hits my center, and he inhales, licking his lips.

I'm more turned on than I've been in years.

"That was so fucking hot." *Did I just say that out loud?*

"No need to be shy around me." He looks as distressed as I feel. "Can I please have a taste, chef?"

His begging makes me want to shove him right between my thighs. But he's worshiping me, and I want to relish in that.

"Just one." I raise a brow at him.

Through my panties, he closes his entire mouth around the hottest and wettest part of me and sucks. The heat in my core bullets to the base of my spine, and I toss my head back, spreading my thighs further.

"You're fucking soaked, doe," he laughs. "I bet you'd feel so right wrapped around me."

"Then what are you waiting for?"

Rising from his knees, he kisses me as my hands roam over his shoulders, fighting off his shirt. He tastes so good. Feels so right. My mind is dizzy as the sweetness of cinnamon and the taste of myself explodes between our lips.

He shucks off his belt, and I help pull down his jeans.

"Wait," he says against my lips.

"I'm done waiting."

"No, doe, I don't have a condom."

*Ugh.* Why? Why now? My mind's blistering with need for him. I rack through all the possible options.

"I—I'm on the pill and all clear."

His eyes are bewildered. "I'm clear too, but, doe…" He sighs heavily. "Are you sure?"

"I'm sure. I'm so sure. I need you." I mean it.

He pushes my panties aside and smiles. "This is about to be all mine, isn't it?" His tone is arrogant and irresistible. There's no trace of the tenderness from before.

"Mhm," I whimper.

Ollie smacks my swollen clit, the sting vibrating through me. "What did I say about using your words, Meadow?"

"All yours," I say impatiently, liking the pain.

"That's right. You won't ever have to guess that I've been here, that I've made this gorgeous cunt all mine." His lips curl into a devilish smirk. "Because you'll be feeling me for days after this."

He is made for me, and I am for him.

I scoot closer and drag the head of his cock along my entrance. His thick and hard erection in my fist is so fucking hot. He's big. How could he not be, given the sheer size of the rest of his body. But every single time I get acquainted with his third leg, it still sends a spell of shock into me.

"Are you going to keep admiring it, or can I use it to make you feel good?"

"A little admiration never hurt anyone," I laugh and notch the tip of him right up against my entrance. Once Ollie is centered right at my core, I throw my arms back again. His hands grip my waist and ass, his lips falling to mine.

"Come here, my girl." He pulls me closer, sliding me over another inch of him as a tremor pulses through my thighs. "Let me take care of you."

He thrusts into me so agonizingly slow that I feel every vein and every inch of smooth skin as he goes. My heart blasts in my rib cage.

He's all man. Brown eyes drenched in darkness. Slicked back waves. He's perfect.

Ollie slouches forward and plunges deeper. The sheer size of him is already making my walls convulse. His eyes refuse to leave my own as his hot breath drums against my lips while he begins to fuck me.

"Ol—" I breathe. I'm wound up to the point of desperation. The familiar burn of my orgasm at the base of my spine starts to rope through me. "Ol, I'm close," I say, surprising even myself. We've just begun, and I'm already on the brink.

He pounds into me. Skin slaps against skin until it's the only sound in the kitchen.

"Hang in there, baby."

He gets harder, practically splitting me open on the counter.

"I—mmm." I whimper and warn. My mind spins out of this dimension. *Fuck.* I'm going to come. I'm actually about to erupt or pass out. "Ollie, if you don't fucking come inside of me right now…" I groan, trying to resist for as long as I can as he pumps in and out of me. We must've spent an hour getting me all worked up, and I can't possibly wait. "I will start threatening you with my knives."

He laughs, sweat gathering on his brow. "Yes, chef. Don't"—he grunts—"need to ask me twice."

My body is tethered between control and the scorching release of my long-awaited orgasm. In a few thrusts, he gives me the look, the one I have been waiting for, and I finally let myself go.

My mind is full of stars, rattling around my skull and stealing my vision. But my tongue is speaking to me. "Seaweed," I breathe.

"What?"

"Seaweed," I repeat.

He whispers into my neck. "That a new nickname?"

"No, that's the recipe—it's mushrooms and seaweed." Excitement bursts out of me as his release trickles down my leg. That's a sensation I haven't felt before.

He laughs. Ollie's heavy body is draped over me, and I let myself close my eyes, savoring the smell of his skin. The cinnamon on his breath.

I want to give him so much. I want to howl his name into the night. Wrap myself in the coarse hair on his chest, drape his heavy arms over my body and keep them there until I regain consciousness. It's absolute madness, but my need for him always has been.

Maddening. Deep. Alive.

"Someone's here," Ollie whispers in my ear, his muscles stiffening. "Doe. I just heard the front door."

His words finally register. "What?"

He shrugs, looking panicked as he starts to grab our clothes off the floor, handing me my shirt and jeans. "Who could it be?" he whispers.

"I have no idea. We're closed today. Only Brooke, Fi, Davina, and I have keys."

Panic gushes through me, sending my heart into a frenzy. Footsteps come closer, heavy and loud as they hit the hardwood out in the dining room. *Oh, fuck.* I can see *The Thistlehill Daily* headlines now, "Head Chef Fucked on Her Day Off." I glance around, looking for a place to hide a six-foot-five man.

"The fridge?"

"Absolutely not." He frowns.

"Oliver, get in the fucking walk-in." I swing open the door and shove him in there, pulling up my pants as I go.

"You're going to pay for this, doe."

"You can use that belt on me later." I give him a wink and shut the door. Slapping my hair into submission and tucking my shirt over my shoulders, I inhale a breath as a figure emerges through the swinging kitchen doors—two figures.

"Fi?"

"Meadow?"

My pastry chef strolls into the kitchen, holding hands with Elspeth. The poor woman's blissful smile falls off her face, and she looks at me with mortification. "What are you doing here?"

"Me?" I glance around. "Uh, just cooking."

"Cooking?" Fi's eyes drop to the boxer briefs at my feet.

"Yep." I kick them underneath the counter. "Hi, Elspeth. Such a surprise to see you."

She gives me an embarrassed wave. "I actually forgot something in the car. I'll be right back. Or, you know, I'll just—yeah." Elspeth shoots Fi a panicked look and speeds out of the kitchen.

Fi and I stare at each other before the tense silence splits open and we're toppling over with laughter.

"Please tell me Ollie is in the walk-in and you're not just some boxer fetishist, bringing his underwear here to cook into a stew."

I stare at her with disgust. "Oh my goodness, Brooke is rubbing off on you, isn't she?"

Fi snorts, wiping eyeliner out of the corners of her eyes. "Says the woman who has a man inside of our fridge."

"That's positively filthy, Fi. What do you take me for, some kind of animal?"

She looks me up and down, settling on a firm nod. "You look happy, chef. There's actually some color in your face, and it's not because one of us is doing something you don't like in the kitchen."

I lower my voice and take a step toward her. "I just needed inspiration for a dish."

"That's what we're callin' it these days?" She hesitates, mouth opening to speak, but she keeps the thought to herself. "I need to apologize to Elspeth. I promised her we'd be alone."

"Were you on a date?"

Fi blushes, pushing the longer strands of her pixie cut out of her eyes. "I wanted to treat her to some of that pear dessert I've been working on for the tasting menu."

"We'll be out of here in just a few," I promise.

Her whole body squirms. "You better not be. The bleach is in the cleaning closet. The pair of you are going to scrub until your bones start peeking through your skin. I'll leave you to it. I have a date I need to get back to—it was going well before my business partner traumatized her." Fi shoots me a wink and turns to leave. "Bye, Ollie!" she shouts as she pushes her way out of the swinging doors.

The fridge door cracks open. Ollie peeks his head out, his lips the slightest shade of blue. I'm definitely going to need to warm him up. "She knows."

"Of course she knows. I mean, they kind of already knew," I chuckle as he comes closer.

"You told them?"

"I can't really keep secrets from those two."

"I like that you told them." Ollie searches my face, smiling beneath his beard. "Now lose the jeans and shirt again, throw on some rubber gloves, and get to work."

"Excuse me?" I jerk my head back in shock.

"That's your payment for shoving me into the fridge butt naked."

"Fine." I roll my eyes, not even attempting to hide the smile plastered onto my face. "But you're taking me home afterward and giving me a long scrub down in the shower."

"Sounds like a dream come true, doe."

I rise onto my tippy toes and connect my lips to his. "Deal."

## Chapter 29
# Meadow

MY PARENTS' HOUSE IS DARK WHEN I LET MYSELF IN, WALKING toward the spare bedroom in the back where Maisie falls asleep four nights a week.

"Hey, honey," Mom whispers, startling me. In the living room, Dad is reading next to a small light, and Mom is knitting in one of the matching leather armchairs. They're rarely awake when I get here.

I check my watch. It's past one. "What are you two doing up?"

"Your dad accidentally made us the caffeinated Earl Grey tea after dinner."

"That's the worst." I smile awkwardly. "Um, I just want to say that I appreciate you taking care of Maisie all these days. I know she's my responsibility—"

"We're happy to do it more often," Mom interrupts. "You know, whenever you'd like to finally enjoy some of your free time."

I smile. "Thank you, but I've got it figured out. This is more than enough, and I don't want to impose on you both. You've already done so much for me with the restaurant."

"You're not imposing, Meadow. She's our granddaughter." Mom frowns. "We want to take care of her."

"And help you. You did a big thing by taking her in the first place," Dad adds.

Sure, it's been years since that happened. But it's still nice to hear. Maybe this is my chance to share some of the uneasiness that's been stewing. It's late, but I rarely get a moment alone with them together.

My dish for Fox is still incomplete, and deep down I know it's because I haven't spoken to my parents about the feelings I had toward my brother or the way my teenage years played out.

It's time to air it all out.

My body is screaming at me to go home, to leave things as they've been for the past seven years. At least we haven't been fighting. I sigh. Just like my cooking, I can't keep operating on autopilot with my parents too.

"Can I share something with you both?" I settle into the couch across from them. Shadows dance along their faces. "I just..." The words fight their way out of my throat. It's time to get it all out, no more holding back. "This is hard to admit, but when I took in Maisie, I knew it was a chance for me to make up for the past. I know I wasn't always the most responsible or good at school and maybe not even the kid you may have wanted—"

"Meadow." Mom drops her yarn and places a hand on her chest. I can't look at her, can't bear to hear her tell me I'm right.

"No, look, I know that after Fox died..." I roll my shoulders, fighting back tears. "I wanted to make him proud. Make you proud. Maisie was the only way to show you that I'd changed. That I could do things right because I wasn't that rebellious seventeen-year-old who left home."

"We knew that." Dad eyes me over his reading glasses and frowns. "You didn't need to take Maisie to prove that to us."

I don't believe him.

"But I did. You two were distraught after Fox passed. Penelope's parents weren't alive. I was the only one who could take Maisie." I inhale, staring my dad in eyes that match my own.

Mom's lip trembles. "When you put it that way—"

"I was never going to be able to live up to your definition of success—the one that Fox managed to achieve so well. I had a chance at a do-over with Maisie. I could show you that our family's version of success was something I could try."

A silence stretches on, and I want them to react in some kind of way that could fix this. But it's not up to them. I need to get this off my chest.

"Meadow, you lost your brother." The words make my lungs feel like they're filled with water. "I know what Fox did for you, what we couldn't—he supported your dreams." Mom's cheeks are red and wet.

"We're sorry that we ever gave you any reason to believe we weren't as proud of you as we were of your brother."

Mom sobs; her cry is like a squeaking door in my chest. Dad glances away. I can barely make out his face in the shadows. What is he thinking? That I'm still foolish?

"We should have supported you from the beginning, but I guess..." Dad rubs the back of his neck, and I wait for the words *I guess because we loved Fox more*, but instead he says, "I won't give you an excuse, because none of them are valid. We had many failures as parents, but doubting you, forcing you into a box you were clearly never meant to belong in was our biggest one. Refusing to pay for culinary school as some morbid way to teach you a lesson—" His voice cracks, and he rolls his lips between his teeth.

Tears run freely now. I'm shocked, stunned that we're finally talking about this. Surprised to see my parents take the blame, admit that our distance hasn't been in my head all these years.

"We always wanted what was best for you, to protect you," Mom sobs. Like I try to protect Maisie. I'd move the earth for her, but I'd never keep her from chasing after her dreams. "When we lost our son, we realized that we had no control over anything anymore."

Something fizzles in the back of my mind. Ollie's soft voice when we sat at the loch, *You deserve to live your life as if it's the first time you're doing it too.*

I can't pretend to understand what it's like to have two children who are so different from each other. The parts of themselves that they may have seen in us both. The way they chose to handle those feelings. I guess maybe I can find a bit of forgiveness in the fact that this is their first time on earth too.

That all of us are really just trying our best with what we have.

"We're sorry for not making it clear that we love you and are proud of you every single day." My parents get up and join me on the couch. Mom strokes my hair like she used to when she'd put me to sleep back in Boston. "We were so afraid that you'd pull away from us if we ever admitted where we went wrong. That we'd lose a second child." Mom squeezes my hands.

I split open, letting the admission sink deep into my bones. I want to go home and cry.

Cry for the teenage girl screaming at the loch, that heartbroken woman in a new country, wailing for her lost love in between culinary classes. The tired chef who never even bothered to get a bed frame for her tiny apartments. The sister clawing at the ground at her brother's funeral and the mother who lost herself.

"I can't imagine what that felt like," I whisper.

"And we can't imagine the responsibility you felt pressured to take on as a twenty-seven-year-old who'd just lost her brother."

My eyes are heavy, and the sobs refuse to calm. I don't hide from them. I want to feel the emotions I've kept bottled up all this time. "Maisie is my whole world. She's why I want Fox Den to succeed. I want her to have every opportunity to attempt any kind of life she may choose. I want her to see that I did. That despite how little you understood, I still pushed through. I want to pay you back so I can be a role model for her."

"You don't owe us anything." My chest is weak. "The money we gave you was never a loan. It was always meant for you. It was the same amount Fox got to start his life with," Dad says.

I blink back the tears.

"Maisie may have been your chance to prove something you didn't need to prove, but our investment in you is our chance to show you that we're sorry. That we never should have withheld something from you. We were only trying to protect you from the things that made our life difficult," Mom explains.

Children really are prisoners of fate—I guess I can understand that. No matter how much I attempt to shield Maisie, life is going to throw things her way that I won't be able to fix. My parents couldn't stop me from chasing my dreams. I don't have to stop myself from having a life with them now. The same one we had before all the talks of college started and left us here, one Macrae down, but with a smaller one in the bed a few feet away.

"Let's keep talking, okay?" I offer my best consolation for the moment. "I want us to be a real family again. Not a distant one."

On the couch, their arms wrap around me. "We want that too."

"Maybe we can start by going to the Thistlehill Festival together, like we used to when you were little." Mom wipes at her splotchy face. We haven't done that since I moved back. It's a small step forward.

"I'd love that."

In their arms, I feel the weight of unspoken words lift. Visions of velvet shank mushrooms with shaved black truffle and crispy seaweed fill my head before the drain of fatigue calls me home.

A recipe for tomorrow.

## Chapter 30
# Meadow

VIBRANT COLORS ADORN EVERY NOOK AND CRANNY OF Thistlehill's cobblestone streets. After picking up treats on Main Street, Maisie, my parents, and I decided to leisurely stroll through the festival grounds, which are crowded with tourists and locals alike.

The scent of freshly cut wood fills my nostrils. Laughter, conversations, and the infectious rhythm of folk music sings through the air.

"It's even bigger than last year." Maisie smiles as she chews her bright purple cotton candy.

"Isn't it?" I squeeze her hand as we edge our way toward the heart of the festival, where men and women are preparing for the legendary caber toss competition.

We pass booths overflowing with games, delicacies, and artisanal goods. Everyone in the Highlands books their spot months in advance, wanting to showcase their small businesses to the tourists who travel up here along the North Coast 500.

"Mom, look." Maisie points her cotton candy ahead of us. "It's Coach Ollie."

I search through the sinewy arms of the competitors and the

towering wooden cabers until my eyes land on him. He's impossible to miss.

An overpowering stature, almost half a head taller than the people around him. Not only is he imposing in every sense of the word, but Ollie Anderson is wearing a kilt.

The Son of Andrew colors, deep blue and white, drape around his waist. Beige socks hit just below his knee, stretching over calves that are almost as thick as one of my thighs. There's a pair of cleats on his feet.

His Thistlehill Tacklers rugby team shirt stretches across his burly shoulders as he chats to Neil and a few of the guys from Blair and Brothers.

"Meadow?" Mom's voice breaks through my focus.

"Huh?"

"We asked if you'd like to go say hello." She shoots me a knowing smile.

"*Pleeeeaaaseee?*" Maisie sings, her face stained with purple. I pull a tissue out of my crossbody bag and wipe her down as she rocks back and forth on her feet.

*Note to self: make all of my obvious staring far less obvious.* "Right, sure, of course."

We wade through the crowd to the field.

Ollie and I have seen each other every single day since he came with me to forage by Loch Flora. Sometimes, he makes a casual excuse to stop by in the morning after I take Maisie to school, usually dropping off a handful of wildflowers. Other times, he waits for me to get off my shift at Fox Den to help carry Maisie upstairs from the car. On those nights, we quietly sit on the porch swing and he rubs the soles of my aching feet.

Small things have started to shift around in my life. My porch is swept without me ever picking up a broom. Maisie's cleats are always scrubbed clean the morning after she stains them at rugby. The Monday nights we spend together never extend my workload beyond whatever dish I make—pans are cleaned, counters scrubbed.

However much he shrugs it off or says he has nothing better to do with his time, I've started to rely on him. We've become a team at playing house. A hazardous game for us to play. For me to enjoy.

I counted this morning, and he'll be gone in twenty-eight days.

The reminder needlepoints a thread of hurt into my heart. We'll have to stop pretending soon.

"Coach Ollie!" Maisie waves at him when we arrive at the audience seats.

He turns to see all of us standing together on the opposite side of the field. His face looks as if it's captured the stray bit of sunshine in the sky. His warm smile hides in his auburn beard. Rings of curls damp with sweat. My favorite.

*Ollie*, my heart sings through the ache.

He jogs over to us, the damn kilt swinging as he crosses the field. "Hey, Mais." He high fives her. "I better go tell them to clear the pitch now that the fiercest competitor has finally arrived." Maisie giggles, sticking out her arm and flexing her muscles. "Meadow," he smiles, his eyes licking over every inch of me. The deep tone of his voice sends a shiver through me. "Ivy, Harris, nice to see you guys. Are you enjoying your day so far?"

"We are." Mom smiles and nudges me with her elbow.

"Good on you, son, for representing Thistlehill." Dad pats Ollie's.

"Maybe I can join a kids league?" Maisie stares out onto the field, mesmerized by the competitors.

Ollie squats down in front of her. "Why don't we petition them to start one for next year?"

"Yes!" She jumps up, and he ruffles the hair on her head. Watching him with her has reminded me of our brief family-planning conversation during our first Monday dinner. Seeing him on the field with her too. The care he puts into everything.

My ovaries are begging to free themselves from my body and wrap around Ollie.

"Your mouth's open, hun," Mom whispers in my ear behind me.

I clip it shut and attempt to brush it off with a casual laugh. "Allergies or something; my nose is clogged."

"Hmm." Dad gives me a concerned frown. "You never had a pollen allergy."

I shrug. Ollie refuses to take his gaze off of me. We must be so obvious. "It was lovely seeing you; good luck with the toss. We're going to go find some seats."

"Leaving so soon?" Ollie asks.

"Why don't we take Maisie for another cone of cotton candy and get us a spot on the bleachers, and you can join us after?" Mom nods suggestively.

"Sounds like a great idea, Ivy," Ollie declares.

*Yeah, they're all conspiring against me.*

"We'll be cheering for you," Dad says proudly. "Maybe tomorrow, after the festival, you can finally stop by our new place? I've been hoping you could come by since you arrived."

Ollie's cheerful disposition flattens a smidge. "You know what, I will, Harris. I promise."

"It's a plan. Now, come on, Mais. What do you say you show Grandpa how much cotton candy you can carry?"

Maisie throws a quick glance my way to check if that's alright, and I return a nod. It's a holiday, after all. She can eat her body weight in sugar. "I'll join you in a few."

They leave Ollie and me at the corner of the field and get swallowed up by the crowd.

"What do you think?" He tosses his hands to his side, showing off his kilt.

"Certainly dressed for the occasion."

He laughs, and it sounds like crackling butter in a pan. My favorite. "It wouldn't hurt you to pay me a compliment, doe. Especially when you're so obviously wondering what's awaiting you beneath this thing." He tugs the corner of the wooly fabric.

Curse him for being able to read me like the back of his own hand. "I already know what's under there."

"True." He smirks. "Last I heard, you were its number one fan."

"Fine." I force a loud exhale and glance around. "You look very nice in your kilt, Ollie."

"There, that wasn't so hard, now was it?" The gleam of mischief in his eyes makes me want to rip that kilt off and bite into what he's hiding under there. Though, knowing him, and knowing me, we'd both like that far too much.

"You're a true townie." I smile, trying to ward off how bittersweet those words feel in my mouth. "Caber toss, rugby coach, poker nights with Neil, flirting with the locals at Tavern," I tease. "Better be careful, or you might give someone the impression that you're from here."

"I'm proud to be from here. I've had a change of heart since returning." He shrugs. "There are two certain someones who helped that happen."

My pulse sings like I'm some kind of jolly, skipping schoolgirl getting to talk to her crush for the first time. In some strange way, I am. "The Cameron twins finally got to you?" I nudge him. "I can't blame you; those ladies are fabulous."

"No." He rolls his eyes at me. "It's because of *my* girls."

I want to shoot back another taunting quip or a silly jab, but I can't ignore the way those words make my intestines purr. The last time I was someone's, I left him at the Inverness airport.

"Your girls?" I swallow the shake in my voice.

"Maisie and you."

The ground beneath my feet turns into a pot of melting wax, encasing my boots and buckling my knees.

We've never been someone's. I made sure of that when I became Maisie's legal guardian. No one to hurt us. No one to leave. Because if I've learned anything in my life, it's that nothing is permanent. No matter how much you love it, no matter how much of your heart that one thing or that one person owns, it doesn't last.

The fluttering butterflies in my gut turn slow, and their giddy wings start to clap against my stomach in a way that makes me feel nauseous.

Sure, Ollie and I didn't get it right the first time, but could we have a real shot at trying again? Could he be there for Maisie? I obviously couldn't prevent them from bonding.

I may not be able to answer the first question, but I'm certain of how to answer the second—he loves her, and she loves him.

Even when an inevitable crash and burn looms over us. Should that keep us from ignoring the little sanctuary we've created? Would it be enough to get him to stay?

Ollie clearly senses that my mind has started to drift, and he touches my hand. "Doe?"

The warmth of his fingers brings me back to the present. His gorgeous smile shimmering in the sun. The damn kilt around his waist.

"How long until this thing starts?"

He looks back. "Twenty minutes?"

Another moment of fun. Would it be so wrong to take advantage of it? I clearly can't protect myself from whatever my heart feels for him. Maybe there's no point in trying.

"Did you forget something in your truck?" I keep my voice to a low simmer, checking to make sure no one in the crowd might hear us.

"No, I don't think—"

"Oliver," I say more urgently. "I think you may have forgotten something"—I glance down at his kilt and back up to him—"in your truck. A *favorite* thing of mine."

"Really? Right now?" A smirk kisses his lips.

"I'm only human, okay? That thing on you…it looks mighty fine."

"Then we better not waste any damn time chatting about it here," he laughs and quickly strides across the field, toward the large parking lot on the other side. I rush after him, keeping a tiny distance between us as we weave through the crowd.

His broad build towers over the other cars. The fabric of his shirt clings to his torso, revealing the defined contours of his back. The veins in his neck and the muscles in his shoulders have gotten bigger since he arrived. The rich tartan pattern around his waist swings with every step, giving me a glimpse of those tree trunk thighs that could easily crush my skull between them—and I may let them.

Okay. I'd totally let them.

We quickly get into the truck. Him in the driver's seat, me in the passenger. Thankfully, it's parked so far back that no one could find us here. Our mouths fuse together as we hungrily feast on each other, like we used to do as teenagers in this very same truck.

"You're a dream, I want—"

"Shut up, we don't have time for that." I reach across the center console to the adjuster on the other side of the driver's seat and yank it up. Ollie's body shoots back, surprise on his face. "What? I have needs, okay?"

He laughs. "Yes, ma'am. Do not let me get in the way of those needs."

I kneel in my seat and drape my front half over the console, my ass probably jutting up in the air. I unlatch the buckle of the leather sporran around his waist. My eyes burn with tunnel vision, adrenaline relentlessly pounding against my chest.

I'm restless and rushing and all too desperate for a taste of him. For a small reminder that this is all for fun, because the past few months with him have been exactly that—filled with joy and laughter and sex that makes my mind split.

I pull apart the woolen tie and move the tartan off his thighs, setting his cock free.

"You really went regimental, huh?" I quirk an eyebrow at him.

"For good luck." He winks at me. "Now, let me at you." Ollie reaches over to my side, clearly ready to strip me out of my clothes, but I swat his hand away.

My mouth waters as I take in his handsome, thick length. "No, I want you. Just you."

And my heart beats his name again. *Ollie.*

"Then don't be kind about it, doe. I fucking want you too." He glances at the thick head of his cock and looks back up at me. "Clearly."

A glisten of precum sits at the tip, and my eyes fill with anticipation as I widen my mouth into an O, close it over him, and suck. The salty taste of him spreads across my tongue. My core flushes with another sear of heat.

"Fuck, fuck, fuck," he groans. I steady my hand on his giant thigh; it looks so small in comparison. Pretty and delicate against the corded muscles in his leg. "Fuck, Meadow, you're desperate for it, aren't you?"

I run my tongue over his bulging veins and suck the tip of his cock again, the way that would always make him stop breathing. The way it's doing now.

I glance up and catch his head tipped back in pleasure. Eyes half shut. We could get caught. But I don't care. I want him. I want this power. I want to know that he's at my mercy—because a part of me feels so powerless with him.

And that feeling is only growing. I'm his. And I'm terrified and desperate and free-falling through all of it at once.

My hand stays firmly on his thigh; the other worms itself from beneath me and wraps around him. I unlatch my lips from his cock and tip my head back up for a second. Ollie doesn't hesitate to swing his palm beneath my jaw and bring my mouth to his, clearly not caring where it just was. The kiss is gentle and tender. So fucking sweet.

"You were made for me, weren't you?" He pulls back, eyes scanning me. Next to the deep, dark desire, there's a genuine question. "I fucking know you were."

I think I know that too.

I glance at my watch. "We don't have much time." I smirk and gather the taste of him on my tongue, spitting onto the head of his cock.

"Meadow," he growls. The darkness in his gaze starts to burn as I lower my mouth back onto him.

His hands tangle in my hair, stroking the strands and massaging the strain in my neck. Surely, my panties and jeans are entirely soaked as I keep pushing him deeper and deeper into my mouth. The tip of his swollen cock hits the back of my throat, and I breathe through my nose, my mind getting lost in the sound of his pleasure. Euphoria and lust are the only things pumping through my veins. I want to get him there.

I want to make him finish.

"Christ, you're so fucking beautiful. So, so good to me."

My eyes widen, and I stare at the lines my nails are making on his thigh. The blue and white tartan brushing over his skin as he starts to punch his hips upward in the driver's seat.

This damn fucking kilt. Did he have to look so sexy in it? Seriously?

I spin my grip along his cock, my mouth connecting with my fist as I try to match his pace. His thrusts turn longer, more unsteady, but I don't stop. He gently strokes my hair as I work myself up and down his shaft.

Out of the corner of my eye, I catch a glimpse of his strong pecs. The rough, virile hair poking out of his shirt. To anyone else, he's the most intimidating man alive. Strong. Monumental. Gorgeous.

To me, he's mine.

"I—" he says breathlessly. "Love, I think I'm going to—" He tries to pull away, but I seal my lips tighter around him. *Love.* The scary four-letter word neither of us has been able to say. A nickname in this case. Likely just in the heat of the moment. But it sings to a part of me. The part that always hoped the love between us would never falter or wither away.

The part that's afraid and knows he is too. The part I want to break through and move past.

I hum against his throbbing cock, feeling it grow thicker and bigger in my mouth. His breathing turns slow.

"Look at me, doe. I—ah," he groans. "I want to see you."

The callused pads of his thumbs push the hair out of my face as I tip my head to the side and feel his cock pulse on my tongue. I smile, giving my head a small shake to edge him on.

*I'm here.*

*I'm here too.* He looks at me before giving in.

His release spreads over my tongue, hot and abrupt. I swallow the taste of him until his body stops shaking beneath my touch.

A large bell sounds on the field. "Fuck, we should hurry back."

"I can't even feel my legs, doe," he sighs, fumbling with the kilt around his waist.

"You have to try," I laugh, checking myself in the mirror, brushing my hair out of my face.

"Wait." He reaches for me. "You really do drive me out of my mind. You're a fucking gift."

The warmth in my body is palpable. I try to enjoy it. "And you better find some boxer briefs to throw under there."

"Jealous?"

"Yes," I huff and climb out of the truck, closing the door

behind me. Ollie joins my side, and we walk hand in hand out of the parking lot.

"I'll keep an eye out for you in the stands?"

"I'll be there."

"Cheer extra loud for me, won't ya?" His cheesy grin returns.

"Win, Ol. For Thistlehill."

I kiss him hard. It's just like when we used to sneak around the festival, whether we were hiding under the bleachers taking sips of beer, or the year he placed second in the caber toss.

We go our separate ways, and I make my way to the stands, beaming and looking for Maisie and my parents—they're impossible to miss with the monster-sized cotton candy in Maisie's hands. I push past a few of the people and take a seat beside my family.

"You're gonna turn into a piece of cotton candy yourself, Mais." I eye my parents with a scolding look.

Dad shrugs. "It's impossible to resist those eyes."

Maisie keeps her focus on the pitch. "They're starting."

Mom leans over, lowers her voice, and says, "You guys planning on making it public soon?"

"What?"

"Meadow, you're my daughter, not an actress."

"It's nothing. Don't worry, I'm not going to drag Mais into it."

Mom's blue eyes fill with sadness as she frowns. "I know you care about her, but I think it's about time you cared about yourself too. If you're happy, dear, be that. Feel it in your gut. Enjoy it. Let it do you some good."

A part of me hesitates. Isn't this what they always wanted? For me to end up with Ollie? "I'm sure you'd be happy if I got back together with Ollie, but he's leaving this month."

The same defeated look I saw on her face two weeks ago returns. "Oh, Meadow. You're right, we were happy for you all those years ago, but not for the reasons you think. When you two were young, and your father and I made your teenage years difficult, it was Ollie who put a smile on your face. He had a way of doing that better than any of us. Still does."

"What if...what if it crashes and burns?" I whisper. "He has a job lined up. His dream job, Mom."

"I know that's why you're both keeping yourself safe, but it's plain to see things may not be working out the way you thought." She doesn't say it outright. That Ollie hasn't brought up his dream job lately. That he's here, committing to the town. That he's talking about next year with my daughter. That somewhere over the past few weeks, I've become his. Again. "Look, Meadow, what if you just let it?"

"Let it what?"

"Crash and burn, as you've put it. What if you let that happen? What then?"

I stare at her, confused. "I don't know. I'd be hurt, and then there's Maisie..."

Mom shakes her hand, winding her arm through mine and pulling me closer. "And so if you don't?"

If I don't *just let it*, let whatever feelings I'm starting to feel again for Ollie, let my daughter keep falling for someone who's going to leave, then we'd be right where we were before he came back home.

"We've all had enough loss in our life, dear. There are certain things we may never get back, but you have a chance now. You can let yourself come back—Ollie too. You can let it happen, and we'll be here for whatever unfolds after you do."

Whether I want to admit it or not, when we broke up, a part of me disappeared too. Not only was Ollie some kind of embodiment of a time when my brother was still alive, when things were easy. But there's something else about being with him that has returned to me over the past few months.

I don't have to be perfect around him. I don't have to pretend I'm fine and try to make things right.

With Ollie, I'm me again.

The pieces of myself I've been searching for all this time are starting to fall back into place. We were foolish for letting each other back in when neither of us had any intention of making our fun permanent. But it's more than that, isn't it? It's not just fun.

Even as I'm wrestling with the idea of ripping back into that hurt, my soul calls out his name. *Ollie*, my heart says. *Take me back to Ollie.*

He's found a way to live within me. In all the corners of my soul. As much as I want to ignore that, I can't. He's made me feel known again. Lit up all of my true colors. Given me a way to realize that, however good I am on my own, I'm myself with him.

I'm better. A better mother to my daughter. A better chef. A better woman to myself.

The town provost steps forward to make an announcement, a mic in her hand. In a booming voice, Jody declares, "Ladies and gents, the time has come! The caber toss competition is about to commence! Prepare tae witness feats of strength and skill that will leave ye in awe!"

The crowd erupts in cheers and applause, shaking the nerves simmering beneath my skin. The sun's warmth caresses my cheeks, and I stay present. The same way I listened to my gut and snuck Ollie back through the parking lot to his truck. *Stay here.* I listen to the sound of my daughter clapping, my parents laughing. I let the smell of freshly cut grass and greasy treats tickle my nose.

I let myself be.

I embrace just *letting it be* for a second.

"First up, we have the three-year reigning champion, Vladislav Petrovsky."

The first competitor steps onto the field. A small man who's as tall as he is wide, his muscles ripple with power as he kicks up the red wool of his kilt and waves at the crowd. Collective breaths inhale in anticipation around me.

He approaches the caber, and the crew around him raises it into an upright position. With a steady grip, the man lifts the caber from a squat and releases it with a mighty heave. The wood spins through the air and collapses onto the ground.

The crowd goes wild. I spot Ollie on the field, looking calm. The competition moves through a few more participants before it's finally his turn.

"Next up, we have Thistlehill's very own, Ollie Anderson," Jody announces, welcoming Ollie onto the pitch.

"There he is," Dad smiles. "Let's go, Anderson!"

"Ollie! Ollie! Ollie!" Maisie claps her hands together and drums her feet on the metal of the bleachers. I join her stomping, smacking my boots into the stand. "Come on, Mom, we gotta be louder. Like you cheer for me on the field."

I join her, shouting his name until our section erupts in a chant: "Ollie! Ollie! Ollie!"

From the field, he spots us standing above everyone. Mom and Dad wave ribbons that match the color of his kilt. Maisie jumps beside me. Ollie catches my eye, and I smile, mouthing, *You got this.*

He shoots me a wink. *This one's for you.*

The whole tough-guy-on-the-field thing still makes my knees weak, the way it did when I'd show up to Fox and Ollie's rugby games. But seeing him all grown up, that look of stark pride and challenge on his face, those damn calves and strong thighs, I want to run out onto the field like some lovestruck fan and drag him by the skin of his neck back into the truck to show him just how wild he drives me.

He stands apart from the rest of the competitors, exuding immense strength. As he plants himself in front of the caber, a hush falls over the crowd. Every move is deliberate and calculated. So fucking sexy.

"Come on," I whisper under my breath, biting my lip to ease the anticipation.

With a surge of power, he hoists the pole into his hands, pressing it close to his chest. The veins in his arms bulge. Ollie breaks into a running start, and with a thunderous roar, he launches the caber into the air.

It rotates. The ground beneath us seems to vibrate. All eyes are fixed on the pole as it soars against the blue sky.

The pole spins in an actual circle before the end hits the ground perfectly, standing straight as a pin for a breath and then collapsing to the ground. The crowd erupts in thunderous applause, chanting his name. The atmosphere is electric, filled with an overwhelming sense of joy and pride from all the locals in the stands. Ollie secured first place for us, there's no point in doubting that.

"Mom!" Maisie tugs on my hand. "Did you see that?"

"I sure did, plum." I nod frantically, unable to wipe the smile from my face.

Ollie flicks the sweat off his face, searches for us in the crowd, and waves us over.

"C'mon, we have to go over there," she pleads, batting her big, round eyes.

Instead of hesitating, instead of looking for an excuse to say no, I say, "Alright. Let's go congratulate Ollie on his toss."

"You guys go on," Mom smiles. "We're gonna watch the rest of the competition from here."

We weave through the bleachers and the crowd on the lawn until Ollie comes into view, striding toward us like some Greek god.

It's like time has slowed. Sweat drips from his shaggy hair, and veins bulge in his arms. His kilt swooshes. My mouth waters again. The taste of him is still on my tongue. Each one of his heavy steps makes the ground beneath my feet shake.

Ugh. He's perfect.

Maisie slips her hand from mine and bolts right at him, dragging me back to this plane. I let her go. Her hair beats in the wind as she runs into Ollie's arms.

He bends down, picking her up off the ground and spinning her.

She squeals in his arms. "Do you think if you throw me in the air I can spin like that caber?"

"Maybe when we're not on solid ground," I laugh.

Ollie shoots me a quick look. *Is this okay?*

*Yes.* I nod.

"Can I really get that strong?"

"All that conditioning is going to pay off, and you'll be able to pick up your mom here and toss her into the air," he teases, booping her nose.

"Let's not go that far," I laugh.

"Maybe I'll be able to win the big fluffy cow then." She cranes her neck, looking at the booths with games. "There's one that looks exactly like Belle, Mom."

"Maybe Ollie here can win it for you," I suggest. "If he's up for a little game of ring toss."

"You mean if *you're* up for getting *crushed* in ring toss. Did you not see what I just did to that caber?" He shoots me a wink.

*Did you forget what I just did to your caber?* I shoot his kilt a look.

*Hush.*

"What do you say, Mais? Think we can kick this caber toss champion's butt?" I give her a little nudge.

"Don't jinx it; they haven't announced the winners yet," Ollie says.

Maisie flails around in his arms, finding her way to the

ground. She grabs my hand, then grabs Ollie's. "Let's go before someone else gets my fluffy cow."

As we make our way through the crowd, which has multiplied since we arrived, I tightly hold Maisie's hand, her small fingers intertwined with mine. She looks between us both with wide eyes filled with excitement. I can't help but smile, grateful to share this special moment with her. With Ollie.

Maybe it's okay to let it crash and burn.

Maybe the hurt I felt once was worth it since it led us back here again.

"You looked yummy out there," I lean over to him and whisper. "Can you keep the kilt a while longer?"

His brown eyes light up. "Whatever you want, doe."

"The kilt." I repeat myself. "On or off."

"Let's win this cow first, shall we? And then Mama Bear can decide what happens with the kilt."

As we approach the game, the cheers and laughter grow louder. Colorful rings hang from the pegs on the wooden structure at the far end of the booth. Eager participants line up to try their luck. We join behind them.

"That one." She points to the furry cow hanging from the top of the booth. It's about as big as she is, beige and brown, with a fringe covering its button eyes. "That's my very own Belle."

"Who's next?" the person working the booth calls out.

"That'll be us," Ollie says, pulling out a couple of pounds and getting rings for us. The worker passes us three rings each, and we line up at the table, readying for our turn. "How do we win that furry beast up there?"

"Three rings in the top section of the board, and it's yours."

"Ladies, why don't you go first?" Ollie nods toward the pegs. "I'll count you down."

"Ready, Mom?"

I lean my weight on my back leg, holding the rings loosely in my hand. "Yes."

"Three, two, one," he announces.

We throw our rings. Both of them smack against the board and collapse to the ground. "Again," Ollie says, counting us down one more time. We throw again—one of Maisie's rings lands at the bottom section, and one of mine sticks to the top.

"Aw, I'm sorry, plum," I give her a squeeze.

"Two more in that top section, and the cow is yers," the worker says.

We throw our rings again but miss the pegs.

"Alright, ye have three more rings, and then it's game over."

Ollie readies at the table. He tosses the first ring, and it hits the top peg and sticks. We clap and cheer for him. Maisie bounces beside him with anticipation. He goes again, missing the top.

"Last one," he says. "Let's do it together." He extends his hand to us, motioning for her and me to put our fingers on the ring.

"Three," I start.

"Two," she continues.

"One," Ollie says, and we let go of the ring, sending it through the air. It clatters against the wood, and by some windfall luck it lands on one of the top pegs.

"Yes!" Maisie screams. "We did it! Together!"

The worker pulls the cow from the hook on the ceiling and hands it to Ollie. We move out of the way to let the other participants play. The kids around us watch Maisie with a jealousy that makes me far too excited.

Okay, it's totally inappropriate, but my big man just won the best prize for my little girl.

I'm the coolest mom here.

Ollie gets down on one knee, coming eye level with her. "Maisie Macrae, may I present you with your steed?"

She laughs, her cheeks burning red. "Thank you!" She takes the cow from Ollie and swings her little arms around his neck in a hug. The sight of them snuggling together is irresistible.

He looks up at me. *You want to get in here?*

*I do.*

*So, come on.*

I glance at the sea of people around us, hesitation pulsating through me. But I remember my mother's words and take the leap. *What if you just let it?* And so I let myself squat down beside them and wrap Maisie in my arms, pressing my chest into her back until Ollie's heavy arms settle on my shoulders.

"I feel so happy, Mommy," she whispers.

"Me too, plum."

"What about you, Ollie?" She pulls back to get a good look at him, even though our cheeks are still all smooshed together. "How are you feeling?"

"The happiest I've been in a long time."

Fox had it right all those years ago when we stood side by side at the sink. *You never know where life may lead you.*

Never did I imagine it would lead me back to this feeling.

A screech pierces through the crowd, the sizzling shock of the speakers above us lighting up with a voice. "Will Ollie Anderson please make his way back to the caber toss field?"

My parents appear beside us. Quickly, I unhinge from the three-way hug and rise to my feet.

"They're looking for you," Dad says. "Something's wrong."

"What?"

"They can't find the caber trophy."

"*Huh?*" Ollie's face is just as confused as mine.

"That thing has been in Thistlehill for two centuries," Dad says. "And Ollie was going to get the chance to take it home for the year, but it's missing."

"I'm sure there's an explanation."

Mom shrugs. "We better go and find out."

## Chapter 31
# Ollie

"No, no, no. It was right here this morning!" Jody frantically pulls off the tablecloth, like she's a magician hoping to reveal the missing trophy. Meadow, Jody, and I are behind Honeydew Market, where awards and flowers are sprawled across multiple tables. "It looks like a ribbon is missing too."

"Surely someone must have seen something," Meadow says.

"If anyone can solve this, it's you." I gently nudge her arm. "You've been reading mysteries for ages."

"Yes, but that's fiction." She shakes her head. "And usually there are clues."

"Please, Meadow." Jody grabs her shoulders. "If I lose this trophy while in office, that's all people will remember me for."

"I doubt that, but I'll help. Has anyone seen Belle here today? Although, I doubt she could carry a trophy in her mouth…"

"The Camerons swore she was locked up in the pasture."

"Okay." Meadow nods. "You stay here and check the festival. Try to figure out if anyone saw anything unusual. Perhaps the kids took it as a prank. Ollie and I will look around town."

"You're a lifesaver. If ye find it, anything Fox Den or

Anderson Distillery ever needs, I'll make it happen. Mark my words," Jody says before frantically running around the building.

That would've been useful when I wanted to build the damn bottling facility.

"Okay, if I were a trophy, where would I hide?" Meadow taps her finger to her lips, puts a hand on her hip, and scans the area.

"What is that lovely brain of yours thinking?"

She plucks a thistle from below the table, running her fingers over the spiky leaves and purple bloom. "The trophy is usually filled with flowers; maybe the culprit left us a trail?"

"Roger that, Detective Beck," I say, following her around the backside of the building until, sure enough, we stumble upon two more thistles. "Someone should give you a trench coat and a notepad," I chuckle, plucking the flowers off the ground and spotting a couple more in front of us. "Actually, I will. I will do the honors of seeing you in just a stereotypical detective coat."

After what happened in my truck, I owe this woman my life. Never had I felt so fucking good before.

She laughs. "Already got my notepad here."

"I can see the next installment of the Highland Murder Series now—*Highland Heist: The Caber Conundrum*."

"Are you sure you didn't bribe Kleptocow to steal the trophy just so you could spend more time with me?" Her lips twinge up into a smile.

"Maybe I did. A lot of apples can fit under this kilt, Macrae." She rolls her beautiful blue eyes at me.

"I checked earlier, *remember*? And all I spotted was a giant ego."

"You're going to name him Giant Ego?"

She scowls. "Come on, we have a mystery to solve."

"We could go back to my truck and look there first. What's the rush?"

"A favor from Jody!" She flicks the thistles at my chest. "Fox Den will surely need one eventually."

We follow the trail of flowers, bringing us farther away from the festival. The music and noise are barely audible. Meadow's nose is scrunched up, her eyebrows knotted. I want nothing more than to kiss her right now.

"You are wildly attractive when you're in the zone."

Her face relaxes, a hint of a smile on the edge of her lips. "Thank you for reminding me of that over the last two months." She slows her pace, her fingertips dancing along my palms.

"So, you gave me a hug today...in public," I say, trying to probe her feelings.

"Yeah."

"Well, it made this afternoon one of my favorites since I've been back." We walk together. "Getting to chat with Neil and the rugby lads before the caber toss, hearing you and Maisie cheer for me in the stands. Then winning that stuffed animal before getting to spend the rest of the afternoon with you." Energy beats through my veins. I hope it takes all fucking day and night to find this trophy. "Best day ever."

"Maisie will probably sleep with that cow every night."

My throat itches to tell her that I want to stay. Hell, I only have a month left, but I can't imagine getting on a plane back to New York and leaving her behind again.

*Just tell her.* It's better to know if we are on the same page.

"I've been thinking about not going back to New York."

She halts. Her eyes find mine, and I hold her gaze, feeling too exposed, too vulnerable. "What?"

"For a while now."

A look of shock crosses over her face. "What about the job?"

"I haven't reached out to Viggle yet. I wanted to talk to you first."

"Oh, Ollie, I think—" My gut flips, awaiting her response. "I think I'd like it if you stayed, but I don't know how that would ever work. What about your friends in New York? Your life over there? Are you really going to sacrifice your big paycheck to come back here?"

The questions I've been wrestling with for weeks all skip off her lips with worry, but my certainty in their answers holds fast. "You're right. I do have friends in the States, and a life there—one that was lonely for so many years. I refused to admit that no amount of career success was ever going to be enough for me."

"Even if it's the success that would come with the director position?"

"I spent almost twenty years making all the money anyone could possibly need. I did the corporate grind, and I gave back to the world. I simply forgot to look inward and take care of what I truly needed."

"Which is?"

"My family back."

"But your friends?"

"Will still be my friends," I assure her. "They love to travel, and I can always go visit them. I know that leaving them behind would be difficult, but I won't make the same mistake I made when I left Thistlehill for the first time. I won't stop prioritizing the relationships that are important to me."

Her blue eyes fill with concern again, and I wish I could answer every single question going through her mind. She's right to be worried. In hindsight, this might seem like a fast and sudden decision, but I'm certain of it. I'm certain of her.

"Okay," she says. "I understand what it's like to give up your dream job and move back here, but I *had* to do that. I gave up being a sous chef at d'Or because I needed to."

"And that's exactly why I believe that I can come back to Thistlehill," I explain. "You have your restaurant, Meadow. You have the thing you always wanted. You have your family and Maisie. You still have a full life here. I lied to myself for years thinking that I couldn't possibly have any of those things in

Thistlehill simply because I didn't feel accepted by my da or because of my heartbreak."

"Let's say you truly will be happy leaving the job behind. What will you do here?"

"Work at the distillery."

Meadow's face scrunches up. "Ollie, that makes me nervous. When we were kids, you never wanted to be at the distillery. You wanted more out of your life than this small town could give you."

"You're right. I did. I wanted more because I was embarrassed that my parents weren't as well-off as yours. I was certain that if I became as successful as your da, then I could be happy. That when we moved abroad together and I got to have everything your family did, plus you...well, I thought I would no longer want for anything."

Her lower lip quivers. "Ol, I didn't realize you felt that way. I know you wanted a better life, but not because of my family—"

"I was a boy, but I'm a man now."

"And what happens when this man realizes that this town of thieving cows and mud and one bar and two restaurants is too small for him?"

"The family I would have here would be big enough," I say with certainty. "I've seen how love can change your life, how it made my friends' lives fuller."

"Maisie and I are not something you can try on for size—"

"Doe," I interrupt.

"No, Ollie, please listen to me." She takes my hand in hers and holds it tight. "Maisie and I cannot cosplay a family like your friends have, only for you to realize you don't want that. The way you have been the past couple of weeks, Ol...it's everything I would've ever wanted in a partner while I was alone or when I first got Maisie, but this is a big decision. This isn't something you can change your mind about."

The sun glows around her and reflects a small beam off a

silver hair on her head. My heart stretches in my chest. She's right. Protective and fierce, and not a damn thing she's saying is invalid. But I'm certain of what I want.

"You will always be enough for me. You and Maisie aren't something I'm going to change my mind about. I love you, Meadow." I finally say the words out loud. They don't feel like a shock or a surprise. The only thing I could ever feel for her is love. "You've given me a chance to redefine success. A chance to feel like I belong in a place that once made me happy. A place where I had my girl and my best friend. A self I haven't been in a long time."

I want more out of life than what I had for the last seventeen years.

"But what happens if you do get tired of Thistlehill?" Meadow looks down at the ground. "What's going to happen when your dad comes back? Sure, you made things right with Callum, but will the rest of your ideas be accepted? What happens if they won't be? What if the distillery doesn't turn a profit and then you won't feel comfortable—"

"Meadow," I say to calm her panicked questions. "I have three million dollars in my bank account. Money is the least of my concerns right now. Truly, I have more than enough."

"Three million dollars?" Her head jerks back in confusion. "What?"

I shrug. "Good investments pay off. Silverman Sachs had bonuses for working me to the bone, and I sold shares of my start-up when we joined the Oceanic Research Organization. Ma and Da never let me make things right after they gave up their travel fund to pay me the year I was deferred from MIT. They put their dreams on hold for me, and I came back for the chance to repay them for their sacrifice."

She traces the lines in my hands. "And you would be happy at the distillery? Happy being around your da?"

"I wanted success for the wrong reasons, Meadow. I wanted

to be rich. I wanted to not end up like my parents, but you know what I've realized? My parents are happy. Sure, there were years of fighting and hostility in the Anderson house, but they love each other. They always had each other. Da believed in his legacy, while I ran away from mine because I thought it wasn't good enough for me."

"And is it good enough for you now?"

The months I've spent at the distillery haven't been easy. Between the difficulties with Callum and the long days to get the bottling facility on track, there were so many times when I felt like I made a mistake coming back. But there were also times, like when I found Meadow's whisky, going through those barrels and seeing a history that I could've been a part of, a legacy that isn't just about status but about heritage and tradition, that made me want to embrace the parts I once threw shame at.

The distillery is beautiful, and it is mine. "I wanted my name smeared across the world, but my name has always been here. My name is already in Thistlehill," I explain. "Not only that, but now our whisky is in resorts all across the world. Something that my hands have touched, the work and labor I put in, the same as my da, has made it out there, doe. That makes me proud. Isn't that the real definition of success? To feel proud of yourself?"

I want to be a good friend, a good son, and a good contributor to society.

A good dad. A good husband.

"It is. It's one I've been struggling to understand as well," she whispers.

I reach for her arm, tracing a path up to her neck. "We can continue trying to understand it together, doe. We always made a good team. Just us against the world, remember?"

Her chest swells with a heavy breath. "Just us." She gives me an uneasy smile. "Okay then. Well, what's the plan now? What happens? Have you worked things out with your parents? I needed to make things right with my family, and I did. After we spoke on my porch a few weeks ago, you made me realize that things had gone unspoken for too long."

"I wanted to talk to you about this first," I explain. "You understand me better than anyone."

"I get that. Are you afraid to talk to your da?"

Unease swarms in my chest. "Maybe a little bit. How am I going to explain to my parents that I felt ashamed of what we had growing up, that I stayed away because of my foolish ego and the fear that if I came back to Thistlehill, I'd end up like them—wanting and sacrificing?"

"You told me that despite everything, my parents would love me and be proud of me. You were right. I know you and Seamus don't always see eye to eye, that he never quite understood this ambitious part of you, but surely, he'll be happy with the changes you've made. I'm certain he will want you back, Ol. You parents missed you as much as I did."

I hope her words are true. "I hope so. Even if Da isn't happy with what I've done, the distillery is in a good place. A much better one than when he left."

"He's older than us, and a traditional man," she smiles, "But Seamus can't deny when things work out for the better. If it would bring you back to Thistlehill, I'm sure he'd let you tear the whole place down and build it again."

I laugh. "I wouldn't go that far. But, doe, do you believe me? Do you understand that I've given this a lot of thought?"

She holds my gaze for a few moments. Nerves build up as I wait for her response. When one doesn't come, I keep talking.

"Honestly, I have fears. I'm not going into this thinking it'll be all sunshine and daisies. New York and Thistlehill are polar opposites. Sure, I'll give up the subway, food delivery, my bodega, and the hustle and bustle, but I won't be spending money left and right to try and keep a drop of serotonin for myself after an exhausting week at the office."

"We could always travel together. Maisie, you, and I. We can go to cities whenever you miss it," she offers, her voice small and hopeful. "I also miss the chaos and the life I had in Paris."

I love that she's already planning a way for us to have a fulfilling life together. Like the one I have been dreaming of for weeks. "That sounds like the perfect solution."

She nods, smiling. "Alright, okay. What's your plan after you tell Seamus? Where are you going to live?"

"I could get my own house, but, Meadow, I'm thirty-five." I twirl the stem of the thistle in my hand, my nerves scratching my throat. "If I move here, I'm making a commitment. I feel like I've fit into your life like a missing puzzle piece. I want to be there for the whole picture. I want to be the one who steps up. I want to support you."

Her smile turns into a look I'd recognize from miles away. Concern and worry. "I don't need—"

"No, Meadow, enough. I'm tired of you saying you don't need anyone to support you. Because we both know you're fine on your own, we do. But listen to me, take my words seriously: I want to be here to take care of the things that you don't want to. I want to help you make Fox Den a success. I want to coach rugby —connecting with that part of me has brought me so much joy, Meadow. I want to feel useful in a way that can't be measured by data points and performance reviews."

I want to bring her coffee in bed and drive Maisie to school. I want the little moments, because they've felt so much bigger than anything I've experienced so far. I want to fit into her life, the way she so easily fits into mine again.

"My house has been two girls for the past seven years. I can't even imagine living with a man, let alone one of your size," she laughs.

"Then we'll have to get a bigger house," I smile.

"Ol, I'm serious. Maisie's going to be a teenager in a blink. Can you really stand to be around that much estrogen?"

I'm thankful for the reprieve of our jokes, even in the midst of such a big conversation. "What do you want me to say, Meadow? I'll grow out my hair to fit in, maybe lose the beard. Maisie's not a fan of it anyway."

She playfully rolls her eyes and reaches for my beard. "This thing isn't going anywhere."

"Neither am I. Look, I'm no fool. I know I have no real idea what it'll be like. Maybe the both of you will hate me. Maybe it'll be easy. But I'll do my best to just be there for you both."

"You've done a really good job at that, Ollie. You've made me feel like I could rely on you, and instead of being afraid of that—though I think I still am a bit afraid—I want the life we can have."

"I'm afraid too, doe. But I want to go through the scary days together."

"Are you going to be okay if those scary days mean letting Maisie braid your hair, or taking care of her when she gets sick, maybe more scraped knees, and, I don't know, even picking up pads at the pharmacy?"

I shoot her a look of disbelief. "What gave you the impression that I'd be opposed to that? You two can roll me in glitter, put ribbons around my ears, and I'll treat you both like princesses—"

"Glitter?" She quirks an eyebrow at me.

"And if you don't want to be princesses, I'll treat you two like starved warriors who have come home from battle. Meadow, listen to me, I want this. I want this life. I want Maisie. I want you. I want to be in a house filled with *Beck* reruns, washing your dishes, helping with math homework, cleaning Maisie's cleats, and carrying my girls to bed."

She hesitates. "That sounds right to me, but I want you to think this through, not just tell me what you think I want to hear. I want everything you just said, and I do believe we can have that life together. But Maisie isn't something that lasts for only another three months. Caring for her is constant. A relationship is endless work. We'll have hard times, maybe just like your parents did, or mine did. Are you ready for that?"

"I'm done being a coward, Meadow. I'm done letting my shame and ego make decisions for me."

"Even if you would be giving up your freedom and some of your independence to fit into my routine?"

"That hasn't been a problem so far. But you're right, again. I get it." However much I hate it, I understand. "We're in our thirties. Neither of us has the time or energy to go through a mess of a relationship like we did the first time."

She nods. "Ollie, I love you too, and I like having you here." She takes my hand in hers and looks at me. My heart feels ready to break. "And don't think I haven't wanted to have this exact conversation. This is important. But I'm afraid of getting hurt again. Of Maisie getting hurt. I know I can't protect her from everything, but I know firsthand how hard it is to have you and then have to live without you."

It's like a knife in my gut. As much as she abandoned me all those years ago, I did the same to her. The stonewalling, the never coming back home. I hurt more than myself, more than Meadow, more than Ma and Da and the Macraes. I deprived myself of the life I could have had in Thistlehill. Of maintaining friendships with Neil and the guys. Of seeing people grow. Of having them see me grow. Of being known. I boarded myself up in nice things because I was so afraid that no one would ever truly understand that small-town boy who wanted bigger things.

The biggest thing, the most important one, is looking right at me. I tilt her face up to mine. "Doe, for seventeen years, I operated with only half of my soul. I don't want to do it again now that I've come back to my other half. I love you. I'm going to take some time to think about what you said and tie up all my loose ends."

"And I'll be here for you when you do." She kisses me, out

in public. Sure, we're far from downtown and nobody is around, but there is no hesitation.

We find another flower along the path and walk for a bit in silence.

She's right.

We're not seventeen and eighteen anymore, planning a life that *may* happen. She's not going to culinary school; I don't have to go off to university. The stakes are real. And it's not as simple as me just moving here.

I need to contemplate what my life would be like in Thistlehill. I need to fully invest in this place, which means I need to stop hiding from the past. I need to make things right with my da. To call Viggle and turn down the position, pay back the signing bonus. I promised Ivy and Harris I'd go over there.

I'll make everything right so Meadow and I can start with a clean slate.

I take another step, and my foot squishes into a large pile.

"You just stepped in shit." Meadow cracks up, ending our serious conversation.

"Ugh." I run over to a patch of grass and rub the bottom of my foot in it.

"If you think that's gross, you won't survive being a dad. One time when I was changing Maisie, she was maybe eight months old, it was two in the morning, and right when I got her diaper off, she projectile pooped all over me."

"What?" I squirm.

"Joys of being a parent. Gotta deal with all the bodily fluids. That's what'll happen if you decide to live here, Ollie. There's going to be a lot more than just cow shit."

"At least I'm good at cleaning."

She laughs. "Look." Her finger lifts over my shoulder. "There are a bunch of flowers by the barn."

"Isn't that the Cameron twins' place?" I ask, eyeing the

bright pink barn and matching two-story house. "I knew it was going to be that damn thieving cow."

"Or maybe it's just Kenna and Lorna trying to lure you here by stealing the trophy," Meadow giggles.

"Only one way to find out."

We hurry down their driveway and peek inside the barn, expecting to find it full of treasure, but it looks mostly empty. There's a beat-up purple tractor, bales of hay and alfalfa, and tools hanging from the walls. A hose is coiled out front. While I spray off my boots, Meadow peers into the empty stalls.

"No sign of the trophy," Meadow says.

A squeal comes from the entrance. "Ye two gettin' frisky in our barn?"

"See, Lorna, I told ye they were a pair." Kenna joins her sister. "Can't blame them. A man in a kilt was my kryptonite back in the day."

Meadow and I share an embarrassed look.

"And they're ready to announce it to the whole town from our barn." Lorna claps her hands together. "We're pure chuffed, aren't we? Let's call *The Thistlehill Daily* ASAP."

Meadow's hands frame her hips, and she narrows her eyes at them. "Do you two or Belle have the trophy?"

"What are ye on 'bout this trophy? We just swung back from the festival for our jackets. There's rain in the forecast."

"The caber toss trophy," I explain as I join Meadow's side. "It's missing. We followed a trail of flowers to your barn."

"Oh, dear." Lorna looks puzzled. "Our darling Belle's been in her pasture all day. What would she need a trophy for?"

Meadow straightens her shoulders and paces, just like Detective Beck. "Suspicious that at the last Town Hall, you two were the only ones to bring up the fact that things have gone missing."

Fuck, she's so hot.

*No. Focus. The trophy.*

"Ye forget our own stuff is disappearin'." Kenna shakes her head at us.

"Or so you claim. Perhaps to cover up your thieving?" Their interrogator crosses her arms, but a hint of a smile dances on her face.

She's enjoying this.

"Ye've been readin' far too many o' them mystery books."

"Lorna! It's like we're the red herring." Kenna nudges her sister.

Meadow scrunches her eyebrows. "Are you sure?"

"We're a pair o' auld lassies. Ye think we've got nae better things tae be doin' than stealin' from the town?"

"Well..." I say.

"No, they're right; this is exactly how the mystery books go." Meadow shrugs her shoulders. "Told you my skills were no use here."

"But what about the trophy?"

"It was probably Vlad," she resigns. "He won it three years in a row. Maybe he knew it was yours?"

"I wonder if Jody found him already."

"We're headed back to the festival. We can give the two of ye a lift. Unless ye fancy a wee tumble in that hay over there?"

Meadow grabs my arm hard, yanking me out of the barn. "Let's go."

## Chapter 32
# Ollie

THE MACRAES' LIVING ROOM IS DRAPED IN EARTH TONES, wooden furniture, and soft, plush cushions. Natural light streams through the large windows at the front of the house, casting shadows across Ivy and Harris's faces as they sit opposite me in two leather armchairs.

"Yeah, that's Boston for you." Harris laughs at a story about me cleaning trash out of the Charles River while I was on campus at MIT.

"It was a good time." I nod, taking a sip of my herbal peppermint tea.

"We're so glad you could stop by," Ivy smiles. "It's great to have you back here."

The conversation is light, but uneasiness ebbs beneath the surface. I wish Meadow was here with me. But deep down, I know that if there is any chance of me moving back here, I cannot avoid Ivy and Harris.

Because Meadow was right yesterday—I can't try the family life on for size. She doesn't deserve that. It's time to clear my conscience and move forward. To finally leave the past in the past.

The nerves in my throat attempt to silence me, but there's no point in pussyfooting around. I've owed the Macraes this for seventeen years. "I have to say that I'm sorry."

"For what? You've got nothing to apologize for." Ivy frowns, but Harris reaches over to his wife's leg and sets his hand on her knee, nodding for me to go on.

"I'm sorry for not coming to Fox's funeral." I swallow and tuck my hands into each other, wringing my fingers together. "I was a jerk for not offering my condolences to you. And I was a coward for not checking in or calling all this time. You were like parents to me."

The weight of my confession spills out into the room. Ivy's blue eyes flood with tears, and she swipes her sleeve beneath her lashes. Harris lends me a tight-lipped smile. Instead of the anger I expect—no, deserve—he leans over to me. "We never held that against you, Ollie."

"I appreciate you saying that," I say. "But I hate how I acted. Your family was important to me, and I allowed myself to forget that because I was hurt. No—because I didn't want to admit that I was hurt, that I missed Meadow, that I missed Fox, that I missed you and my parents."

"It was like we lost our second son before we lost our first." Ivy shakes her leg, a replica of her daughter's nervous habit. "We always loved you like our own, and the only thing that matters now is that you're back."

"Ivy is right, Ol." Harris smiles. "We're just glad you're here now. The past is the past, and we don't want to go on without talking to you. We kept silent with our own daughter for too long, and that caused a rift in our family."

"Meadow mentioned that you all are working on things."

Harris nods. "I'm glad she has you to talk to again. You two were always a good pair. Thankfully, we're in a better place now. Staying focused on the future."

I shift on the small sofa. The cushions creak under my weight. The veil of guilt vanishes from my shoulders.

"I'm thinking about sticking around for longer," I admit. "There's a chance that I still have a life here."

"More like a new life you can begin here." Ivy pats my hand. "I'm going to get us some more tea, okay? Then you can tell us all about what you're thinking." She gets up and moves to the kitchen.

"That's good news," Harris says.

"I never truly told you how much you were a role model to me." The confession is easy. "One of the reasons I went to MIT and worked at Silverman was because you inspired me to. You had this whole life, and I wanted to get a piece of it."

"I know, son. I always carried that around with me, wishing that I could've told you what I know now back then."

"Do you ever regret giving up your life in the States?"

A question I don't deserve an answer to, but I have to know. I need some kind of certainty that there's a chance my life here will work. Harris always had it figured out, and his guidance is still useful to me.

He sighs heavily, taking his glasses off. "When I brought my family here, we were in a state of crisis. Thistlehill was the only thing that brought us closer together. In Boston, stuck to the grind, I never realized the importance of the little things. Seeing smile lines around your wife's eyes. The growth of your kids marked on doorframes. You start to see those milestones as expected parts of life, and you stop cherishing them. I spent a decade convinced that my career was more important than both of my kids." He goes quiet for a second, giving me a tender look. "If I knew then what I know now, I'd have left sooner, spent more time throwing around the footie with my son, been supportive of Meadow's cooking."

I shake my head. "I'm sorry that you lost Fox so soon. That he was taken from your family."

"Your da always had it right, you know that, Ol?" Harris smiles. "He always kept you close as a kid, shared the things he knew with you, made sure you and your ma were taken care of as best as he could. He went to bed with a clear conscience his entire life. It took me so long to understand him. For years, I thought that money, status, and location equaled happiness, but I was wrong. It's the simple, most meaningful things that can't be bought."

"But you all seemed so happy."

"We were, and I actually got to enjoy that when I finally let go of the pride I had about my job in Boston. It wasn't easy. There were days when I felt restless, like I'd made a mistake moving my family to the country that my folks were from, but the kids seemed so happy. They had you; we had your parents. When I stopped searching for fulfillment in my career and made room to find it in my family, I became the most well-off man in the world."

Harris says this like he's talking to a younger version of himself. He isn't wrong. The uncertainty I'm battling is the very thing he's already experienced and learned from.

I don't want to miss out on more years with Meadow and Maisie. I don't want to hear about their life in snippets. Or catch the few years I still have left with my folks over the phone.

I know what I need to do.

"Thank you for telling me that."

"The past is the past, remember?" Harris nods, leaning over the chair and reaching for a box beneath the seat. "Here. This is what I've wanted to give you since I heard you were back." He hands me the wooden box, which is big enough to fit into both of my hands. "It's some of Fox's stuff. Things he'd want you to have."

"No, I can't possibly—"

"You can, and you will. We all got a piece of him after he was gone. He'd want you to have one too."

I hold on to the box, wrapping it in my fingers. "I actually have something for you too." I rise and pull out the small envelope of Polaroids from my jacket. "Photos of all of us when we were younger."

Ivy comes back in. She sets down the tea tray she's carrying, tentatively takes the envelope from me, and unfurls the top.

She blinks hard when she sees the first photo. It's Fox leaning up against their old front door with his book bag, a fox tail dangling off of it. There's one of Fox in woodshop class, holding a saw and wearing a mischievous expression. "I love these," she says.

"I'll be back," I promise, wanting to give them space. "I'm going to be around a lot more often."

"Your parents will be happy to hear that," she smiles, curling up next to her husband.

"There are a couple of things I still need to work out, but I'll tell them soon." Between Meadow and Viggle, I need to have a clear plan for how I'm going to get it right this time. I have yet to repair the relationship with the parents who raised me, loved me, and supported me, even when we didn't see eye to eye.

"Do any of those *things* have to do with Meadow?" she asks through tear-soaked eyes.

"They do."

"Good. You were always good for each other, Ollie."

The words make me feel like I've found my way back to a home I never thought I could return to again. "I love her," I admit. "I never stopped loving her."

"She loves you too."

*She does.* "Do you think that's enough?"

Harris puts his arm around his wife and pulls her close. "It was for us."

I won't lose out on a life with my girls because of some flawed definition of success. The love I've felt the past few weeks—feeling needed, feeling accepted by her—has meant more to me than anything I could ever gain materially.

The air is refreshing as I make my way along the winding trails back to my house.

I climb the steps to my porch, looking over at the old Macrae house. The ghost of laughter fills my ears.

Soon, I'll be living in that house. Making a home with the woman I love. A girl I'll love like my daughter. My parents next door.

A new life. A better one.

When I'm in my room, I set the box down on my bed. Carefully, I unhinge the latch and brace myself for what's inside.

An envelope sits on top of old mementos. Fox's old fox tail. A medallion from our old rugby team. A photograph of Meadow, Fox, and me at the loch.

Who even knows how old we are here.

My eyes sting with tears as I go through all of the ancient charms. Pieces of my life. Pieces of my best friend. I reach for the envelope, tracing the handwriting on the outside. It's addressed to my old apartment in Boston with a return label stuck to the front. I rip through the tape and read.

## Chapter 33
# Ollie
### sixteen years ago

AN UNKNOWN NUMBER FLASHES ACROSS MY SCREEN. COUNTRY code +44. I silence my phone and put it in my pocket. Annoyance swims through my veins. By now, the feeling is a close friend.

*It's not her,* I remind myself. It can't be. I got a new number the moment I got off the plane a few months ago. But who else would be calling me from the UK?

"What's up?" Hannah—at least, I think that's her name—asks with a tipsy giggle.

"Nothing." I shake my head and continue down the sidewalk to my apartment near MIT.

The hasty decision to double my class load this semester, to try and graduate in three years so I don't get left behind, has fried my brain. The one thing I wanted this Saturday was to be left the fuck alone. I wanted to escape for a few hours.

The dingy bar off campus helped. Whatever terrible rock they were playing was loud enough to drain out any thoughts. Now, a block from my apartment, regret shrouds me. I should've left this girl at the bar. For some reason, girls cling to me like the bees used to hover around flowers back home—probably because I look like a heartbroken fool slumping around MIT.

She begged to come see my place, to cheer me up, and for the first time in weeks, I thought, *Fuck it.*

But I don't want her here anymore. I want to be alone.

We turn onto my street, and I pull my keys out of my pocket.

"Ollie," a familiar voice rings out, and my heart stops. "Ol? You hear me?"

At the front door of my building stands Fox Macrae, a University of Edinburgh sweatshirt stretched over his long arms. A new pair of black Air Jordan XXs on his feet. My feet remain cemented to the sidewalk.

"Who's that?" Hannah sings.

*Fuck.* I shake her grip from my forearm and pocket my hands. It's too late.

Fox's eyes scan my face, then hers, then mine again. His nostrils flare with anger. It's a look I've seen many times in scrimmages and rugby games.

"What are you doing here?" I keep my voice level, even as nerves metastasize in my gut.

"What am *I* doing here?" Fox scoffs, dropping his duffel bag on the sidewalk and clasping his hands together in a loud clap. Is *she* here? "Checking if you're fucking alive, Ol."

"Uh, I'm gonna go." Hannah's small voice cuts through the ringing in my ears. I don't protest as she disappears from view.

"Alive and well." I hold my hands out in a dramatic display. "You can leave now."

"Really, man? That's how you're going to welcome your best friend?" He shakes his head. "What the fuck is wrong with you? You haven't been answering any of our calls."

The streetlight flickers above, and I take a step closer to my apartment building's front door. "There's a reason for that."

I can't stomach hearing about Meadow.

Over the past few weeks, I've come up with a million explanations for why she abandoned me at the airport. The same one sticks out through all the rest—she didn't love me.

The evidence was there all along: her wanting to keep us a secret, not wanting to commit to a one-year lease—oh, and sending me that shitty text on the day of our flight.

"Who were you with?" Fox looks distraught. "Who even is that girl?"

Is he going to tell *her* about this? A pain slithers through my chest. *Good.* Maybe she'll get to feel even a fraction of the pain I felt after what she did.

"You don't have the right to ask me that," I snap.

"You know what? It doesn't matter. Ollie, you're like a brother to me. You always have been, alright?" The familiarity in his kind voice is something I had forced out of my head. "Listen, can you just invite me upstairs? Can we talk?"

"Why?"

"What happened between you and my sister—"

"Is none of your business," I bite out defensively.

Of course he's going to take her fucking side. Why wouldn't he? They're bound by blood. I only spent a few years with her. I'm the kid next door.

"You're right." He frowns. "It isn't my business at all. But you're my best friend, and she's my sister, and you two were together." The reminder stings. "If you're anything like Meadow, I know you're hurting, Ol."

"I'm not, not even a little bit," I lie and puff out my chest. He's no bigger than I am, but standing in front of him is making me feel like a speck of dust. "I'm happy here in Boston. Best decision I ever made." I hold my head up high, shaking the sting out of my eyes. The loneliness that's become my closest friend here smiles down at me from the starless sky above. "It was just a meaningless fling. Nothing more. Now, would you move aside?"

He swipes at the messy hair on his forehead and brushes it

back. His shoulders sag. He looks tired. "Please don't act like that. I know you're angry—"

"I'm not *acting* like anything. If anyone was fucking acting, it was your sister. The best actress I know."

A vein bulges above his brow, and his hands curl into fists. He forces a long breath into his lungs and exhales from his mouth. "Meadow's at culinary school."

She got rejected from all of them. Did she try again? Is she in America?

*Can't be.*

Whatever. It doesn't matter. She could've told me, but she chose to bail instead. Like a coward.

"I don't care."

"Le Cordon Bleu," Fox continues, disregarding me. "I dropped her off weeks ago."

The school she considered a mere fantasy. The very same one I urged her to pursue years ago. She told me she had no intention of applying.

I wouldn't have stopped her.

Hell, there are plenty of universities in France I could have transferred to.

We could have made it work. I would have figured it out for her, because I love her.

*Loved.*

"I have to go," I say, trying to push past him to my door. I'd just gotten to a place where I didn't spend every waking second thinking about Meadow Macrae.

Her smile. Her laugh. Her skin. The mere fucking existence of her etched into my brain.

And now her brother.

The reminders keep flooding my head.

*Quiet.* I need quiet.

"No, wait." He stands in front of the door and looks at me.

"As a friend, Ol. As your brother. Please. I'm just asking you to pick up one of her calls. Can you let her explain?"

"She said all she had to say." In one lousy text, mere seconds before the doors closed on our flight to Boston.

Fox huffs. The reaction forces a tic into my jaw. "I understand this is difficult, but you don't need to act like an asshole—"

"Me? The asshole?" Indignation bubbles its way up into my chest. "If anyone's the asshole, Fox, it's your fucking sister."

I regret the words the moment they leave my mouth, but my own anger can't bring myself to take it back. I expect his fist to connect with my jaw or his knee to hit my crotch, but nothing comes. "She fucked up. *She* knows it. *I* know it. *You* know it. But she deserves—"

"She doesn't deserve anything from me. We had a life planned together. Me and her. Then she fucking bailed." My voice cracks, and I feel weak. "She made a choice."

We were supposed to run away from our parents' expectations together. And she did run. Just in the opposite direction of me.

Fox's hand lands on my shoulder and shakes me roughly. "Are you even the same Ollie I knew? I don't understand, man." His voice turns into a sob. "We all do the wrong thing sometimes. We all make bad choices. Doesn't mean we should bask in their aftermath."

My chin tips up to the sky, and I yank his arm off of me. The once-friendly touch now stings my skin.

"What the fuck do you know about choices? Huh?" I yell as shadows dance on the sidewalk beneath us. "Fox Macrae has never made a wrong choice a day in his life. Perfect family. Perfect grades. Perfect everything. Nothing about you was ever fucking wrong. The nerve of you to judge me for how I choose to handle something I didn't even want—"

"And you always wished you had that, didn't you? That's

why you're here. Following in *my* dad's footsteps instead of finding your own." He leans down to snatch the duffel off the ground.

Anger hits me like a tsunami. "Fuck you."

"Fuck you too, man. Fuck you." His shoulder bumps mine as he pushes past me. "Fuck the fact that I missed classes to come here to try and fix things with you. You want to be this guy? Fine. Don't ever fucking talk to me or my sister again. We'll both be better off without you and your fucking ego."

He leaves me by my lonesome. I fumble with my keys and push open the door. My body shakes with frustration all five floors up to my apartment. When I make it inside, I collapse, letting out a sound like a dying animal. I can't feel like this anymore. I don't want to.

I will be better than this.

The Macraes' opinions won't stop me from being the absolute fucking best.

And when I am, when I've graduated at the top of my class, gotten the job at Silverman Sachs, and then eventually, one at Viggle, when I'm richer and more successful than the both of them—then they'll see what they lost out on.

I'll be the one walking through Thistlehill in Air Force 1s and my MIT sweatshirt. I'll have even more money than the Macraes. I'll be better. I won't end up like my father. I won't struggle—ever.

Then she'll see what she missed by letting me go.

# Chapter 34
# Ollie

OLIVER,

Fucking hell that was formal.

Ollie, I've rewritten this letter enough times to have completely used up all the paper in my dorm. Blame Penelope. She's been on a paper crane kick, and all the sheets that were gathering dust in my printer have now been turned into paper birds. All of this is to say, and I'm going to come right out and say it, I'm sorry.

I was out of line when I came to Boston. So were you, but I know you know that already. I was angry at you the last time we talked. Angry because you hurt my second favorite person in the world. Angry because my second favorite person in the world hurt my third favorite person in the world, and the third favorite hurt the second favorite back.

If you're not following, it's:

1. Penelope
2. Meadow
3. you

I've tried calling, but it seems you've switched your number again and I can't seem to convince your parents to give it to me. So that's why I'm writing this terrible letter.

*I wanted to ask for your advice about how I should propose to Pen. I want to make it perfect. I picked out a ring already, but she has no idea. She really is the one, and you were always good at helping me with this stuff.*

*Either way, maybe you could come to the wedding and be my best man? Even if we said all that terrible stuff to each other?*

*Though maybe it would be the most awkward gathering in the universe if Meadow is there too. Because she would be. She's fine, by the way. Working at some extra fancy place where we'd probably not be able to pronounce a single item on the menu and she'd lie and pretend she wasn't feeding us snails and we'd eat them anyway and love it because her food is that damn good.*

*How's Boston? Are you smarter than everyone at MIT? I bet you are. You always have been the smart one out of the two of us.*

*Write back!!! I miss our family of three.*

*PS. I didn't mean it when I called you an asshole. Well, maybe a little bit, but you were acting like one, okay?*

*PSS. If Meadow manages to muster up the courage to call again, don't ignore her. Hear her out. Please.*

A heavy tear drops onto the scribble of writing before me, and I dab it away with the sleeve of my shirt. This letter is all I have left of my best friend. The final sliver of forgiveness I'd been searching for without even realizing it.

A piece that's truly my own. Something that was only between Fox and me. Not Meadow. My best friend and I hurt each other because we were both angry. It's a memory I plan to keep cataloged for myself, because I was a fool. A child. Now, I can make things right.

I memorize the words, imprinting them onto my soul. I've been homesick for seventeen years. I've been running around searching for accolades and success when all I needed was the people I left behind.

*I miss our family of three.*

There's still hope for that.

"Fox, I'll make it right." I throw my words to the ceiling above. "You hear me? I'll take care of them both." My voice cracks. "Your daughter, your parents, my parents, myself. I'm not going to ignore it any longer."

This life is not something for me to try on for size like an old jumper at the back of my closet. This is my future—and it's the perfect fit.

## Chapter 35
# Meadow

"I'm not sure, chef," Brooke says, taking another bite of the lamb leg. "They all taste spectacular."

"Thank you." I straighten at the plating station in front of us. "But we need to decide on which one will complete the menu."

Three dishes lie on the stainless-steel counter. Braised lamb leg with chard and hazelnut. Caramelized veal sweetbread with black truffle and white peppercorn. A twist on a lobster roll, plated on new stoneware from local artisans.

"Tell us about them." Fi inspects the slab of veal more closely. "You had a story behind the cheese dish for Maisie and the velvet shanks for Fox. What do these have?"

"I made the sweetbread at d'Or. It was one of the first dishes of mine that Colette praised."

Brooke nods. "They are similar to what we served there."

I push the veal aside, leaving the lamb and the lobster. "You're right; we'll nix it. Now, the roll is an ode to my parents, and Boston. We'd walk along the Fan Pier together and chow them down as the sun set." I consider the dish Brooke, Fi, and I worked on together—smoked local langoustine with lemon and verbena herb butter and sourdough toast—then the lobster. "But it's probably redundant with our seafood dish."

Fi smiles. "And even though this is the best lobster roll in the world, I will say our dish smokes it out of the water."

"Because of your sourdough." Brooke nudges her.

"And your strong shuck on the shellfish."

"You two are adorable. Guess that leaves the lamb." The same dish I made for Ollie over six weeks ago at our first Monday night dinner. It's gone through endless revisions since then, new nuts and greens and jus. My chefs share a look. "I made this for Ollie on his eighteenth birthday. A small piece of the past. But it's still missing something…it's not quite right."

"Be right back." Brooke runs through the swinging kitchen doors and quickly returns. In her hand, a bottle of Fox Den's exclusive whisky. "I know how to fix it."

Fig and hazelnuts. That hint of sweetness is exactly what this needs. Maybe in the braise? I hesitate as she sets the bottle down on the counter. "A part of me is worried about choosing a dish that reminds me of him. I won't be able to stomach cooking it when he leaves."

"I thought he said he wants to stay?" Fi's eyebrows rise.

I filled them in on our conversation a few days ago. One I haven't been able to shake because it would mean the possibility of a future with Ollie. Not just a way to move on from the past.

"He hasn't turned down the dream job yet." I shrug. "I can't help but take that as a sign of him hesitating."

He deserves time to think things through. Moving back here isn't going to be a walk in the park, and he'll have to truly make peace with giving up this nice job before doing so. The choice I made to come back was easy, but I wasn't given time to think.

Brooke shakes her head. "Meadow, he's thirty-five years old. He had the career, he lived abroad, and he said he's choosing you," she says as if reading my mind.

"Even if he doesn't stay." Fi traces her finger along the stoneware. "If he's full of shit, then it might be nice to have something to remember the good parts of him. The ones that encouraged you to become a chef, to open your own restaurant."

"You're right." I snatch the bottle off the counter. "Can one of you get the morels from the fridge? And some figs? I think this would make more sense as a braise."

"Heard, chef."

"Actually, let's run through the dishes one more time. I want to see the menu altogether."

---

A FEW HOURS LATER, I finish the final plate, drizzling the remainder of the sauce over the whisky-and-morel braised lamb.

I look up. The little whittled fox sits on the plating station, staring back at me.

As much as I hate to admit it, because I'd spent the last seven years convincing myself otherwise, I was missing the discovery and abandoning a fear of failure.

No pressure to be perfect. No pressure to get it just right. No autopilot.

"Yes!" Brooke shimmies her shoulders, moaning over the plate.

"This is the one, Meadow."

"And this amuse-bouche. You've outdone yourself." Fi holds up the dish that came to me as I was finishing off the chard.

A small meadow, edible flowers and roasted nuts that look like logs in spicy honey. A way to start the meal with something that's *just* me beside dishes that commemorate the people who have had the biggest impact on my life.

I look at all of the courses together, imagining how they'd look printed on menus.

The meadow.

Brooke's aubergine caviar with roasted baby parsnips.

Haggis with Double Gloucester pastry, fermented root vegetables, and crowdie for Maisie.

Velvet shanks with black winter truffle, dark sherry, and crispy seaweed for my brother, the shank stems shaped like small foxes lying beside a jus that resembles the loch.

Home-smoked langoustine with lemon and verbena warm herb butter on sourdough toast.

Braised lamb leg, chard, hazelnut, and whisky glaze for Ollie.

Fi's poached apple and caramel bavarois.

Each one tells a story. Of my life. Of how Fox Den came to be.

"It's perfect."

"Honest." Fi nods firmly.

It feels strange to acknowledge and appreciate that the work I've put in is enough, but I don't want to be hard on myself anymore. That killed my creativity. Made me lose myself. Plus, I've spent thirty-four years thinking I need to do more, and it was exhausting. I've missed out on time with my daughter, my friends, on the little discoveries because I was so tied to the idea of perfection. Of not wanting to let anyone down.

Now that I've found this part of myself, I don't want to lose her again.

"Let's call the staff and tell them to come in early on Thursday so we can run through the new dishes. The printers will have the menu done by Monday of next week. We'll be ready for Adair Grant on Saturday."

"There is no way he won't give us Best of Scotland on the spot." Brooke beams, wiping off the counter.

"And if he doesn't, then fuck him," I laugh.

"There's our girl." Fi puts an arm around me. "We should celebrate having you back."

"Beluga and champagne?" Brooke curves a brow at me, and I shoot her a quick nod.

"We deserve it."

"I'll get the fire going in the dining room." Fi leaves us to pull together our extravagant celebratory treat. Brooke and I tidy up the kitchen and join her.

"What if we take a trip after tourist season is done? A small vacation for the three of us," I offer.

"That sounds perfect." The fire crackles in the stone pit, the wood splintering to pieces in the amber glow. "We'll just have to plan it around our cycles, because I can't deal with all three of us PMSing on a beach."

I laugh, but something in the back of my mind tingles.

Brooke notices immediately. "You okay over there?"

"Yeah, totally fine," I shrug. "Just realized my period is late."

"She's been so busy tumbling and rumbling around, she's forgotten." Brooke pokes her finger at my arm and giggles.

"What if you're pregnant?" Fi says.

Impossible. And even if I were—which I'm not—I can't possibly let that play a role in Ollie's decision to stay. Sure, Maisie wasn't a planned situation, and she's the best thing to ever happen to me, but I didn't have a choice.

He does.

"Absolutely not. I'm on the pill." I shake my head. Although I've skipped a few days, especially when I have to rush out of the house after staying up too late with Ollie. "It's just the stress of the tasting menu, and there's a lot going on. Fibroids throw off my periods sometimes. Once I was a month late."

Fi's playful look drops off her face. "Have you been using any other protection?"

Apart from the birth control, not really. But I'm sure it's effective enough, especially with how complicated my uterus is.

"Just the pill."

"Do we need to have a convo about the birds and the bees?" Brooke teases.

"Guys." I set my hand on the table, ending the conversation. "Enough. It's just stress."

"We'll get you a test anyway."

"Don't bother. I'm sure it's around the corner. Actually." I pause. I've been ruminating about this for the past couple of days, and I think it's time to make a real commitment to my well-being. No more panic attacks or kneecapping pressure stressing me out. "I've been enjoying our new schedule. What would you both think if we only kept Fox Den open four nights a week? I realize that tourist season is already in full swing and we're fully booked on weekends, but we'd actually get to enjoy the summer."

It's been difficult to realize that since we run our own business, we can set our own hours. I don't need to work twelve-to-sixteen-hour-days like I did in France to be successful.

I like spending time with Maisie, my parents, and now Ollie. Plus, with the extra time, I'll keep being creative. I can work on specials for the tasting menu, depending on what's in season.

"I never thought I'd see the day!" Brooke faux gasps and holds a hand to her heart. "I'm on board. There's a Wednesday disco night in Inverness that I've been loving."

"Me too." Fi smiles. "Not the disco, but it'll give me more time with…"

"Your girlfriend," Brooke and I tease in unison, making our pastry chef turn tomato red.

Fi rolls her eyes. "You guys are the worst. But yes, fine, I would like to spend more time with Elspeth. Sue me!"

"We're just busting your chops." I pass Fi the bottle of champagne and give her knee a small kick under the table. "We can always change our mind about the hours. We're our own bosses; you guys were right to remind me of that. Whatever you'd like to do, I'm here to try to make it happen."

"We know that." Brooke stretches her legs toward the stone fireplace, wiggling her feet beside the flames. "I did the rat race in France. I worked those hours for years with you. I like having time off. And look, I won't speak for Fi, but I knew there was a chance I'd lose my entire investment when I agreed to open this place. I knew we wouldn't break even for a few years, that the whole thing was a big risk, and I still took the jump because I believe in us."

"I agree." Fi casts a reassuring gaze at me. "If we make money this year, amazing. But most businesses don't for the first three years. I care more about our happiness and fulfillment running this restaurant together. Hell, I get to run a business with my two best friends."

"You consider me a best friend?" Brooke nearly falls off her chair as she swings her head to look at Fi.

The bundle in my stomach dissipates, replaced with that sense of belonging I always used to feel when I cooked. When my simplest pleasure was making the people I love happy with food, with the things I could do for them. But my friends have given me so much more, and it's about time I let myself enjoy it.

"Yes," Fi says begrudgingly, but her smile gives her away. "Being next-door neighbors and sharing a kitchen for over four months will do that. If I'm being honest, you're more like a sister."

"Meadow." Brooke taps the table, getting my attention. "Are you hearing this?"

"I'm hearing it. Fi's a big softie."

Fi shoots me a glare, and Brooke slides out of her seat, mauling her with a hug.

"Get in here." They look over at me, and I join the hug. My best friends. The people I can rely on. Peace sits on my shoulders. This is lovely.

"I love you guys," I say through the cuddle of limbs.

"We love you."

We pass around the bottle of champagne. I hold up a slice of bread with caviar in a salute, and we cheer together.

I'm so utterly and happily complete.

## Chapter 36
## Ollie

"I ALREADY INITIATED A WIRE TRANSFER TO RETURN THE SIGNING bonus," I explain to the head of HR at Viggle, fumbling with the throw blanket at the edge of my bed. The quarter of a million dollars was going to sit in my retirement account anyways. A small price to pay for the chance at a life here.

I'd spend tenfold to not miss out on the opportunity of a future with Meadow.

"Can you please provide some more information about the sudden withdrawal of the offer acceptance? We were certain that the benefits package was going to be very appealing to you."

"Yes, it was well put together," I assure them.

The line goes silent for a moment, and the rep returns. "We can increase your shares and offer a more appropriate title. How does the President of Innovation sound?"

The offer makes me hesitate for a moment, but it's not enough. Nothing will be enough to keep me from the life I'm ready to start. "No, but thank you. At this point, no amount of money or perks will play a role in my decision."

Once again, the call goes silent. I can't even imagine the number of people listening in on my resignation.

"Oliver, once we go ahead with this, there won't be another offer on the table." I freeze at the reminder. But the sound of my full name ringing in my ears is enough. I do not want to spend the rest of my life being called *Oliver* by anyone who isn't my woman. "This is the opportunity of a lifetime."

"It is," I agree. "But my priorities have changed."

When I hang up, a colossal weight lifts off my shoulders. I expect some kind of regret to appear, but it never does. Good. It shouldn't. The life I always needed is so close I can almost taste it.

The only thing left to do is book a flight to pack up my things in New York. Most of my stuff is in storage. I barely even thought about it while I was here. But there are a few pieces of my past that I'd like Meadow and Maisie to see.

Maybe I can bring them with me. The idea expands my chest. I'd get to introduce my found family in New York to the one I have at home. My lips curl at the edges.

After Meadow's tasting menu tomorrow, I'll bring up the idea. A perfect way to celebrate what I'm sure will be a successful night.

Alright. One more call to make before everything is truly finalized.

My ma texted me that they'll be docking in Valencia earlier today. They should be there now. I pick up the phone and dial. They answer on the second ring.

"Ol?"

"It's me, Da."

Ma's voice joins the line. "Is that him?"

"Aye," Da says through the choppy static on the line. "What's wrong?"

I hate that he assumes I'm calling with bad news, but that's something I can repair.

"Nothing, Da, don't worry. Just wanted to tell you that

Callum and I made up. I gave raises to him and Elspeth last month."

"What?" he grumbles. "Does the distillery even have the mon—"

"All's well. We already delivered the second batch of On Cloud Nine shipments. They increased their order amounts. The rich fancy folk can't get enough of our whisky. The bottling facility is saving us time and money by not wasting any more of our product," I say proudly. "Meadow is hosting the Best of Scotland judge tomorrow, and let me tell you, she's going to be a huge success. Our Anderson whisky is going to be a staple of the best restaurant in Scotland."

Although the money will be nothing like Viggle, the distillery will be earning enough to take good care of all of us. No more worrying about finances at the Anderson house.

There's a brief pause, and I check the phone to see if I lost him. No, he's still here. "Ye must be daein' somethin' right."

It's nice to hear him admit that. I pace the floor of my room for this next part.

"I know we didn't get off on the best foot when I came back, and we never really saw eye to eye about me going to the States, but…" I hesitate. This is important. "I didn't want to suffer the way you did when I was a kid. We were always wanting, and I foolishly blamed you for that. It was so selfish and wrong of me, but I was a kid; I didn't know any better."

There's a pause on the line. I've surely hurt his feelings. "Aye, son. Ye're not wrong." The words hit me with surprise. "I poured all of our money into the distillery, wanting to make my dream work. I only hurt yer ma by doing so, keeping her from her goals. And I know it hurt ye as well. We didn't suffer, but we weren't comfortable all the time either."

"Since coming back here, I've realized that material things didn't really give me what I was actually searching for." I sigh.

"What's that?"

"To feel accepted. I wanted to leave Thistlehill because I felt like I was in the wrong family. I'm sorry for saying that, Da. I don't feel that way now, but I was a teenager. I wanted more."

The line fills with silence again. Heavy, unsaid words weigh down the call. "I never quite grasped yer ambitions. The distillery is my home, my plan since I was a lad. I should've heard ye out when ye made suggestions instead of blabbering on about the work ye needed tae put in first."

That means more than he realizes. "I only ever wanted to help our business grow."

"And I thought if it grew beyond my control, I'd lose it."

I guess I can understand that, but the distillery was on the brink of bankruptcy more than once. Maybe it's easier to get stuck in a routine than to take a risk. Meadow said that herself.

"It's not going anywhere now, Da."

"Ol, when ye developed interests beyond my comprehension, I didn't ken how tae connect with ye. I'm a proud man, son. But I was too proud tae admit that I just didn't get ye and that it hurt me when ye didn't take after me. The regret of my life, Ol."

"I think I have taken after you, Da. Your love for the distillery, the work you put in…in some way, I did the same with my career, except I lost my family. You came home every day, and you knew the value of a family. I thought that if I ran toward success, it would give me that same understanding. I was wrong."

"It's not easy being a man, son. Being a provider. Responsibility makes us do things we feel are right, even if they're not the best option. I'm sorry, Ollie."

My mouth hangs open in shock. I expected more pushback; Da's never bent easily. "I'm sorry too, Dad. I'm sorry I held on to a teenage fear all of these years and lost out on time. I'm sorry that I came back to the distillery and acted as if I knew best despite not having been around. I wanted to make you proud. I wanted to make improvements so that you would forgive me."

"Forgive? Ol, no. There's nothing tae forgive. I'm not easy tae change, but if I've learned anything on my trip with yer ma, it's that I should give new things a chance."

Just like I have been giving some old ones a chance.

"Maybe when you get back, we can spend some time getting to know each other some more? Like a fresh start?"

"Aye, son, and ye can teach me how tae use yer fancy contraptions." He laughs, and I do too. The lock in my chest unlatches. "Speakin' of technology, can ye sort out yer ma's laptop? Blasted thing's been broken for a year."

"Only if you agree to make a legacy whisky with me when you get back—a father and son malt."

"Aye. Won't be ready till I'm past eighty."

"I'll be here," I promise. "I'm not going to be leaving Thistlehill, Da."

The line goes silent again. "Was it Meadow?" Ma asks. "Did she finally convince ye?"

"Ye two bairns always belonged together," Da says. "Smart lad."

"You're more excited about Meadow than you are about me moving back home," I tease.

"There was never gonna be one without the other," Ma laughs.

"We're proud of ye, Ol," Da says. Number four of many more to come. I know it. Now the only thing that's missing is wrapping my arms around them both.

"Love you guys. Have fun. I won't keep you. We'll have a big celebration when you're back."

We hang up, and I look across the way to Meadow's house. Through the window of my past and into my future.

Life is about to start all over again. The right way this time.

## Chapter 37
# Meadow

"Fucking brilliant."

Two pink lines stare up at me.

I'm pregnant.

I deteriorate into a fit of laughter on the toilet of Fox Den's employee bathroom. Because of course this would happen on one of the most important nights of my career.

It's positive. *Actually positive.* I blink a few more times, but the lines are still there. I'm going to be a mom. *Again.*

At least the gagging I felt when Brooke plated our seafood course makes more sense. I have never been one to turn down shellfish.

*Fuck. Ollie.* My heart hurts. I can't tell him yet—this can't be the reason he stays in Thistlehill.

I shake my head, tuck the pregnancy test in a wad of toilet paper, and go to toss it in the bin. But then I stop. Deep in my bones, I want this. I want him to want it too.

My pulse thumps rapidly, and I place my hand on my stomach. Does their small heartbeat sync to mine? Christ, I've been stressed about the tasting menu all day.

Maybe it's too early for that. I can't be more than four weeks along. My mind pieces together the past month. Did we conceive in my damn kitchen?

I knew all that coming to my senses was ridiculous. I pocket the test and scrub my hands clean. But I've been on the pill. I guess not as consistently as I should be. I push a heavy inhale into my lungs.

Flashes of chubby baby faces fill my head. The wails. The laughter. There are options. I pause. No, there's only one. It's this. This is right.

"I want this baby."

When I say the words out loud, panic doesn't come.

In the mirror, I peek at my stomach. The skin is soft. No bump. Not for a couple more weeks. There's barely any change at all, but suddenly, everything is different.

"Hi," I whisper. "Hope you're doing okay in there."

For years, I was certain that I'd be content with not having a biological child. Maisie would always be enough, and she is, but now there's an opportunity to have more than enough—with Ollie.

There are a million things that could go wrong with this. Thirty-four isn't exactly the easiest age for a no-issues pregnancy. But even if I only get a few weeks with this little one growing inside of me, they'll still be so loved.

The best-case scenario may still happen. A future where Ollie stays and we have a family together. One where it may not be just his girls.

"Who are you in there?" I ask and glance up to look at myself in the mirror. It's the same question I have been asking myself over the past few weeks. Motherhood is so depersonalizing. But these past few months have taught me a lot about myself. Ollie helped me find a path back to the girl I used to be. He won't let me lose myself again. I'm certain about this decision. It feels right, even though it's terrifying. I want this. I choose this.

I stood in this exact spot on Fox Den's opening night and chewed up my nails, wanting to make sure everything went perfectly. *Now, the only thing that's going to be on my mind is you.*

The baby and the tasting menu.

*Sorry, little one. You're going to learn soon that your mama is a workhorse. I need to get back to work.*

I rush out of the bathroom and throw on my chef's coat. Fox Den's doors opened fifteen minutes ago, and chaos has already ensued.

We've been here all day, prepping. There should be no hiccups today. Our dishes taste amazing—inventive and exciting. We've done our best to impress Adair Grant and earn our place on the Best of Scotland guide.

Everything else is out of my control.

"Chef, Adair Grant just arrived." Davina intercepts me before I make it back to the plating station. "He's seated. Ordered the Anderson exclusive."

"Thanks for the update. Make sure there's eyes on him all night," I nod, itching to get back to the lamb waiting for me before it makes it out to the customers. "Keep his table waxed."

"Heard, chef." Davina pauses for a second before saying, "Your mom called, asked me to tell you to pick up your phone."

The rhythm of chopping knives and sizzling pans dulls in my ears. She'd never bother me at work unless it was important.

"Thank you." I rush to my purse in my locker. Five missed calls. My body freezes as pressure screws into my chest. *Relax. Surely there's a reasonable explanation.* I dial the phone.

"Meadow, is Maisie at the restaurant?" Mom's voice is laced with panic.

"Wh—what? No? She was supposed to be with you."

"We were just getting ready to leave, and one second, she was here, the next, she's not in the house."

My hands tremble uncontrollably. *Stay calm.* "Did you check my place?"

"Yes. We're at the school now, and no one has seen her."

Time seems to slow down, each second stretching into an eternity of torment. I need to stay calm. For Maisie. For her little sibling cooking up in my belly. But the reminders barely register as the ripping rope burn of a panic begins to whack my skin.

*Not now.* This is all one big misunderstanding. It must be.

"Check the rugby pitch, tap class, and check in with her friends." My feet are already shucking off my clogs. I lace up my boots, grab my bag, and throw on my jacket. "Have you called Ollie?"

"He's checking the distillery now."

Okay. That doesn't leave many other places around town. "I'll head home and make sure she hasn't gone back there. Call me if you find anything."

"Meadow, I'm so—"

"No, don't." I grab my keys. My voice comes out with more bite than I intended. "Everything will be okay."

*It has to be.*

A lump rises in my throat, making it difficult to swallow. The town isn't that large. She has to be around and safe.

*Find Maisie*, my mind blares over and over again. *Just find Maisie. You can panic and process later.*

I sprint back to the kitchen, finding Brooke. Fi rushes my side. "What's wrong?"

"Maisie is missing." My voice trembles. Worst-case scenarios flash through my mind, fueling the anguish. Hundreds of new people came through town this week. What if—

*No. Stop it.*

"We'll grab our coats, we'll come help." Brooke's eyes fill with worry.

"Please stay here. Make sure tonight goes well. There's four of us looking. It'll be fine," I reassure myself.

"No, Meadow, we can—"

"Look, I know. I know you want to help, but we've worked too hard on this. Just man the ship, both of you, and I can find my daughter. I'm sure this is one huge misunderstanding. I trust you."

And I do. I have a team for a reason.

"We'll take care of things here," Fi promises.

Brooke wraps me in a quick hug. "We got this, Meadow. Go find our girl."

Wind and rain hit my face as I sprint out the back door and rush into my car. Rainclouds are heavy in the sky. It's been gloomy all day. Thankfully, it's not dark. I should be able to find her without a problem.

*Don't cry, Meadow. Be strong for Maisie.*

Dammit. I should've gotten her a phone like all the other parents. What was I fucking thinking? I slam my hands on the steering wheel.

I need to calm down.

I need help.

*I need Ollie.*

MEADOW

meet me at urs asap

The drive to my house is torture. I scan the sides of the roads, making sure she isn't walking there.

*Please let her be safe and sound. Please let this all be a misunderstanding.*

Ollie's truck isn't there when I park in my driveway.

"Maisie!" I yell. My hands tremble as I fumble with the keys to the front door. My fingers feel useless as I struggle to unlock it. Once I do, I rush to open all the doors in my house, looking for her.

Nothing.

My heart is in my throat as I run to the Andersons'.

"Maisie!" I scream around Ollie's yard, but there's no response. Only silence. She's not out here. I run up his front steps and throw open the door.

I rush to flick on all the lights. "Maisie? Plum, are you here?"

Nothing. More silence is my only companion.

I slump against the kitchen table. Tears refuse to stop falling in droves, splashing against Ollie's laptop. I grab the edge of my chef's coat and try to wipe them up with shaking hands, but his computer screen flickers on.

In front of me, there are flights from Inverness to New York.

*He's leaving.*

My heart shatters into a million pieces. How could he leave us after he promised to stay? What about our life together? What about the baby?

*I don't have time for this.*

There's no room for self-pity or sorrow or heartbreak. My daughter's safety and well-being are my sole focus now.

I ditch the computer and run out the door, slamming into Ollie's chest.

"Doe, I got here as fast as I could. Maisie's nowhere around the distillery." His face is pale and haggard, dread laced behind those brown eyes.

"Move out of my way." I push past him, but he grabs my shoulders. "Get off of me."

"What is going on? Meadow? Is she okay?" His voice is thick with the suggestion of something I can't stand right now. Maisie has to be okay. She has to be.

I cough through the sobs in my throat.

"You lied. You were going to do the same thing I did to you. Just leave." Anger gushes out of me. "It doesn't matter. None of this matters. I need to find Maisie. Now move."

"Meadow, that isn't what it looks like." Ollie tilts my jaw up to his face, which is shrouded in seriousness. My phone rings, and I yank away from him, my feet carrying me back out into the front yard.

"Did you find her?" I say into the receiver.

My mom's voice comes from the other line. "No. Nothing."

"She's not here either."

"We asked Lorna and Kenna to search too. They were already out looking for Belle."

My mind spins wildly. Maisie's small voice fills my ears: *I bet she could be my best friend.*

There's no fucking way.

"Belle is missing?" I clarify.

"Yes, but that's not—"

"I have an idea; I'll call you back. Keep looking for her." I hang up the phone. "Maisie loves that cow. She has to be with her. See, everything's fine. She has to be with Belle."

Ollie nods, already walking to his truck. "I'll drive."

"Fine, just buckle your seatbelt."

We speed over to the Camerons' house in silence. Each second passes like quicksand. I keep my eyes on the road but my mind is short-circuiting.

He attempts to break the silence. "Meadow, what you saw—"

"Ollie, please, I don't care. I just want to find my daughter. We can talk about that later." At the end of the day, it doesn't matter. Whatever he chooses to do, whatever he thought he wanted but realized he couldn't commit to isn't my problem. I figured it out on my own once and I'll figure it out again.

He parks the car on the Camerons' road. "You're right, let's focus on finding our girl," he says, and we rush out into the mud.

The rain pours down relentlessly as we sprint across the muddy pasture, our footsteps muffled by the thunderous downpour. We first check the barn, behind hay bales and inside the empty stalls. *Nothing.*

"Didn't they have a shed on the edge of the property? We saw it once when we were younger," Ollie suggests.

"Who knows if it's still there." I'm starting to feel helpless.

"We have to check."

"Maisie!" I scream.

"Maisie!" Ollie yells. "There's something over there." He points, jolting off to the edge of the farm.

She has to be there.

She just has to be.

A small building comes into view. The wind whips around, taking our cries of her name with it. We reach the small shed, yank open the heavy door, and a sound wrenches from my gut that barely sounds like it belongs to me.

In the small space, my daughter is curled up against Belle. The pair is surrounded by a pile of junk.

"Maisie!" I let out a sob of happiness, falling to my knees in the mud. *She's okay. She's okay.*

"Mommy?" Maisie blinks up at me as the cow lifts her head and huffs. I crawl through the shed until my arms find my girl and I squeeze the air out of her lungs.

"Plum, I was so worried." I rub my thumbs over her face, checking her for any marks or scrapes.

She yawns, rubbing at her puffy eyes. "I fell asleep."

"I love you so much." I place a million kisses on her cold face, never wanting to let her go. Ollie drops to the ground beside us and slings his arms around us both. I want to push him away, but I can't. The heavy weight of his touch is the only thing keeping me together.

"Love you too." She lets out a small sob. "What's wrong? What happened? Why are you crying, Mommy?"

"How'd you get here?" I look around the shack and gawk. There's the caber toss trophy, Brooke's clutch, some towels and jackets. My shiny red pot and Perry and Jerry, Betty's garden gnomes. It's everything that has gone missing around town. This

## Falling for Meadow 429

dang cow really did have a secret lair. "Have you been taking this stuff?"

"No, Belle has. I was getting ready at Gran's, and I realized my fox tail was missing. When I looked outside, I saw Belle pick it up with her mouth. I think it fell off my backpack," she explains through another yawn. "I chased after her, and she brought me here. But then it started raining really hard. So I just laid down on Belle, and I must've fallen asleep."

"Oh, plum, I'm just so glad you're safe."

"We were so worried about you," Ollie says, the terror in his face fading away.

"Let's get you home." I stand, pulling her into my arms.

"Okay."

"I can carry her," he offers.

"I got it," I whisper.

Maisie murmurs, and I hike her up on my hip. My knees buckle, and I almost collapse onto the ground as the adrenaline fizzles into exhaustion. Ollie lands a steadying hand on my lower back. He doesn't drop it from my waist the entire walk back to his truck.

"Do you want to swing back by the restaurant?" he whispers.

I press Maisie into my chest one more time before buckling her into the back seat. "No, I want to be with my daughter. Fi and Brooke can handle it."

As he drives us home, I pull out my phone, steadying my muddy fingers on the screen.

> MEADOW
> 
> found maisie. she's safe
> 
> thx for manning the ship tonight

> FI
> 
> Thank god, we were so worried

**BROOKE**

so glad she's okay

grant left ten mins ago, ordered second helpings of dessert and left a big tip

**MEADOW**

good sign

ily both

**FI**

Love you

**BROOKE**

love you!

## Chapter 38
# Ollie

MY RAIN-SOAKED, MUDDY CLOTHES CLING TO MY BODY, mirroring the dampness in my soul as I pace on my porch. I should've told Meadow last night that I was staying in Scotland. Timing has never been our strong suit. A heavy drumbeat of regret and longing thumps in my chest.

At least we found Maisie.

After what feels like hours, her front door creaks open, and she waves me over.

I rush through the rain to her side. "Is she alright? That fucking cow, I can't believe it."

"She's asleep. Ollie, thank you for your help, for looking for her, but I'm exhausted. Let's just talk about things in the morning." Her arms fold over her chest, and she shies away from me. She's shutting me out—no, protecting herself. My world distorts, as if I'm looking through a dram of whisky.

*Look at me, my girl.* "This can't wait."

"I can't take you telling me you're leaving. Not right now."

"I'm staying, doe, I swear."

Her mesmerizing blue eyes connect with mine, scanning them for a hint of truth. My mouth ticks up. *I promise.*

"But I saw the flight—"

"I was waiting until after the tasting to tell you. I called Viggle yesterday; I turned down the job. I talked to my parents. I'm moving back. I'm staying in Thistlehill, with you, Meadow. With you and Maisie."

"Then why are you going to New York?" The wind outside bats around her hair, and she remains steadfast in her spot.

"I need to go back and pack up my things. I wanted to bring you and Maisie with me." She bites her lip, her foot tapping up a frenzy on the porch. "Look, when your mom called to tell me that Maisie was missing, my world split apart. I would've ripped the Highlands to pieces with my bare hands to find her and bring her home to you. I love that kid with every fiber of my being. I want to be here to watch her grow up. I want to keep her safe from that damn cow. I want to make sure you're both okay. I won't leave my girls."

"Not even if—"

"Meadow, I love you." I cradle her face in both of my hands, keeping her eyes on mine. "I love you so fucking much it hurts to be apart from you. I will not lose you."

The evening glow kisses her skin. "You can't change your mind about this once you commit, Ollie. There's not going to be a third chance here."

"I know that, and it's exactly why I'm here. I lost you once, doe. I'm not going to lose you again, or that little girl. You're the reason my heart beats, even after all these years." Her hand reaches up to my fingers, cupping them with her palm. "I'm not going anywhere without you. It wouldn't even be possible. You're my home."

"And you choose this life?"

She's been the air in my lungs the past few months. The confrontation to my ghosts, the light in all the darkness. "Meadow, I choose you and this life. I would choose you in every life. I'll be your lover, your chore boy, your fighter, your best friend, your rock, and your patience when yours starts to break. I'll be your man. I can promise you that."

Our lips finally meet, and my future is resting on her tongue.

"I love you too," she sighs against my lips and pulls me closer.

My hand rakes through her hair, rubbing its silky texture between my fingers. "There's one more thing. One last question that I get to ask you for the first time." I go to kneel in front of her, but she follows me down to the damp wood on the porch.

"What are you doing?"

I look into her hopeful eyes, and I'm back on the stone path outside this house, seeing the most beautiful girl in the world for the first time. "Meadow Macrae, would you do me the honor of becoming my wife? Will you let me devote myself to you and Maisie and keep you both safe and away from harm? To keep laughter in your bellies and smiles on your faces and be here when the tears come? To be the best Kristofer Hivju look-alike you've ever seen?"

She snorts, punching me in the bicep. "Yes, Ollie. My answer is yes, but I have to speak with Maisie first, okay?" She looks at me with a cheerful expression that could keep me on my knees forever. "She gets the final sign-off on all big life decisions. "

"We can take our time. Right now, I'm going to carry you up to bed and not let go. I'll never let go again."

Meadow pauses for a second, taking a breath. "That's good, because there's another thing I'm going to need to talk to my daughter about since—um, I genuinely have no idea how to say this, so I'm just going to come out and say it."

"What is it?"

"I'm pregnant." A burst of joy illuminates deep within me. "I —is that too much? I just found out tonight."

"I thought you couldn't—"

"I thought so too."

"But you're on the pill?"

"I haven't been super diligent about that. Ollie, I promise, this isn't some way to get you to stay."

"Meadow," I interrupt her. My head spins like I've ridden a roller coaster twenty times over. Between Maisie missing, finding her, telling Meadow I'm staying, getting engaged, and now finding out I'm going to become a dad—it's like every single nightmare and dream I've ever had has come true in one night. "The woman I love is carrying my child."

My future flashes in front of my eyes. The silver in my beard and the gray in Meadow's hair. Maisie, older, with a little peach beside our plum. My eyes burn.

"And you're not upset?" She bites her lip, looking nervous. "You want this? Me? Us? A whole family?"

"I do, doe." I stroke her hair, planting a kiss along her jaw. "I don't think I've ever wanted anything as badly as this."

"Can I be honest?" Her eyes cast downward. "This baby terrifies me, Ol, and not because of your giant-sized genetics." She tries to crack a joke, but I can tell she's serious. "I spent the past few months reconnecting with my old self, the woman I was before I was a mom, and a newborn is going to be a lot of work, even with my extra days off. I don't want to give up my restaurant or my career and go back on autopilot." Her hands shake, and I can tell she's scared to share this with me. But she won't lift a single finger the entire time—not during her pregnancy or after. "I put someone else's needs before my own for so long, and I just don't want to lose myself again."

"Meadow, those fears are so valid. But this is *our* baby. You won't be alone ever now that I'm around. You made me remember the importance of family," I heave. "Now you're giving me one of my own."

"That doesn't scare you?"

"Maybe a little. But I had my big career, and now I'll be working at the distillery. A job that won't be all-consuming. Da and I are going to run it together. Which means that I can be the primary caretaker of our baby."

"Primary caretaker?"

"Yes, ma'am. For you, for Maisie, and for our baby. It's about fucking time you put your feet up and let someone else do all the work you've burdened yourself with for years."

Meadow's lip trembles. "Do you even understand how much work a newborn is? It's sleepless nights, nappies, screaming, crying."

"Sounds perfect to me. Besides, you learned; I'll learn too. We always were good at learning together. Plus, we have a whole village here. We can figure it out."

"That's true," she smiles.

"This baby is my responsibility, Meadow. I will not be one of those passive fucking fathers who makes promises they can't keep. I'll learn everything I can, try hard, and give my all to ensure that your dreams and career come first. You did this role on your own for seven years. Let it be my turn to be a caretaker. And if I get no sleep and have to crawl out of bed next to you every night, I'd do that until all the hairs on my head and beard turn gray."

"We're doing this?" She places my hand on her stomach. "An Anderson-Macrae baby is going to be a lot."

"And I have a lot to give." I kiss her forehead. "Especially for another member of our zombie apocalypse team."

## Chapter 39
# Meadow

By the time the whistle blows, the tension in the air is bubbling like a boiling pot of water. The final game of the season has been fierce. The Thistlehill Tacklers are locked in a close battle with the Riverrun Runners. The score is neck and neck, with each team pushing themselves to the limit. Honestly, kids' sports are far more intense than adult games. These tots have been throwing elbows and patching up bloody noses all afternoon. My eyes track Maisie on the field as she unleashes a high kick that sends the footie soaring through the air.

The ball sails over the heads of the opposing team, landing perfectly between the goalposts. The crowd of parents and townies erupts in cheers as her incredible kick secures the winning points.

"Mom, we won! We won!" Maisie runs over and swings her arms around me. "Did you see that?"

Her uniform is drenched in mud, but I can still see the small ribbon tied to her sleeve.

The weather outside is crisp, with a gentle breeze carrying the scent of fresh grass. The vibrant blue sky above us is dotted with clouds clustered together, which almost resemble the kids all running around and celebrating their win against Riverrun.

"You're a rugby star, plum."

Ever since she ran away with Madame Kleptocow, I haven't been able to stop keeping a close eye on Maisie. My protectiveness has grown tenfold. The sheer realization that I could lose her, or that I could lose this baby, has made me realize two important things—I love my family and the one I'm going to have with Ollie, and life is way too short for me to be hung up on making mistakes.

"Can Coach Ollie come celebrate with us?" She looks over at him and waves, a smile lighting up her face. He returns her hello from the sidelines.

*I'm going to tell her.* I shoot him a look through the crowd of people gathered around him.

*I'll be right here.*

"Of course." I brush the sweaty strands of hair out of her face. He's been spending more time at the house as a small trial period. Most nights, we curl up by the fire together, and Ollie tells Maisie stories about Fox that I've forgotten. I like her having this piece of her dad.

He doesn't spend the night when she's around. Not yet anyway. But we haven't been shy about holding hands or exchanging small kisses in front of her. It's not exactly easy to resist my almost-husband. Being with Ollie makes it feel like we'll be forever young.

Before Maisie's game today, he and I agreed that I would put the question to her and get the most important seal of approval.

"What would you think if Ollie was around a lot more?" I kneel down in front of her, swiping my thumb over the mud on her cheek.

"What do you mean?" Her brows knot. "We see him every day. Are you two…" She snickers under her breath. "In *looooooove*?"

Nothing gets past her. "How would you feel about that?"

Beneath the grass stains and muddy knees, her eyes sparkle. "He's funny, and I really like having him at the house with us. We get to play jokes on him and make him try all sorts of different food."

"That's true," I laugh.

"And if you get married and Coach Ollie is coaching summer league, we can get all the girls on the team to be flower girls at your wedding. He can put little flowers in our hair." She reaches for her own braid, the one Ollie and I helped her with this morning. He's been taking diligent notes on hair care as part of his fatherly duties. Along with reading all the gentle parenting books I own. "Just like this."

I glance over at my future husband, who's watching us from a distance. *I think she's on board.*

"Would you be okay if Ollie moved in with us? To our house?"

"I don't know," she says sternly, grabbing my shoulders and making her face all serious. "When Cece's mommy moved in with her new daddy, they made Cece a little sibling. Am I going to get one?"

I want to tell her that she may be a big sister soon, but I have to wait until after my first trimester. There are still a few things I can protect my girl from, even if most of them are out of my control.

"Do you want a sibling, Mais?"

She nods her head seriously. "At least ten."

"*Ten?*"

"Ten. Then I'll get to have my own rugby team, and I can coach all of them like Ollie coaches me."

I snort before the fear of God works itself into my veins—ten Ollie-sized babies may actually tear me to pieces. The idea of one is quite frightening, given how tall we both are.

"We'll see about that." I stand and pull her hand into mine.

"Are you sure you're okay with this, kiddo? If Ollie and Mommy get married, and you're not happy, then you can tell me whenever, okay? I can make things like before." A possibility that I hope is plan Z, but Maisie's life is about to change as much as my own. She deserves some autonomy in the decisions that affect her. I know what it's like to have your parents decide your future for you. I won't do that to her.

"Mommy, if you're happy, then I'm happy." She smiles and pulls me off the pitch toward Ollie.

"I am, Mais."

There's a big surprise waiting for her at home—a massive Highland cow Jellycat, which Ollie insisted on buying at the toy store in Inverness, new cleats, and a big, sparkly pink cake. Maybe we got ahead of ourselves a bit by assuming the Thistlehill Tacklers would win today, but with Maisie on their team, there was no other possibility.

"I guess, until the summer season starts, what should I call Coach Ollie? You know, since he's going to be your *huuuuuuusband*."

"Whatever you're comfortable with."

She thinks for a moment. "I like Ollie."

"Good. He'll be our Ollie."

## Chapter 40
# Ollie

"Mais." I nod her over and squat down in front of her. "I made you something." A moving-in gift. I hand Maisie the wooden bowl I carved from a fallen birch tree in our backyard. There are forty-seven tiny hearts engraved in the shiny bowl. "For when Belle stops by. We'll have to tie it down though, so she doesn't take it," I laugh.

The Cameron twins, at my insistence, have put a tracker on their furry beast. Meadow and I couldn't keep Maisie from wanting to be around the damn cow, so the next best compromise was a GPS we can track from our phones.

"It's *udderly* cute," Maisie whispers, searching for her mom. "Can we put it by the porch?"

"Maybe by the back door?" The last place the five-hundred-kilo cow needs to be is at our front door.

"I'm going to go do that right now, and you can cut up one of the apples you got at the store."

"Herd." I shoot her an overexaggerated wink.

"What?"

"Get it, like *heard*?" I point to my ear. "But instead, it's *herd*, because cows travel in herds."

"Belle travels alone." She shakes her head at me, one hand on her hip. Sassy like her ma. "Your puns need work, but don't worry, Ollie, I'll help you with them." She hugs me and sprints into the house.

*Our house.*

"Are you already being a bad influence on Maisie?" Meadow strides toward me, wearing a blue jumper that matches her eyes. My pulse spikes, the way it does each time I see the goddess who's growing my baby.

"Nothing hits your ego quite like getting bested by a seven-year-old."

She shrugs. "Get used to it. In a few years, I'm sure she'll be outsmarting the whole household."

"We'll have to board up her windows so she won't sneak any boys in."

"Luckily, my *fiancé* is the best woodworker in town."

"In and out of the bedroom."

She rolls her eyes, but the blush on her cheeks is obvious. We haven't been able to keep our hands off of each other since finding out about the wee 'un. In her hand, she's holding an old cigar box.

"Hey," I scold her and pluck the box from her. "What did I tell you about carrying anything?"

"It's only photos." She softly slaps me across the chest. "You didn't have much to move in the first place."

"Nice that everyone decided to pitch in though."

Turns out those forty-seven steps are the perfect distance between our houses to host our friends and family. Neil and the crew are throwing a footie around, Brooke humbling them with every failed pass. Fi is helping Elspeth set up the band in front of our house. Even Kleptocow is here for the celebration, standing at the edge of the forest. *How can something so cute be so devious?*

"That's Thistlehill for ya." Meadow steals a quick kiss from me. We pull apart to find Maisie cheering on the stairs. "Think she'll ever stop doing that?"

I hope not. "She just likes seeing her ma happy."

"We gotta get the lamb kebabs on the grill if we're gonna feed everyone."

"Maybe they can wait a sec?" I pull her close and grab her arse. So fucking juicy. "I got something for you upstairs. We have ten babysitters on standby."

"What are you hiding up there?"

"A little housewarming present."

This time, she grabs a handful of my behind. "I wouldn't necessarily call your thing *little*, but—"

"Always such a smartass."

Meadow laughs. A song I'll be hearing for the rest of my life. "Hey, Brooke, can you watch Maisie for a second?"

"Of course. Get over here, kiddo, and let your Aunt Brooke tell you about the time your mommy over there karaoked on top of the Eiffel Tower," she calls from a creaky lawn chair on the grass.

"Brooke." Meadow's chef voice sends a jolt through her friend. Brooke waves her off as she latches her arm around Maisie. "Let's go."

I stand flummoxed. "Sorry, I'm going to need more details than that."

"You'll have to serve me a whole bottle of Anderson whisky to loosen these lips. And too bad for you, that won't be happening anytime soon."

"I can coax it out of you in other ways."

We enter the house and go up the stairs, and in our bedroom is the giant white box with a copper-colored bow I placed on the bed earlier today.

"This is a big box! You got another you in here?"

"Stop gabbing and just open it." I roll my eyes and nudge her forward. "Actually, wait—start with the little one first."

She picks up the smaller of the boxes, undoes the ribbon, and plucks out the small wooden frame I made. Behind the glass is the Polaroid I took of her all those years ago, when she told me about her dreams of owning her own restaurant.

Without saying a word, she slides the closet door open, kneels, and takes out a cotton knife roll. My eyebrows knot. "What are you..." She holds up a knife—not just any knife, but the Japanese blade I bought her all those years ago. "You really do still have it."

"I couldn't get rid of it."

I set the frame down on the nightstand and run my finger over the photograph. "I kept this in my wallet all these years. I would've never admitted it then, but it was like you were always there with me in the States. That absolutely fucking creepy?"

Meadow looks at me, tears welling in her eyes. "I hate these pregnancy hormones."

"Maybe you're just a big softie, doe."

"Shut up." She frowns and holds out her knife at me. "What's in the big box?"

"Open it," I laugh.

She uses the blade to cut the ribbon and unwraps the box without any care for the paper. "Stop," she exclaims, swinging her head back to look at me. "Copper All-Clads?" She breaks open the box and pulls out one of the saucepans, hugging it to her chest. "I've been wanting the copper ones for years. They have such better heat conductivity."

"Aren't they *pantastic*?"

"I love you, Ollie. But Maisie is right; we need to work on your puns."

A car horn honks outside. I look out the window and see Ivy and Harris drive up, my parents in the back seat. "They're here. Come on, you can play with your new pans later."

"Are you nervous?" Meadow asks, care apparent in her voice.

"No," I assure her. "This reunion is overdue."

Outside, Ma ducks out of the car as Meadow and I walk hand in hand down the driveway. "Ollie, we've missed you," she says. Her typically pale skin is flush and glowing for what seems like the first time in ages. My heart is full. She finally got her trip. Clearly, you can get everything you want out of life at any age. From the back seat, my da lumbers out.

His nose is burnt red, and the creases around his eyes look more relaxed.

"I've missed you too." I drop Meadow's hand and embrace my ma. Another pair of arms slings around us, and when I expect to find my lady, I see that it's my da.

Hugging me.

"Son, I'm glad you're here like you said you would be," he whispers and exchanges another look with my ma. They both seem lighter.

"Glad to be here," I say. And I mean it.

We don't let go of each other for a while. The hug is a real, big, warm one that smells of sunscreen, oak, and the slight tinge of plane. This is nothing like the half-hearted, complacent hug we shared three months ago when I returned to Thistlehill—it's almost like a promise without words.

An embrace that says we're a family again. It feels good.

"Nan, Pops, Ollie is moving in!" Maisie yells, sprinting toward us, intercepting our hug. We make room for her as she snuggles up close between the three of us.

"You've gotten so big, our wee rugby champion." Ma kneels, kissing Maisie's cheeks until my sweet girl squalls with laughter.

"I'm going to be as tall as my mom," she laughs.

"You sure are." Ma smiles and glances over at Meadow with a warm wave. "It was the whisky contract that brought ye together, aye?" she teases. "Ivy and I knew we could get you both matched up again." Our parents are about as devious as we are.

"Aye, yer ma thought it would be good for you to have a friend here." Da shrugs and looks a bit embarrassed that we've caught on to his schemes.

"Well, she was right. I'm glad you asked me to take over that contract. Not only did it help me reconnect with Meadow, but—" I stop for a moment. I haven't spoken this frankly or been this vulnerable with my parents in decades. But there's no point in hiding behind words now. Not when I'll be around for good. "It also helped me remember why Anderson Distillery is the best in the Highlands."

Da's eyes gleam beneath the sun above. That swell of pride I'd seen only a few times before is obvious now. Nothing is lost in translation. "Speaking of which, let me get a taste of that exclusive Anderson malt that's being served up at Fox Den."

"The judge for the Best of Scotland guide actually surveyed our restaurant. But we won't find out if we made it until the end of summer." Meadow shrugs. She hasn't been too stressed about the results of Adair Grant's visit to Fox Den the last two weeks.

"Aye. It'll be the on that guide without a doubt." He nods.

Ma joins him. "Our bright kids, working together. What a joy."

We finish up our welcome backs. Ma fills us in on their trip while Meadow asks her about all the different food they ate. Ivy and Harris toss the footie around with Maisie as Da and I watch our two families reunite.

"It's like nothing changed," Da laughs. "Can almost hear ye wee bairns playing out here, the way ye did all those years ago."

"There will be a lot more laughter between our houses from now on." More shared memories. More small moments to share together.

Da nods his head toward our house and says, "Can we talk, just us two?"

Nerves bubble up in my chest, but when my eyes meet Meadow's and she gives me a soft smile that says, *You got this,* I feel the strain vanish.

"Over a dram?"

"Aye."

A part of me is still nervous that Da and I will resort to our old ways and the sweet taste of their return will go sour. Despite our conversation on the phone, there's still a lot that hasn't been made right between us. Things that only time will fix.

We walk up the old creaking porch stairs of my childhood home. When I push open the front door, Da freezes. "Where's our table?"

*Right.* There wasn't exactly a good time to mention that I broke this thing right after they left. "The old one had issues." I gloss over the way it shattered between my and Meadow's weight. "So, I built a new one."

Da walks over to it and runs his fingers over the wood, his scrutinizing gaze looking over every inch of it. I prepare myself for a snide remark or an argument, but he surprises me when he says, "Doesn't even wiggle anymore. Nice work, Ol. Yer Ma will be happy 'bout it."

My chest collapses on an exhale of relief. *You're not a kid anymore, Ol. We're men here, together. Things are different.* "Have a seat, and I'll grab us a bottle of Fox Den's exclusive whisky."

"Aye." He nods. "Ye kept it nice in here, Ol. Thank ye."

"Don't worry about it." I join him and pour us two drams of whisky. "You look good, Da. The sun definitely did its work on you."

"Burnt me to a crisp, but it was worth it."

"We'll have to send you on a three-month vacation every year." I tip my glass to his. "You seem happy."

"*Happy* doesn't even begin to cut it. I pushed this trip off far too long, and I was a fool to dae that. Yer ma and I haven't been

## Falling for Meadow 447

this content in years." He swipes at the back of his neck, looking uncharacteristically calm. No brutish crease in his brow or frown on his lips. The perpetual concern in his eyes seems to have faded away. "I never understood why ye or yer ma wanted tae travel the world. I thought we had everything we needed in Thistlehill—but we don't have one of them steam sauna things." He lets out a laugh that is hearty and full. "Have ye used one of those? My bones have never been happier."

"There's a lot more out there, Da," I concede. "But there's a lot of good here too. I felt like Thistlehill was too small for me but maybe it's about balance, right? Anderson men here and out there could do a lot of good."

Da nods in agreement. The distillery is doing well. On Cloud Nine has promised a steady stream of orders. The Anderson legacy will live on, and it'll be because of my ideas and Da's whisky.

The kitchen I first sat in when I arrived doesn't feel as grim now. There are fresh flowers on the sill. The sound of laughter in the walls. It feels like home. "Aye. Now that our whisky'll be all over the world"—he holds up the amber liquor between us and marvels at the colors—"everyone will be coming tae Thistlehill tae get a taste of it."

A sense of pride shoots through me at his words. "It's too good to keep it to ourselves."

"That's right," he says, and I savor the recognition I always wanted from him. "I was too afraid tae see that and take a risk on our product. There were opportunities, lad, but I couldn't stomach change the way ye could. Ye were always braver than yer old man."

Little does he know I picked up all of my stubborn determination from him. Da never gave up on the distillery, and I never gave up on my dreams. Our dedication led us back to each other. "You still have a lot to teach me," I admit.

"Aye, ye have a lot tae teach me. But maybe I'll stay away

from the damn computer and ye can handle the ordering system," he jokes. "Callum's sung yer praises about the bottling facility."

"Wish he told me," I sigh.

"Hard tae share yer feelings here, son. We're a proud pair, he and I, but we've got our bairns tae keep us on our toes." He takes a sip of the whisky, savoring the taste. "This ain't easy for me to so say, but I should've been learnin' from ye too."

The regret in his voice is obvious, but we don't have to live our lives that way anymore. I run my hand over the grain in the table, seeing all the possibilities still in front of us. "Maybe, Da, we had to do things our own way. I had to go to the States, and you had to get in a sauna."

Da's laugh leaps out of him so fast it sends him reeling back. He swipes at the happy tears in his eyes and slams a steadying palm on the table. "With all the business ye've managed for us, we could get one of those steamers for the shed out back."

"Aye." I grin. "We can even take a trip as a family. If you'd like to."

"I'm sorry, Ol. Ye deserve to hear that in person. Yer ma's always on about how I'm a stubborn bull, and she's right. I let my pride keep me from improving my life, my wife's, and yers. I ken ye was ashamed of—"

"No, Da," I interrupt. "I was wrong. I thought money was going to be the answer to all my problems. All I really needed was to be seen and understood by you."

"Well, ye will be now, lad. Ye didn't need to prove it by taking over the distillery, but ye did Gran Craig proud. Did me proud as well," he says surely, and a smile creases his face.

I shake my head. "You both made sacrifices so I could chase my dreams. Now we can start working on a new dream together."

He finishes his dram and sets it on the table. "That sounds like a plan tae me."

A dream that won't mean being overworked and stressed. No quarterly goals overshadowing every waking moment of our lives. No bosses who see you as a means to an end rather than a person. Corporate capitalism, while effective in generating wealth, often prioritizes profits over people. My life is fuller than it ever was when I was stranded at a desk, working myself to a pulp.

Now, life will be filled with rest, laughter, memories, and small moments, which are more important than a fancy title or a big paycheck.

My legacy. My family. My home.

I take another sip of whisky. Success sure does taste sweet.

*The End*

# Epilogue
## Ollie

***two months later***

"What is this surprise? Are we going to repeat what we did in the kitchen last night? Because if we are, I hope you got me a bigger apron," I tease my woman as she pulls me through the kitchen of Fox Den.

She's been hiding something all week, and she hasn't been covert about it. My detective skills are simply not as good as hers, no matter how much *Beck* we've managed to pack into our late nights together the past few months.

"You're going to love it."

"I would've been happy to spend my birthday lying around with you, Maisie, and the little peach." I place my hand on her pregnant belly. Her bump is barely visible. We hit the second trimester last week, and I've been anxiously stuffing my head with parenting books and baby-proofing the house to be ready for the big day.

Maisie's taking her older sister duties very seriously. She and I decorated Fox's old room to welcome the new baby. Da cried the most when I told him he was going to be doubling his Pop duties. He and I have been making up for lost time. Meadow and Ma join us for lunch most days at the distillery.

Da and I bottled up our first cask together, a single malt in a sherry. I plan on giving it to Meadow on our ten-year wedding anniversary.

She smiles at me, squeezing my hand. "More like a lemon now."

"Explains why we had those citrus pancakes this morning," I tease.

"I'm not sure that's how cravings work."

"The second we're off citrus, you let me know, and I'll stock the fridge with whatever the little lemon wants." This woman has made me the happiest man alive. "Maybe, also, you can finally listen to me about getting off your feet."

She sucks her teeth, shaking her head. "You can't keep me in the reclined position forever."

"I can try."

Meadow insists on her four days a week at the restaurant. The summer season has been busy, and Fox Den is packed every night, but we savor the three days a week she's not feeding the locals and tourists. Whether we're spending the mornings skipping stones at the loch with Maisie, driving to Inverness for the farmers market so Meadow can get her fill of all the fresh crops, or helping my parents out with their new garden.

It's a slower life. Mine. One where every day feels longer. Small gifts of time.

"Can you at least pretend to be excited?"

"Of course I'm excited, doe. I just didn't need you making such a fuss about me," I say and let her lead me through the swinging kitchen doors. The dining room lights are turned off. "Some after-hours fun?" I squeeze her juicy arse. Her body has grown more irresistible, stretching and growing to support our baby.

"Ollie!" Meadow scolds.

The lights flick on. "Surprise!" A burst of celebration explodes in front of us.

"Happy birthday!" Maisie bullets toward me, sporting plaits with pink bows that I helped put into her hair this morning. Meadow has been teaching me how to braid her hair and I'm certain the technique is improving. I lift her and swing her around, cataloging the people in front of me, familiar faces all smiling at me.

My past and my present joining together.

"Meadow? What is this?"

"Happy birthday," she beams and pushes me further into the room.

"We have a trip to New York in two weeks," I remind her. The surprise fills me with overwhelming joy. I knew that keeping my friendships back in New York would be a challenge, one that I was ready to take on, but I didn't think I'd get to see everyone today, of all days.

"Yes," she says. "But I reached out to a few people through your LinkedIn, and, well, the plans just happened. Your friends were very insistent. I can see why they're important to you."

My heart splits at the seams. "Doe," I sigh.

"If you're going to be back here, Ollie, I'm going to make sure that you're happy too. As happy as you've made me."

If there was ever a moment that confirms I did the right thing, it's now. "I love you," I whisper.

"Love you, Papa Bear. Let's go say hi to everyone; I want formal introductions."

"Uncle Olliepop!" Kaia waves at me, standing beside her parents. Luca Navarro, in his classic suit, looking entirely out of place at the Den, shoots me a head tilt. At his side, Avery Soko, her blonde hair pulled high above her head, lights up.

Without letting go of Meadow's hand in mine and Maisie in my arms, I stride toward my friends. "You're here! In Scotland. I'm honestly blown away."

"Your lovely lady here organized all of this." Avery smiles at Meadow and wraps her arms around me. Then she turns to my woman. "It's nice to finally meet you. This is my husband, Luca."

My former boss extends his hand. "Your restaurant is very beautiful," he remarks. "We can't wait to try out the entire menu."

Meadow shakes his hand. "Thank you."

Avery glances at the formal handshake and stretches out her arms for a hug. "I promise he's less stiff after you get a drink or two in him," she giggles as she wraps her arms around Meadow.

"Well, Mr. Navarro, you'll surely enjoy the Anderson whisky then," my lady laughs over Avery's shoulder.

"It's the best in all of Scotland," I brag.

"Happy birthday, old guy!" Matthew's voice comes from behind me. His heavy hand lands on my shoulder, and I spin to face him and Molly Greene. They're wearing matching knitted jumpers. "And congratulations on your engagement." They both grin at Meadow.

"You're here too?" My voice cracks; I'm entirely overwhelmed. I look back at my woman in shock, and she nods softly.

"It was so good to have your whisky at The Griffin, we had to come check out the distillery ourselves," Matthew laughs.

"How's it going over there?"

"We've never been better. Molly here has done an incredible job with all of the inn's activities. We're even hosting a LARPing event next month."

Meadow raises a brow. "LARPing?"

"Live action role play," I explain, noticing the faint tinge of excitement in her eyes.

"Well, we'll have to make a stop since we'll be there in two weeks." She nods surely.

"You'll love it," Molly replies. "We can find the perfect costumes for all three of you."

The past and the present together. A future filled with plans I can experience rather than daydream about.

"We wouldn't miss it," I promise.

Matthew wraps his arm around his wife. "Guess we all ended up where we needed to, didn't we, Ave?"

Her smile glistens. "We always did make a good team."

"Ollie, are you crying?" Maisie's voice reels me back to my emotions. My nose stings with the onslaught of tears. "Oh, goodness, I'm so overwhelmed I almost didn't introduce you to my second lady." I hike the little plum up in my arms. "This is Maisie, everyone. Our girl. She just turned eight last month."

They all say their hellos as she shyly buries herself in my neck. "I think you'd love to meet our little girl, Kaia," Avery says and calls her daughter over.

"Hi," Maisie waves. "I like your turtle necklace."

"I like your shirt," Kaia laughs, looking at Maisie's Thistlehill Tacklers jersey. I set Maisie down and let them run off through the legs of adults.

"Lily and Nico flew out too," Molly announces. "A perfect stop for them before they tour Vietnam this month."

"My brother was very insistent," Luca nods. "I don't blame him. The conservation efforts here sparked my interest too. Avery and I are going to do some wildlife tours with Kaia."

"That sounds incredible."

"Robert is here too." Matthew nods to the back.

The best part of New York was all of my friends. A substitute family for the one I get to have today.

"Bobbie!" I call across the room to one of my oldest buds. Even if we don't talk every day, we can always pick up where we left off. He shoots me a neutral thumbs-up and leans forward to talk to Brooke. Ha! Maybe Bobbie's internet girlfriend didn't work out and he'll be the next one to find love in

Thistlehill. Fi and Elspeth are holding hands, chatting with Callum and Jody.

"Happy?" Meadow asks.

"I don't have the words."

"Big man!" Nico Navarro joins his brother's side. In his hand is his beautiful fiancée, Lily Rodin. "Gotta say, we're a bit mad at you for not telling us about this place sooner."

Last I heard, Nico was remotely leading a team at Viggle on an application that helps detect plagiarizing, an idea inspired by his lady. We would've likely crossed paths at some point had I taken that job, but now we can meet here.

"Seriously." Lily tosses her long black hair over her shoulders and leans in. "Do you think those guys would be down for an interview?" She points to Neil and the rugby crew. "I've already come up with a brilliant new idea for a novel set in the Highlands, and the whole battered rugby player thing could really spark some *interest*."

Meadow nudges me. "I'm sure Ollie's lads would be happy to help with the research."

"If you make it a cozy mystery, Meadow here would be your biggest fan."

Lily's eyes light up. "Now that I can do."

"You must be Lily Rodin." My woman smiles. "I have to be honest, I looked up your books online, and they're quite a success."

Lily has had more international bestsellers since unveiling her pen name, Zoe Mona. Her books are filled with passion and based on all of her and Nico's adventures.

"Lily is a romance-writing genius," Nico boasts. "We've been traveling the world as she writes her stories."

"More like my fiancé here distracts me as I try to write my stories," she teases him and pinches his side.

"Distraction or inspiration; call it what you want," Nico laughs.

I lean over to Meadow. "We know a thing or two about inspiration, don't we?"

"Ollie! Ollie! Kaia and I are going to be best friends." Maisie and Kaia's arms are linked. Kaia is shorter than Maisie and a few years younger, but the two are very obviously ecstatic about their new friendship. "We're going to be pen pals after she goes back to America."

"Is that right?" I squat down and give them both a little tickle, sending them running away with screaming laughter.

"It only makes sense that our kids would be the best of friends," Avery laughs.

She's right. Now, I'll have a link to every bit of my life. All the people who shaped it and helped make me who I am are in one room, a grand reminder of how the people who care about us will always find a way to make things work.

"Thank you all for coming here, to my hometown, to Thistlehill. We're going to have to give you a whole tour," I say and look at Meadow. "Show you where the whisky is made and the loch we go to."

"As long as you guys don't mind some mud," Meadow laughs.

I shoot Luca a look as he glances down at his shiny dress shoes. Avery notices her husband's panicked expression and laughs. "We'd love that," she says.

"Fun is worth a little mess sometimes, isn't it?" Molly giggles.

My heart fills with joy. "Thank you all, again. I'm just immensely grateful that you could be here."

"We couldn't miss your birthday or the chance to congratulate you on your engagement," Avery says.

"Thank you so much." I pull Meadow even closer to me.

Robert joins our circle, Brooke smiling brightly beside him. "We could never miss commemorating the day you were welcomed into this world or your pending nuptials."

"Bobbie, come here." I hug him, and more arms sling around us. "You're the best."

"I am quite ordinary, Ol, but I appreciate your compliments," he says in a flat tone. "It is a pleasure to see where you come from."

"You're always welcome here," I promise. My friends. My family.

"There's something else we can celebrate today." Brooke's voice breaks through the chatter. "Meadow, Fi! We just got the email from Adair Grant."

My lady shoots me a look—all nerves and excitement.

*You got it.*

She shrugs. *And if I didn't, it doesn't matter.*

"We got it!" Fi scans her phone. "We made it onto the guide." She flashes the screen to Meadow, whose hands shoot up to her mouth.

"They ranked us first, Ol." Her voice cracks.

"I knew it."

"Okay, this is feeling very much like another hug situation," Ave laughs. We all pile together again. I've never felt more whole than I do at this moment.

"Happy birthday, my Ollie," Meadow whispers through the limbs and smiles between us.

"Congratulations, my doe."

# Bonus Epilogue
## Meadow

*ten years later*

Behind the thick glass, fog rolls over the tarmac like a thick blanket. The muffled whoosh of an airplane can be heard over the dragging of suitcases and chatter of travelers.

Maisie's fingers nervously drum against her thigh—a habit she picked up from Ollie. She's as tall as me now. Muscular and strong after years of rugby. Her chestnut hair sits in two French braids that Ollie helped her with this morning. A Thistlehill Tacklers sweatshirt hangs off her shoulders.

My plum, my world, is off to college. It doesn't feel real. A full-ride scholarship to play Division I rugby in the States. Harvard University. With Ollie as her coach, she became one of the best kickers this town has ever seen. Scouts and university offers poured in. It was inevitable, and yet, it doesn't feel remotely real.

My chest fills with a bittersweet sadness.

"Mom, I think you're more nervous than I am," Maisie smiles, wrapping her hand around my fingers and squeezing them.

"Not nervous," I assure her. She shoots me a look like she doesn't believe me. "Okay, maybe a little bit."

"I'm nervous too, but I'll be good. You taught me how to be strong, remember?"

"I know." My eyes sting. She's right. Maisie is a wonderful young woman who doesn't need me anymore. Who am I kidding? I need her.

But she needs to chase her dreams, the way I went after mine.

Even if I wish I could go back and just get one more day with her when she was small enough to be comfortably perched on my hip as we made soup, or when she was four and would fall asleep on the couch and have to be carried to bed. Or when she won the championship this year and ran to me and picked me up, swinging me around.

Time slipped by too fast.

My fingers find the cool metal wrapped around my neck, and I rub my thumb across the chain.

*I hope I didn't mess her up too much, big brother.*

Maisie turns to Ollie, who's walking back from picking up snacks for the flight. "Keep an eye on her, Dad? She won't admit it, but I know Mom's going to start crying as soon as we board."

My husband slips an arm around my shoulders, pulling me in close and kissing my temple. "Aye, I'll be crying too, Mais."

"Mom, Mom!" Adelaide claps, holding up a Toblerone bar that is the size of her nine-year-old arm. Her dark auburn plaits match her sister's. Those shimmering brown eyes like her father's. "Dad said I can get the extra big one to share with Maisie."

Maisie squats down in front of her sister and ruffles her hair. "Thanks, Addie. I'm going to miss you so much."

"And me?" Fox joins his sisters, popping open his bag of sour straws. When he was a baby, he used to pluck the lemon rinds from the counter and suck on them.

"And you." Maisie pulls her siblings into a hug.

Alright. No point in holding back the tears anymore. I fish a packet of tissues from my carry-on and swipe away the tears rolling down my cheeks.

"Oh, doe." Ollie rubs my shoulder. "We'll go visit, and she'll come back home."

"I know, it's just happening so fast," I whisper, watching our kids giggling together.

"Mom, did you know we are going to be about a thousand meters in the air, and that means we may enter the stratosphere?" My son is obsessed with the sky. On more than one occasion, I've found him trying to slip outside to watch the stars.

"That so?"

"Yeah, there are five layers of the atmosphere." He pulls out a book from his backpack, flips through the pages, and stands. At ten years old, he's taller than all the kids in his class. He shows us his geography textbook. "After Boston, I hope I can go to all of the states."

"You will," Ollie promises. "You'll travel just like your ma and I have. Especially since Mrs. Michelin Star will be taking more trips to perfect her new menu." He kisses me on the cheek.

The announcement that Fox Den received its first star came last month, and as rewarding as it felt to pop bottles of champagne with Fi and Brooke, there are no accolades I could ever receive that would feel as good as coming home to Ollie and our kids every night. Our new house, which Ollie built for us, looks out over our spot at the loch. Every morning, I get to enjoy tea on the porch with my husband until the kids get up and slowly walk outside to join us.

I like the life I'm living. I'm no longer constantly searching for validation with my career, but finding the happiness in slowing down and appreciating each moment.

"Now boarding for Heathrow to Logan," the airline employee says into the speaker.

Ollie scoops up all the carry-on suitcases. I grab Addie's hand while Maisie grabs Fox's, and as a family we all stroll onto our next adventure.

# Also By Kels & Denise Stone

### Perks & Benefits Series:

**Water Under the Bridge**

Workplace Romance, Avery and Luca's Story

**Our Scorching Summer**

Friends to Lovers Romance, Lily and Nico's Story

**On Cloud Nine**

Fake Dating Romance, Molly and Matthew's Story

**Falling for Meadow**

Small Town Romance, Ollie & Meadow's Story

### The Hastings Series:

**Close Knit**

Sports Romance

# Acknowledgments

We did it. Four books. Four unique love stories featuring characters from diverse backgrounds. Thank you, reader, for joining us on this journey through the entire Perks & Benefits series. Words cannot fully express our gratitude for your support, time, and readership.

When we set out to write these books, we were two burned-out corporate women with a dream—a dream that wouldn't just make our childhood selves proud (lil K & D are cheering for getting to say they're authors), but would also create change. It was a tall order, but you, our readers, have shown us it's possible. Through every interaction, you've resonated with our characters, felt a connection with their dreams and personal struggles, and changed our lives in the process.

We are grateful to our editor, Caroline A., who saw our potential from the first book and has stayed with us ever since. You have understood our vision, our stories, and helped us believe in ourselves. We eagerly anticipate countless dinners in the city with you. Our third Stone Sister for life.

Caroline K., it's been a pleasure working with you. Your attention to detail is unparalleled, and we appreciate how carefully you handle our words.

Thank you to our proofreader, Isabella. Our beta team: Nicole McCrane, Isabella F., Logan Chisholm, Sophia and Lizzie Moore. Thanks for being the first readers to fall in love with Ollie and Meadow, and for providing invaluable feedback. You all deserve a slow-motion video of Ollie running toward you in his kilt.

While we acknowledge that no words can truly do justice to the beauty of Scotland, a visit sparked a profound appreciation for its culture and landscapes. As we transpose a fictional small town into your captivating Highlands escape, we have endeavored to portray it with justice, love, and respect. After months of research, we hope we've managed to capture even a fraction of the charm that Scotland so uniquely possesses. Thank you, the Highlands, for your beauty.

# Playlist

"Over-the-Ocean Call" by Lizzy McAlpine
"You Should Probably Leave" by Chris Stapleton
"When We Were Young" by Adele
"All I Wanted" by Paramore
"right where you left me – bonus track" by Taylor Swift
"Heather On The Hill" by Nathan Evans
"All My Love" by Noah Kahan
"In The Kitchen" by Renee Rapp
"Erase" by Omar Apollo
"Woman" by Mumford & Sons
"I, Carrion (Icarian)" by Hozier
"Everything I Am Is Yours" by Villagers
"Surround Me" by LÉON
"Eyes on Fire" by Blue Foundation
"I Think I Like It When It Rains" by WILLIS
"Sweet Creature" by Harry Styles
"Coming Home" By Leon Bridges
"Sweet Nothing (feat. Florence Welch)" by Calvin Harris
"This Love (Taylor's Version)" by Taylor Swift
"Little Life" by Cordelia

## About The Authors

Kels & Denise are authors, best friends, and the definition of the found family trope. The pair bonded over their love for romance and turned all their late-night chats into writing together. Their love for storytelling morphed into writing strong heroines and rugged, swoon-worthy love interests with lots of dirty talk. While Kels travels the world with her high-school-sweetheart husband, Denise is making her way through every restaurant with her boyfriend.

Stay in touch!
@authorkelsdenisestone
kelsdenisestone.com

Join our newsletter *The Sticky Note*
kelsdenisestone.com/the-sticky-note
Join our Patreon for exclusive content

Made in United States
Orlando, FL
04 June 2024